Twin River II

FOUR STARS: *Twin River II: Have Weapons Will Travel* is a thrilling trip into history. The second book in a trilogy by author Michael Fields is a relentless action adventure in the seedy world of organized crime. Once Palladin leaves Philadelphia and arrives in Barree, a lot of sinister events happen near the town's Twin River … Matt's transformation from bullied teenager to hardened criminal is chilling throughout the novel … Fields paints such a clear image with his writing, the novel can easily be adapted as a mob drama similar to *The Sopranos* … *Twin River II* also benefits from Fields' acerbic writing which mixes brutally violent scenes with sarcastically funny dialogue … *Twin River II: Have Weapons Will Travel* is a book that will take readers on an unforgettable journey into the dark side of small-town life.

—Ella Vincent, *Pacific Book Review*

RECOMMENDED: If readers have not read the author's first book, *Twin River*, prepared to be floored: a nonchalant, casual scene turns dark without a moments notice. From this moment onward, Fields has his audience captivated and eager to discover how a sympathetic, *Catcher In The Rye*-loving fourteen-year old Wesley Palladin steps into his father's shoes and evolves into a prolific hitman . . . The frenetic, breakneck pace of the action is exhilarating . . . Entertaining dialogue to keep the readers engaged is icing on the cake . . . For those who enjoy a good thriller and mob story, this is a highly recommended jolt of energy that leaves readers awaiting *Twin River III, A Death at One Thousand Steps.*

—Mihir Shah, *The US Review Of Books*

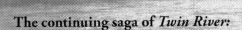

The continuing saga of *Twin River*:

Visit author's website at:
www.michaelfieldsauthor.com

Twin River II

Have Weapons Will Travel

Michael Fields

TWIN RIVER II
HAVE WEAPONS WILL TRAVEL

iUniverse books may be ordered through booksellers or by contacting:

iUniverse
1663 Liberty Drive
Bloomington, IN 47403
www.iuniverse.com
1-800-Authors (1-800-288-4677)

ISBN: 978-1-4917-4446-8 (sc)
ISBN: 978-1-4917-4445-1 (e)

Library of Congress Control Number: 2014915081

Printed in the United States of America.

iUniverse rev. date: 01/29/2015

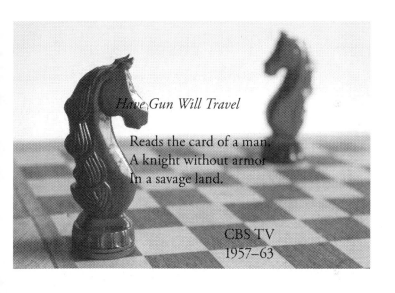

Have Gun Will Travel

Reads the card of a man,
A knight without armor
In a savage land.

CBS TV
1957–63

Chapter One

Ormond Beach, Florida
August 1966

Meandering a slow course through lush vegetation, marshland, and pristine forest, the dark waters of the Tomoka River flow past Ormond Beach before emptying into the Halifax River. Green-and-black-ridged alligators dot the banks, rattlesnakes lie camouflaged in rotting mangrove trunks, and bobcats hunt for prey in the deserted Timucuan village of Nocoroco. The river is a sanctuary for manatees and bald eagles. Red and black drum, snook, sea trout, tarpon, and black bass inhabit its waters.

Motor chugging in the gray dawn light, a jon boat moved slowly up the Tomoka. Water sprayed in the air, leaving a moist sheen over a chess piece—a solitary black knight—painted on the side of the boat. Next to the knight, the logo, Have Weapons Will Travel, was stenciled in bold red letters. Waves from the jon boat splashed against the dense tangle of mangrove roots. Across the river on the bank, flat and heavy in the mud, a ten-foot gator blinked and slid into the water.

Beads of perspiration glistening on his forehead, fourteen-year-old Wesley Palladin sat in the front of the jon boat. His brown hair was cut short. He had narrow eyes and a sunburnt face. The boy was five ten and had broad shoulders and strong, dexterous hands. He was holding a six-foot graphite rod and an antique black Mitchell 320 spinning rod. A white foam float tied to the line swung with the motion of the boat. Wesley's blue T-shirt was wet and stuck to his skin. The identical black knight and logo, Have Weapons Will Travel, were sewn neatly, prominently, on the front of his T-shirt. Wesley nodded to his dad, who sat in the back of the boat with his hand on the trolling motor.

"Why'd we have to get out of Philadelphia so fast? I didn't have time to pack."

"It was getting hot."

"It's hot here!"

"I know," his dad said. "It's stifling and humid. But you get used to it. The heat in Philadelphia is unpredictable. It can come up real sudden. Before you can react, you're dead. Even in the middle of winter."

Mr. Palladin was middle-aged and had muscular shoulders and arms. In the shade of a wide-brimmed Panama hat, his face was deeply lined and unshaven. Almost invisible in the shadows, his blue eyes were sharp and clear, constantly shifting, focusing on the boy, the docks, the mangroves, the receding strength of the Tomoka tide, and the salient humped lids and glassy eyes of the submerged gator now motionless in the current. Mr. Palladin wore jeans and a camo crewneck T-shirt that remained neat and dry in the morning heat. The black knight and logo, Have Weapons Will Travel, were in the upper corner of his T-shirt. The boy studied his father.

"Dad, did you take the company's name from the TV program?"

"What TV program, kiddo?" he asked. He always said the word *kiddo* lightly, approvingly.

"You know. The show we used to watch, *Have Gun Will Travel*."

"No, I didn't take our name from any TV show. I've used this company name for six years. When I retire, the name will be yours. You'll own the company."

"Will you teach me about weapons?"

"Of course. Today we'll start with the simple fishhook."

"Dad, a hook catches stupid fish. It isn't any kind of real weapon."

"Everything within reach is a weapon, kiddo. Now quit with all the questions, and get ready to catch some fish. And fish aren't stupid. If you think like that, you'll never catch a hog."

"I'll catch me a hog today," Wesley said. "But I have one more question."

"You're wasting time. If you don't catch fish, you won't eat dinner tonight."

"I know that." Wesley sat quietly and waited. Mr. Palladin shrugged his shoulders.

"What's the question?"

"The hero of *Have Gun Will Travel* ... Paladin. Did you take his name?"

"No. His name begins with *pal*; ours begins with *pall*. *Pal* is the same as friend. *Pall*, our name, has nothing to do with friendship. Palladin is pronounced the same way as *pall*bearer." The boy straightened; his eyes opened wide.

"You carry the dead around?"

"I have contracts. People die. On some occasions, I attend the funeral and do my duty as a *pall*bearer. When I finish burying the dead, I get paid. Usually it's a lot of money. You'll find out soon enough."

"If you get paid so much, why do you rent that cheap office above Yummy Restaurant in Chinatown?"

"That office is not cheap. And the food's great." Palladin shifted his position on the seat. The boy pointed at the logo on his dad's shirt.

"*Have Gun Will Travel* is good TV, but I like *The Rifleman* better."

"I like it better too," Palladin said. "Chuck Connors is a great man. He's the first actor I've seen on TV who tackles real-life problems."

"Like shooting bank robbers and rustlers?"

"No, not shooting bank robbers and rustlers. Anyone can shoot someone else. You just lift your gun and pull the trigger till the noise stops. What the Rifleman did was way more difficult. In fact, this was the first time the TV producers and sponsors permitted it. The Rifleman had to raise a troublesome kid all by himself ... without his mother. If I could tell him half of what I've been through with you, the show would still be on prime time."

The sun rose in a sudden display of brightness. The red orb burned away the mist, thin wispy lines rising off the water, thickening the layers of moisture over the Tomoka. A roar of noise shattered the brightness. Wesley Palladin lifted his hand over his eyes and watched a line of dark helmeted figures thunder their motorcycles across the I-92 bridge. Within seconds, the roar diminished to a hum; the heavy morning silence returned.

Below the bridge, numerous docks lined the bank. Some docks were weathered wooden planks that tilted close to the water; others were sturdy state-of-the-art structures. Red mangroves grew dense along the shore. Looming behind the mangroves, Yellow Pines and Swamp Bay evergreens cloaked the river-front mansions in deep, tropical shadows.

Spanning across a marsh before jutting into the river, the newest dock was metal and had a towering yacht moored on the side. A red-and-white umbrella and red lounge chairs were in the center. The dock ended with an ornate circular platform that held two large potted palm trees with massive drooping leaves. The planks of the dock cut a wide path through the marsh of needle-sharp saw grass, cattails, and flat lily pads before extending a silver fist into the placid waters of the Tomoka.

Mr. Palladin slowed the trolling motor; the incoming tide drifted the boat toward the dock. Then, suddenly, beginning soft and distant, a lively clarinet and flute melody filled the morning air. Wesley looked toward the bank.

"What is it, Dad?"

"Classical music," Mr. Palladin said. "It's *Billy the Kid*. A famous composer, Copeland, wrote the music."

"How do you know it?"

"I heard it at the home of my employer. We were discussing my latest contract. The contract took me out of Philadelphia, which I hate to do. While we negotiated, I listened to the percussion and bass drums. They got very intense. I think it was when the posse was shooting at Billy. My employer said I would hear *Billy the Kid* in the near future. He said I would grow to like it."

"Maybe you'll grow to like *Billy the Kid*, Dad, but it doesn't sound right when we're out here trying to catch fish."

"Give the *Kid* some time, kiddo. He'll start sounding pretty good."

"I doubt it," Wesley said emphatically. "I never cared for your music. I like popular music. The *Ballad of the Green Berets* is number one now. I'm always humming it. *Silver wings upon their chest. These are men, America's best.*"

"Stop it. You'll scare the fish away."

"And I also like *Monday, Monday* and *California Dreamin'*. And I love *Help* and *Yesterday.*"

"Those damn bugs."

"The Beatles, Dad. They have a great name. They took it to honor Buddy Holly and the Crickets."

"More bugs, Wesley. I read that the Beatles's concerts smell like urine."

"Because …"

"Because, Wesley, the girls get to screaming and crying. When they get completely wild and lose control, they piss in their panties."

"That's crazy," Wesley objected "You don't know what you're talking about."

The music grew louder. Tracing the sound of the clarinets and flutes and now trumpets, Wesley saw a grand veranda with white pillars and the protruding spires of a four-story mansion through gaps in the thick, verdant foliage. Meandering through the trees, a stone path shaded by hanging palms and thick palmetto plants ended at the dock. Painted in an alarming red tint, No Trespassing signs lined the bank.

"It's posted, Dad."

"The owner can buy the land but not the water."

"I've never seen a dock this big," Wesley said. "It's beautiful."

"No, it's ugly, kiddo. A rich man's toy. But the fish appreciate the shade. They're waiting in ambush back in those shadows." Turning the trolling motor, Mr. Palladin maneuvered the boat parallel to the dock. "Get the bait on. Hook the shiner high above the tail and—"

"I know what to do," Wesley interrupted. He lowered his hand into the aerated minnow bucket. Smooth bodies smacked against his fingers; some silver shiners jumped in the air.

"They're hard to grab onto. Why did you get monster shiners?"

"My daddy always said, 'big bait for big fish.'"

"I got a real big one," Wesley said. He squeezed the eight-inch river shiner in the palm of his hand, turned it around, and stuck the barb of the hook through the meaty flesh below the dorsal fin. Standing, swinging the rod to the side, he adroitly cast the shiner. The white float plopped quietly on the water; the current sucked it toward the dark shadows under the dock.

The shiner surfaced, gulping for air; its tail swished through the water, creating a series of small ripples. Then it swam erratically, the float jerking to the right, to the left. Suddenly there was an explosion of bubbles; a cavernous mouth closed around the shiner. Escalating from soft to frantic, percussion notes from the mansion reverberated down the stone path. As the booming percussion intensified, the white float sank in the dark water.

"Money!" Wesley exclaimed, setting the hook. The rod bent. The line ran straight toward the dock and then suddenly angled upward. Wesley stared in amazement. Breaking free, the glistening body of a massive black bass twisted in the air and dropped back into the water with a loud cracking splash. Across the river, the ten-foot gator lurched forward and moved with predator precision toward the noise.

"Money!" Wesley shouted again. The line made a whirring noise ripping off the spool.

"Tighten the drag," his dad instructed. He revved the trolling motor, fighting the current, but the boat drifted closer to the two potted palm trees. Then a loud, angry shout sounded over the tense, riveting percussion music.

"Hey, you dumb-shits! Get off my property!" Wearing a purple silk bathrobe, a man hurried down the path.

"Dad," Wesley said hesitatingly.

"Keep your attention on the fish."

"Hey! Are you deaf! Or daft! I'm talkin' to you dumb-shits!"

The folds of his purple silk bathrobe swinging in the air, the heavyset man jumped onto the dock and stomped across the marsh. Striking a cadence with the timpani drums in the background, marching awkwardly forward, he ducked under the umbrella. His bald head gleamed in the light. Large, thin-frame designer sunglasses hid his eyes. His lips were thick and red and wet with liquid. There was a Highland Park bottle of scotch in his hand.

"Dad . . ."

"You heard me. Don't be distracted. I've always taught you to concentrate on what you're doing."

Wesley nodded. The rod was heavy in his hands as he struggled to turn the fish. Perspiration dripped from his forehead, thin beads flowing into his eyes. Wesley blinked rapidly and wiped his forearm across his brow. The current pulled the boat toward the dock. The sounds of percussion were replaced by a solo trumpet, the notes clear and vibrant in the heavy air. The massive outline of the drooping purple bathrobe loomed closer.

"I spent more money building this dock than you'll make in your lifetime. Now I plan to enjoy my peace and quiet." The man sneered, lifted the Highland Park, and drank. After he emptied the bottle, he pointed at them and spoke in a commanding tone. "I'm tellin' you to fish somewhere else. Get that fuckin' piece of scrap away from my dock!"

Mr. Palladin didn't say anything. Sitting in a relaxed manner, he held the boat steady with the trolling motor. His narrow eyes were keenly focused on the man and the belt that squeezed into his white, fleshy stomach. The leather holster attached to the belt held a single-action revolver with a golden grip.

The bass spooked and ripped off line; the drag made a steady clicking noise. Wesley's eyes darted from the man to the fishing line; his hands were wet and slippery. The sound of the trumpet lingering in the background, the voice shouted from the dock.

"You've got the whole damn river to do your fishin'. I'm not warnin' you again!"

"Dad."

"You heard me. Pay attention to what you're doing. Hold that rod tight, or you're gonna drop it."

The man stood there, stomping his foot. His face reddening, glaring at the boy, he lost his grip on the Highland Park Scotch. The bottle splashed in the water and drifted under the dock. A smug expression forming on his face, the man reached under the folds of his silk bathrobe and removed the Colt .45 from the holster. The barrel had an engraving that glistened red in the sunlight. Mr. Palladin stared at the man and the Colt in his hand. As he focused on the cylinder chambers, the solo trumpet in the background became stronger, menacing in tone.

The tide flowed with a low, gurgling noise. A snowy egret glided over the dock. The breeze picked up, flapping the leaves of the palm trees. Approaching from the opposite bank, the half-submerged body of the gator created V-shaped ripples on the water. The tide crested, stilling the flow of current. Thin legs protruding from the mud, a little blue heron perched motionless on the bank. The trolling motor made a smooth humming sound. The man leveled the gun.

"You can't say I didn't warn you," he announced. The man stepped forward, balanced his feet, and leaned into a shooting position. The breeze lingered; the palm leaves swung back and forth. The fishing rod tight in his hands, Wesley stared at the circular void of the gun barrel.

"Dad," he said again. Mr. Palladin didn't move or say anything. Not taking his eyes off the gun, the boy sat down.

"Fuck it," the man said. He burped; small whiskey bubbles formed on his lower lip. From the mansion, the timpani and bass drums echoed loudly and produced a booming thunder that shook the mangroves. A grim smile spreading ear to ear, the man fired the gun rapidly. Wings flapping, the little blue heron took flight.

Exhaling a burst of air, Wesley heard himself scream. Muscles tight, body frozen motionless, he watched three bullets walk little circles toward the jon boat. The fourth bullet hit inside the pointed bow. Sparks flew in the air; a metal shard ricocheted into the boy's leg, burning a hole in the jean fabric. His face drained of color. Wesley felt a wetness soak through his boxer shorts. He dropped the fishing rod and rubbed at the rip in his jeans. The man laughed as the rod disappeared in the current.

"You son of a whore," Mr. Palladin cursed. "My daddy gave me that Mitchell 320."

Clicking the trolling motor into reverse, Mr. Palladin backed the boat away from the dock. A Plano two-tray tackle box, a grainy, waterlogged oar, and a heavy-duty fishing rod lay next to his sand-specked combat boots. The rod was five feet long; the saltwater reel had braided two-hundred-pound-test line. Tied to the line, a sturdy ten-inch lure, shaped like a mullet, had two pearly eyes protruding from its head. Attached to the lure, flashing lethal, razor-sharp barbs in the sunlight, two polished-silver Stinger 5/0 treble hooks swung back and forth. Mr. Palladin slowed the motor.

"You're still too close!" the man shouted. "Get the hell out of here!"

Ignoring him, Mr. Palladin clicked off the trolling motor and reached for the fishing rod. He grasped the heavy rod with both hands, and with a deft, powerful side cast, he sent the lure with pearly eyes racing in a straight line toward the figure on the dock.

"What the fuck!" the man exclaimed. As the whistling noise of the lure grew louder, the man jerked his hand in the air. The gun fired again, and a hole ripped through the red umbrella. The mullet-shaped lure hit him solidly. One treble hook lodged in his earlobe; the second hook stuck in the fleshy part of his neck. His throat muscles convulsing, the man opened his mouth and made a deep guttural noise.

"Fish on," Mr. Palladin muttered to his son. Balancing himself, his biceps bulging, Mr. Palladin pumped the rod hard. Pulled by the treble hooks, the man's skin stretched outward in a grotesque coned pattern. He fired the gun wildly. The bullet sliced through his calf muscle as he was lifted off the dock. Trumpets sounded from the mansion.

His scream echoing along the Tomoka, the purple bathrobe billowing behind him, the trumpets and stentorian drums pounding rapidly in the background, the heavyset man plunged headfirst into the river. Water filled his mouth. His thin-frame designer sunglasses broke loose and drifted away. Mr. Palladin looked at Wesley, who sat quietly massaging his leg with both hands, eyes wide and teary.

"Your bass put up a better fight," he commented in a disappointed tone. Shoulder muscles tightening, Mr.

Palladin reeled the heavy body to the boat. The man beat the river with his arms; dark water spilled from his mouth and spouted from his nostrils. Blood oozed around the treble hooks in his ear and neck. Then the man calmed; the thrashing movement of his arms stopped.

"You bastards," he gasped. "Time to stop playin' wit' you." Straining, stretching his arm around the heavy line dangling from his ear, the man raised the Colt and pointed it at Mr. Palladin. Staring at Palladin's face, the cold granite expression, he hesitated, shifted the gun, and aimed at the boy. A smile formed on the man's face.

"Don't worry, kiddo," Mr. Palladin said.

"Fuck you both," the man said, pulling the trigger. The gun clicked empty; the smile vanished. Moving quickly, Mr. Palladin grabbed the Colt from the man's grip and dropped it in the boat. Then he cranked the reel twice, tightening the line, elevating the man's head out of the current. He turned to Wesley.

"Pick up the oar," Mr. Palladin ordered. "Club him with it."

"What?"

"Are you *deaf* or *daft*, Wesley? I said club him! Club him with all you got!"

"Yes, Dad," he said quietly, a note of apprehension in his voice.

Wesley picked up the oar with both hands and lifted it over his head. The man's face was red and blustery, his eyes oval and extremely white. Wesley swung the oar downward. It hit the man weakly on the cheek. The flat side of the oar slid into the river; water sprayed in the air. The man sank but quickly resurfaced, his mouth spitting water, his chin lacerated with a red, broken line.

"Don't," he sputtered, lifting his hand in the air. The palm was pink and fleshy. His index finger had an enormous diamond ring. "Please. I'm sorry." Trumpet and flute notes floated a dull sound over the dock. Moving erratically, the diamond radiated sunlight. Wesley squinted at the blinding flashes of light.

"What should I do, Dad?" As Wesley turned, his dad cracked him sharply in the head. Wesley lost his balance and grabbed the side of the boat. Through the sudden ringing noise in his ears, Wesley heard the words as from a great distance.

"Next time I'll *clock* you so hard you'll forget the time of day. Now quit acting like a baby. Club him like you mean it!"

Wesley straightened. He clamped his mouth shut, set his jaws against the ringing sound, and focused on the bald head bobbing in the water. The music from the mansion reached a heightened crescendo when suddenly, the violent, passionate *Billy the Kid* ballet ended with the slamming of a door. Except for the rhythmic lapping of the waves against the jon boat, there was extreme silence. A woman's voice called out.

"Henry!" The voice paused and then called louder. "Henry, your breakfast is ready!"

Eyes opening wide, the man turned his head and looked toward the sound. Wesley blinked, refocused, and squeezed the grainy handle. The skin over his knuckles stretched tight and turned a pale purple. The woman's strident voice resonated in his ears. His entire body trembling with anticipation, Wesley raised the oar with fierce deliberation and swore.

"Fuck you, Henry."

Knees flexed, biceps pumped, he brought the oar down with great force. There was a dull, clunking sound. When Wesley lifted the oar, he saw a deep gash in the man's head; a yellowish, jellylike matter oozed from the gash. Wesley dropped the oar in the boat.

"You should have done that the first time," his dad admonished. He handed the heavy-duty fishing rod to Wesley. "Keep hold of him."

Mr. Palladin started the trolling motor and moved the boat slowly away from the dock. The line tightened; the rod bent in half. Mr. Palladin steered the boat toward the opposite bank, toward the snout and two gator eyes suspended motionless in the water.

Wesley sat down. The handle buried in his stomach, he tightened his grip on the rod. He watched the man's body float to the surface and flop over before sinking again. The purple robe loosened from the body and floated away. His dad slowed and then stopped the trolling motor. The jon boat drifted quietly toward the gator. Mr. Palladin took his skinning knife from the sheath.

"Bring Henry up," he directed.

Wesley reeled in the heavy mass. When the body was next to the boat, Mr. Palladin grabbed the arm, exposing the naked chest and stomach. With a quick motion, he sliced the knife through the bloated stomach. Intestines, blood, and bile spilled into the water. His grip tightening on Henry's arm, Mr. Palladin grabbed the mullet lure and ripped out the treble hooks. Pieces of white skin and a jagged earlobe hung from the silver barbs. Palladin released his grip, and Henry's body dropped into the Tomoka. Henry's hand flopped up and down with the rolling motion of the waves. Bloody fingers and a diamond that cast a dull crimson glow pointed feebly at the knight logo on the side of the jon boat.

A thick, oily slick spread outward from the body; the gator submerged. Unable to blink, Wesley studied the black current now dazzling with sunlight. Suddenly, the green snout and eyes appeared at Henry's side. Gigantic jaws opened, and rows of crusted teeth locked around Henry.

"*El lagarto*," Mr. Palladin said with respect.

"What?" Wesley asked.

"Lizard," Mr. Palladin answered. "It's what the Spanish conquistadors called the alligator. The Spanish are long gone from here. *El lagarto's* been around for thirty million years." Palladin squinted in the light. "Pay attention, kiddo. Gators are unique survivors. Even though they got seventy-plus teeth in those jaws, gators don't chew and enjoy food like normal predators. They rip up their victim and swallow whole sections."

There was a violent swirl of water. The Tomoka tide turned to a boil of blood and bubbles. Henry's right leg shot high in the air. The left leg followed, but it was detached from the body. The leg drifted momentarily in the current and then was pulled under. On the opposite side of the river, shielding her eyes from the sun, the woman walked to the circular end of the dock and stood in the shade of the two palm trees.

"Henry," she called in a loud, angry tone. "Henry, your eggs Benedict *Florentine* is getting cold!"

Mr. Palladin shook his head, cranked the motor, and raced the jon boat toward the I-92 bridge. When he reached the bridge, he tossed the anchor onto the wide cement pillar. Rocking back and forth as the wake smashed against the side of the boat, Wesley had his head lowered. Mr. Palladin stared at him.

"Look at me," he said. Wesley lifted his head and met his gaze.

"What?"

"Maybe it was wrong. Maybe I shouldn't have smacked you like that. But you have to understand something, son. Never show weakness. The privileged with all their wealth have the idea that they own everything. But this water flowing by the boat is not theirs. It belongs to everyone. It belongs to you and me. The Tomoka, this whole river, belongs to you and me. If someone, anyone, tries to take what's yours, you stop him. By any means, you stop him. Do you understand?"

"Yes," Wesley answered in a soft voice.

"Say it like you mean it!" Horns blew; traffic raced over the bridge.

"Yes!" Wesley shouted above the echo of bridge traffic. He saw the gun next to the blood-stained oar and picked it up. "How'd you know?"

"It's a classic Colt Frontier. It's the gun that made Billy the Kid famous. The Colt has six rounds. For safety reasons, you should keep a chamber empty. But Henry was an amateur. He loaded all six rounds, and you can bet your life I counted each one of them. Henry fired three in the water, number four hit the boat, number five put a hole in the umbrella, and he wasted the last one shooting himself in the leg. It was simple mathematics, son."

"Simple math!" Wesley said in a high-pitched, strained voice. "I thought he was going to kill me!"

"First off, pay close attention to your adversary. Henry was out of shape and a little drunk. His shooting form was weak. I reckoned he was pretending tough and trying to scare us off. I reckoned he wouldn't kill us."

"You could have told me that before I pissed my pants." Wesley frowned and pulled at the wet smear on his crotch.

"Quit acting like one of those girls at the Beatles's concert," Mr. Palladin remarked dryly. He stared at Wesley, who had his head lowered. "Okay, I'm sorry. I should have told you what I was thinking. But Henry got on my bad side real fast. No one has the right to threaten family, to threaten the young and innocent."

"I'm not so innocent after what I done."

"You're right. Mr. Henry was a scumbag. You lost your innocence when you smashed his brains out and fed him to a real predator."

Reaching for the treble hooks on the mullet lure, Mr. Palladin removed the pieces of skin and earlobe and tossed them in the river. Perched on a crossbeam, a screeching seagull swooped down and grabbed the earlobe. The seagull returned to the beam. Mr. Palladin studied the boy.

"Were you afraid?"

"No."

"Then why'd you drop my daddy's Mitchell 320 in the river?" Mr. Palladin asked. A loud horn sounded from the bridge. A truck horn answered with a longer blast. Young Palladin hesitated.

"Maybe I was afraid. But only a little bit afraid."

"Under the circumstances, I guess I can understand you being a *little* bit afraid." Mr. Palladin removed a silver flask tucked under his belt. It gleamed in the morning light. He unscrewed the cap and handed Wesley the flask. "Take a drink of this."

"What is it?"

"Ole Smokey."

"What?" Wesley asked. Holding the flask to his lips, he was immediately aware of the aroma. "It smells sweet."

"It's better than sweet," Mr. Palladin said. "Tennessee moonshine is the best. Take a drink."

"Okay." Wesley tilted the flask, and the smooth clear liquid filled his mouth, flowed down his throat, and cramped his chest and lungs with a sudden warmth. He squinted, and his face lost all color. Mr. Palladin smiled.

"How do you like it?"

"Wow," Wesley answered. Crimson blotches formed on his pale face. Shuttering, Wesley handed the flask back to his dad. "It's real good. I felt hot for a while, but now I don't feel much of anything."

"Are you still feeling a *little bit* afraid?" Palladin asked. Glassy-eyed, his lips a dull purple, Wesley clumsily moved his head up and down. Palladin glared at him. "Is your tongue tied in a knot? Answer the question. Are you still afraid?"

"I don't know."

"Take another drink," Mr. Palladin instructed. He held the flask to the boy's lips and poured the Ole Smokey in his mouth. Wesley gulped most of it, some spilling down his chin. Jagged bolts of lightning clouded his vision. He took a deep breath and gagged.

"Wow," he said again. His eyes rolled; beads of perspiration formed on his brow.

"What about now?"

"I'm not afraid." Wesley began shouting. "Gators! Snakes! Dinosaurs! I ain't afraid of nothing!" Winded and red-faced, he grasped the side of the boat and steadied himself.

"That's the way to think, kiddo. There's more than enough bad things in the world to make a person sick. Even a strong person. I don't want you being afraid of any of it. Being afraid only weakens you. Makes you nervous and insecure. And it don't change the outcome. Do you understand?"

"Yes, I understand. I'm sorry I was a little bit afraid. It won't happen again."

"You're damn right it won't happen again," his dad agreed. He replaced the flask under his belt and handed the gun to Wesley. "The Colt's yours now. With the engraving and that golden grip, it looks to be more expensive than this boat and my Mitchell 320 at the bottom of the river." Mr. Palladin saw the scrolling and the glint of red letters on the barrel. "What's written on the gun?" Wesley turned the Colt in his palm and read the words.

"*Omerta*," Wesley said. "What's *Omerta*?"

"The Mafia code of silence. The Philly families swear by it. First, they'll never snitch. Second, they handle their own problems. Mostly their own killings. It's kind of what you did with the oar."

"Should I take the Omerta oath now?"

"That's not necessary."

"When did you take the oath, Dad?"

"Who said I did?"

"I just thought …"

"Don't think so much when you're drinking Ole Smokey." Mr. Palladin looked at the troubled expression on the boy's face. The gun crimped his wrist. "How does the Colt feel?"

"It's heavy."

"Heavy is good. There's less kick when you shoot. Give me that." Mr. Palladin took the Colt. Then he opened the tackle box and removed a pink, eight-by-ten, anti-stat Ziploc bag. Searching through the numerous cartridges inside, he selected a Long Colt, slid it in the chamber, and handed the gun back to Wesley.

"Who do you want me to kill now?" Wesley joked halfheartedly. Palladin didn't laugh. He pointed to a log jutting into the Tomoka. Sunning itself, a ten-inch painted turtle lay at the end of the log. The turtle's neck, bright orange lines patterned the length of its skin, stretched out of the smooth shell.

"Kill that turtle," Palladin ordered. Wesley focused on the log; two oval, glassy eyes stared in his direction.

"I can't shoot no helpless turtle."

"I said shoot it. Or I'll clock you a good one." Palladin waited, and then he issued the directives. "Stand up. Spread your feet apart. Pull the hammer back. Aim and shoot."

Staring at the turtle, Wesley got to his feet. He positioned his feet solidly, pulled back the hammer, and aimed the Colt. The orange lines on the turtle's neck blazed over the log, reflecting brightly in the river below. Wesley blinked and pulled the trigger. The explosion knocked him of his feet. The echo of noise reverberated through the mangroves. Wesley sat up and peered over the side of the boat. The painted turtle was motionless, the orange-streaked neck was stretched longer, two oval eyes stared at him.

"I missed it!" he muttered.

"I reckoned you would," Palladin said. "If you're curious about what happened, the turtle was never in any danger. You shot a hole in the mud. But don't worry. Now that you know training's important, you just might take it seriously when we start."

"I sure will take it seriously," Wesley said. "I'll take it real serious." He slid the Colt under his belt. A ripple of movement in the water caught his eye. The shiny black body of a manatee broke the surface. There was a long, white festering scar on its side.

"The manatee," Wesley said, pointing. "Did a gator bite it?"

"No, that's no gator bite. That's from a propeller blade. The Tomoka is a manatee sanctuary. But the privileged don't care. They race their yachts up and down the river. The manatee are defenseless. They get hit. They live with their scars. And like the rest of us, they die with their scars."

Mr. Palladin started the trolling motor, and the jon boat spun away from the bridge. Wesley swayed awkwardly, hiccupped a steamy burst of Ole Smokey fumes, and grabbed the side of the boat with both hands. He laughed and began to hum.

"This river is your river. This river is my river."

"What?"

"This river belongs to you and me." Wesley continued to hum. Then he said, "Woody G. sings that song, Dad. He thinks just like you... and now me." Mr. Palladin stared at the boy. Wesley smiled. "I mean about us being part of the Tomoka."

"I know Woody G. And Woody G. never sounded that terrible. And he was singing about the land, not the water. You're buzzed, aren't you?"

"I feel kind of dizzy. Are we going home now?"

"Did you catch any fish yet?"

"No, but—"

"We're going to hit a few more docks. You need to catch dinner. And you'll need to use the gator rod since you dropped my daddy's rod."

"The gator rod's way too heavy ..." Wesley started to complain. Then he sat back, smiled, and hummed to himself. *"This river is your river. This river is my river. This river belongs to you and me."*

A hot breeze blew over the Tomoka. The heavy scent of the sea and vegetation from the salt marsh and oyster beds hung in the air. Narrow waterways, dotted with giant leather ferns, flowed into the main channel. At the mouth of a large stream, a solitary mullet sailed in the air, splashed down, and sailed again, its body silver over the brackish water. Suddenly a dark shadow swooped low; the bald eagle's golden talons snatched the mullet out of the air. As the raptor soared upward, Mr. Palladin watched the mullet twist and turn, its body dripping water that sparkled crystals descending in the sunlight.

"I love this place," Mr. Palladin whispered to himself. He idled the trolling motor, pausing the jon boat, and turned to Wesley. "The school mailed the grade reports. I read yours before we left. Your teachers had nothing but praise for your work. They noted that you're intelligent, perceptive, and attentive to details. Your English teacher Mr. Glendenning gave you an A+. He said you love to read."

"Yes, I love reading almost as much as you love practicing with your weapons. Mr. Glendenning told me books could take me to places I could never get to on my own. But he's not at the school now. He resigned. He got a new job in Edinboro.

"That's quite a promotion. Edinboro's a prestigious teacher's college in Pennsylvania. I met Glendenning once. He was kind of slow-paced and nerdy."

"If he was nerdy, then I'm nerdy too."

"You are—" Palladin paused, noticing the combative expression on Wesley's face.

"What were you saying about me?"

"I was going to say you were a little nerdy, but you're not anymore." Palladin played with the trolling motor for a moment. "So you love to read. That's good. What are you reading now?"

"*Catcher in the Rye*. Mr. Glendenning gave me the book before he left. It's about Holden Caulfield, this young teenager—"

"I know that book," Palladin interrupted. "The language is vulgar. And Holden's a whiner. A neurotic complainer. You won't learn anything from him. Put the *Catcher* away. You don't want to end up like Holden. Read Thoreau and you might learn something."

"I started *Catcher in the Rye*, and I'm going to finish it," Wesley stated firmly. "I'm learning good stuff already. What's Thoreau going to teach me?"

"He'll teach you his quintessential views on nature. Thoreau isolated himself in a cabin near Walden Pond. He worshipped the beauty, peace, and harmony he witnessed every day on his walks. He concluded that all men, even all nations, should live that way … in peace and harmony. When you read Thoreau, I want you to form your own conclusions. I just watched an eagle snatch a mullet out of the air. The act was not peaceful, but there was perfect harmony and beauty between predator and prey. It's nature's version of murder. The author of peace and non-violence missed that. Or ignored it. Nature survives on destruction. The best and the strongest destroy and survive."

"Like the gator that don't chew?"

"Like the gator that don't chew and the eagle that dropped out of a beautiful blue sky … And now, of course, you with nothing but an old oar," Palladin said proudly. He clicked on the trolling motor. The jon boat moved forward; Palladin took a quick swig of moonshine. "There's another reason I have trouble with Thoreau. He contends that water *is the only drink for a wise man*."

"He's crazy to think that. Even Holden Caulfield drank, and he was underage."

"I told you to forget about the *Catcher*. You'll never be weak like him." Palladin angled the jon boat toward an abandoned pier that had planks of wood collapsing in the river. A cooter, neck stretched in the air, green eyes luminous, turned toward the noise. Then, feet and claws scratching the wood, the yellow-streaked shell slid into the water. Shielding his eyes with his hand, Wesley looked up through the blaze of sunshine.

"Dad, can I have another taste of Ole Hickory?"

"No, you can't. And it's not Ole Hickory. It's Ole Smokey."

"But I need something. I'm worried."

"About what?"

"About the lady on the dock. She's going to be lonely now. Did I have to hit Henry so hard?"

"Don't worry about stuff like that. What's done is done. My daddy always said when you do the right thing, you don't have to explain yourself to no one."

Wesley stared at him. Pulling at the rip in his jeans, he saw the bruise on his leg. There was the sound of a motor, and a houseboat cruised around the bend and down the middle of the Tomoka. When it neared the jon boat, a tall, slender teenage girl in a pink bikini walked to the railing. Seeing how the pink fabric stretched around the perfect form of her breasts, Wesley grinned.

"Wow," he exclaimed loudly, waving his hands in the air. "Wow! You're beautiful!" Wesley watched the bikini fabric stretch tighter when the girl lifted her hands and cupped them around her mouth.

"You're cute," she called, scanning the logo on his T-shirt. "And you look tough. What kind of *weapons* do you carry?"

"The best and the biggest," he boasted. Ole Smokey heat rose in his throat, flushed his face. "But nowhere as pretty as those two you're pointing at me."

"Ha! Ha! You're funny." She laughed and clapped her hands. "Do you want to come ride with me for a while?"

"Dad …"

"I'm gonna slap you silly."

"Oh." Wesley stood quickly and shouted at the boat. "I'm sorry. My dad won't let me." The girl waved; the houseboat cruised by. Mr. Palladin shook his head.

"You'd better hope those powerful *weapons* you're bragging about can put some fish in the cooler."

Wesley looked at the heavy rod with the mullet lure and large treble hooks. He frowned. Mr. Palladin guided the jon boat toward the abandoned pier. Beyond the pier, a fallen palm tree lay deep in the channel. Partially submerged in its outer branches, the purple folds of a bathrobe fluffed softly with the motion of the waves.

"Dad, what's this eggs Benedict Florentine that Henry was planning to eat for breakfast?"

"Son, you ask so many questions." Mr. Palladin clicked off the trolling motor in front of the pier. "Eggs Benedict Florentine is poached eggs with spinach and a sweet yellow sauce all stacked on sourdough toast."

"It sounds tasty. I'm feeling real hungry. I did hard work today. The hardest I've ever done my whole life."

"Since the food's already prepared, maybe we should go back to Henry's dock and invite ourselves up to his mansion for breakfast."

"No!" Wesley barked. "I won't be eating no dead man's food!" He noticed the wily expression on his dad's face and calmed quickly. "Besides, the toast is probably cold and all soggy by now."

"Then maybe you should catch us something fresh before it gets too hot to fish."

"Okay," Wesley said. He cut off the mullet lure, rigged the gator rod with a float and shiner, and made an awkward cast toward the barnacled planks. The white float smacked down and bobbed high in the water. Seconds passed; there was a swirling boil, and the float disappeared with a loud plopping sound. Instantly alert, Wesley gripped the rod tightly. Watching the line slice through the water, he counted in a dramatic voice.

"One … two … three … four … five!" Wesley braced himself and set the hook. The weight and power of the fish bent the rod tip. Wesley's body was jerked forward, his knee cracking into the side of the boat. A burning pain shot the length of his leg. Opening his mouth wide and fierce, Wesley prepared to bellow. Then he saw the smile on his dad's face, and he smiled too.

"Money!" Wesley shouted in a voice that echoed up and down the Tomoka.

Chapter Two

Polecat Hollow/Twin River High School
Alexandria, Pennsylvania
Thursday Morning
November 1980

A short distance from Martins Gas Station on Route 22, Polecat Hollow Road wound through forest and steep hills. At the Route 22 turn-off, Polecat Hollow began as black tar and asphalt. After four miles, it disintegrated into dirt and potholes. Isolated and primitive, the abandoned Calvin property was at the end of the road. It consisted of an old wooden three-story house, a barn, and a large circular holding pen constructed of logs and warped planks of wood. Its legs lashed together, bloody cuts crisscrossing its head, a goat was tethered with barbed wire inside the holding pen. Bleating at long intervals, the goat wobbled on shaky legs. The sound carried across the yard and into the trees.

Thrashing noisily, three immense hogs, their bellies swinging low to the ground, wandered in a broken line toward the Calvin property. As they neared the wooden enclosure, the bleating noise reached a piercing crescendo. Moving faster, crashing against each other, the hogs charged through the broken gate into the pen. Short legs propelling her into the lead, a two-hundred-pound sow reached the goat first. Mouth dripping foam, she crushed the bloody head in her jaws. Seconds later, the two slower sows ripped into the goat's body.

On the other side of the Calvin farm, dragging its three-hundred-pound body over weeds and brush, a solitary male hog rooted through mounds of sod. Stiff bristles covered its head and snout. Four-inch tusks, sharpened by continual grinding, bent upward. The hog sniffed the air and snorted loudly.

Thirty yards away, marching down the middle of a weed-covered path, a mother possum led five baby possums in a straight, orderly line. The small possums, less than a foot in body length, covered in gray woolly fur, moved in a precise, mechanical manner.

Hooves kicking up dirt, the hog trotted to the end of the line and began to gorge itself on soft bodies. In a very slow motion, the mother possum turned at the commotion. The baby possums were gone; the massive shadow of the hog loomed over her. The mother possum bared its teeth, bubbles formed around its extended mouth, and the animal dropped to the ground in a curled, lifeless position. During its sudden demise, a vile odor secreted from the possum's anus. The satiated hog, its mouth filled with gray strands of fur, gristle, and pools of blood, gored the body with its tusk and then crushed the possum in its jaws. The stench of death and decay lingered in the air as the sun rose over the mountain and covered the path with a warm, glowing light.

Located on the road to the Calvin property, the Wilson farm was the only other dwelling in Polecat Hollow. It was home to Mr. Wilson and Wayne and Becky Wilson, sophomores at Twin River High School. Under the glare of a spotlight attached to the barn door, Wayne raked straw and cow manure. Wearing a heavy flannel shirt, blue jeans, and boots crusted with crap, Wayne scraped the rake over the ground and hummed Kenny Rogers's *Coward of the County*.

Wayne was tall with strong legs and a muscular upper body; his face and arms had a deep tan. The light growth of hair under his nose formed a fuzzy line. Breathing the fresh, fecund aroma of the barn, Wayne hummed quietly.

> *Twenty years of crawlin' was bottled up inside him.*
> *He wasn't holdin' nothing back; he let 'em have it all.*

Wayne stopped humming, leaned the rake against the wall, and walked outside to a rusted basketball rim nailed above the entrance to the barn. The rim had no net, and the screws on the support were loose. Wayne picked up the basketball, half-buried in a pile of straw, and began shooting. As Wayne practiced, he heard a faint bleating sound from the Calvin property. Shaking his head, he stepped back and made a long shot. The morning sun rose and flashed a golden glow over the perfectly even rows of corn spreading out from the barn. Wayne made four straight shots, and then he stepped to the edge of the corn and made two more. There was a loud engine noise. The Twin River school bus came down the road and turned around in his drive. The door swung open, and an elderly man wearing a Pirates baseball cap called to him.

"You making your shots this morning?"

"Thanks for asking, Mr. Isenberg. So far I've made them all."

"That's great. Keep it up, Wayne. Any smart coach would have you on the varsity team."

"Mr. Eckin ain't so smart. He never played any sports. And he's always late for practice. He stays in his office drinking Mountain Dew and eating pizza and chili dogs."

"He could miss practice altogether, Wayne. His older brother's on the school board. You just keep on practicing like you do." The driver waved, closed the door, and grinding gears, he drove away. Moving into the corn, Wayne broadcast loudly.

"Five seconds on the clock." Then he started to count. "Five, four, three." Wayne shot over the corn stalks. "Two!" The ball rotated in a high arc. When a sudden, shrill bleating sound echoed from across the hill, Wayne was momentarily distracted. Then he heard the ball clang through the rim.

"One!" he shouted. The bleating sound abruptly stopped. Raising his fists in the air, Wayne ran to the house and jumped onto the porch. Once inside, he climbed the steps and knocked quietly on the bedroom door.

"Becky," he whispered. "Becky."

"Come in."

Wayne opened the door. Becky sat on the edge of the bed. Her brown hair was long, reaching her shoulders. Her face was clear; her blue eyes glistened. Her breasts and the prominent bulge of her stomach filled the pink dress she wore. The dress was patterned with clusters of roses with large red petals. There was a suitcase at her feet.

"Where are you going?" Wayne asked. He sat next to her and took her hand.

"Dad's taking me to Uncle Hector's. He doesn't want anyone at Twin River to see me in my condition."

"You can stay here like you've been doing."

"Dad saw Cain's truck driving past the house these last two nights."

"I know," Wayne said. "I've been watching through the window. "Wayne squeezed Becky's hand. "I should have killed that bastard when I had the chance."

"You shot out his knee, didn't you? That had to hurt more than dying." Becky smiled. "And you're home safe. Not in any jail or anything."

"So far I'm safe," Wayne said. Bright sunlight flooded the room with light, casting a glow on her face. "I just hate it when you're not here."

"Burnt Cabins isn't far. I'll have the baby there. I'll be fine. I mean we'll be fine."

"I promise to visit you often." Wayne sat quietly, massaging his fingers across her wrist.

"You should go now. You'll be late for school."

"I just might stay home today."

"Dad wouldn't permit that."

"I know that. Dad's been counting for a long time. I haven't missed a day of school in four years. But I'd miss one for you." Becky shook her head; Wayne frowned.

Releasing Becky's hand, Wayne kissed her on the cheek. Then he got up and left the bedroom. Halfway down the steps, he turned to go back. Before he moved, he saw Becky at the railing. She waved at him. Waving back, Wayne ran out of the house and jumped on his bicycle. As he pedaled down Polecat Hollow Road, he heard engine noise and saw a line of Winnebago Chieftains and construction vehicles coming in his direction.

"What the hell's going on at the Calvin farm?" he muttered to himself, breaking and steering the bicycle to the side of the road.

Two miles from Polecat Hollow, sunlight blanketed Twin River High School. Situated at the confluence of the

Juniata and Little Juniata Rivers, the school was a two-story rectangular building. The front courtyard had a brick display case, a flagpole, and a faculty parking area. Across a narrow ditch, State Route 305 ran parallel to the school. A huge gray smokestack and a large student parking lot were to the right of the building.

Directly behind the school, a landscaped area of green sod angled sharply toward the Juniata River. Placed meticulously into the sod, flat stones painted in blue-and-gold letters spelled the words "TWIN RIVER." Next to the school's name, narrow steps constructed of weathered railroad ties slanted a precipitous path to the muddy bank. Small in the distance, crafted of four symmetrical stone arches, a train bridge spanned the river.

Opposite the school, the dark cliffs and forested bluffs of Redemption Mountain dropped deep shadows over the river. A domed church and the towering Flaming Cross were at its summit. A narrow, circuitous road wound up the side of the mountain. Jutting out of the rock, large stone tablets, each displaying one of the Ten Commandments, were placed at equidistant intervals along the road.

Just below the school at the pool where the two rivers merged, Blood Mountain rose sharply out of turbulent, swirling rapids. Clouds of mist formed at the base of the mountain. The Shadows of Death, as the mist was called by the first settlers, sent voluminous clouds that covered the pine trees at the summit. Vultures flew in and out of the mist.

Freshman Heather Wainwright wore a blue-and-gold Twin River sweatshirt and dark slacks. She was five feet eight inches tall and mature both socially and physically for her age. Her engaging personality made her popular with the girls; the natural beauty of her face and spontaneous smile made her popular with the boys. As she buttoned her lined jacket, Heather looked at the chorus and music trophies and gallery of pictures that filled the over-sized wall cabinet. A door opened, and the aroma of bacon and toast drifted in from the kitchen. Heather's mother rushed into the room. Carol wore a yellow dress. Her face was round and dimpled.

"We're running out of space," she observed, a cheerful expression on her face. "We'll have to add an extension to the house soon."

"We can get rid of some of these older trophies."

"We're not getting rid of anything. Your dad and I like the trophies and pictures here by the entrance. Visitors can see how talented you are."

"I'm not talented. I just practice a lot." Heather grabbed her book bag and turned to her mom. "Yesterday Mrs. Michaels pulled me aside. She congratulated me. She said I would have the major solo in the holiday concert."

"That's great. That's great news to begin the day with." Carol was quiet for a moment. There was a bright glow in her eyes. "What song did you choose?"

"*Home for the Holidays.*"

"That's my favorite song. I can't wait for the concert. Gram and Pap will be so proud."

"I love to see them in the front row," Heather said. "We'll be practicing late tonight." She kissed her mom and opened the door.

"Call when you're finished. Dad will pick you up."

"It's not that far. I'll walk home."

"But it's so dark at that time."

"You and Dad worry too much. I've walked to and from Twin River for years."

"Then be careful. We'll have the Christmas lights on for you."

"Okay," Heather smiled. She went out to the road that was bordered by rows of corn. The morning air was brisk and clear. Crows sounded periodic caws from deep in the corn. As Heather approached the one-lane, iron bridge, she saw a dark vehicle approaching. It moved slowly and stopped in the middle of the bridge.

Two men sat in the front seat. One puffed on a cigarette. Wearing identical blue guard uniforms, both men stared at her through the smoke. Their faces were dull and sinister. As she walked by the hood of the car, the window lowered. Clouds of smoke swirled out. Heather read "Green Hollow Correctional Camp" on the side. Suddenly the door cracked open in front of her, striking her knee. Heather cried out.

A loud horn sounded from the other side of the bridge. The bus driver honked and blinked the lights to high beams. The car door blocking Heather slammed shut; the vehicle moved forward. In a heightened state of frenzy, the crows cawed bitterly from the corn field. Heather ran off the bridge. Without looking back, she hurried up the hill to Twin River High School. Yellow busses were lining up in front of the school. Breathing heavily, Heather rushed to join the crowd of students.

"Are you out of your mind?" Luther Cicconi asked. A Marlboro dangled from his mouth; thin lines of smoke rose through his dark, shaggy mustache. He had a muscular, tall physique. "You can't be grabbing anyone in broad daylight!"

"But …" Max Wright stammered, rolling up the window. He had a crew cut, long face, and shifty eyes. His body was thin, his hands wrinkled and boney. "But she was beautiful. And she moved real pretty. Like a …"

"Like a what?" Luther asked. He bumped the car off the bridge and drove around the school bus.

"Like a dancer," Max said. "Even under that heavy coat, she was shapely. She would be a star in the videos. Isn't Nathaniel ready to open the business again?"

"Yes, he's ready." Luther puffed on the Marlboro. "Nathaniel figured we lost thousands of dollars when that fucker Jeffery squealed on us. The state police freed the girls and closed both cabins. Plus, they confiscated the video equipment. Nathaniel told me that cabins weren't in his plans anymore. His new ideas for the business are great."

"What ideas? All I know is that the FritoLay van is out and we're using a Minnie Winnie to pick up the girls. I don't know where we're keepin' them or nothin'."

"You're going to love this, Max. Nathaniel bought the Calvin property at the end of Polecat Hollow. He's fencing it off and modernizing the house and barn. Work is starting this morning. We won't have to drive all over hell and back. And he's got a great name for our new location. You'll never guess it."

"Sure, I can. It'll be named the Max and Luther Fuck Club," Max bellowed.

"It's not named any fuck club," Luther said. "It's called Happy Hollow Hunt Club. Nathaniel bought four custom Winnebago Chieftains. They're the expensive, deluxe models. He's having them transported to the barn today. Nathaniel's all excited. He's got video orders coming in already."

"It's about time. We can surprise Nathaniel with this girl. I know lots about her. I've seen her picture in the papers. She's famous. She won the singing award at the Huntingdon Country Fair last year. I was packed in the last row. I could hardly breathe. But I heard every word."

"What's her name?"

"Heather something. I'll call my brother Oliver. Don't forget he's the number one police officer in Huntingdon County. He'll find out all we need to know about Heather's schedule and where she lives."

"You're in a hurry."

"I sure am," Max agreed quickly. "I'm missin' all that money we made from the videos. And maybe I'm missin' foolin' around and havin' fun with the girls after the videos. We got to fetch Heather tonight."

"Call Oliver as soon as we get to the corrections camp."

"I will," Max said enthusiastically, a wide, sloppy grin on his face. "Heather will be comfortable and singin' in my arms tonight. I can teach her my favorite country songs like *Sugar Daddy* and *Good Ole Boys Like Me*."

"What the hell you mumbling about?" Luther asked, blowing smoke into the windshield. Max coughed and sang pitifully.

> *I guess we're all gonna be what we're gonna be*
> *So what do you do with good ol' boys like me?*

Standing and pedaling furiously down Route 305, Wayne Wilson zipped past the 15 mph yellow traffic sign, turned into the school entrance, and dropped his bicycle behind the towering smokestack. When he glanced into the vo-ag classroom and saw the students stand for the Pledge of Allegiance, Wayne sprinted toward the back exit. There was a crack in the door.

Yes, he said to himself. Wayne pushed open the door, rushed into the hallway, and stopped abruptly. Two boys wearing black sweatshirts and red athletic pants were standing at the entrance to the furnace room. Each boy leaned on a crutch. The tips of the crutch were sharpened and left scratch lines in the tile.

Identical twins, Cain and Abel Towers had similar six-foot-four-inch muscular bodies. They both had black hair, narrow green eyes, and scowling mouths. Abel wore black Converse sneakers; Cain had black suede Hush Puppies on his feet.

"We've been waiting for you, Wayne." Cain lifted his crutch and stuck the sharpened point in Wayne's face.

"Yeah," Abel said. "It's been weeks since we last seen ya. I notice you didn't bring your gun. You were full of surprises that day—playin' your stupid *Coward in the County* song and shootin' us in the knee like you did. Well, I got somethin' I've been waitin' to show ya." Abel grabbed Wayne in a choke hold. "Do you wanna see up close what you did?"

Abel pulled up the zipper on the athletic pants, exposing a dark bulbous knee swollen twice its size. The skin was stretched tight around a ten-inch purple scar that bisected the kneecap. Abel pushed Wayne's nose into the scar.

"Can you see it good and clear?" Abel asked. "Can you tell there's no bone anymore? The bone was sawed off and replaced by a metal tube and socket." Abel tightened his choke hold. Wayne's face turned red; his eyes bulged.

"Wait a minute," Cain said, pushing Abel away. "We need to talk to this farm-fuck about his sister, Becky." Cain stuck the point of his crutch under Wayne's chin. "Before Becky disappeared, did she tell you, Wayne? Did she tell you she's carrying my baby? I need to find her, Wayne. Why's Becky hiding from us?"

Wayne didn't say anything. Maneuvering the crutch, Cain lifted Wayne's chin high in the air. Blood dripped from the sharpened point. The speaker clicked, and the notes of the National Anthem echoed down the hall.

"*Oh, say can you see by the dawn's early light.*" Cain moved closer to Wayne and shouted above the music.

"We need to find your sister, Wayne. We don't mean any harm to Becky, do we, Abel?"

"No, no harm. We're all family now. Wayne, think of me as your brother."

"I'm not your brother," Wayne muttered angrily.

"But we are too brothers," Abel said. Turning his crutch sideways, he swung it into Wayne's abdomen. Wayne gave a muffled cry. Abel was readying the crutch again when the door to the furnace room opened and Gene Brooks stepped into the hall.

The school custodian wore neat gray slacks and a blue, long-sleeved shirt rolled up to the elbows. He was six-feet-two-inches tall, had an agile, muscular frame, and sharp facial features. Gene watched as Abel made a sour face and lowered the crutch. Leaning forward, Cain twisted the point of his crutch slightly, slicing into Wayne's chin. Gene ripped the crutch out of his hands and tossed it into the furnace room.

"What the hell's going on?"

"Nothing," Cain said. "Wayne was curious about our replacement knees. Abel was showing him his new scar." Cain smirked. "Tell him, Wayne. Tell him it was nothing." The concluding notes, "*o'er the land of the free and the home of the brave,*" sounded in the hall. A student began reading the morning announcements.

"Yeah, it was nothing," Wayne said, wiping at the blood on his chin. "I'm late. I should go to class." Wayne walked down the hall. Abel lowered the zipper on his athletic pants, covering the swollen leg. The student announcer invited everyone to "have a great day." When the speakers clicked off, Gene looked at Cain and Abel.

"Do you invalids need help getting to class?" he asked.

"Don't call us invalids," Cain said.

"Yeah, that ain't polite," Abel said. "Don't call us that. We're as strong as anyone in this school."

"Stronger," Cain said. He and Abel limped down the hall. Abel stopped at the water fountain.

"That bastard janitor," Abel said.

"Mr. Brooks isn't the problem right now."

"Yeah, I know. What are we gonna do about Wayne?"

"We waited long enough. I think it's time we killed the farm-fuck. Tonight, after rehab, we'll make a visit to Polecat Hollow."

"What about Becky?"

"She can wait," Cain answered. "First things first." He turned and limped down the hall. Scraping his crutch along the floor, Abel followed him.

"We got to get your crutch back."

"I don't need no fuckin' crutch," Cain said.

Room 8 in Twin River High School had four large windows that faced Route 305. A 1980 calendar lay flat on the teacher's desk cluttered with multicolored pens, a copy of the November 6 *Philadelphia Inquirer*, and a blue Twin River discipline pad. A silver pencil sharpener was screwed to the corner of the desk. A large trash can was under it.

Working at the blackboard, substitute teacher Miss Victoria Stanley wore a long-sleeved white blouse and a blue ruffled skirt dotted with yellow butterflies. She had a narrow face; silver-framed glasses rested midway down her pointed nose. She finished writing, put the chalk in the tray, and clapped the dust off her hands. Victoria was reviewing the instructions when the bell rang.

SIT DOWN IN ASSIGNED SEAT
STUDY HALL MEANS STUDY
NO TALKING
NO HALL PASSES

There was the sudden congestion of bodies in the hall, lockers slamming, loud laughing and talking. Students began filing into the room. Some paused, read the instructions, and wandered to their seats. Sophomore Matt Henry stopped and glanced at *The Philadelphia Inquirer*. Noticing the small but bold-print advertisement, "Have Weapons Will Travel," on the corner of the page, he sat in the front desk.

Matt was fourteen years old, five feet eight inches tall. He had brown hair that fell over his forehead and covered his ears. His face was clear, soft in the light. His large brown eyes were bright and gleamed with intensity. Matt wore a medium Twin River sweatshirt, old jeans, and orange Pro-Keds.

Matt's best friend, Conner Brooks, walked into the room, nodded to Matt, and sat across from him. Conner was also a sophomore, fourteen years old, and an even six feet. His black hair was thick, cut neatly to the top of his ears. He had a high forehead and blue eyes. Conner wore the school sweatshirt, jeans, and a pair of white Pro-Keds.

"Conner," Matt said, "can you meet me at the bike stand after school? I want to go to the Cicconi house."

"Sure. What's at the Cicconi house?"

"You'll see when we get there," Matt said.

The students were in their seats when the bell rang. Miss Victoria Stanley pointed to the blackboard and read the instructions in a raspy tone. She also added that no student would be excused from the room. Then she raised her voice and warned everyone.

"If you didn't bring any work, I will present you with a copy of *Webster's Dictionary*. You will write down fifty complex words and definitions and turn the paper in at the end of the period. Any student talking or causing trouble will be sent to the office." Victoria scrutinized the rows of student faces for a moment and sat down. She leaned forward and opened *The Philadelphia Inquirer*.

As he worked on his book report, "The Chicken Thief Soldier, A Death at Valley Forge," Matt followed Victoria's progress on the newspaper. When she reached the comic section, grinning profusely, she whispered, "Oh, dear me, Lucy. Let Linus have his silly blanket." Making a chuckling sound, she folded the paper. Matt immediately got to his feet and walked to the desk. Victoria looked up; her lips barely moved.

"I told you there would be no hall passes."

"I don't need a hall pass," Matt said.

"Then why are you here?"

"*The Philadelphia Inquirer* … is that your newspaper?"

"Yes, of course, it's my newspaper. It's the only one I read. The local paper is worthless. They print slanderous garbage in their "Opinion Line." When I read it on Saturday, I see nothing but ignorant and rude statements. Last month someone called in and stated that Violet, the new substitute teacher at TR, was mean and looked like she had just crawled out of a grave. I mean that dumb caller couldn't even get my name right. And the editors printed it!"

"That's not polite to print your name if it's not accurate," Matt stated. He paused for a moment, shuffling his feet together. "I wanted permission to borrow your newspaper for a few minutes. I saw a headline and would like to read the article."

"What headline?"

"About the presidential election." Pointing to the column, Matt read the first lines. "Voter turnout in recent election is the lowest in decades. Only 52.6 percent of eligible voters participated."

"I always read the important section of the newspaper first," Victoria said. "I didn't get to that article yet. But I'm delighted Ronald Reagan won the election. You like the new president, don't you?" She glanced at the seating chart and picked out his name. "Don't you, Matt Henry?"

"I liked him in the movie *Bedtime for Bonzo*. Reagan was a psychologist, and he gave tests to Bonzo, who was a chimp. He was funny—"

"Our newly elected president was funny?"

"No, the chimp was funny."

"Oh," Victoria said. "Here." She handed him the newspaper. "When you've finished the article, return *The Philadelphia Inquirer* to my desk. And don't crinkle the pages."

"Crinkle?"

"Be careful to keep the pages folded nice and smooth."

"Okay," Matt said. As he returned to his seat, Conner looked up and rolled his eyes. Matt sat, straightened the newspaper, and focused his attention on the advertisement in the corner of the page.

Have Weapons Will Travel
Guaranteed Protection
Individual, Home, or Business

Palladin
131 N 10th Street
Philadelphia, PA 19107

Matt picked up his pencil and began to copy the information in his notebook. Then there was a loud engine noise on Route 305. Turning toward the windows, Miss Victoria Stanley stood and looked at the black garbage truck, "Landis Sanitation" printed on the side. Clouds of exhaust rose in the air and drifted toward the school. Pushing her chair away from the desk, Victoria moved quickly and slammed the window shut. Matt moved just as quickly. He ripped out the ad, folded it, and slid it into his pocket.

The noise on the road lessened, the smoke settled, and the Landis Sanitation truck disappeared down the hill. Victoria returned to the desk and sat down. Waiting a few minutes, folding the ripped page carefully, Matt stood, walked across the floor, and returned the newspaper to its spot on the desk. Victoria raised her skinny hand and straightened her glasses.

"What do you think you're doing, young man?" she asked curtly.

"Returning the newspaper like you said to."

"What is the matter with you, Mr. Matt Henry?"

"Nothing."

"Nothing!" she snapped. "I instructed you to return my *Philadelphia Inquirer* the same way you received it. Is that correct?"

"Yes."

"Then why did you rip it to pieces?"

"I didn't—"

"Don't talk to me in that tone of voice. I see the corner page is ripped out. You're a sneak and a thief and a liar. What would your mother say to that?"

"It wouldn't bother her," Matt said in a soft voice. "It wouldn't bother her at all."

"Well, let's just walk down to the office and call her."

"You can't call her."

"What do you mean, I can't call her?"

Matt didn't answer. Everyone in the class was looking at him and Miss Victoria Stanley. As the silence intensified, Conner leaned forward.

"You can't call her," he blurted. "No one can call her. She's dead."

"Is that right?" Victoria asked incredulously.

"She died fourteen years ago," Matt said. "You shouldn't be doing that."

"Doing what?"

"You shouldn't be talking about my mom."

"Don't tell me …" Victoria began. The lines of small bumps on her forehead hardened, turned a shade of pink. "There must be someone at your house who can correct your bad habits. I'll call your dad."

"You can't do that either," Conner volunteered. "Mr. Henry's on vacation. Matt's staying at my house. My dad's the custodian here. You can call him."

"I'm not calling no toilet cleaner about a discipline problem," Victoria broadcast loudly. Then she pointed her finger at Matt. "When's your dad coming back?"

"I don't expect him back anytime soon."

"Well, isn't that just too convenient—no father or mother to keep you on the straight path. There's no excuse for what you did. You tore up my newspaper, and that's destruction of property." Victoria straightened the blue discipline pad on the desk and began writing. After signing it, she ripped the page from the pad and handed it to Matt.

"I didn't mean to cause a problem."

"Just shut up and take this to the office! Maybe the principal can deal with a boy who tells lies about a dead mother and delinquent father."

Grimacing, holding back the *Go to Hell* response burning his lips, Matt took the paper. He grabbed his books, left the room, and walked down the hall. Situated near the main entrance, the Twin River office had see-through glass walls. The interior had a wooden rack with rows of faculty mail slots, some cushioned chairs, and a counter with a swinging door. The secretary's desk, a large work area, and a closed door with a black plaque, "MR. ARTHUR PORT, HIGH SCHOOL PRINCIPAL," on the front, were on the other side of the counter.

Matt entered the office, put the discipline report on the counter, and sat on a cushioned chair. Talking on the phone at her desk, the secretary didn't look up. The principal's door opened. Arthur Port walked to the counter, scanned the office, and picked up the discipline report.

Dressed in a blue coat and tie, Mr. Port was in his sixties and walked with a limp. His tan face was deeply lined; his brow was furrowed. Reading quickly, the principal lowered the discipline report and looked at Matt slumped in the chair. The boy's face was gloomy, eyes downcast.

"I see you've got yourself on the wrong side of the substitute teacher. What happened, Matt?"

"Miss Stanley wrote me up for ripping her newspaper. Then she said something about Mom. She said she was going to call my mom and tell her I was a sneak and a liar." Matt lowered his head, shuffling his shoes on the floor.

"Were you rude to the teacher?"

"No."

"Did you use any profanity?"

"I wanted to, but I didn't."

"Fair enough," the principal said. "It's nearly lunchtime, Matt. Go on down and be the first in line."

"There's no detention?"

"No, Matt. Enjoy your lunch."

Matt stood, nodded to Mr. Port, and walked to the door. The principal waited a few moments, rolled up the discipline paper, and tossed it in the air. It banked off the side of the counter and landed in the trash can.

A few minutes before the end of class, Conner grabbed the Mead CAREBEARS notebook from the desk of freckled, curly-haired Suzy Pickles sitting across from him. Turning through the notebook, Conner ripped out the first blank page, covered it with his forearm, and wrote quickly. When the change-of-class bell rang and students rushed for the door, Conner slipped the page onto Victoria's desk. The message scribbled in heavy, dark letters was brief. It read, "For immediate release to the Opinion Line. The substitute teacher at TR is a real bitch."

At lunchtime, sophomore Alice Byrd waited in the hall as students raced past each other to get a place in line. Alice was medium height. She had long brown hair and brown eyes that sparkled. Alice wore a blue blouse and matching slacks. The top buttons of her blouse were open, revealing clear, smooth skin and the shadow cleavage of prominent breasts. From inside the cafeteria, the sounds of talking and laughter and the noise of sliding trays filled the hallway.

Carrying a ham-and-cheese sandwich and a milk carton, Matt Henry walked past the potbellied cafeteria monitor,

Mr. Haverhill, who was standing half-asleep at the exit. Matt came up behind Alice and took her hand.

"I brought your lunch," he said. Noticing Mr. Haverhill's head slump lower on his chest, he led Alice down the hall.

"Where are we going?"

"It's a nice day. You can eat outside in the fresh air."

"What about your lunch?"

"I already ate. I came down early."

A heavy chain was wrapped around the push-bar at the exit. Matt saw the open padlock and dropped the chain to the floor, and he and Alice stepped outside into bright sunshine. They walked quickly around the corner of the building and across the road to the baseball field. Matt was still holding her hand when he led her down the cement steps to the dugout. Alice sat on the wooden bench. Matt sat next to her.

"Now what?" she asked. Matt gave her the sandwich.

"I'm going to watch you eat like I do every day."

"That must be boring," Alice said. She peeled off the wrapper and took a bite of the ham-and-cheese sandwich.

"No, it's not boring." Matt watched when she swallowed, saw how the muscles in her throat moved, saw how the fabric of her blue blouse lifted slightly.

"I'll eat quickly. We have to get back before the bell rings." She took another bite of the sandwich and threw the remainder in a trash barrel. Matt gave her the milk carton.

"Alice, I have something to tell you. I won't see you at lunch tomorrow. I'm missing school. But it's important. I'm taking the train to Philadelphia."

"That's so far away. Why are you going there? Is your dad there?"

"No, Mr. Henry's not in Philadelphia," Matt said. "I have to see a man. His name's Palladin. I want him to come to Alexandria and work in the bank."

"Can't you just phone him?" she asked. Matt shook his head.

"Mr. Henry said I should talk to him personally."

"I'll miss you," Alice said. She drank some of the milk, dropped the carton in the barrel, and moved closer to Matt.

"I'll miss you more," Matt said. He put his arm around her shoulders, leaned forward, and kissed her. Her lips were moist and milky. As he moved his tongue deeper, the milk turned warm and sweet. Matt felt his heart beating faster. The hardening muscles of his chest brushed against the soft cushion of her breasts. Matt took a long, slow breath. The three-minute warning bell rang from a far distance. Locked in their embrace, Matt and Alice slid further into the shadows of the dugout.

As the dismissal bell rang at the end of classes, Twin River principal Arthur Port and school custodian Gene Brooks walked through the back exit, crossed the road, and stood on the bank overlooking the Juniata. Across the river, the black rock, shrubs, and pine trees of Redemption Mountain rose high in the air. A dark cloud covered the sun, and when the cloud drifted by, bright rays of light reflected off the towering cross at the summit. Covering his eyes from the glare, the principal stared at the Flaming Cross.

"Gene, you've worked here a long time. Did you ever think about the significance of the school's location?"

"What do you mean?"

"Well, think about it. The school's an integral part of a triangle. On Redemption Mountain, we have faith. Here at Twin River we have reason. And on Blood Mountain, we have …"

"Death!" Gene finished the sentence. "We have the Shadows of Death. Is that what you meant?"

"No, but I see your point. Faith and reason can help us understand the complexities of death."

"There are no complexities, Mr. Port. Death has a finality beyond faith and reason. The grim reaper stalks us relentlessly, haphazardly at times, and swings his razor-sharp scythe. If not sooner, then later. If you don't prepare yourself, take the necessary precautions, it'll be sooner."

"That's too gloomy for me."

"Gloomy or not, I've seen it happen enough times to believe it's true."

"Is that what you learned in Vietnam?"

"In Vietnam I learned how to kill swiftly and quietly."

"With those knives I've seen in your house?"

"Arkansas toothpicks," Gene said. "In the jungle—well, I should say anywhere—the throwing knife was my weapon of choice."

"Matt's been staying with you and Conner since his father disappeared. Is that what you're teaching him?"

"Matt's a great kid. I'm teaching him hunting skills. And shooting skills. I'm teaching him just like I taught Conner. Conner's an expert marksman. Matt will be too."

"I saw Matt in the office today. He looked upset, dejected, kind of *hopeless*. Do you think he's worried about his dad?"

"No, he's not worried about Mr. Henry. The bank manager has been gone for weeks. It would be best if he never returned."

"I don't agree, Gene. I think a kid needs his parents when he's growing up." Mr. Port was pensive for a moment. "I was glad to hear that Lucy returned home."

"It was difficult without her," Gene said. "I missed her. And Conner really missed her. Now that she's back, it's like we're a family again."

"That's why I think Matt needs his father. His mother died in childbirth. Mr. Henry is all the family he has."

"I don't like to talk about that man," Gene said. He glanced at Blood Mountain. Dark clouds covered the summit. Only the outer limbs of the towering pine tree were visible. Winged forms shook loose from the branches, and a line of vultures circled through the shadows. Deep in thought, Gene followed their flight as they swooped toward the rapids. Mr. Port spoke and interrupted his reverie.

"Gene … Gene!"

"What?" Gene turned away from Blood Mountain. They exchanged glances. "I'm sorry. I was distracted. What was it?"

"I was going to say the Reverend Towers's sons, Cain and Abel, are back in school. They recovered real fast from those knee replacements. With their return, I think the quiet times at Twin River are over. They're like ticking bombs. Those twins are good examples of what can happen when you grow up without a mother. I remember that one of the boys found Irene Towers at the base of Redemption Mountain. Her death was devastating to the family. The Reverend Towers hasn't fully recovered from the loss."

"It's changed him. He's become a mean-spirited person," Gene said. "I hear in his sermons he talks more about revenge than he does about forgiveness."

"The complexities of death," Mr. Port said. "If we abandon faith and reason, we lose *hope*. We're left with revenge in our thoughts. Then we become totally lost."

Chapter Three

Green Hollow Correctional Camp
Thursday Morning

Built on fifty acres at the edge of a heavily forested game preserve, Green Hollow Correctional Camp for juvenile offenders was located twenty miles from Twin River High School. It had an athletic field, basketball court, administration building, two classrooms, cafeteria, dormitory with bunk beds, and a shooting range. The dog pen next to the basketball court was constructed of a rickety wooden fence. Some standing, ears pricked back, some sitting, jaws low to the ground, five healthy pit bulls occupied the pen.

The camp itself was enclosed by a chain-link fence with coils of barbed wire clamped to the top. Many of the original coils had broken off and lay at the base of the fence. An imposing gate, elevated speed bump, and air-conditioned guard station marked the entrance to the camp. The sparkling water of Globe Run flowed behind the camp. Throughout the day, native brook trout smacked flies and insects floating on the surface.

On Thursday morning, the sky was blue; the air was brisk. Dressed in the camp uniform of brown shirt and pants, Ira Hays was on the basketball court playing horse. Ira was sixteen years old, six feet tall, and very athletic. He had a light complexion and hawkish eyes. Ira had stenciled

Pittsburgh Penguins on the front of his shirt. Standing at the foul line, Jamal Pritchett, a hulking Negro from North Philadelphia with Chocolate Thunder scratched on his shirt, dribbled the ball adroitly from hand to hand. Ira looked at him.

"What's this *Chocolate Thunder* stuff, Jamal?"

"You never been to Philadelphia, have you? Darrel Dawkins is the Thunder. He dunked the ball so hard last year in Kansas City that the whole backboard came crashing to the floor. When he did it again in Philadelphia, the NBA officers got real worried. They said all that flying glass was dangerous and that the cleanup delayed the game too much. You know what they did about the problem?" Jamal stared at Ira, who shook his head. "The NBA spent all this money and invented the break-away rim."

"We got no break-away rims here, Jamal? And we got no glass backboards. You planning to dunk the ball, maybe bend the rim, and win this game?"

"That's exactly how I'm gonna win. Because I know one thing for sure."

"What's that?"

"Penguins don't dunk. They can't even jump."

"You're wrong as usual, Jamal. I saw a penguin jump seven feet out of the water and land on an iceberg."

"Where'd you see that?

"Pittsburgh Zoo."

"Ira, you're so full of shit. Pay close attention, and watch the Thunder gravitate." Jamal took two giant steps, jumped at the basket, and slammed the ball powerfully into the side of the rim. The ball bounced away. His body twisting precariously, Jamal hung onto the rim with both hands. It made a harsh, grating noise. Jamal released his grip and dropped lightly to the cement. Ira retrieved the ball.

"Nice try, Thunder." Ira walked to the corner, and setting his feet, he shot the ball high in the air. The seams rotating slowly, the ball descended and rattled through the chain net. Ira laughed, retrieved the ball, and passed it to Jamal. There was a large plastic Mineral Springs bottle on the ground. Ira picked it up, gulped down the water, and tossed the bottle into a rust-coated trash barrel. Wiping his lips, he looked at Jamal.

"You miss," he said. "You out."

"I'm never out." Jamal dribbled once, twice, aimed, and shot a line drive from the corner. The ball ricocheted off the rim, rolled across the dirt field, and hit the barbed wire at the fence. There was a hissing sound. One of the pit bulls barked loudly.

"Shit," Jamal said.

"You suck so bad." Ira laughed, walking toward the fence. "I got the ball.

"Let it be," Jamal cautioned. "You know the rules, Ira. Don't go near the fence."

"I signed it out. I got to return it." Ira hesitated and then began running to the fence. Snapping jaws, the four other pit bulls snarled and charged against the boards of the pen.

Glancing in their direction, Ira pulled the ball out of the barbed wire. Sprinting back to the basketball court, Ira saw Jamal on the way to the dormitory. Dressed in their blue guard uniforms, their eyes focused on Ira, Luther Cicconi and Max Wright stood in the center circle. Luther was smoking a Marlboro. Max stepped forward.

"What the hell do you think you're doin'?" he sneered.

Ira didn't answer. He held the deflated ball against his chest. Then he lowered his head and started to walk around them. Luther grabbed his arm, stopping him at the edge of the center circle.

"Not so fast," he said. He spun Ira around and brushed his hand across the brown shirt. "Pittsburgh Penguin," he read slowly. "Why you defacing state property? No one will want to wear a shitty shirt with Penguin written on it."

"I'll pay for the shirt. I'll take it with me when I go home."

"You're not going home anytime soon," Max pronounced.

"Wait a minute," Luther said. "If Ira cooperates, we could see him leaving the camp sometime next year. What do you think, Ira? Do you want to cooperate?"

"Cooperate how?"

"It seems your girlfriend, Lisa, has gone missing. We have a job for her. A good-paying job. You can help us find her."

"I don't know where she is."

"Oh, Lisa was here, Ira. Right here in this camp. But Dan Boonie, the stupid new guard, helped her get away."

"I don't know anything about that." Ira looked past Luther at Jamal, who had reached the dormitory and was watching them.

"We think you do know," Luther said. "And each day we don't find out about Lisa's whereabouts, it's going to be twenty-four hours of hell for you."

"I said I don't know anything. The last time I saw Lisa was at the Pittsburgh train station. That's all I know."

"That's all you know about your favorite pussy?" Luther asked. "I guess you are pretty stupid. And look how dumb you write. You spelled Pittsburgh Penguins all wrong because you never completely dotted your *i*'s. Hold him, Max." Luther inhaled deeply, the cigarette glowing brightly. Max clamped Ira's arms tight behind his back.

"The prisoner ain't goin' nowhere."

"Make sure he doesn't," Luther said. Taking the Marlboro from his lips, he stuck the flaming ash on the *i* in Pittsburgh and held it there. A round hole burned in the cloth; the jagged edges flared brightly, and a line of smoke rose in the air.

"It's looking good," Luther observed. He pressed the cigarette deeper. The bright ash seared the skin. A sweet smell rose in the air. Ira gagged, the red veins on his neck pulsing, ballooning in size.

"Don't forget the other *i*, Luther. You know what the experts say. Two *eyes* is better than one." Max guffawed and strengthened his grip.

Luther nodded, slid the Marlboro between his lips, and inhaled a mouthful of smoke. The ash brightened. Luther studied it for a second, exhaled, and then pressed the cigarette over the *i* in Penguin. Wispy lines of smoke lifted in the air. The fabric disintegrated; the burning ash reached the skin. Ira gave out a muffled cry and gagged. Mineral Springs gushed from his mouth and spattered across Luther's shirt. Luther swore and punched Ira in the gut.

Standing on the dormitory steps, Jamal watched the three bodies on the basketball court. He saw Ira collapse between the two guards and took off running.

"Hey!" he shouted. Luther turned at the noise and saw Jamal.

"Well, we're about done here, Max." He dropped the Marlboro to the cement, leaned down, and got in Ira's face. "The next time we won't be so nice. Just remember, Ira. When you tell us where Lisa is, your troubles will go away."

Luther straightened, and he and Max Wright walked toward the administration building. Breathing hard, Jamal reached the basketball court. Glancing at the black holes and blood smears scorched in Ira's shirt, he bent down and lifted Ira to his feet.

"You all right, man?" Max asked. Ira didn't answer. Jamal took him by the shoulder and helped him walk to the dormitory.

Chapter Four

Philadelphia, Pennsylvania
Thursday Morning

Wesley Palladin was twenty-eight years old. His six-foot-one-inch body frame had a lithe, muscular tone. He had a healthy tan; his hair was thick and black. His mustache curved up at the corners and was neatly trimmed. Palladin often had a gun belt and Colt .45 on his waist. The word *Omerta* was skillfully engraved in red on the barrel.

It was two o'clock Thursday morning. Palladin was dressed in jeans, black jungle boots, and a green M-65 field jacket recently purchased at Philadelphia's Goldberg Army & Navy Surplus Store on Chestnut Street. Swinging a flashlight and striding between the memorials at Morris Cemetery in Phoenixville, Palladin stopped suddenly in front of a three-foot-high granite tombstone. There was a cross at the top of the tombstone. The inscription under the cross caught his eye.

In Memory of our Beloved Son
Henry Hightower
1964–1980

"This one," Palladin said.

"We've checked dozens of tombstones," Amos Williams complained. Amos was short and stocky, and he was also wearing an army surplus jacket, boots, and pants. His shoulders were broad, and his neck was thick. "Why did you pick this grave?"

"Henry's sixteen years old," Palladin said. "The age is right."

"When are you going to tell me why we need a stiff?"

"We can talk about it later," Palladin said.

"If you remember—"

"Just remind me," Palladin said. "You selected the diggers. Can you trust them?"

"They always get amnesia once I pay them. But Curtis and Trevor have never dug up a corpse before."

Amos whistled. There was talking and the clanging of shovels, and two men dressed in dark hooded sweatshirts walked to the tombstone. The shorter one had a black body bag over his shoulder. Trevor, the taller, heavier one spoke.

"Let me get this straight," he said in a strident tone. "You expect us to do all this digging, desecrate a grave, and probably damn our souls to hellfire for three hundred dollars? No way, Dog!" Trevor stuck his shovel in the earth and stood there defiantly.

"Now what do I do?" Amos asked Palladin.

"They're your men. Bargain with them."

"Okay," Amos said, facing Trevor. "Four hundred dollars."

"Not enough, Dog." Curtis threw his shovel on the grave and walked away with Trevor. Palladin clapped his hands.

"Eight hundred dollars," he said. "Apiece."

Curtis stopped in his tracks. He hurried back, picked up his shovel, and started digging. Trevor was right next to him throwing shovelfuls of dirt onto a pile. After ten minutes, they had dug out the outline of a hole. After another ten minutes, an acrid stench filled the hole. Backing away, Amos disappeared in a grove of trees. He lit a match. A thin line of smoke curled in the air, and Amos began to cough. Shaking his head, Wesley stood quietly and watched as the two hooded diggers descended deeper into the earth. There was a clunking sound. Trevor coughed, gagged, and then threw up.

"We found the coffin," Curtis muttered.

"Open it. Slide the body in the bag. Then jump out of there and fill the hole."

"You're damn crazy!" Trevor kneeled over and threw up again. Regaining his balance, he banged the shovel against the coffin. The noise echoed through the cemetery. Covering his nose, Palladin walked away from the grave and joined Amos in the trees.

Later that day driving through the afternoon traffic on Route 30W, dressed in identical brown coats, tan shirts, and dark-chocolate ties, Wesley Palladin and his associate Amos Williams sat comfortably in a silver 1980 Cadillac Eldorado Biarritz. Under its sleek elongated hood, the Eldorado had a Diesel 368 with a four-barrel Quadrajet carburetor. Smooth-riding, climate controlled, and soundproof, the Biarritz model had a plush leather interior with fine wood paneling. Amos opened the glove compartment and checked inside.

"What are you searching for?"

"A strong drink."

"We're working on the most important contract of my career, Amos. We'll be finished by three. Then you can drink." Palladin glanced over. Amos closed the compartment.

"We got a contract, and I don't see your Colt."

"I got the derringer under my belt."

"I wouldn't carry a derringer for nothing." Amos stared at Palladin, the dark shadows on his face. "You're looking a bit tired today."

"Sometimes I have trouble sleeping."

"I never thought you had trouble doing anything." Glancing out the window, Amos noticed a blonde driving a silver-and-black Ford Thunderbird in the next lane. He whistled and waved. The blonde accelerated.

"She wasn't your type," Palladin said.

"Sure she was," Amos said. He stared as the Thunderbird cut across the lane and exited. "Palladin, I was wondering. When are we going to do the Purgatory contract?"

"You still concerned about those damn mutts?" Palladin said.

"Puppies," Amos corrected. "It wasn't right what happened. My cousin bought a Great Pyrenees from one of those Lancaster puppy farms. It had some kind of disease. In twenty-four hours, the disease killed the puppy and their two dachshunds. The kids are hurt the most. What kind of person would raise and sell sick puppies? We need to visit the farm and straighten things out."

"Let's finish this Romano job," Palladin said. "Then we'll go to Purgatory."

"My cousin will appreciate that." Amos slid his hand across the gaudy leather dash. "What the hell prompted you to buy this car?"

"In 1973, I saw my first Eldorado in *Live and Let Die*. I watched the movie five times. Then I made my final decision."

"Wesley, it's nothing but a *pimpmobile*. Your daddy would turn over in his grave if he saw you in this car."

"I loved my daddy," Palladin said. "But he was a hoarder. He didn't know how to spend all the money he earned."

"And you do?"

"That's right."

"Your old man was a funny, stubborn guy. He did his contracts one way. His way. Clean and professional. How old were you when you began your killing career?"

"I was fourteen, Amos. Dad whacked me on the side of the head and made me kill this rich bastard when we were bass fishing in Florida. I still have nightmares about Henry."

"Henry! That name sounds familiar. How'd it go? I'll bet you enjoyed it."

"Hell, no. I didn't enjoy it, Amos. Well, maybe I enjoyed it a little. As a reward, Dad gave me Henry's Colt."

"The one with *Omerta* on it?"

"Yes."

"I never heard that whole story. We should talk about it sometime. I guess I don't know a lot of things about your old man. I don't even know why we got along so well."

"He thought highly of you, Amos. He respected your loyalty."

"Oh, loyalty. That was easy. I learned early on not to cross Mr. Palladin." Amos made a face, and he sneezed.

"You catching a cold or something?" Palladin asked.

"After working in an icebox cemetery all morning, what do you expect?"

"What work? You were hiding in the trees smoking Kools."

"The menthol helped with all the stink in the air. And I wasn't hiding. I was on lookout. No one in the history of my family was ever arrested for grave robbing."

"It had to be done."

"So you say." Amos sat silently for a moment. With heavy truck and car traffic on Route 30, the only sound in the Eldorado was the soft humming of the heater. "I shouldn't complain. We've been busy ever since the Gentle Don was murdered."

"For twenty-two years Angelo Bruno ran the Philly mob. Then he's killed in his car in front of his house on Snyder Avenue. It was a cowardly hit. Angelo was shot in the back of the head. He had a wife and two kids."

"His consigliere, Tony Bananas, orchestrated the murder."

"Omerta," Palladin said. "Tony the Banana Man broke the oath. His body was found in a car trunk in New York City. He had hundred-dollar bills stuffed down his throat and up his ass. The mob payment for greed." Palladin thumped down on the gas. Motor purring smoothly, the Eldorado raced past a line of trucks.

"I thought you might have been in on that contract."

"No. I wouldn't have wasted any Ben Franklins on the Banana Man."

"Everything's been in flux since the murder." Amos reached for a Kool, sniffed the menthol, and put the Kool back in his shirt pocket. "So who you working for now?"

"You don't need that information."

"It's Scavone, isn't it? You're going in with Nicodemo Scavone. He's got those two goons we had a run-in with. They were ready to kill you—and me."

"Noodles and Loco are total idiots. When I *clocked* Loco in the head, he forgot the time of day."

"I don't want to see either one of them. They only show up to hurt people."

"That's what I do."

"You never hurt anyone, Wesley Palladin. You just kill them. Today it's that lawyer, Caesar Romano."

"Not just him, Amos. The contract's for the entire family. I never did a family-style execution before."

"Neither have I," Amos said. "What'd Romano do that was so terrible?"

"After the don's murder, Romano had the books. He took advantage of the confusion. He started collecting the mob's money, and there was a lot of it stashed around."

"What's with all the video equipment?"

"Scavone wants everything recorded. He wants to see Romano bawling and pissing his pants in front of his wife and boy. The don gave me a precise murder sequence. He wants the boy done first, slowly with lots of blood. Then the wife. 'Make it last a long time,' he said. And then he wants me to cut Caesar's throat and let him bleed out. He wants the camera zoomed in close for that. Scavone called it the 'grand finale.'"

"Why all the drama?"

"He's just doing what he thinks he needs to do to stay on top. Scavone plans to show the video to family members and associates. Scare the hell out of everyone. There's only one showing. Then he's destroying the video." Palladin glanced at Amos. "Did you get the Halloween stuff?"

"Sure, I got the vials of fake blood and that rubber skin patch. I had to run to King of Prussia. What's going on?"

"Nothing," Palladin said. He turned the Eldorado off Route 30 onto Morris Avenue. "We have to make a quick stop at Bryn Mawr College."

Traffic was slow. Palladin blew the horn and pulled around a Mercedes. A police officer on the corner stiffened and stared at the Eldorado. Palladin kept his eyes on the road; Amos smiled and waved at the officer.

"We sure got his attention. I'll bet the local fuzz don't see any Bryn Mawr billionaires driving pimpmobiles through town." He laughed and settled back on the cushioned seat.

When the Eldorado turned onto Merion Street, Amos lowered the window and gawked at the two towers in front of a massive medieval stone building. The leafy branches of a weeping hemlock dropped gray shadows over the crafted layers of masonry.

"What the hell is that?"

"Rockefeller Residence Hall," Palladin said. "Wait till you see the next building." He drove down the street and approached a sprawling stone complex with similar towers. Covering a large section of the building, a Japanese linden lofted thick, twisted branches over the golf-green lawn.

"It's like a castle," Amos said. "Or a fortress."

Palladin slowed when he neared the corner of Merion and New Gulph Road. Cars were tightly parked in front of Dalton Hall. He scrutinized each vehicle, eventually stopping and double-parking next to a blue Pontiac Sunbird. A red-and-white sticker on the bumper read, "Reagan for President—Bush for Vice President!"

Palladin unsnapped the cover of the leather sheath attached to his belt and pulled out a Minnesota ice pick. It had a grooved wooden handle capped with a metal cover; the high-carbon steel of the pick was tapered to an extremely sharp point. Reaching to the inside pocket of his coat, Palladin pulled out a side-opening stiletto switchblade. He pressed the button, and the silver blade swung out. Holding the switchblade in his right hand and the ice pick in the left, he hesitated a moment. Then he closed the switchblade and put it back in his pocket.

"This won't take long." Palladin checked the rows of windows in Dalton Hall and stepped outside. Moving quickly, he walked around the Sunbird, puncturing each tire. Palladin left the ice pick slanting out of the fourth tire and got back in the Eldorado. Amos gave him a quizzical look.

"Last night we did some grave robbing. This afternoon, simple vandalism. What's next?"

"Caesar Romano and his family. We're making a fortune on this one. Romano's multimillion-dollar estate is close by. We're right on schedule."

"Whose car did you just trash?"

"The Sunbird belongs to Jane Romano, Caesar's wife."

"You just said she's listed on the contract?"

"Yes, Jane's on the contract, but she didn't steal any of the money. Scavone wants Caesar to watch her die. He wants him to suffer. But I won't harm her just to please Scavone. By the time she has those tires repaired and gets home, we'll be long gone."

"You sure you got the right vehicle?"

"Why?"

"You said that Romano owns a million-dollar estate and lives in Bryn Mawr. People here don't drive five-thousand-dollar Sunbirds."

"I met Jane last week," Palladin said. "She's frugal."

"Is she pretty too?"

"She's a knockout," Palladin said. "A total knockout!" Bright sunlight flashed off the windshield. His mind racing, Palladin thought back to Saturday when Mr. Scavone celebrated his wife's birthday at the Valley Forge Sheraton.

The parking lot at the Sheraton was filled. Along with prominent guests, more than thirty made members and fifty associates of Scavone's Philly mob attended the celebration. Dressed in a dark, elegant suit crafted by Enzo Custom Clothiers on Rittenhouse Square, matched with a red silk shirt and white tie, Palladin arrived late and was informed that valet parking was closed.

There was a thunder of noise behind him, and a polished, oversized motorcycle cruised by. Prominent on his black jacket, the driver had the red-and-white colors and the Harpy insignia of the Warlocks Motorcycle Club. Roaring to a stop, the Warlock parked in a narrow space near the entrance. Palladin was about to leave when a young attendant hurried over and guaranteed Palladin he would find a parking spot.

"I'll do anything to drive a genuine pimpmobile," he said. Palladin thanked him, walked into the Sheraton, and took the elevator to the ballroom on the top floor. At the receiving line, Palladin congratulated Don Scavone and his wife. The Don had a smooth but hard face. He was medium height and strong physically. He wore a luxurious navy suit.

"Vicuna," Palladin said respectfully. "How many of those small llama, do you think, Don Scavone, were sheared to produce such an exquisite suit?"

"Too many." Scavone smiled. "I went to Peru. To the Andes. I had to see the source of the fleece. It was freezing, but the animals were protected from the cold by this very soft, unique fur. After the sheering ceremony, which followed strict Incan tradition, I understood why vicuna was so precious."

"And expensive," Palladin commented. "I would say your garment would exceed fifty thousand dollars."

"The price is of no consequence."

"Not to you," Palladin said. "The important consequence is what you project to others, to everyone in this hall."

"What do I project, Mr. Palladin?"

"The best of the best."

"Not the most cunning, the most ruthless?"

"That is already understood." Palladin looked past Don Scavone at the congregation of spectators in the massive hall. "That was understood before these people entered the Sheraton."

"Very perceptive. The best of the best. I like that. I would say that is the primary reason you are in my employment. Tell me something, Mr. Palladin. Are you afraid of me?"

"Not in the least."

"Are you afraid of anyone?"

"No," Palladin said. He stared into the don's eyes. "My daddy always taught me that fear made a person weak. He told me to avoid any association with weak people."

"Your daddy was gifted."

"The best of the best," Palladin said in a soft voice.

There was a steady tapping sound. The noise level in the hall abated. When the sound of clarinets and flutes drifted through the speakers, Palladin's eyes opened wide. Don Scavone noted the look of surprise on his face.

"You know this music?"

"Billy," Palladin said. "*Billy the Kid.*"

"That's why you are special, Mr. Palladin. In this hall of hundreds, you are one of two, three, maybe four people who know classical ballet. I acquired my taste for the classical from my previous boss. *Billy the Kid* is one of my favorites."

"Mine too."

"Why is that?"

"The ballet starts off lightly, peacefully, but when the percussion and drums reach full intensity, I hear the guns discharge. I can see the shootout between the Kid and Pat Garrett. I feel it throughout my body. I feel that someone is actually being murdered."

"That's the genius of Copeland, the composer. The producer. The director of flawless performances." Don

Scavone talked in a low, mild voice. "You mentioned murder, Mr. Palladin. I've already explained the details of your contract. Like Copeland, you're now a producer and director. Let me show you the star of your very important video production. I'll be listening to *Billy the Kid* when I watch it."

Taking Palladin by the arm, Scavone pulled him aside and motioned furtively to a tall man dressed in a single-breasted white tuxedo. The shawl collar of his jacket was accentuated by a pink butterfly bow tie. The man's hawkish face was flushed; his ears and nose were large. His black hair was groomed neatly. The man was gesticulating with his hands to a circle of associates. He laughed loudly, the strident sound obfuscating the perfect melody of violins in the background.

"That ostentatious lawyer is Caesar Romano," Scavone whispered. "Make the movie soon. I'm dying to watch it." A smile on his face, the don walked back to his wife. Palladin started across the crowded floor in the direction of the bar. When he slid past the man in the white tuxedo, he noticed a Valley Forge Military Academy pin on his lapel. The laughter in the circle grew louder. Palladin squeezed by the exuberant groups of birthday wishers and approached the bar. He slowed when he saw the lady at the end of the line.

Wearing a radiant red dress, showing regal posture, she stood apart from the crowd of noisy, pushy associates. She was five feet ten inches tall, very slender, very angular. *Very beautiful*, Palladin thought. With calm celerity, he moved behind her. When they reached the bar, he stepped ahead.

"I would like the honor of buying your drink."

"You must be new to Philly," she commented. "Mr. Scavone pays for everything."

"That's true for the other guests," Palladin asserted. "But Mr. Scavone will not have the honor of paying for your drink." Palladin placed a hundred-dollar bill on the bar. The waiter, dressed in a pale blue tuxedo, scooped it up quickly.

"What can I serve you?" he asked in a polite voice.

At first, the lady did not respond. She looked at Palladin, studying his features, the narrow dark eyes, the fashionable mustache, the inviting smile.

"Please," Palladin said. The lady shrugged her shoulders.

"Old-fashioned," she said.

"No, you're not," Palladin stated. "Maybe in another fifty or hundred years. Right now, at this very moment in time, there's nothing old-fashioned about you. You're titillating and vibrant. Plus, you're attractive to a degree that makes every other woman look dull and boring." He stared intently at her face. She had a glint in her eyes.

"The old-fashioned is for my husband."

"Your husband's a fool," Palladin said.

"You don't know my husband."

"But I do. Your husband's ignorant. He should be serving you. What would you like? I would recommend champagne. I see a bottle of Bollinger Grande Annee. I think you would enjoy it. James Bond ordered a bottle in the film *Live and Let Die.* I always keep two bottles at my office. It's very good."

The lady put her hand to her chin. The waiter stood there, his hands on the bar. When he saw the smile forming on the lady's face, he smiled too. He saw the man in the debonair black suit smile, reach up, and twist the end of his mustache.

"I would prefer something with a little more kick," the lady said in a soft, provocative voice. "Please mix me a Manhattan. The perfect Manhattan."

"I think I would enjoy a kick too. Mix me a Manhattan, also."

"Do you prefer Maker's Mark or Highland Park?"

"Highland Park would constitute a Rob Roy," the lady answered. "Please use Maker's Mark." Turning to Palladin, she offered her hand. He immediately noticed the gold wedding band. "I'm Jane Romano." Palladin hesitated. A barely perceptible frown forming on his face, he took her hand, caressed it, avoided touching the ring.

"I'm Palladin," he said. "Wesley Palladin."

"You're employed by Mr. Scavone?"

"Yes."

"Through my husband, I've met many of the don's associates and contract people. You don't look like them. You look very young."

"I started at a early age." Palladin released her hand. "What about you?"

"I teach at Bryn Mawr College. I work in the same department as President Woodrow Wilson did."

"Our twenty-eighth president. That would put you in the school's history department."

"Yes, Mr. Palladin. Woodrow Wilson was our school's first professor of history. Bryn Mawr was small then—forty-two students and three classroom buildings. He was paid fifteen hundred dollars a year."

"I couldn't survive a week on that salary." Palladin smiled and studied her face, the smoothness of the skin, the texture of her lips. "I'm extremely sorry to see you're married. Is your husband employed at the college?"

"No, he works for Mr. Scavone. Caesar makes a lot of money doing whatever he does. But … I probably shouldn't be talking about him."

"Why?" Palladin asked. "Anything you say is safe with me."

"Okay, it's not like I've never talked about it before. Simply put, Caesar's a spendthrift. He's careless with money. If a neighbor has a new gate, Caesar buys a bigger gate. If a neighbor puts in a pond, Caesar digs up the yard and makes a colossal lake. I guess we can afford it." Jane was quiet for a moment. Then her eyes brightened.

"At least he's good to our teenage son, Cody. Caesar's spent extra money and enrolled Cody in a prestigious school. My son has to wear a military uniform all the time. He's so handsome in it. He's not a perfect kid, just a great kid. Whatever weaknesses Caesar has, Cody is just the opposite."

"Then he must take after his mother," Palladin said. The compliment brought a smile to her face.

Their bodies in close proximity, Jane and Palladin talked in whispered tones. Some of Scavone's made family members and the one Warlock guest moved past them. Carrying a tray with three drinks, the waiter returned. He removed an old-fashioned from the tray and placed it on the bar. Then he carefully lowered two finely ribbed Manhattan skyscraper cocktail glasses in front of Palladin. One glass had a cherry, stem protruding from the top; the other had a sliver of orange. The waiter clapped his hands together.

"There," he said approvingly. "Perfect drinks for the perfect couple. I took special care and mixed them myself. The cherry Manhattan is for the beautiful lady."

"I appreciate your attention," Palladin said. He placed another hundred-dollar bill on the bar.

"My pleasure." As the waiter picked up the bill, Jane Romano stared at Palladin.

"You're just like my husband."

"Why do you say that?"

"Tossing all that money around. You're a spendthrift just like he is."

"I disagree strongly, Mrs. Romano. I spend my money with much forethought. I don't waste it on inanimate ornamental gates or large ponds."

"How do you spend it then?"

"On the lovely … alluring … fanciful … sophisticated. And most important of all … caring."

"Why include caring?"

"It was very evident in your voice when you talked about Cody."

"He's my son. I don't know if I would have the same feeling toward a stranger."

"Maybe I was a stranger twenty minutes ago, but I don't think I'm a stranger anymore. I've seen how you were watching me, listening to me. I think you know exactly who I am." Palladin handed her the glass with the cherry on the bottom.

"I have drawn some conclusions." Her eyes were steady, her voice smooth.

"Please tell me."

"What if I offend you?"

"You won't."

"Will you stop me if I say anything that's not accurate?"

"Of course." Palladin lifted his glass. Jane tasted her Manhattan and began.

"First, you have expensive tastes, Mr. Palladin. Second, you're knowledgeable in many subjects. Third, you're extremely competent. You complete your contracts with fatal efficiency."

"The first observations were obvious. How did you arrive at the third?"

"If you were not competent—and, I should add, loyal—Mr. Scavone would not have invited you to his reception."

"Go on."

"You're extremely ruthless," Jane said. There was a herald of resounding trumpets in the background, and then *Billy the Kid* clicked off.

"Why ruthless?"

"You survived the bloodbath after the murder of Philadelphia's feared and revered Gentle Don, Angelo Bruno."

"I was lucky." Palladin finished his drink. When he put the glass down, he noticed two fresh Manhattans on the bar. The waiter winked at him and left. Jane studied Palladin..

"I don't see you as a person who needs luck, Mr. Palladin. There's something else. You're very subtle, but your eyes are constantly moving. You see the whole room. Checking this person. Checking that person. I believe you are working now. I believe your next contract is in the room. Probably enjoying his last drink. Or might it be her last drink?" She spun the glass in her hand, the ribbed grooves in the crystal glittering in the light. "Mr. Scavone is a spiteful person. He would derive much pleasure in bringing the victim to the assassin."

"Yes, I'm sure he would. I take it you don't like our host."

"I hate him. He's a crude person. He's also unfaithful to his wife. I know this from personal experience. He has made several awkward advances."

"How unfortunate," Palladin said. "What about your husband?"

"Caesar was pleased. He took it as a compliment to his good taste."

A band began playing *Lady* in the background. Jane Romano turned her head. The crowd of people parted. Mr. Scavone and his wife walked romantically to the dance floor.

> *Lady, I'm your knight in shining armor, and*
> *I love you.*
> *You have made me what I am, and I am*
> *yours.*
> *My love, there's so many ways I want to say*
> *I love you.*

An enigmatic expression clouding her face, Jane finished the Manhattan. Removing the stem and sliding the cherry between her lips, she placed the glass on the bar.

"I apologize, Mr. Palladin. The Maker's Mark made me somewhat expressive. But you didn't make any attempt to stop me."

"You gave me no reason to. It's getting too noisy in here. Let's go somewhere quiet."

"My husband's waiting for his drink."

"I think we both agree that your husband's a fool, a shallow, self-indulgent fool." Moving the old-fashioned to the side, Palladin picked up the two Manhattan skyscraper glasses. "Let him get his own drink." Walking slowly, holding the glasses perfectly level, Palladin led her through the crowd, out the door, and down the hall to the elevators.

"What quiet place are we going to?"

"I'm sorry, Jane. You were so intriguing I forgot to mention it." Palladin stopped at the elevator doors and pressed a button. "I usually rent a suite on these occasions."

"A suite," Jane said. She smiled. Kenny Roger's voice carried down the corridor. *You're the love of my life, you're my lady.* The associates clapped enthusiastically. The doors slid open; Jane and Palladin walked inside. A pleasant aroma filled the closed confines of the heated elevator.

"I sense something very exquisite, like the sweetest, bluest lilac."

"A touch of Highland Lilac," she said.

"Cultivated and exported from Rochester, New York. I'll be sure to put Highland Lilac on my gift list."

"You never stop, do you?"

"No," Palladin said. There was a pinging noise, a smooth cessation of motion, and the doors slid open. As they walked down the empty hallway, Palladin handed Jane her cocktail glass and removed the platinum door card from his pocket.

"I'm talking to you," Amos said in a loud voice. A puzzled expression on his face, Palladin looked at Amos.

"Sorry, Amos. I was daydreaming. What is it?" Palladin drove through an intersection and exited the Bryn Mawr campus.

"I was curious. You went out of your way to spare Jane Romano? Are you still going to whack the rest of the family?"

"Do I have a choice? Scavone and I shook hands. He gave me half the payment. When the videocassette's in his hands, I get the other half. That was the deal. It's about Omerta, a man's honor. My daddy never broke a deal. And I won't either."

"The hell with Omerta," Amos said. "There's a boy involved here."

"Cody's not a boy. He's a teenager." Palladin raced down a straight stretch of country road. Approaching a covered bridge, he braked and drove slowly through the wooden structure. Pigeons flew from the rafters. As he exited the other end, he took a cassette from the door compartment, slid it into the player, and turned up the volume.

"*Live and Let Die*," Palladin said. "It's my favorite song. It was nominated for the Academy Award in 1974. It didn't win. I've never accepted that vote by academy members." The notes boomed flawlessly through the sound system.

> *When you were young and your heart was an*
>   *open book,*
> *You used to say live and let live …*
> *But if the ever-changing world in which we*
>   *live in*
> *Makes you give in and cry, say live and let die.*

Palladin was humming the words as he steered the Eldorado around a sharp bend and up a hill. During the refrain, he accelerated the Eldorado, racing wildly down the hill, and sang with fervour.

"*You know you did, you know you did, you know you did … live and let **die**.*" The music ended; the tape made a clicking sound. Palladin popped it out of the slot and drove toward the Romano estate in silence.

Chapter Five

Twin River
Thursday Afternoon

Cindy Hoover pushed open the door to the girls' room and walked to the silver-framed mirror above the sink. Cindy was a five nine sophomore who sang in the chorus and played center for the basketball team. She had brown hair and a clear, vibrant face. Opening her purse, she took out a tube of Maybelline pink blush and was applying it to her lips when Alice Byrd walked in.

"Where were you?" Cindy asked. "Conner and I were looking for you at lunch."

"Matt felt very romantic today. He treated me to lunch in the baseball dugout." Alice laughed. "How was the movie last night?"

"As soon as we got to the Huntingdon Theatre, Conner and I had an argument." Cindy replaced the tube in her purse and patted her lips with a tissue. "He wanted to watch *Caddyshack*. And I wanted to watch *The Blue Lagoon*."

"Wow, Christopher Atkins swimming in the nude. I wanted to go with Matt last Saturday, but my parents said it had an R rating."

"*Caddyshack* was R rated too. Conner tried to explain to me why he wanted to see it so bad. First, he said it was hilarious. Then he said when the movie ended, people ran off the golf course dancing and shouting, 'We're all going to get laid!' He said *laid* so loud the people in the ticket line turned and stared at us."

"What'd you do?"

"I had to think quickly. I told him that Brooke Shields was topless in *The Blue Lagoon*. You should have seen the look on his face. When we got to the booth, he bought two tickets to watch Brooke Shields. I enjoyed the movie, but Conner was disappointed."

"Why?"

"Brooke had long brown hair. Conner complained that it covered her boobs. He said it was held there with invisible tape. I said I was sorry about that. I promised Conner I would buy the tickets to *Caddyshack*. Maybe you and Matt can go with us."

"Probably not," Alice said. "Matt told me he was going to Philadelphia tomorrow. Is Conner going?"

"Tomorrow's Friday. I doubt that Conner would skip school." Cindy checked the mirror again. The bell rang, and she and Alice walked to the door.

At two thirty Thursday afternoon, Matt Henry exited the front doors of Twin River High School and went to the cordoned area reserved for bicycles. He pulled out his bike from the dozens parked there, sat on the seat, and waited. Within minutes, Conner joined Matt and lifted his bicycle off the rack. The school doors swung open. Pushing and shoving, the students formed lines at the curb. The first yellow bus turned the corner and headed in their direction. Matt spun out in front of it; the bus driver honked the horn. Conner jumped on his bicycle and rushed after Matt.

"What's the hurry?"

"I want to get to the Cicconi place before the bus. First we have to stop at the house."

"Why stop at the house?"

"I need the Winchester." Matt lowered his head and pedaled down the hill.

"What do you need a gun for?" Conner shouted and raced after him. Matt only pedaled faster.

Matt raced down River Road and turned down the driveway to the rustic, two-story wooden house. Conner was a short distance behind him. The garage next to the house slanted at an angle. A rusty basketball rim was above the door; a red Radio Flyer wagon was chained to the roof. The sides of the garage were covered with turtle shells nailed to the wood in neat rows. A thick-skinned snapping turtle's head peered out from under the largest shell. The turtle's jaws clamped down on a ripped T-shirt stained with blood.

As soon as Matt dropped his bicycle in the yard, SenSay began barking loudly. The small collie had smooth fur and a long tail that whipped back and forth. The dog was brown except for the white paws, white chest, and streak of white the length of its back. Matt climbed the steps to the porch and opened the door. SenSay yelped and jumped at him.

"Down, SenSay." Matt filled the collie's bowl with water and put food in the empty dish. Then he went to the gun cabinet, unlocked it, and grabbed the Winchester. Conner was waiting when he came down the steps.

The yellow bus lumbered down the road and stopped at the dirt driveway. Carrying textbooks and Mead notebooks, Lilly and Jack Cicconi got out and stood next to the mailbox. Lilly was twelve years old. She wore a blue blouse and skirt; she had a blue scarf pulled low over her forehead. Jack was a year younger. He had a slim build and poor posture. He wore dark-framed glasses. When the bus was far down the road, Lilly grabbed Jack's hand, and they walked down the driveway.

Matt and Conner stood on a hill in a grove of pine trees. Below them, thick gray smoke rose from the chimney of the wooden three-story house. A black car, "Green Hollow Correctional Camp" written in white letters on the door, was parked at the garage. Sliding the Winchester from his shoulder, Matt held it at his side. He nudged Conner and pointed to Lilly and Jack as they approached the house.

"Do you know why Lilly always wears that scarf?" he asked. Conner shook his head. "It's because she has bruises on her forehead."

Lilly and Jack reached the bottom step to the porch. Matt watched them closely. A green arrowhead hung from a rawhide cord around his neck. Matt gripped the arrowhead; the sharp edges jabbed into his skin. He spoke in an angry tone.

"And Jack wore dark glasses all day because his eye was swollen."

The front door opened. Smoking a cigarette, Luther Cicconi walked across the porch and waited on the top step. His blue correctional camp shirt was unbuttoned and smeared with wet spots.

"You're late again!" he shouted. Taking a deep puff of the Marlboro, Luther swung out and hit Jack on the head. The dark-framed glasses spun in the air and landed in the dirt. Lilly screamed and dropped her notebook. Luther knocked her down. When she reached for the notebook, he stepped on her hand, pinning it to the wood. Lilly squirmed under the weight and screamed again.

The shrill noise echoed up the hillside. Sliding the arrowhead inside his sweatshirt, Matt raised the Winchester to his shoulder and scoped Luther on the porch. His eyes opening wide, Conner stepped closer.

"Matt, what the hell you doing?"

"I'm going to kill him," Matt muttered. Beads of perspiration formed on his forehead. A firm grip on the Winchester, he focused intently on the burning circle of ash hanging from Luther's mouth. Pressure began to build around his eyes and nose. Thin lines formed on his pupils; a drop of blood leaked from his nostril. Taking an even breath, his chest barely moving, Matt squeezed the trigger. The clicking sound exploded in his ears. Matt lowered the Winchester and fell back against the tree. In the clearing below, the door to the house slammed shut. Matt straightened, took a deep breath, and wiped at his nose.

"I've been practicing for weeks now, Conner. When will your dad give me real ammunition?"

"You won't get any until he thinks you're ready. Hell, if he saw you aim at someone like you just did, he'd never give you ammunition. Would you have shot Luther Cicconi just now?"

"Would you have?"

"No," Conner answered. "I hated what he did. But I would never shoot him."

"Why?"

"Because I never miss what I aim at," Conner stated. "I couldn't live with myself if I killed someone."

"I don't know if I think like you."

"What do you mean?"

"I couldn't live with myself if I let him get away with hurting his kids."

"Then you would kill him?"

"I …" Matt began. The door banged open at the house, and Luther walked onto the porch. He had a bottle of beer in his hand. Matt glared at him. *I would enjoy killing the bastard*, Matt thought to himself. Conner looked at the dark expression on Matt's face.

"When Dad came back from the war, he was angry all the time. I imagine he would have killed Cicconi without giving it a thought."

"Your dad's changed."

"I know. I'm glad he did change. Mom saw it right away. It's the reason she returned home."

"I liked him better the old way," Matt said. Conner stared at Matt, his gaze focusing on the section of rawhide cord around his neck.

"When you put your hand under your sweatshirt, Matt, you grabbed hold of something. What was it?"

"An arrowhead," Matt said. "An old arrowhead I found." Matt's eyes narrowed. Looking past Conner, he saw the cliffs on Blood Mountain. Vultures flew in and out of the Shadows of Death that masked the entrance to the cave.

> *The boy crawled through the narrow opening. A skeleton leaned against the far wall. The boy saw the rawhide cord and green arrowhead tangled in the rib cage. The boy's hand trembled, yet he reached through the rib cage and grabbed onto the arrowhead. When he put the cord around his neck, the arrowhead was light and cool against his skin.*

"What did you say it was, Matt?"

"An arrowhead." Matt lifted his sweatshirt and showed Conner the chipped stone sharpened to a point.

"It's different. It's green. Where'd you find it?"

"On Blood Mountain I took it off a skeleton. Matthew Simonton's skeleton."

"That's why you went down the cliffs that day. You found the cave. Dad said the Indians killed Matthew's dad and sister. Matthew went on a murdering rampage. Then he disappeared."

"He died in the cave. I was scared when I saw his skeleton. I couldn't move for a long time. The Shadows of Death drifted inside and covered us both. I took deep breaths and gradually calmed. I began to understand why Matthew had to kill the people who hurt him. I slid my fingers between the ribs and took the arrowhead. It was smooth and weightless. It's hard to explain, but sometimes the arrowhead feels heavy. Real heavy."

"Did it feel heavy when you saw Luther Cicconi hit the kids?"

"Yes," Matt said. "I wanted to stop him. He reminded me of Mr. Henry. I hate Mr. Henry. I hate Mr. Cicconi." Matt stared at the figure on the porch. Light, crying sounds emanated from the open door. Luther glanced at the hillside and drank heavily. Matt saw the bloated face, the gulping movement of the throat.

"And children will rise up against parents and cause them to be put to death," Matt mumbled.

"What?" Conner asked.

"It's from the Bible. When Mr. Henry was drunk, he made me read to him. That was the last passage he heard before he went on vacation." Matt shouldered the Winchester. Reaching into his pocket, he pulled out a ripped piece of paper.

"Here's something I want you to read, Conner. It's from Miss Victoria's newspaper." He gave the paper to Conner, who scanned the lines.

"Palladin - Have Weapons Will Travel." Conner shook his head and gave the paper back. "What's it mean?"

"It means I'm going to hire Palladin to work in the bank. With Mr. Henry gone, Mr. Abrams is in charge. He doesn't know anything because Mr. Henry never let him do anything important. I think Palladin should be director of security. Since the house is empty, I'll pay him for home security too. And even my own personal security."

"That's crazy. You don't need personal security. Dad would never let anything happen to you."

"I'm going back to my home in Barree, Conner."

"You can't leave. You just moved in with us."

"I've made up my mind."

"Is it because you're angry with Dad? I heard you two arguing last night."

"Yeah, we argued some. But I was planning to leave before that."

"It's a bad idea, you being alone in that big house," Conner said. They walked down the hill to the bicycles. "Let's go back. I have basketball practice."

They pushed off and started down the road. The bicycle tires made a scratching noise on the gravel. The setting sun momentarily flared crimson on Blood Mountain. There was a dim halo and then darkness. Flashing bright on Redemption Mountain across the river, the lights of the Flaming Cross blinked on. Conner pointed to the ruddy glow.

"You can see the Reverend Towers's cross from anywhere in the county."

"He planned it that way," Matt commented. "His church services are packed. The light draws people like moths to a fire. None of them sees the danger."

"What danger?"

"The reverend's sons, Cain and Abel. The day of the school shooting Abel tried to drag me into the restroom. I don't know what he would have done. And Cain got Becky Wilson pregnant. That's why Wayne shot him in the knee. He shot Abel too. They're both pissed. There's bad things happening in Twin River. Someone's going to get hurt, maybe even killed. That's why I have to hire Palladin. I'm going to take the train to Philadelphia tomorrow."

"Tomorrow's a school day."

"So what!" Matt exclaimed angrily. "Just another boring day with boring teachers who tell you to shut up all the time and make fun of your mom." Matt hesitated and then spoke in a calmer voice. "Conner, I was hoping you'd come with me to Philadelphia. I already bought two train tickets."

"How could I go? Dad would know right away. And Mom would kill me if I played hooky. And besides, how would you get to the train station?"

"I called Abrams. He agreed to pick me up at nine thirty at the bridge. The train leaves Huntingdon at ten forty." Matt spoke in an excited voice. "I studied the Philadelphia map in the library and found Palladin's office right away. It's in Chinatown. I have to do this. I have to find Palladin. I know I can convince him to work at the bank. But I don't think I can do it alone. I need you to come with me."

Conner remained silent. He and Matt reached the intersection, one road leading to the school and the other leading to his house. Conner braked in the middle of the intersection and looked at Matt.

"There's no way I can go to Philadelphia," he said softly, apologetically. Then Conner pushed off on the bicycle and pedaled toward Twin River High School.

Chapter Six

Redemption Mountain
Thursday Evening

The Reverend Towers's residence on the banks of the Juniata River was a sprawling four-story stone house with seventeen rooms. The yard was landscaped with rows of maple and pine trees, a flower garden of peonies and roses with a large nativity scene, and a fish pond. Large golden and red-and-white koi swam in the pond. Bobbing with the waves, Noah's Ark floated in the center. Giraffe, hippopotamus, camel, elephant, and ostrich heads protruded from the rows of windows. Monkeys, dogs, cats, turtles, and a lone snake were scattered over the decks. Doves roosted on the railings.

Next to the pond, a large eastern hemlock had speakers camouflaged in its branches. The blissful notes of *Bringing in the Sheaves* drifted softly through the air. Star-shaped white-and-pink mountain laurel blossoms carpeted the ground.

Fastened on steel pipes, two Chiclets glass gum containers filled with rabbit pellets were spiked in the ground. The decks of Noah's Ark were littered with brown pellets. A dog and a monkey had been knocked over by the projectiles. Whacked off the railing, one baby dove with a cracked wing floated in the water and was occasionally sucked in and spat out by the ravenous, oval-mouthed koi.

Purring occasionally, two black cats reclined in the bed of laurel blossoms, their green eyes open wide and riveted on the pond.

Next to the driveway, the parking lot had numbered spaces for two hundred cars. There was a row of 1980 Ford ten-seat passenger vans, "Church of the Flaming Cross" written in bold letters on the side. Across the street from the lot, Commandment Road led to the summit of Redemption Mountain.

The Reverend Jeremiah Towers got in a van, started the engine, and turned onto Commandment Road. The reverend had a bony six-foot-one-inch frame. His face was gaunt, lined with deep wrinkles. He wore a black suit, black shirt, and black bow tie.

Leaning forward, avoiding the glare of the setting sun, the reverend slowed at the line of stone commandments. His lips barely moving, he read each tablet, ending with the Tenth Commandment, "You shall not covet your neighbor's wife or property." The gate was open, and Jeremiah drove through it into the church compound.

The Reverend Towers parked the van in front of a large portal carved out of the mountainside. A golden sign, "Catacombs of Rapture" written in black, hung above the portal. Jeremiah entered the catacomb, coughed at the chilly air tinged with formaldehyde, and pushed the switch on the wall. The fluorescent lights flickered into brightness, illuminating the four passageways that separated the burial chambers. Each chamber had an ivory cross, the name of the deceased, and relevant dates engraved on the glass. Some chambers had a formal picture next to the inscription.

Walking carefully, his body trembling from the rush of cold air, the Reverend Jeremiah Towers approached a chamber with a gold cross above it. The inscription on the door was written in bold letters:

Irene Towers
1935 - 1980
Beloved Wife of Jeremiah Towers
Beloved Mother of Cain and Abel Towers

His shoes scraping the stone floor, Jeremiah slowed; there was a clicking noise. A spotlight flashed on the tomb, and his wife's favorite Gospel message, *Bringing in the Sheaves*, played softly from a row of recessed speakers. Jeremiah Towers stopped in front of the glass door. His body wavered; music and song filled the passageway. The spotlight magnified the inscription on the glass; the sudden brightness blinded him.

> *Sowing in the morning, sowing seeds of kindness,*
> *Sowing in the noontide, and the dewy eve;*
> *Waiting for the harvest, and the time of reaping,*
> *We shall come rejoicing, bringing in the sheaves.*

His head swaying, Jeremiah began singing the notes, "*Waiting for the harvest, and the time of reaping.*" The reverend sang in a high-pitched voice. Tears streamed down his face and dropped onto his black suit.

From outside, from the direction of the Flaming Cross, a shrill scream filtered into the catacombs. The sound lingered in the frigid air. Shivering, the Reverend Jeremiah Towers fell to his knees. *Bringing in the Sheaves* looped through its final rotation and stopped. The reverend's labored breathing made a fragile, wheezing noise in the eerie, morgue-like silence.

Then another clicking sound echoed through the stillness. A tape began playing; there was the sound of familiar voices. Jeremiah Towers looked up, his eyes searching the passageway. As the reverend listened to the voices, his face reddened. His heart beat rapidly. Eyes blazing, he emitted an agonized scream and collapsed to the stone floor.

Evening settled over Redemption Mountain. Racing a 1969 poppy-pink Ford Ranchero past each of the Ten Commandments, Cain Towers drove through the gate and parked the truck next to a gravel path. Stepping out of the Ranchero, Abel saw the church van.

"The reverend's at the catacombs."

"He's always crying in there. He'll be *Bringing in the Sheaves* on his deathbed."

"The reverend really misses Irene. He loved his wife more than anything."

"Irene was a silly whore," Cain snapped angrily. "She wasn't our real mother. She ridiculed me, complaining and whining all the time. She always said, 'In one ear and out the other,' when I didn't do her stupid jobs exactly as she demanded. I got sick of hearing her squeaky voice. So just forget Irene. We're done with her."

"But the reverend …"

"Forget the reverend too. He's an old man, all skin and bones. He's nothing but a scarecrow."

Cain took the Sharpfinger skinning knife from his belt and placed it on the seat. Then he shut the door of the Ranchero and started down the path. Scratching his crutch through the gravel, Abel followed closely behind. As the sky darkened, the timing mechanism at the base of the cross was activated. Making a popping sound, the bulbs lit consecutively; radiant light streamed toward the heavens in a dazzling display of brilliance. Within seconds, the Flaming Cross was a towering beacon, spreading a warm glow across the valleys and farmland.

The path twisted around pine trees, large boulders, and mountain laurel shrubs. It narrowed and ended at a row of wooden benches at the base of the cross. Cain and Abel walked to the closest bench. Eight yards of slanting ground separated the bench from the edge of the cliff and the sharp descent to the darkness of rocks and river below. In the distance, there was a rumbling sound, an advancing cone of light, and a train raced across the sturdy, vaulted stone bridge. The rumbling diminished, and a howling noise echoed through the night.

"What's that?" Abel said.

"People are careless and let their dogs run loose." Cain stared at his twin brother. "Packs of dogs are all over these mountains. Remember, we trapped us some."

"Yeah," Abel said. "But I ain't never heard them so close before."

Abel leaned his crutch against the bench and positioned both hands on the wooden back support. Taking a deep breath, he slowly lowered his body, keeping his good knee straight, bending the replacement knee. He stopped the downward push when the burn of muscle and tendon became intolerable, shot the length of his body, and ignited the dark space at the base of his brain. Cain did the same stretch. They repeated it ten times. After they had finished their exercises, Abel stared at his twin brother.

"I smell wine. You been drinkin' again?"

"Maybe I had a little."

"Maybe that's why your leg don't hurt so much," Abel reasoned. "And what about the voices? You're not talkin' much about the voices."

"The voices have been quiet lately."

"That's never happened before. In the desert you always heard stuff."

"This isn't Death Valley, Abel. Things have changed. It might have something to do with Becky being pregnant. I never brought life into the world before. The voices mostly instructed me in ways to destroy life."

"You think they're angry?"

"I don't know," Cain said. "But I hear the clearest voices through moments of extreme pain. So let's get started. You're first, Abel."

"Why me all the time?"

"Because God likes to hear you scream."

"I don't scream." Abel pulled a pill container from his pocket and shook it. "Shit!" he exclaimed, and he threw the container over the cliff. Cain laughed.

"Don't you remember, Abel? You took all your pills the first two days of rehab."

"I thought I had one left." Abel hesitated. "What about that fucker Wayne? Tell me the plan."

"I already told you."

"I know you told me, but I don't remember it all."

"Abel, pay attention this time. We'll grab Wayne tonight and take him to the Calvin farm. We'll cut him up with the Sharpfinger and leave him wired in the pen. The hogs will smell the blood and come for him. That's the plan. Any questions?"

"How do you know the hogs will come?"

"How many animals have we left in the pen?"

"I forget. Maybe seven or eight."

"There were two dogs, a cat, a deer, and the last animal was a goat. The hogs ate them all. What did we find in the pen the next morning?"

"Not much. Just some fur and pools of blood." Abel was quiet for a moment. "We've been leavin' all those animals, but we ain't never seen no hogs."

"And you'd better pray that you never see no hogs," Cain said sarcastically. "Quit wasting time. Get on the bench. Lie on your stomach."

"Why can't we do the first exercises all over again? They don't hurt so much."

"Because we want to walk tomorrow. Not sometime next year. When I force that knee to bend, sure, it may hurt a little, but that's what does the most good."

"It hurts more than a little. It hurts like hell."

"It's that fear of pain that makes you weak, Abel. Remember the first day of rehab when the lady therapist said you couldn't do any damage to your knee? Well, she was right. The knee's solid metal now. You can't hurt it."

"I know that. But you press down on my leg so hard that I can't even breathe."

"Yes, I do. Now get on your stomach. And this time don't scream like a girl."

Abel groaned. His lips pressed together; a look of gloom spread over his face. Gingerly, he lay flat on his stomach on the wooden boards. Cain positioned himself, reached for the extended leg, and grasped the ankle in a powerful grip. Abel closed his eyes; his chest and abdominal muscles turned steel-hard.

I won't scream! I won't scream! Abel swore to himself. He stared at the calming light of the Flaming Cross. *I won't scream!*

Cain pushed the foot down slowly, forcibly. It lowered two, three, four inches, and stuck. Cain pushed harder. The tendons resisted. Using all the strength, Cain pushed and twisted and bent the ankle. The leg tightened.

"Your leg is getting hard as a rock," Cain muttered. Cursing loudly, he pushed it lower, locked it into position, and began counting long seconds.

Abel's muscles went into spasms. His chest elevated and smacked down again and again. Lightning flashed in front of his face. Abel was blinded by hot tears. Then he lost his vision; the Flaming Cross disappeared in darkness.

Cain mouthed the numbers carefully, accurately. On the count of thirty, he relaxed for ten seconds. Then he tightened his grip on Abel's ankle. Planting his chest on Abel's leg, Cain crunched down with the weight of his two-hundred-pound frame. The leg lowered another inch.

Suddenly, Abel's body came to life, convulsing violently on the bench. The wooden planks vibrated and cracked loudly under the pounding weight. In the cold mountain air, Abel's face dripped moisture. His mouth twisting, he emitted a blood-curdling scream that echoed across the compound, echoed into the Catacombs of Rapture. Panting heavily, Abel was exhausted. He swore; bubbles of foam spewed from his mouth.

"I'll cripple that bastard Wayne! Just like he did me! I'll cripple that bastard!"

Cain held the leg in the vise of his grip. Listening to Abel's rant, he smiled and released the ankle. Swiping at the tears streaming down his cheeks, Abel slowly got to his feet. A look of relief flashed over his face.

"It stops hurting as soon as you let go."

"It's metal, Abel. That's what you need your mind to be—strong as metal."

"It didn't take so long this time."

"How would you know?"

"What do you mean by that?"

"You passed out. When you came to, you screamed like a girl."

"The hell I did. Get on the bench, Cain. It's your turn to do some sufferin'." Abel grinned. Cain grinned back at him and lay on the bench.

Strong as metal, Cain thought. He rested his head on his forearm and gazed at the dark shadows of bats gliding in and out of the burning brilliance of the Flaming Cross. Abel growled loudly and grabbed onto Cain's foot with both hands.

"I didn't scream," Abel whispered. Perspiration gleaming on his forehead, Abel pushed the leg down with all his strength and weight. When the muscles and rock-hard sinews resisted, Abel pushed down harder and shouted in Cain's ear, "I didn't scream!"

Cain felt the burning coals rip through his body. The fire surged upward into the dark space where the voices waited. An agony of seconds passed; Cain focused on the cross ablaze in the night sky. There was a brief interlude of absolute calm. Then the voices shrieked with a passion and power beyond anything he had ever experienced. Listening to every syllable, Cain thought fondly about Becky and his son, about destruction and the delicate beauty and necessity of death. A severe smile on his face, Cain rejoiced when he saw a sudden flare-up of movement in the shadows of the towering White Pines and shorter Possum Pines behind the cross.

Mushrooming from the branches, myriad Pale Beauty moths took flight. One-inch wings whipping the air, the moths swarmed from the dark sanctuary of the pines.

Reaching the radiant beams of the cross, the soft white bodies flew into the bright haven and disappeared. As they moved through the light, their darting, ghostly shadows generated the slightest wave patterns.

Sensing the activity at the cross, flying swiftly from the river and the rocky cliffs, big brown bats ravenously dove in and out of the halo of light. Emitting intense sounds, tracking the source of the returning echoes, and feverishly changing direction, the bats snatched their Pale Beauty prey with infinite skill and grace. One solitary hunter, a larger, furry hoary bat, fifteen-inch wingspan, paused on its migration south to gorge itself. As the killing frenzy intensified, thin, translucent wings fluttered from the brilliant glow to the darkness below.

At the bench, Abel twisted the swollen foot, and muttering curses, he threw his weight against Cain's leg, slowly pushing it downward. Oblivious to Abel's rants and fierce pressure, Cain stared into the light of the cross. Feeling extreme pleasure, he stretched out his hand; diminutive, lacy membranes fell lightly through the air, soon covering the open palm with a twisted, silken veil.

Chorus practice was over at seven thirty. The students collected their belongings and left Twin River High School through the back exit. The chorus teacher, Mrs. Michaels, closed the stage curtains and went to her office. There was one vehicle, lights on, motor running, parked at the curb. Heather Wainwright walked through the auditorium and entered the hallway. Cindy Hoover stood at the exit.

"Hi, Heather," Cindy said. "My dad's waiting for me. Do you need a ride?"

"No, I'm just going down the road."

"Your solo, *Home for the Holidays*, was great tonight," Cindy said. "You'll be the star of the holiday concert."

"I'm no star," Heather said, smiling, her face reddening. "But I did tell my parents. They're excited."

"We're all excited." Cindy pushed open the door. "Good night."

"Good night," Heather said. She walked down the deserted hall, opened the locker, and pulled out her jacket. It was a short walk down the hall to the exit.

The night was cool and dark. Across the river, the Flaming Cross was bright in the evening sky. There was one light in the corner of the empty parking lot. Heather walked around the building, past the baseball field, and past the illuminated display case on the front grounds.

The security lights from the school cast a dim glow on Route 305, but when Heather walked down the hill, the road turned to dark shadows. Two houses across the street had porch lights. One of them clicked off. Heather saw the one-lane bridge at the bottom of the hill, and beyond it, the bright Christmas lights outlining her porch.

As Heather approached the bridge, a dark Minnie Winnie pulled out from River Road. It turned onto Route 305, slowed, and then stopped. Both doors banged open, and two men stepped out. Heather turned quickly toward the school.

"Heather," Max Wright said quietly. The girl stopped when she heard her name.

Luther held a gauze pad saturated with chloroform. Max reached Heather first and grabbed her around the waist. Then Luther smothered her screams with the thick, soft pad. They carried Heather's limp body to the Winnebago and lowered her onto the floor in the back. Slamming the door shut, Luther lit a Marlboro. He got in the driver's seat and pulled onto the road. Max sat back, a jubilant smile on his face.

"What a great piece of luck seeing Heather on the road this morning. I guess we're back in the video business. How many girls do we got to collect?"

"Three or four." Luther took a deep puff from the Marlboro. "We're off to a good start with Heather. We'll keep beating on Ira until he gives us Lisa. And Alice Byrd will be girl number three. She lives in Barree. She's fooling around with the banker's son, Matt Henry. He's a skinny wimp. He won't be any trouble. But even if he causes a problem, Alice is worth it. I've seen her on a bicycle. Her body moves perfectly."

"I've seen her too," Max said. "And you're right. She has the sweetest body." Max's face turned serious. "I'm thinkin' that maybe I should star in the first video. What do you think, Luther?"

"Nathaniel prefers young, handsome actors. But I'll put in a good word for you."

"Thanks," Max said. "I'll start workin' on my script tonight."

"Don't start jacking off yet. You know Nathaniel. He makes all the decisions."

"It's time I had more input," Max said. "Nathaniel selected Jeffery. Now Jeffery's loose out there. And he's a danger because Nathaniel introduced us nice and proper. If the state police ever pick Jeffery up, he can identify us."

"Don't worry about him, Max. Nathaniel has a ten-thousand-dollar bounty on him. If Jeffery shows up in this area, he's dead."

"I never liked Jeffery. The bastard was a little too cute, too sweet-faced to have the stomach for the job. He didn't do any video with the girls."

"Relax. Business is starting up. We'll make money with Heather. She's a cutie."

"She sure is," Max said. Luther saw the shadow on the road and blew the horn.

"Roadkill." Luther accelerated the Minnie Winnie and flattened a snarling gray possum into the asphalt. Jostled in the back, Heather moaned and rolled on her side.

Chapter Seven

Twin River
Thursday Evening

"You're here early," Conner said, walking toward Wayne Wilson, who was shooting baskets in the empty gym. Conner wore blue shorts and a white T-shirt with the numbers *01* on the front.

"I didn't go home after school." Wayne took a jump shot; the ball swished. "I finished my barn work this morning. And besides, the house is empty. Dad won't be home till late tonight."

"Where is he?" Conner passed the ball back to Wayne.

"He took Becky to his brother's house in Burnt Cabins." Wayne shot the ball. It swished again. When Conner passed it back, he noticed the bruise on Wayne's chin.

"What happened to your face? Cut yourself shaving?"

"It's nothing. Cain Towers sharpened the end of his crutch and made it into a weapon. He jabbed me in the chin with it this morning. Your dad showed up. He took the crutch away and threw it in the furnace room."

"Cain and Abel are bullies. I'd stay away from them."

"I try to," Wayne said. "But even with their busted knees, they seem to be everywhere." Wayne kept shooting; every ball swished the net.

"You never miss," Conner said.

"I practice every morning."

The gym door burst open, and players ran onto the floor. Fifteen minutes later, holding a slice of pizza in his hand, Coach Eckin emerged from his office. He stuffed the pizza in his mouth, chewed earnestly, and then blew the whistle. The players began running the first of ten laps. Wayne and Conner took off sprinting and were half-a-floor length in front of the group. Randy Parks, the sheriff's son, a tall, muscular player, walked through the first lap and then sat down next to Coach Eckin on the bleacher.

After sixty minutes of drills and conditioning, the players divided into teams. As the scrimmage began, Sheriff Parks cracked open the exit door. The sheriff was dressed in a tailored blue shirt and designer jeans. He was six feet three inches tall and broad-shouldered. He wore a brand-new Stetson cowboy hat, bone-white alligator boots, and a wide belt holding an eight-inch barrel Smith & Wesson 686. Except for a dark bruise under his left eye, the sheriff's face was unblemished.

Noticing Conner Brooks at the far end of the court, Sheriff Parks removed the Smith & Wesson from the holster. His eyes narrow slits, Parks leveled the barrel through the crack in the door and aimed at Conner Brooks.

"You little bastard," he snarled. "You're just like your dad." As Conner ran down the floor, the barrel angled slightly ahead of the *01* on his jersey. The bruise under Parks's eye throbbed. The sheriff blinked rapidly, tracking Conner's movement. Coach Eckin blew his whistle, the shrill noise echoing off the walls.

"Foul!" Eckin shouted. All the players jumped to a stop. Sheriff Parks holstered the Smith & Wesson, pushed open the door, and stepped inside the gym. Coach Eckin saw him and walked over.

"How's Randy doing?" the sheriff asked, shaking hands.

"He's doing great. Randy should average twenty-plus points a game."

"He's good, but he'll never top his old man," Parks said, his face brightening. "I averaged 27.8 points a game. I still have the school scoring record, forty-three points against Glendale." The sheriff surveyed the court. A short, chunky kid shot an air ball. It went through the hands of a lanky kid, bounced off his forehead, and went out of bounds. Sheriff Parks laughed.

"It looks like you've got only one athlete on the floor."

"And that would be your son," Coach Eckin said. He pointed to a player jumping high and securing a rebound. "That farm boy, Wayne Wilson, might help us. All that barn work has made him pretty strong."

Wayne held the ball over his head. He glanced at Randy shouting and clapping his hands. Wayne threw the ball to another player. Sheriff Parks made a face.

"That was a dumb pass," he barked. Coach Eckin nodded his head.

"Wayne's got a lot to learn. He should have passed the ball to Randy."

"You got that right," Parks said. He watched his son shoot a three over Conner's outstretched hand. The ball went cleanly through the basket. Randy clapped his hands.

"In your face, dumb-shit!" Randy taunted.

"Yeah, you tell him!" Sheriff Parks shouted, giving a high thumbs-up. The next time down the court Randy faked and rose confidently in his jump. Conner waited. When the ball left Randy's hand, he swatted it into the wall and glanced at the sheriff.

"What about that hothead Brooks?" the sheriff asked.

"He's a loser. But you know that. You arrested him last month, didn't you?"

"Yeah, he was racing the jeep past the school. When I stopped him, the tough guy resisted arrest. I punched him pretty good. Got him under control. If the state police hadn't interfered, he'd still be in jail."

"He's a pain in the ass," Eckin said. "Sure, he'll mug and foul the hell out of you playing defense. But he don't know where the basket is on offense. He doesn't understand you put the ball through the hoop to win the game. I may have to cut him."

"What choice do you have?" The sheriff watched Randy shoot over two defenders. The ball bricked off the glass. "I got to do heavy police work tonight. Is it okay to take Randy home now?"

"No problem with that. We're only going another twenty minutes."

"Thanks," Sheriff Parks said.

Coach Eckin called Randy over. The sheriff high-fived Randy, and father and son left the gym together. Eckin blew the whistle and put a substitute on the floor. Thirty minutes later, after a series of sprints and push-ups, he dismissed the team.

Conner and Wayne went to their lockers. Clouds of hot mist from the shower filled the small room. After hanging their shirts and shorts on hooks, they joined the other players in the shower stalls. Wayne carried a plastic bottle in his hand. When he unscrewed the cap and poured a blue liquid over his head, Conner laughed.

"What's that you're using, Wayne? It smells like flowers."

"The newest Old Spice. Becky bought it for me. She swore I needed something strong after the barn work."

"Let me try that?" a voice asked. Wayne tossed the bottle toward the voice. Soon, all the players were passing the bottle of Old Spice around. A thin boy caught the bottle and sniffed the cap.

"It don't smell like flowers to me. It smells like shit."

"It's hurting my nose," a low voice sounded from the mist.

"It smells like pussy to me," a squeaky voice said.

"How would you know about pussy, Sal?" There was no quick answer. Sal remained silent. The only sound was water splashing off the cement floor. Then a loud voice from deep in the steam shouted in a booming voice.

"Because Sylvester sleeps with his mama's panties over his face."

Laughing, the players wandered out of the showers, one spigot still blasting clouds of hot spray. They toweled down and dressed quickly. Wayne dropped the half-empty bottle of Old Spice into his gym bag, and he and Conner walked to the parking lot. Conner saw his dad's orange Jeep Wagoneer. It was caked in mud and had a *Dukes of Hazzard* logo and large *01* painted on the side. His dad's Winchester 94 was racked above the rear window. There was noise on the road, and Conner saw the gaudy pink Ford Ranchero race past the school. He turned to Wayne.

"There's no sense you riding the bicycle to Polecat Hollow. Dad can take you home."

"No, thanks," Wayne said. "After that practice and those sprints, the fresh air will feel good."

Wayne pulled his bicycle off the rack. It was a 1959 Schwinn Deluxe Hornet that his dad had found at the Hartslog dump. Repaired and repainted, the radiant black Schwinn had an oval mirror and a chrome hi-lo beam headlight. The front tire was bald. After securing the gym bag to the double-hinged carrier, Wayne got on the seat. He hesitated, staring at Conner.

"What's wrong, Wayne?"

"Nothing's wrong, but ... maybe you don't feel the same." Wayne's face was clear in the beams of light from the jeep. His hair glistened from the Old Spice. "With the farm work and all the troubles at home, basketball's the only real fun I have."

Conner didn't say anything. He watched Wayne pedal past the jeep, wave at Gene, and head for the exit. When Wayne turned onto Route 305, Conner pushed his bicycle to the jeep, tossed it in the back, and got in the front seat.

"How was practice?" his dad asked.

"It was great, Dad. I got scored on only once." Conner's face beamed with pride; Gene nodded and started the jeep.

The sky over Twin River was pitch black. Across the Juniata River, the Flaming Cross cast a dazzling halo of light that covered the summit of Redemption Mountain and the surrounding countryside with a brilliant glow.

There was a chill in the night air. Headlights flashing, a truck roared down Route 22. Wayne waited for it to pass and turned the Schwinn into Polecat Hollow. Dark shadows fell over the road. Wayne hit a pothole, and the light on his handlebar shook up and down. Wayne drove through another pothole; the light slanted and remained pointed at the front tire. When Wayne reached to tighten the clamp, he saw a dark body racing toward him. Before he could straighten, a heavy fist knocked him off the bicycle. Wayne's shoulder cracked against the asphalt; his head slid into the pothole.

Chapter Eight

Polecat Hollow
Thursday Evening

Abel howled and kicked Wayne in the face. Cain grabbed the handlebars and threw the Schwinn into the brush. The gym bag flew off, hit a tree, and ripped open, the contents littering the ground. Cain turned and looked at Wayne's twisted body. When he saw Abel pulling out the Sharpfinger, he grabbed his arm.

"Don't cut him, Abel."

"Why? I've' been thinkin' all night how I was gonna slash his face."

"Not on the road. We don't want the hogs sniffing blood out here. Pick him up. Throw him in the Ranchero."

"I guess I can wait. We're gonna have us some fun tonight." Abel lifted Wayne to his shoulders and tossed him in the truck bed. "Cain, you notice I ain't usin' my crutch anymore? I left it on the mountain."

"I noticed that. You're doing much better," he complimented.

"I figured if my twin brother can walk without a crutch, then so can I."

Cain and Abel got in the poppy-red Ranchero, drove down Polecat Hollow, past the Wilson house, which was completely dark, and onto the dirt road. Turning the bend, Cain saw the two massive stone pillars and the newly constructed arch that loomed high over the road. Steel fencing jutted out from the pillars. No Trespassing signs were wired to the fence.

"What the hell is this?" Cain muttered.

"Shit, I don't know." Abel shrugged his shoulders.

Racing under the arch, Cain drove erratically, the truck bouncing through the ditches. A smile on his face, Abel was silent, his hand outstretched, pinging the blade of the Sharpfinger off the dash. At the Calvin house, Cain drove to the large barn and stopped. The door was open; spotlights flooded the interior with a soft, yellow glow.

"Look at that, would ya?" Abel said.

The barn had been emptied. The walls were painted blue and had murals of scantily-clad women. The women were young and beautiful and posing in the most provocative positions. A wooden platform filled the center section of the barn. Four silver Winnebago Chieftains, an orange "flying W" painted on the sides, were parked on the platform. There were two plush sofas, cushioned chairs, a bar, and recessed floor lights in the open space between the Chieftains. Abel made a whistling noise through his lips.

"Let's go in and check out those babes."

"Not now," Cain said. "Let's get Wayne trussed up first." Cain drove past the barn. As he approached the holding pen, a cloud drifted across the moon, darkening the shadows around the expansive yard and tree line behind it. Crickets bombarded the yard with a fluctuating crescendo of noise.

Leaving the lights on, Cain parked the Ranchero in front of the slanting gate of the holding pen. While Abel pulled Wayne's body out of the bed of the truck, Cain cleared the planks of wood from the entrance. Then he and Abel walked to the far end of the pen. There was a coil of barbed wire on the ground. As Abel lowered the body next to the wire, Wayne's head brushed against his face. Abel leaned closer, buried his nose in Wayne's hair, and sniffed.

"Smells good."

"What the hell you doing, Abel?"

"Smells like Old Spice," Abel explained, an amused look on his face. "It's the same shampoo that I use." Abel nudged Wayne in the shoulder. Wayne's head rolled to the side, hit against the warped board, and was still. Abel studied the face, the half-closed, bloodshot eyes; he nudged Wayne again. Cain stood there impatiently.

"Leave the boy be, and go get the Sharpfinger in the truck."

"He ain't movin', Cain. I think you hit him too hard. I think you kilt him."

"Don't be such a dumb-ass. There's nothing wrong with Wayne."

"What'd you mean?"

"Wayne's smart. He don't like being hit. He's playing possum."

"How can you tell?"

"Because you only smell Old Spice, Abel. You don't smell ammonia or anything like shit, do you? When people die suddenly, that's what they do. They shit and piss themselves."

"Yeah, I remember now. That's what Abbey Lee did all over her panties back in Death Valley." Abel stepped closer to Wayne and spread his legs apart. "Let's give a little test." Abel moved quickly and kicked Wayne in the groin.

Wayne's eyes opened wide, and he screamed. His hands dropped and cupped his groin. His body trembling, Wayne crouched against the warped boards. Abel bent over the boy, clapping his hands and laughing.

"You had me fooled for a while, playin' possum like that." Abel ripped off Wayne's clothes. Then he took the wire and wrapped it around Wayne's chest and arms. He twisted the wire tight, slicing deep into the flesh. Blood flowed uneven lines over the pale skin and dripped to the dirt. Cain stepped closer.

"I'll finish with him, Abel. You get the Sharpfinger in the truck so I can start the cutting. The design is real important. I need to make exact triangles and circles on his chest and back."

"Are the voices telling you what to do again?"

"Yes. The voices began shouting at me on the mountain. Louder than ever before!" Cain took the wire and twisted the end around a wooden plank, securing it to the pen.

"I'll get that Sharpfinger." Abel became animated; his face lively and jovial. "When we finish cutting, Wayne, can we stay and watch the hogs?"

"Bad idea, Abel."

"Why?"

"The hogs won't come near the pen if they smell us."

"But—"

"Okay," Cain interrupted. "We'll wait in the Ranchero. But only an hour."

"Great," Abel said. He started across the pen. At the gate, he heard a rustling, scraping noise in the brush and moved faster. Then he heard the sound of a car horn blaring from Polecat Hollow Road, and he stopped in his tracks.

"Dad," Conner Brooks said as the jeep rumbled across the one-lane bridge below Twin River High School, "can we turn around and catch up to Wayne?"

"He said he didn't want a ride."

"I know, but I'm worried about him. I saw Cain's pink truck race by the school right before Wayne left."

"The twins were bullying Wayne this morning," Gene said. Crossing the bridge, he pulled to the side of the road. "We'll go back and make sure he's all right."

"Can we hurry?" Conner asked.

Gene nodded. As he spun the jeep around, a car pulled onto the other end of the bridge. It advanced to the middle and stopped, and the passenger door opened. A heavyset figure stepped out, unzipped his pants, and began urinating in the river. Conner leaned out the window and shouted at the man. When the man didn't respond, Conner stepped onto the road and shouted louder.

"Hey!"

"Whoopee!" the man brayed. He fell down and crawled on his hands and knees to the car. The door slammed; the car moved forward and stalled. The engine started grinding, and the car jerked into motion. When it reached Conner, a lady, her face plain and wrinkled, looked out the window.

"Sorry," she said. "He's had too much to drink … again."

"Whoopee!" sounded from inside the truck. Shaking her head, the lady drove off the bridge; Conner raced back to the jeep.

"Fuckin' redneck," Conner mumbled, slamming the door.

"Don't use that language," Gene said.

"Dad, we eat fish from the Little Juniata."

"I know," Gene said. "But I don't care if it's red neck, blue neck, or yellow neck. Don't use that language. I want you to tell me right now that you'll stop talking like that."

"I'll try to stop, Dad."

"Okay," he said. "Let's find Wayne."

Gene spun onto the road and headed back toward the school. He went through Alexandria, past the Main Street Café, crossed the bridge over the Juniata River, and turned onto Route 22. After going only a short distance, he swerved into Polecat Hollow. The headlights bounced a flashing light through the darkness. There was movement, and a deer raced across the road in front of them. Gene braked; Conner sat nervously.

"Can we go faster, please?"

"Hold on tight and keep your eyes open. We don't want to hit anyone."

Gene bounced the jeep over a series of potholes. After a four-minute drive, he stopped the jeep in front of the Wilson house. The porch was dark. Some wooden chairs and an old high-backed rocker sat in the shadows. Gene looked at Conner.

"We didn't pass him on the road. Wayne's probably sleeping."

"I don't see his bicycle." Conner reached over and hit the horn. The blast shattered the quiet; the house remained dark. Conner pressed the horn and held it down. The resounding blare echoed across the barnyard and cornfields. Gene waited a moment and removed his son's hand from the horn.

"That's enough, Conner. Wayne's not here."

"He was on his way home. Maybe he stopped at Martins for a snack. We should check the store, Dad."

"Let's do that," Gene said. He turned the wheel and raced the jeep down the road.

Listening to the distant blare of the horn, Abel stood motionless by the Ford Ranchero. When the noise stopped, he opened the door and grabbed the Sharpfinger. On the way through the gate, he again heard a snorting sound. The thick brush parted; Abel saw a dark head, gristle patches of hair, and two glaring red eyes.

"Cain!" he screamed. "It's a fuckin' hog! Get the hell out of there!" Abel limped clumsily back to the Ranchero, dropped the Sharpfinger on the seat, jumped inside, and started the engine. Staring through the windshield, he saw the hog trot out of the brush. Abel's mouth dropped open.

"Holy shit," he swore. "A fuckin' big hog!"

Standing four-plus feet high, the hog lifted its head and pawed the ground. Its curled tusks caught the glare of the headlights. The hog made a loud grunting noise, and in a blur of motion, it charged the poppy-pink Ranchero. The skull smashed into the front grill, splintering a headlight. Cowering in his seat, Abel blew the horn loudly.

"Holy shit!" Abel swore again. The hog straightened and stood menacingly in the glare of the solitary light. Hands trembling, his knee throbbing, Abel shifted into reverse. In the rearview mirror, he watched Cain climb over the fence and run in a spasmodic motion for the truck. Shaking its head, its belly swinging back and forth, the hog snorted and trotted around the front fender. When it rumbled past his door, Abel saw gobs of foam spewing from the hog's mouth.

"Hurry, Cain!" Abel shouted, pounding the horn. "It's comin' at you!"

Only yards from the rear gate of the truck, Cain saw the charging hog. As Cain jumped wildly, the hog swiped. The curved tusk made contact with the less mobile, dragging foot and ripped off the Hush Puppy. Cain toppled over the gate, rolled the length of the bed, and beat his hand on the window. Abel shifted gears once, twice, smashed the pedal to the floor, and wheels spinning dirt and grass in the air, he spun the truck around.

Making wheezing and grunting noises, the hog stood motionless. A fresh scent drifted from the holding pen. The hog lifted its head in the air and sniffed. As it trotted toward the warped planks of wood, the scent became stronger.

The horn blasting against the side of the pen, Wayne opened his eyes and struggled to his feet. When he tried to breathe, the wire cut deep into his ribs. Wayne leaned against the warped planks of wood. With the horn still blasting, the truck sped across the yard. As the headlight disappeared, a deep silence settled over the barnyard. Then Wayne heard the snorting noise. The enraged hog charged against the side of the pen; its tusks and snout pushed through the gap in the wood, stopping inches from Wayne's exposed leg.

"The fucker's not chasing us," Abel said, braking to a stop at the front gate. Cain opened the door and climbed onto the front seat.

"Do you still want to stay and watch the hogs work?"

"Hell, no!" Abel drove down the road. When he approached the Wilson property, he accelerated past the empty house. "What do you think will happen to Wayne?"

"I imagine the same thing that happened to the goat."

"The hogs will munch him good," Abel reasoned. "There won't be any body parts left to bury." Driving down the road, he felt a hard object scratching into his pants. He shifted his weight and slid out the Sharpfinger. Cain watched him drop it on the floor.

"Don't tell me you were sitting on that knife the whole time? You're lucky you didn't cut off your nuts." Cain laughed at him; Abel sat quietly. Slowing at the stop sign on Route 22, he looked at his brother.

"It was one crazy fuckin' night," Abel said. A smirk forming on his face, he looked directly at Cain. "All I know for sure is that I got out of that pen free and clear."

"What are you talking about?"

"I mean I'm still wearing both my shoes, but you only got one Hush Puppy." Abel pointed at the ripped sock and laughed loudly. Headlights were coming down the road. Abel spun out in front of them, shifted gears, and raced down Route 22.

The hog's snout squeezed deeper into the gap. His body trembling, the wire barbs piercing his flesh, Wayne stepped away from the curved tusks. The hog sniffed and scratched against the plank. The wood began to splinter. Grimacing, biting his lip, Wayne straightened and moved his feet slowly in a tight circle. As the wire uncoiled, the barbs pulled off patches of skin. The line of gashes on Wayne's arms and chest turned dark and filled with blood.

A cold, dry wind blew over the farm and holding pen. It swept across the open ground into the tree line, rattling thin branches, rustling leaves as it whisked up the hillside. Heavy, dark predators, their bellies scraping the ground, the three sows grunted and dug hooves into the burrow. Weighing two hundred pounds, the biggest sow buried her snout deep into the dirt and bit into the clawed paw of a mole. Jerked in the air, the mole squirmed briefly before a smaller sow latched onto its furry hind section.

As the sows ripped the mole in half, devouring skin and bloody innards, a gust of wind shook the branches overhead. Leaves broke off and twisted through the air, some dropping into the crushed burrow. The sows raised their heads, catching the fresh scent. Then, smashing bodies against each other, the sows stampeded down the hillside.

The cloud slid past the moon; the holding pen shimmered with gray shadows. Blood streaming from the cuts across his chest and abdomen, Wayne turned another full circle, and the last coil of wire fell to the ground. Listening to the rumbling noise on the hillside, Wayne grabbed his boxer shorts from the pile of clothes. The rumbling noise grew louder; the three sows crashed through the tree line that bordered the holding pen.

Bright moonlight flooded the flat interior of the pen. Wayne slid on his shorts, the cotton fabric soaking up blood. Moving carefully around the coil of wire, Wayne climbed onto the bottom plank. There was erratic grunting and a splintering impact at his feet. The hog's grizzled snout widened the gap in the bottom planks, its tusk swiping across Wayne's ankle. Wayne screamed out.

A shrill roaring noise erupted at the other end of the holding pen. Shattering the loose boards at the gate, the three sows charged through the opening, charged in a broken line across the flat ground. The smallest sow, caught between two massive swirling bodies, clipped her hooves together, stumbled, and was squeezed to the back. She squealed. The scent of blood was heavy in the air.

Chapter Nine

Romano Estate
Bryn Mawr, Philadelphia
Thursday Afternoon

"We'll be at the Romano estate in a few minutes," Palladin said. He drove down Twin Arch Lane. Wide stretches of grass were bordered by sturdy wood fencing. Horses grazed inside. One black stallion had its head over the top board of the fence. As the Cadillac approached, the horse dropped puddles on the ground and raced away. Amos laughed.

"The pimpmobile strikes again."

Twin Arch Lane dissected a grove of evergreen trees. Dark shadows falling over the hood of the Cadillac, Palladin drove through the grove and stopped in front of a wrought iron gate intricately carved with images of conch shells and silver bodies of dolphins. There was a keyboard on the side of the gate.

"This is it," Palladin said. "Punch in 3553, and we'll go inside."

"It's good to see how well you've prepared," Amos commented. He stepped outside the Eldorado, walked to the gate, and shrugged his shoulders. After pushing the gate open, he returned to the car.

"Someone opened it for us. Who else is involved?"

"Your guess is as good as mine."

"Noodles and Loco," Amos said. "I'll bet they're here to check on us. To guarantee the job is done Scavone's way."

Palladin was quiet. He drove through the gate onto a paved road. The road circled around a large lake that had gold fountains gushing water in the air. Mallards bobbed in and out of the water spray. Maple trees and thick shrubbery bordered the lake. Palladin parked the Eldorado under a vaulting portico, and he and Amos stepped outside.

"Want me to get the video camera?"

"Yes. Go in the back entrance. If Noodles and Loco are there, just set up the camera and wait. I'll handle them."

"Okay." Amos pulled the bulky JVC VHS camcorder and heavy tripod from the trunk. Balancing the equipment, Amos slid the Browning Mark I from his holster. "Just in case," he said, walking to the corner of the house.

Reaching in the trunk, Palladin opened the Halloween bag and removed the contents. He dropped some plastic vials in his coat pocket and placed the swollen patch of rubbery skin under his belt.

Palladin crossed the porch and looked through the picture window at the spacious living room. A five-tier chandelier cast a dazzling light over the wide expanse of coppery-amber mahogany floor and the antique mahogany table against the wall. The table held a silver tray, crystal glasses, and a bottle of Maker's Mark. There was a thick decorative Valley Forge buff-and-blue candle set at each end of the table.

The living room also had an L-shaped sectional sofa, recliner chairs, mahogany end tables, and a stone fireplace. Logs of ornamental firewood were stacked on the hearth next to the copper screen. Bedded in a terra cotta lava bowl, an immense yucca cane, narrow green leaves scraping the ceiling, accentuated one corner of the room. The other corner had a smaller bird of purgatory plant. Each end table had exotic bonsai trees sprouting from rectangular resin stone pots.

Leaning against the stone wall, holding a half-empty glass of Maker's Mark in his hand, Noodles loitered at the fireplace. He was tall and thin, and he wore a fine tailored black suit, black tie, and white shirt. Straggly lines of brown hair were combed over the round, empty area on the top of his head.

With a pudgy body and short, stocky legs, Loco stood next to the sofa. He wore a black sweatshirt, baggy green pants, and scruffy tennis shoes. He had a red Phillies cap pushed low over his forehead. There was a jagged scar above his left eye.

Bound with packing tape, Caesar Romano slumped on the sofa. The fabric of his white tuxedo was slashed and soaked with blood. There were tears running down Caesar's face. Loco and Noodles both looked up when Amos walked into the room. Nodding in their direction, Amos began setting up the camera.

The loud roar of a motor sounded from the gate. Palladin turned his head. A shiny red Corvette raced around the lake, swerved erratically, and spun into the grass at the entrance to the portico. The tires left wide grooves before the Corvette jumped back onto the pavement and skidded to a stop directly behind the Eldorado. The door swung open, and a boy in a school uniform, blue shirt, black tie, and pleated slacks, jumped out. The knot on his tie was loose; the shirt was unbuttoned at the neck. The boy was tall and angular. His eyes were lively, his face unblemished. Palladin moved away from the window and stepped in front of the teenager.

"You have handsome features just like your mother," Palladin said.

"I hear that a lot, sir. Have you met her?"

"I met Jane last Saturday."

"I'm Cody," the boy said.

"I'm glad to meet you, Cody. I'm Palladin." They shook hands; Cody's eyes were riveted on the Cadillac Eldorado.

"Is this car yours, sir?"

"Yes."

"I never thought I'd see a pimpmobile in my driveway." The boy laughed. He noticed the expression on Palladin's face. "I'm sorry, sir. I didn't mean anything derogatory. I think it's a great car, sir. How does it handle?"

"See for yourself." Palladin threw him the keys. "Take a drive around the lake."

"Great!" Cody jumped in the front seat, started the engine, and floored it. The Eldorado sped out of the portico, rounded the sharp curves smoothly, scattered the ducks at the edge of the lake, and returned within seconds. Cody jumped out and gave the keys back to Palladin.

"I never would have believed it was that fast, sir. And that smooth too. And it's quiet like … like a church inside."

"I'm satisfied with it. I had it going an easy one hundred on the turnpike last week."

"That's incredible, sir."

"What about your Corvette?"

"Oh, it's fast too, sir. But I don't race it. I just got it for graduation."

"You look pretty young. When did you graduate?"

"Oh, not for two years, sir," the boy replied, laughing. "But Dad didn't want to wait. He got a big bonus from the law firm, so he bought it for me. When I pass my driver's test, I'll be able to take it to school."

"Valley Forge Military Academy," Palladin said.

"How did you know, sir?"

"Your uniform. Last year I visited the campus. "Courage. Honor. Conquer." I like the motto. Especially the 'Conquer' part. I wasn't there long. I walked around for a while. Went to the May Becker Memorial Library. Her husband founded the academy, didn't he?"

"Yes, Lieutenant General Milton Baker."

"What was the lieutenant general's problem?"

"Problem, sir? What do you mean?"

"His preference for incorporating British customs and ceremonies at Valley Forge. Baker's a brazen Anglophile."

"Not too brazen, sir. We practice … we respect many West Point traditions too. But last week at assembly, the Commandant of Cadets said the British were true gentlemen. They had a strict code."

"What code?"

"During the fighting they ordered their soldiers to fire carefully, not to aim at officers." Cody had a serious expression on his face. Palladin frowned and spoke in a calm voice.

"My daddy told me that many British officers were entitled land owners with little military training. They bought their commissions and used them recklessly. They ordered the lower classes into battle after battle, into total annihilation, with little or no remorse."

"But the British officers followed the code. Because of this code, George Washington survived the war and became our first president."

"I don't understand."

"At the Battle of Brandywine, Captain Ferguson, a Scotsman, an excellent marksman, had General Washington in his sights. The captain lowered his gun. He refused to shoot an officer who was doing his official duty. He felt it was a dishonorable act. The Commandant of Cadets said the Americans fought differently."

"In what way?"

"The Americans hid behind trees and shot at anyone, soldiers and officers. They fought like Indians."

"Whatever your Commandant of Cadets said about codes, about honor or dishonor, the British lost. They were defeated and humiliated."

"I realize that." Cody paused for a moment. "What were you looking for in the library, sir?"

"Traces of ... you might refer to them as Holden Caulfield's footprints."

"*Catcher in the Rye*." Cody laughed. "Yeah, Salinger attended Valley Forge. He said most of the students and all the teachers in the school were phonies. In the book, Holden said things about his roommate that I could see were true about mine."

"What things?"

"My roommate's always lying. He's always pretending to be better than everyone else."

"Phony people are very clever. It's not easy to recognize who's for real and who's not." Palladin stared at the boy. "Cody, are you a phony?"

"No. I don't think I am." Cody shook his head. Palladin stepped closer and continued to stare into his face.

"By the end of the afternoon, we'll both know if you're a phony or not."

"I don't understand," Cody said, narrow worry lines appearing on his forehead. "What do you mean?"

"You'll find out soon enough," Palladin said. He took a step back. "Did you read the whole book, *Catcher in the Rye*?"

"I read it twice. The first time I missed so much of the meaning."

"What do you think about Mr. Caulfield?"

"I like Holden Caulfield. I like him a lot. Holden wanted to protect the kids who were running and playing in this field of rye. The field was on the edge of a cliff. It was real dangerous to play there. But the kids didn't know that. Holden wanted to be ready to catch them if they fell off the cliff. That's what he wanted more than anything. He wanted to save the lives of the innocent. What do you think, sir? Isn't that a good thing?"

"*If a body catch a body coming through the rye*," Palladin quoted. "They're memorable words, Cody. But I think you need to understand something important. A person needs to catch himself first before he can catch others. Holden was weak and depressed. And he did fall. Holden wasn't much good to anyone, even to his sister Phoebe."

"Maybe you're right, sir. But I still like Holden. He was a rebel. He used vulgar language all the time. That's one of the reasons libraries ban his book. But the language didn't bother me."

"Cody, I would think the language would bother you—a little," Palladin said, pointing to the insignia on the boy's blue uniform. "I see you're an officer."

"Master sergeant, sir," the boy said proudly. "How do you know about rank?"

"Before I went to Vietnam, my daddy taught me all about officers and rank. He made me memorize the insignia. I can tell every rank from sergeant to general."

"Why did he want you to know about rank, sir?"

"I asked him that very question." Palladin smiled. "My daddy advised me never to shoot just any soldier. He said only shoot the officers."

"Ha, sir," the boy said, laughing. "You got me there."

"Not yet," Palladin said. Hearing loud voices from inside the house, he grabbed the boy's arm and backed him against the door. Palladin's face turned dark; he spoke in a rough, crude voice. "Listen carefully, Cody. Things are going to get ugly pretty fuckin' fast."

"I—"

"Shut up and listen." Palladin slapped him across the face. Cody struggled; his face reddened. "Are you paying attention, Master Sergeant?"

"Yes, sir."

"From this point on, just obey my orders. Don't think. Don't argue. And for Christ's sake, don't resist. Just do exactly what I say."

"I don't understand."

"You don't need to understand, Cody. Just be an obedient soldier and follow orders. If you don't, you will die. Right here in your house. You will die. Nod your head if you understand this." Cody nodded. The front door slammed open, and Loco ran out.

"What the hell you doing out here, Palladin? We've got the camera and everything set up for the big show. I see you got the kid." Loco moved closer and punched Cody in the stomach, dropping him to his knees. Then he grabbed the boy's tie and dragged him through the door.

Still standing at the fireplace, Noodles had refilled his glass; bourbon was spilling over the sides. Across the room, Amos stood behind the tripod and video camera. Struggling to stand, Cody saw the bloodied figure on the sofa.

"Dad!" he cried. Loco punched him in the chest. Cody fell to the floor and started crawling to his dad.

"Turn on the fuckin' camera," Loco instructed. "Mr. Scavone's gonna enjoy watching this." Loco gave an enthusiastic thumbs-up signal to Amos, who looked at

Palladin. Shaking his head, Palladin walked slowly toward Loco.

"Leave the kid alone," he said.

"Don't interfere, Palladin."

"You're the one interfering. It's my contract. I don't need you here. I don't want you here. So get the hell out before I work on your face again."

"You son of a bitch!" Loco shouted. He swung his fist blindly. Palladin let it flash by; then he hit Loco in the face, sending the Phillies cap through the air, splitting Loco's lip, and knocking out two teeth. Loco fell to the floor.

Noodles dropped the glass of Maker's Mark. It shattered on the stone hearth. He drunkenly pulled out his Beretta and raised it toward Palladin. Reaching under his belt, Palladin slipped out the derringer, aimed, and fired. The bullet put a hole in the middle of Noodles's forehead. The gun falling from his hand, a look of surprise on his face, Noodles grimaced. His body dropped heavily into the fireplace. Amos lowered his Browning.

"You're damn fast with that toy gun," Amos said. He put the Browning back in his holster. Using his elbows for support, Loco lifted himself off the floor.

"You're dead!" Loco sneered, spitting globs of blood. He slid his hand down his leg and reached for the drop gun on his ankle.

Palladin grabbed Loco's wrist. Wrenching it with considerable force, he mutilated the ligaments, ripping tiny carpal bones from the joints, releasing the lubricating synovial fluid. Loco bellowed; blood sprayed over his sweatshirt. Palladin removed the drop gun and threw it across the floor. It disappeared under the sofa.

Loco cradled his wrist against his chest and began making alternate shrieking and moaning noises. Palladin picked up the Phillies cap and carefully placed it on Loco's head. Loco's wrist was dark and swollen. Blood dripped from the fingernails. He began to wail. Palladin frowned.

"I'm sorry, Loco. Mr. Scavone wouldn't want to hear you bawling like this."

Palladin dropped to one knee and grabbed Loco's head. Twisting it in a sharp, powerful motion, he snapped the neck. Loco, his eyes closing tightly, lay still on the floor. Palladin stood and surveyed the living room.

"It's too bright in here." Palladin reached over and turned the dial on the wall switch, dimming the lights on the chandelier. Then he walked to the middle of the room, stepped over Loco's body, and grabbed Cody by the neck.

"Start the camera!" he ordered. "Make sure Romano's in the picture. And I don't want any part of Loco in this video." Amos focused the lens, hit the button, and the red record light flashed on.

"I got you and Cody. I got Caesar Romano looking bloody and miserable on the sofa in the background. I'll keep everything at waist level."

"Good," Palladin said. Choking Cody, he dragged him across the floor and threw him into the plush recliner. His hand on the camera, Amos stood behind the recliner.

Palladin punched the boy in the chest, caught his breath, and punched him again. The thud from the contact echoed into the JVC microphone. Amos shouted at him from behind the camera. His hand twitched slightly.

"I thought your daddy told you never—"

"Be quiet and videotape!" Palladin said, anger rising in his voice. He punched Cody again, leaned close, and muttered in his ear, "Pay close attention, Master Sergeant … when you feel pressure on your throat, fall to the floor …

stay there ... don't breathe ... don't move an inch ... just be dead."

Cody sat frozen in the chair. Except for the dark splotches of blood, his face was pale. Out of the corner of his eye, Palladin watched the red light on the JVC camera. His hand hidden by the back of the chair, he reached in his jacket and took out two plastic vials. Then with his other hand, he removed the switchblade from his inside pocket, clicked it open, and held it high in the air. The stiletto flashed silver in the dim light. Palladin stared into the camera.

"Your first victim, Don Scavone." Palladin paused. Then flicking the caps off the vials, he swiped the stiletto across Cody's throat. Blood squirted in the air, squirted over his hand and brown suit and tan shirt. Cody made a gagging noise, grabbed his throat, and rolled to the floor, where he lay perfectly still.

"Now I'll slice Caesar's throat for you." Palladin lifted the stiletto in clear view; blood dripped onto the handle. He smiled a wide smile that stretched his mustache. There was a horn blast from the front portico, and the smile disappeared.

"Who the hell is that?" Palladin asked. Amos put the camera on pause, ran to the door, and looked through the peephole.

"It's our two diggers, Curtis and Trevor," he said. "They parked the truck, and now they're walking up the steps with Henry Hightower's body bag. I'll handle it." Amos opened the door and closed it behind him. There were words, fragments of a heated conversation. Then there was a loud shout, and Amos opened the door.

"We have a slight problem."

"What problem?" Palladin asked, stepping onto the porch. Trevor approached and addressed Palladin in a squeaky voice.

"We brought Henry Hightower's body, and we even brought the gasoline like you said." Trevor pointed to the container on the porch. "On the drive here, Curtis and I talked it over, and we decided for all the extra work, we deserve more money. That's what it is, Dog," Trevor said complacently.

"That's right, Dog." Curtis blinked and nodded his head. The black bag was slung over his shoulder. Both diggers were wearing the same hooded sweatshirts. Their pants and shoes were caked with mud. They reeked of alcohol.

"We made a deal last night," Palladin said. He held the stiletto tight against his pants. "Eight hundred dollars apiece. That's all you—"

"It's not enough money for what we did!" Curtis cut him off. "We dug the grave. We got the gasoline. We watched the body all night and all morning. It stinks real bad."

"A deal's a deal," Palladin said. He smiled. "But I could stick in something extra if that's what you want."

"I'm glad you're starting to see things our way." Curtis smiled too, shifting the weight of the body bag on his shoulder. "We want an extra five hundred dollars. Apiece."

"This piece will have to do." Palladin swung the stiletto and stuck the point in Curtis's buttock. His eyes blinking out of control, Curtis screamed and dropped the body bag on the steps. Palladin twisted the stiletto once, scraping the point against bone, and then pulled it out. Clicking it shut, he slid the switchblade into his pocket.

"What the hell, Dog!" Trevor shouted, throwing his arm around his fellow digger.

"Fuck you, Dog! Fuck you, Dog!" Curtis bellowed. He collapsed to one knee and pressed his hand against the hole in his pants. Seeing the blood flowing through his fingers, Curtis began crying. Trevor lifted him into the truck, pushed him across the seat, and jumped in. Starting the engine, spinning tires, he raced the truck for the exit.

"I'm sorry about that," Amos said. He and Palladin returned to the living room.

"Let's get back to work," Palladin said. He looked at Cody lying perfectly still on the floor. His eyes were open wide and tearful. "You don't need to see this," Palladin muttered. He walked over and smashed Cody's head into the mahogany. Straightening, Palladin looked at Amos. "We need to finish before Jane Romano gets her tires fixed."

"That's right. We're on a tight schedule." Amos stepped behind the tripod and started the camera."

Caesar Romano was slumped on the sofa. The streaks of blood on his ripped shirt formed dark lines that pooled at his waist. Wet bubbles of saliva leaked from the tape on his mouth. Palladin turned his back to the camera, retrieved the switchblade, and walked slowly toward the sofa. Amos called to him in an agitated voice.

"You're in the way, Palladin. I can't see what you're doing to Caesar."

"Be patient, Amos." Palladin pulled out the patch of rubbery skin and peeled off the adhesive cover. Then he hit the release button; the silver stiletto flashed from the handle. Raising the stiletto, he stepped in front of Romano, leaned forward, and slapped the skin patch on Romano's neck.

"Be sure you get this," Palladin directed. In a lightning-quick motion, he swung the stiletto across Romano's throat, cutting through the thin fabric, releasing a thick, bubbly liquid. After hitting Romano sharply on the head, Palladin stepped adroitly out of the way. Romano was unconscious; his neck was disfigured and coated in crimson. Amos zoomed in on the mangled, bloody throat.

"I got it," he said.

"The grand finale," Palladin said dryly. He waited a few seconds. "Turn it off."

His hand twitching slightly, Amos hit the button; the red light went dark. Opening the side, Amos pulled out the cassette from the JVC recorder. Palladin walked to the table, took the bottle of Maker's Mark, and filled a glass. Lifting the glass, he drained it. When Amos came over and handed him the cassette, Palladin slid it inside his coat pocket.

"I think I deserve one of those." Amos reached for the bottle. "Maybe I'd better have a double." He filled a glass, raised it to his mouth, and drank it in one gulp. Slamming the empty glass on the table, he refilled it, bourbon spilling over the table. While he was drinking, Palladin walked to the sofa, lifted Romano's body, and threw it over his shoulder. Amos shook his head.

"What the hell you doing with Caesar? Scavone's not going to like this."

"Don't worry about Scavone. When you've finished your double or triple or whatever you feel the need to gulp down, bring the boy out."

Palladin carried Romano to the portico, opened the door of the Cadillac, and dropped the body in the backseat. Amos came down the steps with Cody. Palladin helped him slide the boy's body next to Romano's. His buff-and-blue military uniform was caked with blood. Cody's head flopped to the side and rested on his father's chest.

"Now what?" Amos asked.

"Put Henry Hightower on the sofa."

Amos shrugged his shoulders and laughed. He grabbed the corner of the black bag, dragged it into the living room, and plopped it on the sofa. Following behind him, Palladin carried the gas container into the room, opened it, and poured gasoline over the mahogany. Leaving a trail of gasoline, Palladin took the container to the kitchen and dropped it open by the door. Then he turned the knobs on the gas range and returned to the living room. Amos reached in his pocket and handed Palladin his lighter.

"It might just work," he said. "Noodles and Loco weren't in the original contract, but now we have three bodies to burn. Scavone will like that number. Sometimes you're a genius like your father. We could get paid after all. Can we go now?"

"In a minute." Palladin walked past him to the fireplace. He reached into Noodles's coat pocket, removed the set of car keys, and gave them to Amos. "Follow me in Noodles's car. We'll leave it at Bryn Mawr. It'll take campus police days to track the owner." Amos nodded and walked toward the video camera.

"Let it burn," Palladin said.

"I guess that means we're out of the movie business." Amos turned and rushed out the door. Palladin waited. When he heard the car pull away, he grabbed the bottle of Maker's Mark and walked to the porch. He clicked the lighter once, twice. On the third try, a bright flame appeared, and he tossed the lighter in the living room.

Moments later, followed by a white 1980 Pontiac Grand Am, Palladin drove the Cadillac Eldorado through the ornate entrance gate. At the Romano estate, clouds of smoke billowed in the air. A sudden gust of wind carried the smoke over the lake; the mallards quacked loudly and circled into the blue sky.

A mile down Twin Arch Lane, Palladin looked up and saw a car racing toward the Eldorado. He slowed and moved closer to the berm. The car sped by. It was a blue Pontiac Sunbird. Palladin caught a glimpse of the woman behind the wheel. For the briefest moment, their eyes met, and he saw her smile.

Engine idling, Palladin waited at the entrance to the Bryn Mawr visitor parking lot. Amos walked between a line of cars, opened the door, and got in the front seat. He took the Maker's Mark bottle off the carpet and took a drink. Palladin drove down Morris Avenue. When he turned onto Route 30, Amos lowered the bottle.

"I feel really stupid," he said. "Let me see that switchblade."

"Here." Palladin took the switchblade out of his pocket. Putting the bottle of Maker's Mark between his legs, snatching the switchblade out of Palladin's hand, Amos clicked it open and slid the stiletto over his palm. He studied the fresh wrinkle on his skin. Then he smiled and returned the switchblade to Palladin.

"It's worthless. The point's sharp enough, but the blade's so dull it wouldn't cut through cheese."

"It had you fooled, cameraman."

"I couldn't see it clearly. You dimmed the damn lights." Amos grabbed the bottle, took a swig, and stared out the window. He spoke in a cautious voice.

"You planned to kill Caesar Romano all along, didn't you?"

"Yes. I had the contract on him. Plus, I was beginning to hate the man."

"It's not like you to change your plans. What happened?"

"Maybe because Romano cared about his son. Caesar bought Cody a Corvette."

"You and this thing with expensive cars," Amos remarked. He drank and sat there quietly for a moment. "You really had me scared. Especially when you kept hitting the kid. My hand was shaking. That's never happened to me before. I thought you were going to kill the boy."

"*If a body catch a body …*" Palladin whispered.

"What?"

"Nothing, Amos. It was a conversation I had with Cody. I'm sorry about your hand shaking, but I needed to make it look real. If you were convinced, maybe Scavone would be convinced too. He had to think Cody was dead. Only then would he scratch the boy's name off the list."

"I don't care how you explain today, Palladin. I didn't like none of it. You left me hanging out in the cold. Just like that damn trip to the cemetery. Why didn't you tell me what you were planning?"

"I don't know. My daddy never told me nothing. I grew up having to figure everything out on my own. Maybe that's it, Amos. You have to figure out the difficult things yourself. You have to think about them. Think hard about them."

"So your daddy never told you anything. You had to figure out the difficult things yourself." Amos smiled. His eyes brightened, and a smug look crossed his face. "Then let me tell you something, Wesley. You're not so smart." Amos sat quietly, staring at the traffic, the smile frozen in place.

"What do you mean, I'm not so smart?" Palladin asked, an annoyed look on his face. Still smiling, Amos turned.

"Do you remember Joey Battista."

"What about Joey?"

"You remember him?

"Sure, I remember him. Dad said he was ambitious and greedy. He went against the don and tried to move his people into Atlantic City."

"How long ago?"

"I don't know … maybe ten, fifteen years."

"Where is he now?"

"He's alive and enjoying the good life. Dad said he escaped to Sicily."

"Is that what your dad said?" Amos nodded, lifted the bottle, and drank with the smile still plastered on his face. He began to cough and lowered the bottle. Wesley waited for the coughing to subside.

"Are you going to tell me or not? Why the hell are we talking about Joey Battista?"

"Okay," Amos said. "I guess at the age of fourteen you were too young to figure out the *difficult things*. See if this will help you. Joey's middle name was Henry. At the time the hit was put out on him, Joey was hiding out in a nice estate on the Tomoko River. One morning he suddenly disappeared off his million-dollar dock."

"Son of a bitch," Palladin muttered, his grip tightening on the steering wheel. "Did Joey Batiste like classical music?"

"I never met him. Your dad never met him. But I heard that Joey always played opera and ballet music for his dinner guests. It was all show. Joey was a cheap hood and a phony. He didn't understand anything classical."

"On the morning he passed away, Joey played something loud. *Billy the Kid*. I can still hear it." Palladin shook his head. "What the hell! I did my dad's contract, and I didn't know it until now."

"Wesley, like I said, you're not as smart as you think you are. You should have been suspicious when you saw *Omerta* on Henry's Colt. But, everything considered, I guess Mr.

Palladin started you in the business the right way. Your dad was for real. There was nothing phony about him. He knew exactly what he was doing. And you can bet he had good reasons for doing it his way." Amos took a long drink; his shoulders relaxed, and he burped.

"Save some for me." Palladin grabbed the bottle, took a drink, and handed it back to Amos. "What a day! It's time to relax and enjoy the sound quality in my pimpmobile, as you call it." Palladin pulled out the cassette again and slipped Wings into the player. He and Amos listened through the song twice.

> *When you were young and your heart was an*
> *   open book,*
> *You used to say live and let live.*
> *You know you did, you know you did, you*
> *   know you did.*

The music ended. Palladin removed the cassette. Except for the soft, steady breathing from the backseat, the interior of the Cadillac was extremely quiet.

"Church-like quiet," Palladin said.

"What?"

"Cody took the pimpmobile for a test ride. He was impressed. He told me it was church-like quiet inside."

"Your pimpmobile is quiet and peaceful," Amos said. "Scavone's contract called for morgue-quiet. I prefer church-quiet like it is now." Amos nudged Palladin in the shoulder and sniffed. "But you can't mistake the odor of blood. It smells like a morgue in here. And, unfortunately, one of them … I think the old man shit his pants."

"That shows you the effectiveness of my grand finale," Palladin said. "This will help a little." He hit a button. A lace curtain slid out from the corners of the backseat, moved over the windows, and closed directly behind the front seats.

"Much better." Amos smiled. His face was flushed, his nose red from the bourbon. Shadowy trees and dark hillsides loomed closer to the Cadillac. Amos reached his hand forward and began hitting the padded dash in a quick, rhythmic pattern. Then he drank bourbon and sang in a loud, booming, awful voice.

*"Live and let **live**. You know you did! You know you did!"* Amos dropped the empty bottle on the floor. Sitting back, he put a Kool in his mouth but didn't light it.

"Tell me one thing, Wesley Palladin. You said you were disappointed Wings didn't win the Academy Award in 1974. Which song did win?"

"I don't remember."

"Sure, you remember," Amos said in a confident tone. "Tell me what it was."

"You won't believe it."

"Let me decide. Go on. Tell me."

"The Way We Were." Palladin had a disgusted look on his face. A wide smile spreading from ear to ear, Amos began to sing with drunken fervor.

"Memories light the corners of my mind …"

"Stop it!" Palladin blasted the horn. "Stop it now!"

"I remember that song like it was yesterday." Amos continued to smile. "My wife, daughter, and even my son cried during the movie."

"Did you cry?"

"Hell no," Amos answered, frowning at Palladin. "Well, maybe a little at the end when Streisand and Redford called it quits on that sidewalk in New York City. Streisand sang in a haunting, beautiful voice. *The Way We Were* is a pretty damn good song."

"No, it's not a pretty damn good song, Amos. It doesn't have the quality nor the substance of Wings. It's weak and sentimental." The traffic leading into Philadelphia began to back up. Palladin drove slowly.

"Amos, we need a break from all this. What do you think about a quick fishing trip to Lake Wallenpaupack? Stripers will be all over the lake."

"I'll pass on that, Wesley. I'm leaving Philly. After what just happened, I don't think it's a safe place to be. I'm visiting my sister in St. Cloud. You should come down."

"Maybe I will. We could go to Ormond Beach and fish the Tomoka River."

"You'd go back there, the same place where you wasted Joey Henry Battista?"

"Sure, I'd go back. The bass under that million-dollar dock were huge." Palladin laughed. "I'll call you as soon as I figure out what I'm doing. A vacation sounds like a good idea right now."

It was late afternoon when Palladin entered North Philadelphia. He dropped Amos off at his house on Frankford Avenue in Fishtown. Then he drove a few blocks to the Liberty Bar and stopped at the curb. A man wearing a black trench coat with a fur collar stood at the door. He was smoking a cigar. Palladin rolled down the window.

"Yoh, Victor."

"Yoh, Palladin." Checking out the lines of the Eldorado, Victor walked to the curb. He noticed the blood on Palladin's shirt. "Any sign of Noodles and my brother, Loco? They were due back hours ago."

"Maybe they got stuck in traffic." Palladin removed the videocassette from his pocket. "Mr. Scavone is waiting for this."

"He told me to expect you," Victor said, taking the cassette. "You sure you haven't seen Loco? I know you two don't get along."

"Things change quickly in our business, Victor. You'll be glad to hear the good news."

"What good news?"

"I had a brief talk with your brother. Loco and I patched up our differences. We shook hands on it." Palladin stared at Victor. Victor blew smoke in the air and turned the cassette in his hand.

"Why don't you come in the bar and give the video to Mr. Scavone personally?"

"I don't have time."

"But I'm sure the boss would appreciate hearing your story. He really likes to know the details. You could answer all his questions."

"I told you I don't have time. I'm late. I've got a date."

"I see you got the curtains closed. Is your honey in the backseat?"

"Not yet," Palladin said. He closed the window and pulled away from the curb.

Chapter Ten

Polecat Hollow
Thursday Evening

Gene stopped the jeep in front of Martins, and Conner ran inside. Conner searched the four aisles of the store and then waited in line as one customer bought ten gallons of gas, another customer ordered two hot dogs with ketchup and onions, and a third customer paid for a cup of coffee with a twenty-dollar bill. The customer was carefully counting her change when Conner pushed past her.

"Do you know Wayne Wilson?" he asked the cashier.

"Yes," she said. "He's cute. He always comes in the store."

"Was Wayne here tonight?"

"No, he wasn't. And Becky, his sister, hasn't been in for weeks. I meant to ask him about her."

"Thanks," Conner said. He ran to the exit and got in the jeep. "The cashier hasn't seen Wayne tonight."

Gene drove past the gas pumps and turned right on Route 22. As the jeep approached Polecat Hollow, Conner saw the poppy-pink Ranchero at the intersection.

Caught in their headlights, the truck pulled out and raced down the road.

"Dad," Conner said.

"I know, son. It's Cain and Abel." Gene turned into Polecat Hollow. He was driving fast when the jeep hit a pothole and bounced in the air. The headlights flashed across the trees and low brush; Conner saw a metallic glint.

"Dad!" he called excitedly. "Stop!"

Gene braked hard. Conner took the flashlight out of the glove compartment and ran back to the pothole. Swinging the light into the woods, he saw the handlebars protruding through the branches.

"Wayne!" Conner shouted. He jumped a ditch and crashed through the brush. Pushing branches that whipped across his face, Conner tripped on the back wheel of the bicycle and fell awkwardly. Gene helped him to his feet.

"It's Wayne's bicycle," Conner said. His heart was beating fast. He swung the light in a circle and saw the gym bag, towel, and bottle of Old Spice in the roots of a tree. Conner grabbed the bag and replaced the items.

"Cain and Abel just drove out," Gene said, walking back through the brush. "Besides the Wilson home, there's only one other property back here."

"The Calvin farm," Conner said. He picked up the bicycle and followed Gene to the jeep. Opening the door, Conner set the bicycle on top of his and threw the bag behind the seat. Gene grabbed the Winchester and a box of cartridges and gave them to Conner.

"I keep three cartridges in the Winchester. You'd better put two more in." Opening the box quickly, Conner removed two hollow-point cartridges and slid them in the magazine.

"I'm ready, Dad. What do you think happened?"

"I don't know what happened." Gene waited for Conner to get seated; then he started the jeep. "But you'd better be prepared for anything. None of it good. There are four of the biggest damn hogs you're ever going to see back there."

Gene sped through Polecat Hollow, past the Wilson house, and under the new arch. Approaching the Calvin farm, he swerved through the gate, knocking over the mailbox. As he raced past the red glow of the barn, the headlights flashed on the holding pen. Gene saw Matt's bloodied, naked body trapped on the top planks of the pen.

"Fuck!" Gene cursed. A massive hog charged at the lower section of the pen. The planks collapsed under Matt, creating a gap in the wood. Gene slammed on the brakes; the jeep stopped thirty yards from the holding pen.

"I'll get the hog's attention," Gene said. "First chance you get, shoot its neck out." Leaving the key in the ignition and the headlights on, Gene leapt from the jeep and ran toward the pen.

"Dad!" Conner cried, grabbing the Winchester. He jumped down and moved quickly to the front of the jeep. Planting his feet, steadying himself, he leveled the Winchester. The hog scratched at the toppled rubble of wood. Wayne hung onto the top plank with one hand. His feet swung wildly back and forth.

"Hey!" Gene yelled, waving his arms and clapping his hands. The hog's ears pricked up; its eyes flared red. Conner aimed at the thick black throat. The hog snorted; its stunted legs, hooves digging deep in the earth, propelled the massive weight forward.

"Shoot!" Gene shouted.

The Winchester moving, adjusting to the charging target, Conner was applying soft pressure on the trigger when he heard the shrill, squealing noise inside the pen. The three sows began crashing heavy bodies against the wood. There was a cry for help; Conner watched the pale body shake loose and fall, as if in slow motion. The body suddenly accelerating, Wayne slammed into the debris of smashed planks on the ground. He lay there motionless, his head bloodied and tilted to the side.

"Damn it! Shoot!" his dad shouted above the noise of the charging hog.

Gene stood there, a tall silhouette in the glare of the jeep's headlights. Gobs of mucus and foam swirling from its snout, the hog's massive body grew larger as it closed to six … five … four yards. The silhouette crouched and then remained perfectly still. In the clamorous frenzy of its charge, the hog raised its head, elevating its pointed tusks high in the air.

"Fuckin' hog!" Conner slurred, blocking out the noise.

With Wayne, the hog, and his dad in clear sight, Conner squeezed the trigger. A dull, hollow echo resonated in his ears. With a smooth, continuous motion, Conner stroked the lever and fired again. Two small holes opened in the hog's neck and blasted out craters of flesh and gristle on the other side. Blood gushing out of the holes, the hog rolled to the ground and stopped, its body a dark, rotund mass of wrenching blubber, at Gene's feet.

"Fuckin' hog," Conner said again, sweat pouring down his face. Shivering in the cold night air, Conner stared unblinking at his dad, who turned slowly and met his gaze. Conner's chest heaved. Looking past his dad, he saw Wayne's body.

Wayne lay flat on the ground. His head was perilously close to the warped planks of the holding pen. Loud snorting and high-pitched squealing filled the inside of the pen. Crushing their bodies against each other, the three sows charged repeatedly into the wooden barrier. The lead sow smashed her jaws through the widening gap. Sniffing blood, she lunged.

Wayne struggled to move. The black body loomed closer. Grizzled lids covered her eye sockets. Her snout was inches from Wayne. She grunted a hot stench into his face and surged forward. Covering his head, Wayne pressed his body into the earth.

Then there was a loud crack from the Winchester; the sow's eye exploded a white jelly substance. Jaws snapping, neck twisting, the sow roared. Grabbing a loose plank of wood, Wayne swung it into her snout. She bit into the wood, shredding it, and charged again. Covering his head with his arms, Wayne heard Mr. Brooks's voice.

"I got you." Gene picked Wayne up, tossed him over his shoulder, and ran toward the jeep. Directly behind him, the side of the pen collapsed; the two smaller sows burst by the blind one. Their bellies rolling and scraping the ground, they charged after Gene.

"Dad!" Conner shouted. "They're too close! I can't shoot!"

"Get in the jeep! Get the door!" Gene ran furiously. The lead sow swiped her tusks high in the air. His head sliding low on Gene's back, his eyes blinking, Wayne saw the tusks rising and falling a few feet from his face.

"Damn it!" Conner swore. Running to the jeep, he jumped in the front seat and kicked the passenger door open. Starting the engine, he stared helplessly through the windshield. Caught in the light, his dad struggled to hold the bouncing, slippery body on his shoulder. Perspiration sprayed in the air; Gene's pace slowed slightly. Wayne's exposed hands and head jounced wildly, vulnerably through space. Directly behind him and Gene, the lead hog was partially hidden in dark shadow. Blood sprayed from Wayne's body. Crimson droplets hitting against its snout, the massive hog scrambled faster. Conner measured the distance. His mind racing, Conner grabbed the wheel in a death grip.

The big fucker's too fast … too close, he swore fearfully. Gunning the engine, Conner turned the wheel sharply, swerved around his dad, and smashed into the heavy, grizzled body. Tires spinning grooves in the grass, the jeep jerked to a stop.

"Yes!" Conner shouted when he saw his dad slide into the front seat. Closing the door, Gene released his grip on the boy. A dazed look on his face, Wayne lifted his head.

"Let's get you in the back." Gene helped Wayne crawl over the headrest and onto the seat. When Wayne straightened, his shoulder brushed against the bicycle. Making a clicking sound, the bald tire spun a slow circle.

"My Schwinn," Wayne said, a perplexed look on his face. He placed his hand on the tire, stopping it, leaving a blood smear on the rubber. Gene reached for the bag and pulled out the towel.

"Here." Gene placed the towel over the cuts on Wayne's chest.

Making grunting sounds, their tusks scratching lines in the orange paint, the massive swine brushed aggressively against the door. Legs collapsing and straightening, the blind sow wandered in their direction. Gene looked at Conner.

"Can you put us in reverse?"

"Be happy to, Dad." Conner shifted gears, hit the gas pedal, and the jeep moved backward. Drool falling from their open jaws, the sows followed. Gene switched on the high beams. Blasted by the bright light, the sows stopped and lowered their heads. Only the blind sow followed the jeep. Gene took the Winchester.

"Stop here," Gene said in a nonchalant voice. When Conner braked in front of the barn, Gene stepped out of the jeep. Blood dripping from the scarred snout, the sow shuffled clumsy hooves directly at the light. Gene raised the Winchester.

"This is for you, Wayne." Aiming quickly, he shot a hole in the sow's good eye and got back in the jeep. Wayne clapped his hands when the massive body leaned awkwardly and fell to the ground.

The moon was bright and flooded the barnyard with a silver glow. A black mammoth on the dirt, the sow's body heaved up and down; blood poured from its eye sockets and pooled under its head. The two other sows trotted out of sight. Conner saw a dark object in the grass. Rushing out of the jeep, he ran over, picked it up, and returned.

"What is it?" Gene asked.

"A Hush Puppy," Conner said, holding the shoe in the air. "I hate Abel Towers. But I hate Cain even more." When he placed the shoe on the seat, he glimpsed the interior of the barn. The spotlight cast a warm glow over four colorful Winnebago Chieftains and the floor-to-ceiling murals on the wall. Wayne jumped to attention in the backseat.

"No way is this real!" Wayne blurted. Eyes opening wide, he gawked at a bikini-clad woman stretching her glistening-moist and perfectly tan body seductively on the sands of a tropical beach.

"No way!" he exclaimed. "She's so hot and wet. Can we get a closer look? I feel fine now. Honest. Nothing hurts me anymore." Wayne had a huge smile on his face. Gene nudged Conner in the shoulder.

"Get us out of here."

"Now!"

"Right now," Gene said. "And drive carefully. Wayne's in a state of shock."

Nodding his head, taking a quick glance at the smooth tan lines, Conner turned the jeep around and drove slowly down the road. Wayne sat quietly next to his Schwinn. Even though the line of gashes on his chest and arms dripped blood, he had a lingering smile on his face. Reaching out, Wayne spun the bicycle tire.

Except for the noise of the motor and the steady clicking sound, the jeep was quiet. Conner was careful when he approached a pothole and doubly careful on the curves. Gene stared at the empty stretch of road.

"That was great shooting back there," he said softly. "I'm proud of you."

"I was real scared. I was sweating so much my eyes were cloudy."

"It's natural to be scared, son. Just so you keep your aim steady."

"I knew I could take the hog down." Conner spoke in an excited voice. "Then Wayne fell, and at the same time, the damn hog charged so fast at you. That's when I felt myself boiling inside. My heart was beating wild and hurting too. Then somehow I thought clearly. The night turned dead quiet. That's just how I thought … dead quiet. In the silence, I found I could do exactly what you always told me to do. *Stay calm. Stay focused.* I didn't hear squealing or any noise when I shot that hog. Two times I shot that hog right in the neck where you told me. And I never heard nothing. You taught me everything I know, Dad."

The jeep bumped onto the asphalt road. The lights were on at the Wilson house. As they approached, Gene saw Mr. Wilson on the rocking chair. Conner stopped the jeep in the dirt drive. He, Gene, and Wayne stepped out and walked to the porch. When Mr. Wilson saw Wayne in his ripped shorts, saw his bruised body and the blood-soaked towel, he rushed to him. His lips trembling, he used his shirtsleeve to wipe at the blood on Wayne's forehead.

"What the hell happened?" Mr. Wilson asked in a strained voice.

Chapter Eleven

Polecat Hollow/Barree
Thursday Evening

Holding the bloody towel in place, Mr. Wilson helped Wayne to the porch. Gene leaned the Schwinn against the railing. Conner carried the gym bag up the steps and handed it to Wayne. The line of cuts on Wayne's upper body were crimson in the harsh glare of the porch light.

"What happened?" Mr. Wilson asked again.

"Dad, I'm a mess. I smell bad. I need a shower. Mr. Brooks and Conner can tell you everything." Wayne pushed the door open and disappeared into the house. Gene glanced at Mr. Wilson.

"When Wayne's cleaned up, we can take him to my brother Andrew's church. Joyce can tend to him. She may send him to the emergency room."

"How was he cut like that?"

"This will take some time," Gene said. "Conner and I will explain everything." Gene sat down and motioned Conner to one of the wooden chairs. Wilson lowered himself into the rocking chair. When he leaned back, it made a steady, creaking noise.

Starting with basketball practice at Twin River, Conner, Gene, and Mr. Wilson talked back and forth for a long time. Asking numerous questions, at times swearing and shaking his head, Mr. Wilson become more and more agitated.

"What's this about the Reverend Towers's sons, Cain and Abel?"

"They took Wayne to the holding pen," Conner explained. "They coiled barbed wire around him and wrapped the end of the wire to the boards so Wayne couldn't move very far." The creaking noise stopped. Conner glanced at Mr. Wilson, who sat straight and hard. The look of concern on Wilson's face was now fierce and angry.

"What did you just say?"

"Cain and Abel left Wayne for the hogs." Conner pulled the Hush Puppy from his coat pocket and gave it to Mr. Wilson. "This is Cain's shoe. He lost it at the pen."

"Cain and Abel tried to kill my son!" Mr. Wilson exclaimed. Tossing the shoe on the floor, he got up suddenly, the rocking chair crashing against the wall, and stomped down the steps. He was halfway to the barn when Wayne pushed the door open.

"Dad! Dad! Where you going?"

Mr. Wilson stopped at the barn door. His entire body trembling, he stood there for a moment. Then shaking his head, he turned and walked back to the porch.

"What were you going to do, Dad?"

"Nothing," he said. "Nothing right now. We have to look after you."

"I'm fine, Dad." Wayne was dressed in jeans and a blue flannel shirt; his hair was wet. Conner began to laugh.

"What?" Gene asked.

"Can't you smell it?" Conner looked at their faces. "It's that sweet flower smell stinking up the porch."

"Old Spice." Wayne smiled. "I feel alive again."

"You're lucky to be alive," Gene commented. "Mr. Wilson, we need to report this to the sheriff."

"Yeah, we need to do that. I'll call him now. I'll tell him to meet us in Barree." Mr. Wilson went inside the house to the living room and picked up the phone.

Dressed smartly in his blue uniform, Deputy Oliver Wright sat at his desk in the Huntingdon Sheriff's Office on North Penn Street. His short, stout body supported an oversized head. He had an unlit cigar squeezed between his fleshy lips. Puffing on it, he made a sucking noise. The phone rang as Sheriff Parks walked into the room. Holding the phone tight against his ear, chewing on the cigar, Oliver listened for a few moments and then held out the phone.

"Who is it?"

"Wilson out in Polecat Hollow. It's some kind of bullshit story about his son Wayne being kidnapped and damn near killed. He said it was the Reverend Towers's sons, Cain and Abel, who done it. He wants them arrested."

The sheriff shook his head, grabbed the phone, and asked a series of questions. After a few minutes, he threw up his arms in disgust and replaced the phone.

"Are they all crazy out there in the Hollow?"

"Hello," Oliver answered smartly. "Ain't that kinda' obvious?"

"Nothing's obvious at Polecat Hollow," the sheriff said. "What with the Calvin brothers disappearing like they did, there's nothing but damn mystery back there. Here's what we're going to do. I'm meeting Mr. Wilson and Wayne at the Holy Waters Church in Barree."

"It ain't Sunday. Why go to church now?"

"Because the school nurse lives there. She's checking Wayne for serious injury. I want you to interview the Reverend Towers at Redemption Mountain. Don't bother him too much. Just find out if he knows where Cain and

Abel were tonight. Then come over to the church and report to me."

"I'll just call in that report," Oliver said. "I'm not going near Pastor Brooks's church."

"Why are you so worried about meeting the pastor?"

"The two of us had a little incident at the hospital when Dan Boonie busted his leg riding that motorcycle too fast. Pastor Brooks went berserk, and I had to calm him down. Don't you worry none. I'll do a proper interview with the Reverend Towers." Straightening his deputy's cap, Oliver opened the door and walked to the black-and-white police cruiser.

The Barree Holy Waters Church was on the banks of the Little Juniata River. It was a narrow wooden structure with stained-glass windows on the side and a lofty steeple in the front. A ten-passenger 1971 Ford Econoline van, "Holy Waters Church" printed in bold white letters on the door, was parked in the back. Pastor Brooks and his wife, Joyce, resided in the church basement, which consisted of a kitchen, bedroom, bathroom, and large living room.

Mr. Wilson and Gene parked their vehicles in front of the church. An ornamental lamp under the steeple illuminated the sidewalk; a dimmer light filtered through the colorful stained-glass windows. Gene led Mr. Wilson and the two boys up the weathered, wooden steps and opened the door. Pastor Brooks was sitting in the last pew with his neighbor Dan Boonie and a young girl.

Dressed in a long-sleeve white shirt and neatly pressed trousers, Andrew Brooks was thirty-two and slightly overweight. He had a soft oval face with deep-set gray eyes. The teenage girl next to him had long black hair. She wore patched jeans and a Pittsburgh Penguins sweatshirt with a skating penguin on the front. She was five eleven and well proportioned. The white beak and black head of the Penguin pushed prominently forward when she stood.

Standing next to Lisa, Dan Boonie, a guard at the Green Hollow Correctional Camp, had short blond hair and a trim, muscular body. His pants leg was ripped, showing a bulky white cast that went from his knee to his ankle. He wore a blue-and-gold Twin River varsity jacket.

Andrew introduced the girl, Lisa Hendricks; she went down the line and politely shook everyone's hand. Andrew informed them that Joyce was in the basement, so Mr. Wilson, Wayne, and Conner headed for the staircase. Andrew motioned to his brother.

"We have a problem, Gene. Can we talk to you for a second?"

"Sure. What's the problem?"

"It concerns Lisa."

"She must be from Pittsburgh," Gene said, staring at the penguin.

"Yes, Lisa came to visit her boyfriend, Ira Hayes, at Green Hollow Camp."

"Why was Ira sent there?"

"It was a misunderstanding," Lisa answered quickly. "My dad came home early and caught Ira and me on the porch. When he grabbed me, Ira punched him."

"It sounds like your dad's very protective."

"My dad's a Pittsburgh police officer."

"Oh," Gene said.

"I met Ira," Dan volunteered. "It wasn't his fault. He doesn't belong at Green Hollow. Now, he's in trouble with Luther Cicconi and Max Wright."

"Luther and Max are perverts," Lisa said. "When I went to visit Ira, they tricked me and took me to Muddy

Run. They hurt me. Dan helped me get away. They nearly killed Dan."

"They ran me off the mountain road. That's how I broke my leg."

"Why didn't you report it?"

"My parents did report it. Luther and Max said they were at Green Hollow the whole time. Sheriff Parks believed them. He told my parents that I was out racing the motorcycle and lost control. Now Luther and Max are looking for Lisa."

"They think Ira knows where I am. They're going to beat the information out of him."

"What do you want me to do?" Gene asked.

"Pastor Brooks said you were in the war," Lisa answered. "That you knew what to do in bad situations. He said you would help get Ira out of the camp."

"A prison break?"

"I guess you could call it that," Lisa admitted.

"What do you think, Gene?" Andrew asked. "Can you help?"

"I'm more concerned about you. How can you be involved in a prison break? You're a pastor for Christ's sake!"

"I know I'm a pastor. You're standing in the church I built. But I can't sit around and see Ira and Lisa hurt."

"Come over here," Gene said. He and Andrew walked to the door and faced each other. Sometimes they talked quietly, Andrew's head nodding up and down in agreement. Other times, the exchanges were angry; neither brother backed away.

"No," Gene said in a loud voice. "I'm not going near that camp. You drive the church van. That's why you bought it!"

"But we'll need you if there's trouble."

"Do it right, and there won't be any trouble."

"Go over everything one more time," Andrew requested. Gene moved closer. They spoke in whispers. After five minutes, they returned to the pew. Bright lights flashed in front of the church. Gene heard the squawk of a police radio. A door slammed; Gene shook his head.

"Sheriff Parks has arrived."

"Why's he coming here?" Lisa asked, a worried expression on her face.

"He's here to take Mr. Wilson's statement," Gene said. Lisa wrung her hands nervously.

"I can't let the sheriff see me. Luther alerted the local police to pick me up."

"You can stay at my house," Dan said.

"I hope you can help us." Lisa leaned forward, the penguin's beak and head pressing against Gene's chest. She kissed Gene on the cheek and rushed to the back exit.

Limping, Dan followed her. They walked down the alley to a large fenced yard. A spotlight on the porch lit up the area. When Dan opened the gate, an extremely large, white shaggy dog jumped up and placed its paws on Dan's shoulders. A red tongue flopped out of its mouth and slapped Dan on the chin. Lisa began laughing.

"This is Ruggs," Dan said.

"He's huge."

"He's an Irish wolfhound," Dan said. "The wolfhound's the best hunting dog, but he doesn't use scent like hound dogs. He's got the sharpest eyes. Ruggs is my guardian angel. He saved my life on the mountain." They walked to the green Kawasaki Z650 parked at the porch. "After the accident when I got home from the hospital, Dad was excited. He took me outside, pulled the tarp off the Kawasaki, and said, 'Let the good times roll.' The motorcycle's great. It's got power, and it's steady on the turns." Dan rubbed his hand across the seat; Lisa looked at the blue-and-gold jacket.

"Is that your official riding jacket?"

"Yes," Dan said. "I wear it all the time. I love sports. I had great years at Twin River." Dan led Lisa to the house. Ruggs barked once and reclined next to the Kawasaki.

At Holy Waters Church, Sheriff Parks pushed the door open. Wearing his Stetson cowboy hat and white gator boots, his Smith & Wesson 686 prominent on his hip, the sheriff looked first at Andrew … and then at Gene.

"What the hell are you doing here?"

"Please refrain from swearing in God's house," Andrew said. The sheriff ignored him and walked down the center aisle.

"I asked you a question, Mr. Brooks. What the hell are you doing here?" Sheriff Parks stopped directly in front of Gene.

"I was at the Calvin farm and saw what happened to Wayne."

"What actually did happen to Wayne? The old man called my office and made outrageous accusations about Cain and Abel trying to kill his son. Where's Wayne now?"

"In the basement," Andrew said. "Joyce is tending to his wounds."

"Then let's go down there and see what trouble the boy's gotten himself into. Running around late at night, damn teenagers are always up to no good." Sheriff Parks stomped down the steps. Gene grabbed Andrew's arm.

"Did you see that little knot above the sheriff's eye?"

"It was more than a little knot, Gene."

"I did that. The bastard hit Conner."

Gene and Andrew entered the basement and joined the group. Wayne was sitting on a table. His arms and neck were tan; his chest was pale. A white bandage was wrapped around his abdomen. A clear ointment covered the line of gashes on his chest and arms.

Conner and Joyce stood next to the table. Joyce wore a white blouse with "Twin River School District" sewed on the front pocket. She had short brown hair; her face was aged with deep wrinkles. Mr. Wilson talked to Sheriff Parks at the sofa. Parks was writing on his notepad. When Mr. Wilson finished, the sheriff closed the notepad.

"And you're saying that Cain and Abel Towers took Wayne to the abandoned Calvin property, where they wired him to the holding pen and left him for the hogs?"

"That's what I'm saying."

"That's quite an accusation. Do you have any witnesses?"

"I saw the hogs chasing after Wayne," Conner answered quickly. "Wayne barely escaped from the pen."

"Did you actually see Cain and Abel put Wayne in the holding pen?"

"No."

"Did you see Cain and Abel lead the hogs into the pen?"

"No, but Dad and I saw Cain and Abel leaving Polecat Hollow."

"That don't mean nothing," Sheriff Parks said. The phone rang; Joyce picked it up. The voice at the other end was loud.

"It's for you," she said to Parks. "It's your deputy."

"Excuse me." Stretching the cord, the sheriff took the phone. As he listened, he nodded slowly. After a few minutes, he asked, "Are you sure about that?" The answer was a loud, emphatic echo in the room.

"Yes, I'm sure!"

Watching Wayne closely, Sheriff Parks replaced the phone. Wayne stepped down from the table and put on his shirt. Hand resting on the Smith & Wesson, Parks continued to stare at him.

"What kind of lies you telling everyone, boy?"

"I didn't tell any lies," Wayne said, his face turning red.

"My deputy just had a long session with the Reverend Towers. The reverend, a man of God like you, Pastor Brooks, said that Cain and Abel were at home all night."

"He's lying," Wayne said.

"I don't think so. You see, Wayne, Cain and Abel have difficulty walking with those replacement knees. The reverend said the boys did rehab early in the evening. He said the knees hurt so much after rehab that Cain and Abel could hardly walk."

"They were moving pretty fast at the holding pen," Wayne said.

"That's only your words … while we have three good people telling the opposite."

"Cain and Abel lie their way out of everything," Gene said. "They're the biggest troublemakers at Twin River."

"I never had much regard for your opinion," Sheriff Parks said. "You should be the last one talking about troublemakers. You are—"

"You don't believe my son!" Mr. Wilson interrupted.

"I'm saying facts are facts!" The sheriff was shouting now. "After listening to all these stories, I'm thinking Wayne and Conner were up to no good fooling around in that holding pen. These two country boys got no smarts at all. Look at the numbers! Four hogs against two farm boys. Who's gonna win that fight?"

"Wayne and Conner told the truth," Mr. Wilson said. "That's all you got to say about attempted murder?"

"Oh, I got more to say about it." Sheriff Parks had a smirk on his face. "I got lots more to say. I'm thinking I should charge these farm boys for lying and making false statements … maybe give them some jail time."

"Get the hell out of my church," Pastor Brooks said.

"You listen here—"

"No, you listen here, Rosco," Gene growled. "You stay away from Wayne and Conner. If I ever see you near them, I'll put another knot on your head."

"Hit the bastard now," Joyce Brooks blurted out.

"Punch his face, Dad!" Conner shouted excitedly. Then he added quickly, "We've got reliable witnesses right here, Sheriff Rosco. They'll swear under oath that you tripped and smashed your face on the steps."

Sheriff Parks stood there with his mouth open, his face flushed. Fists clenched, Gene advanced. Andrew and Mr. Wilson jumped on either side. The sheriff turned suddenly.

"Fuck you all!" he shouted, scurrying up the steps. On the floor upstairs, there was the sound of gator boots stomping down the aisle and the sound of the door slamming. Then the engine started, and the blaring noise of the siren echoed through Barree. Mr. Wilson approached Wayne.

"You should go home and get some rest." He turned toward Pastor Brooks and Joyce. "Thanks for taking care of Wayne."

"Let us know if you need anything," Joyce said. They all shook hands. Mr. Wilson, Gene, and the boys started up the stairs. Wayne looked at Conner.

"Your dad was calling the sheriff Rosco. Who's this Rosco guy?"

"Oh, him," Conner said. "He's the halfwit police officer in *Dukes of Hazzard*. My dad loves watching that show." Conner laughed. He and Wayne left the church. Reaching the end of the sidewalk, Wayne grabbed Conner's hand and pumped it up and down.

"Back at the pen, I buried my face in the dirt and thought I was a goner," he said matter-of-factly. "Thanks for saving my life." Wayne punched Conner lightly on the shoulder and went to the truck; Conner walked to the jeep. Standing under the church steeple, Mr. Wilson turned and faced Gene.

"I'll bet you love Conner as much as I do my son."

"More," Gene said, "if that's possible." He nodded to Mr. Wilson and walked across the yard. The night was black and cold. The Little Juniata made soft gurgling sounds, the water flowing swiftly and bubbling around the rocks. Gene took a deep breath, climbed inside the orange *Dukes of Hazzard* jeep, and started the engine. Conner looked at the spots of blood on Gene's shirt.

"I'll never forget tonight, Dad."

"Neither will I." Gene crossed the one-lane bridge and turned onto River Road. Three deer grazed along the bank of the Little Juniata. One of them looked up. The other two continued munching grass. Conner stared at them.

"Dad, I'm sorry. Something's really been bothering me."

"What?"

"I didn't plan to, but I said the *f*— word again. I'm not sure. But I think I said it twice."

"I warned you about using that language. When did it happen?"

"When I saw the hog charging at you, I got excited and blurted out *fuckin' hog* right before I killed it."

"I don't understand you sometimes, son." Gene had a smile on his face. "I don't know what the *fuck* I'm going to do with you."

Gene laughed. Then Conner laughed. The waters of the Juniata River glistened with moonlight. Stationary in the depths of the river, the North Star reflected a solitary light that shimmered and grew brighter as the current passed over it. A silver body rose from the water, curved in the light, and splashed down in the river.

"Did you see it?" Gene asked. "Now's the time to catch big trout."

"You see everything," Conner said, staring through the windshield. "Dad, did you have an argument with Matt?"

"We discussed some things. Why?"

"He's planning to leave. He's going back to the banker's mansion."

"I thought he might do that. I wish he wouldn't. Matt's had a rough time."

"I know," Conner said. "He's got so much stuff bothering him. When he first came, he had nightmares every night. He told me …"

"What?"

"He had nothing to live for. That he'd be better off dead. I don't understand him."

"You don't have to understand anything, son. He's your friend. And mine too. Just be there when he needs you."

The waters of the Little Juniata glistened in the moonlight. Tree frogs croaked along River Road. The return croaks were shrill and piercing. As Gene approached the house, he saw bright light shining from the windows. Hands on her hips, Lucy stood waiting on the porch. Gene parked the jeep, and he and Conner climbed the steps.

"Matt packed his suitcase, grabbed SenSay, and left," Lucy said.

"I figured he might do that," Gene said.

"And you didn't try to talk him out of it?"

"I did try," Gene said. "I tried awfully hard to keep him here."

"What about you, Conner? He listens to you."

"No, he don't, Mom. Matt don't listen to anyone. But I'll keep trying."

Conner was quiet for a moment. He lowered his head, studied the cracks in the steps, and shuffled his feet back and forth. Glancing up, he spoke in a subdued voice.

"Mom, what would happen if, by some kind of accident, some really strange accident, I had to skip school for a day or two?"

"Jeez, I'll tell you what would happen," Lucy answered quickly. "I'd tan your hide and then turn you over to your dad to finish the job."

"That's about right," Gene said. "Nothing good comes from skipping school."

Conner's shoulders slumped. Without saying another word, he walked into the house and climbed the steps in a slow crawl. Reaching his bedroom, he sat down on the mattress, lowered his chin in his hands, and stared at the empty bed across the room.

Mr. Wilson parked the truck in the drive and went directly to the barn. Wayne followed a few steps behind. They walked to a small workroom. After he pulled the string on the overhead light, Mr. Wilson lifted a floorboard next to a wooden cabinet. He reached in the space under the board, found the key, and unlocked the cabinet. His Smith & Wesson Victory Model was on the top shelf. Mr. Wilson picked up the gun, shifted it in his hand.

"It's not loaded," he said, looking at Wayne.

"I'm sorry. I did some practicing."

"No, Wayne, don't be sorry. You practicing how to shoot is a good thing. But always keep your weapon loaded." Mr. Wilson took some cartridges from an open box and filled the empty chambers. Closing the cabinet door, he gripped the gun firmly.

"Feels better now." Mr. Wilson pulled the string on the light, and he and Wayne walked in the dark. When they reached the porch steps, Wayne paused.

"Where are you taking the gun, Dad?"

"Right now I'm keeping it right on my bed stand. Then come this weekend, I'm taking it to Redemption Mountain." Mr. Wilson leaned down and picked up the Hush Puppy. "I'm gonna return this lost shoe to its rightful owner. Then I'm gonna kill the son of a bitch."

Chapter Twelve

Barree/Philadelphia
Friday Morning

At six in the morning, Lucy Brooks was preparing a breakfast of eggs, bacon, and toast when Gene came into the kitchen. He kissed Lucy, grabbed a piece of bacon, and sat at the table. Conner came downstairs, grabbed two pieces of bacon, and sat opposite him. There was the sound of a car engine in the drive. Conner looked at his dad.

"Who's coming here so early?"

"Maybe some fishermen," Gene said. He walked to the front porch just as the car door opened and a middle-aged man stepped cautiously out of a 1975 pea-green Volkswagen Rabbit. The man wore a coat and tie and was holding onto a briefcase. He had a rotund face, a rotund body, and short legs.

"I've driven a long way," the man said. "Please say I found the right house. Please say your name is Gene Books."

"That's my name."

"Thank the Lord," the man said. "I'm plum tuckered out. The drive was nerve-wracking. What a terrible place you have here in central Pennsylvania. Nothing is flat and straight like the beautiful and scenic New Jersey Pinelands." The stubby man's voice was loud and carried into the kitchen. Both Lucy and Conner looked out the window. He glanced at them and spoke even louder.

"You have forests and hills and big animals stopping and staring at you from the middle of the road. And when you blow the horn at them, they don't pay no attention to the racket. I had to detour because of them. I pray I never have to visit this area again. Oh, excuse me. I'm complaining too much and forgetting my manners." Swinging the briefcase in his hand, he climbed the steps. "My name's Charlie. Charlie Wickenburg. Of the law firm Royal, Burns, and Wickenburg." Charlie and Gene shook hands.

"Why are you here, Charlie?"

"I assume you are acquainted with James Junior Jackson?"

"Yes, I know JJ. What about him?"

"He's the one who gave me directions to this place."

"So, why are you here, Charlie?"

"Why am I here? Why am I here? I'll tell you why." Charlie paused, caught his breath. "I have the least seniority at the firm, so I get the crappy assignments. That's why. Not you, Mr. Brooks. You're not crappy. It's just that I'm tired and hungry. I drove all the way from Wildwood, New Jersey. Can I come inside and sit down with you for a few minutes? It won't take long. Basically, I just need you to sign some papers."

"What papers?" Gene asked. Charlie ignored the question. His nose in the air, he started for the screen door.

"Is that Maxwell House coffee I smell?" Charlie asked. Pushing the door open and entering the kitchen, he walked to Lucy and Conner, made the same introductions, dropped his briefcase on the table, and sat down.

"Can I help you?" Lucy asked

"I've been driving all night. My mouth is dry and chalky. Can I please have some Maxwell House? And no need to mess up the taste with sugar and cream. Just keep it black." He winked at Lucy. "Good to the last drop!"

"It's not Maxwell House," Conner said. "It's Folgers."

"What'd you say?" Charlie asked, making a face. Lucy set an empty plate and a cup of coffee in front of him.

"Bless you, mama," he said. Charlie took a long drink. Gene sat down, and Lucy filled his cup. Conner reached for the carton of milk. When Lucy placed a platter of fried eggs and another platter piled high with toast on the table, Charlie moved fast and filled his plate with four eggs and two pieces of toast. Then he looked around, a bit confused.

"Where is it?" he said.

"Where is what?" Conner asked.

"Oh, never you mind," Charlie said. He reached over, grabbed Conner's fork, and began filling his face with eggs and toast. He ate the meal silently and with gusto. After he wiped his plate spotless with a crust of toast, he had another cup of coffee. Then he punched his stomach lightly with his fist and burped.

"Are you okay?" Conner asked. Charlie ignored the question and pushed the dish away. Opening the briefcase, he pulled out a stack of papers.

"Now that I'm not starving anymore, we can get down to business." The folds on Charlie's forehead contracted, and he spoke in a sorrowful voice. "Gene Brooks, Lucy Brooks, and you, Conner Brooks, I am the bearer of bad news."

"You said you came from Wildwood, New Jersey?" Gene asked. He stared at Charlie Wickenburg. "Something serious has happened to Lieutenant Chase Butler?"

"Yes, Mr. Brooks," Charlie said. He fiddled with the papers. His chubby cheeks puffed out. His eyes were pink and glassy. "Lieutenant Chase Butler drowned. His funeral was last week." There was silence for a moment. Conner moved slowly out of his chair.

"Dad, that's terrible. We were just there."

"I know, son. It doesn't seem right. Lieutenant Chase survived a terrible war. I don't understand it, Charlie. The lieutenant grew up at the shore. He was an expert swimmer."

"It was an accident, I think. Maybe cramps. I don't know the details. The body was in the water for a long time." Charlie sneezed suddenly. Wiping his face with his sleeve, he restacked the pile of papers. "Here are the simple facts. Chase Butler was divorced. His wife and two sons did have the decency to attend the funeral service but not the burial service. It seems you, Mr. Brooks, were his only friend. In his will, he left you his house. I have the deed. After you sign the papers, the property is yours."

"I'm not comfortable with that. I can't take his home from the family."

"Like I told you, Mr. Brooks, not one member of the immediate family attended the burial service. His former wife did inquire about monetary funds. Mr. Butler donated everything to a charity, the South Jersey Humane Society. But he wanted you to have his home in Wildwood. He made that very clear in his will. In his memory and to honor his last request, I am going to insist that you sign these documents."

Charlie moved Gene's dish and placed the papers in front of him. Lucy walked over, placed her hand on Gene's shoulder, and whispered in his ear. Nodding his head, Gene signed the documents in duplicate, giving the white originals to Charlie.

"That's it, then." Charlie gave Gene a large brown envelope. "This has the door key and your deed with all the house information. Chase Butler thought highly of you, Mr.

Brooks. He left money with a neighbor to take care of the property. Richard Harris—that's his name—will handle maintenance and pay all the utility bills for the next two years."

"I never expected anything from Chase. Why did he—"

"You were his best friend, Mr. Brooks. Chase valued that more than anything." There was a moment of silence. The aroma of coffee was heavy in the room. Making a scraping noise, Charlie pushed his chair away from the table. He picked up his briefcase and got to his feet very slowly. Lucy walked over and shook his hand.

"Thank you, Mr. Wickenburg," she said.

"No thanks necessary. Just doing my job. But I do need to thank you for a most wonderful breakfast." Then he nodded to Conner. "Good to the last drop! Don't you forget that, son." Charlie did some kind of half salute and left the house. When the pea-green Volkswagen was far down the road, Conner turned to his mom.

"What did you whisper to Dad?"

"I said the sooner he signed the papers, the sooner Charlie would return to the beautiful and scenic Pinelands." Lucy laughed. "What animals do you think he was talking about blocking the roads?"

"Probably some farmer's cows," Conner said.

At nine thirty in the morning, Matt waited in the shadows of the bridge. Impatient and restless, he checked every car that entered and left. When the Landis Sanitation truck thundered by, he stepped back and held his nose. Matt watched the cloud of black exhaust smoke climb the hill to the school. A horn blew, and Mr. Abrams drove a two-door yellow Toyota Celica onto the bridge. Matt got in the passenger seat. Abrams was pulling away when there was loud shouting.

"Who's this?" he asked, braking suddenly. Waving his hands in the air, a figure ran down the hill from the school. Matt's face broke into a wide smile.

"It's Conner Brooks," Matt said, pushing the door open. "What are you doing, Conner? You said you couldn't go."

"I changed my mind." Conner jumped in the backseat and slammed the door. "You're my best friend, Matt. I'm tripping with you to Philadelphia."

"You're tripping all right." Matt laughed. "Did anyone see you?"

"No, I snuck out through the furnace room. But when I was running through the parking lot, I saw a state police car turn into the school. It parked right in front of the office, and Sergeant Delaware Smith stepped out. I stayed low and kept running. I was afraid he would arrest me."

"For skipping school?"

"Yeah," Conner said. "It's the first big law I've ever broken."

"I don't like the sound of this," Mr. Abrams said. "It's like I'm an accomplice to a crime. Matt, are you sure Mr. Henry directed you to skip school and go on this trip?"

"Yes," Matt said. "I'm to meet with Mr. Palladin. The man's an expert on security. Mr. Henry is offering him a job at the bank." Upon hearing this, Mr. Abrams braked suddenly.

"Whose job?" he asked.

"It's a new position, Mr. Abrams. It's director of security."

"We've never had one of those." Listening to every word from the banker's son, Abrams drove slowly through Alexandria and turned onto Route 22.

"Mr. Henry says we have to keep up with the times. Every day you read about bank robberies. This summer, a sheriff's deputy was killed when five armed men robbed the Security Bank in Norco, California. And just this Memorial Day, robbers hit a bank near Boston. They got away with fifteen million dollars."

"We don't have that kind of money in our bank."

"That's not the point, Mr. Abrams. We need to be sure our customers' money is protected. Mr. Henry has made plans."

"I'd like to see these plans."

"I'm sure he'll be sending you a copy soon," Matt said. Mr. Abrams pulled the Toyota Celica into the parking lot next to the train station. Matt and Conner jumped out.

"Thanks for the ride." Matt shook hands with Mr. Abrams. When Matt tried to pull away, Abrams gripped his hand tightly.

"You better be sure Mr. Henry knows what you're up to."

"He knows everything. He chose Mr. Palladin over all the other security firms because Palladin gets results. He's a real professional."

"I can't wait to meet this man, this Mr. Palladin from Philadelphia." Releasing Matt's hand, Mr. Abrams backed the Celica out of the parking place. Matt and Conner walked to the station platform.

"Have Weapons Will Travel," Conner said. "I can't wait to meet Palladin either."

The *Pennsylvanian* arrived at Philadelphia's Thirtieth Street Station at three in the afternoon. Matt led Conner to the SEPTA window and bought two tickets. They hurried down a worn cement staircase and boarded the Regional

Line. The conductor took their tickets, and at the second stop, they got off at the Market East Station.

Pausing on the narrow platform, Matt and Conner were jostled by the anxious people racing toward the exit. Throwing up hot air and dust, trains rumbled by. Conner was bumped in the back by a heavyset man, and then his sneaker was crushed by the wheels of the man's heavier piece of luggage. Conner grabbed Matt by the shoulder.

"I hate this place."

"You have to move out of the way."

"So someone else can hit me?"

"I see the exit."

Matt led Conner through swinging doors and up two flights of grimy stairs to the main station. There were shops, small restaurants, and benches filled with people. Matt pointed to the sign, "Exit To 10th & Filbert Streets." Joining the flow of bodies, they climbed the steps. A Metro security guard in a blue uniform stood at the door. They walked past him and out the swinging door into bright sunshine. Stopping suddenly, shielding his eyes, Conner was smacked in the shins by a wheelchair. The thin-lipped lady sitting on the cushion leaned forward.

"Wake up and move your ass out of my way," she squeaked in a high-pitched voice. An elderly man in a heavy overcoat pushed the wheelchair past Conner.

"You can't just hang out in the middle of the sidewalk," Matt advised. "Move with the flow."

Conner followed Matt down Filbert Street to Tenth Street. The Greyhound bus terminal, a multistory, squared cement building, was on the corner. Horns honking, blue-and-white busses were backed up on Filbert Street. Matt and Conner wandered into the dense crowd of people loitering around the terminal entrance.

"Watch your wallet," Matt whispered.

"I don't have a wallet."

"Neither do I," Matt said.

Breaking out of the crowd, they walked along a cement wall toward a blue "Bus Crossing" sign. There were three wide lanes at the exit. Clutching a paper bag, wearing a ragged trench coat with a soiled T-shirt under it, a man with an extremely long beard staggered down the middle lane. He lifted the bag to his lips, drank, coughed, and spat on the pavement.

"Hurry," Conner said as they approached the man, who eyed them closely.

"Hey!" the man shouted. "Can you spare a dime?"

"Don't talk to him," Matt instructed. He and Conner walked faster.

"Hey!" he shouted again, stepping on the sidewalk, blocking their path.

"Hurry up!" Conner said. Swerving around the bearded man, he and Matt walked through a heavy, wet cloud of sweat and alcohol. Conner covered his nose and tripped. He heard a loud shout behind him. Turning, Conner saw the man raise the bag over his head.

"You cheap bastards!" Face turning red, the man wound up and threw the bag.

"Duck!" Conner said, pushing Matt on the shoulder. The bag flew over their heads. Hitting the middle of the sidewalk, the brown paper tore apart, and glass exploded over the cement. Conner stopped and faced the man.

"You dumb fucker!" Conner shouted. The bearded man raised his fist, took two quick steps in their direction, and stopped, panting loudly. Matt and Conner hurried down the street.

"What the hell is wrong with these people?" Conner asked.

Matt didn't say anything. They walked down Tenth Street. The cobbled bricks were uneven under their feet. Conner stumbled into an elderly Chinese man. The man muttered something and kept walking. Conner shook his head.

"Matt, this isn't right."

"What?"

"Nobody's speaking English," Conner said. Matt raised his hand and pointed to a wide, colorful banner strung across Tenth Street. It had red Chinese letters, the mythical phoenix, and a menacing dragon spewing flames on the pedestrians.

"Of course, nobody's speaking English," Matt said. "We're in Chinatown."

"It still isn't right," Conner mumbled. He followed Matt under the banner. They walked past restaurants, pharmacies, massage parlors, and grocery stores. A spicy, sweet aroma hung over the street. Matt looked at the expression on Conner's face.

"You ain't in Twin River anymore."

"I know," Conner said. "This is crazy here. I hate it."

"You can't hate a place after being in it just a few minutes."

"Yes, I can," Conner said. "Thousands of people walking around, and no one sees you. The only person who showed any interest in us was a bum with a bottle. And he tried to brain us with it."

"It's your fault, Conner, you cheap *bastard*. You have coins in your pocket. Couldn't you give the bum a dime?"

Matt laughed. He slowed and studied the numbers on the shops and restaurants. When he came to the corner of

Tenth and Cherry Streets, he stopped and pointed at a three-story narrow redbrick building.

"This is the place," Matt said.

A white sign, "Yummy Noodle House," was above the door. Bright red Chinese characters and a bowl with two protruding sticks were under the name. There was a row of windows on the second floor. "Have Weapons Will Travel" was stenciled on the lone window on the top floor. Matt walked around the corner to a solid wooden door. He turned the handle; it was locked. Conner pointed to the intercom. Matt reached up and pressed the button. There was a squawking noise. The video camera above the door focused on them.

"What is it?"

"We're looking for Mr. Palladin."

"What do you want? Are you cub scouts? I'm not buying any cookies today." The intercom switched off; Matt pressed the button again.

"Go away," the voice said.

"I need to talk to Mr. Palladin."

"Why?" the voice asked. "And it's not *Pal*. It's *Pall*-adin."

"Okay, Mr. *Pall*-adin," Matt stretched the word. "We want to contract you for a job. A job in a bank. We'll pay you a lot of money." There was a pause … a loud cough. The lock on the door made an annoying buzzing sound.

"Come upstairs," the voice said.

Chapter Thirteen

Green Hollow Correctional Camp
Friday Noon

His Pittsburgh Penguins cap tilted to the side, Ira Hayes sat stoically on the examination table in the camp's one-room infirmary. Shelly Baker, a forty-four year old nurse on call from JC Blair Hospital in Huntingdon, finished the stitch above Ira's left eye and covered it with a bandage. She had brown hair and brown eyes, and she smiled a lot. Staring at the blackened holes disfiguring the neatly stenciled Pittsburgh Penguins on the front of his uniform, she opened a tube of ointment.

"Unbutton your shirt, please."

Ira undid the buttons, dropping the shirt on the table. Shelly first checked the multicolored bruise under his ribs. Then she cleaned the two jagged circles festering on the pale skin of his chest. She gingerly applied the ointment.

"Cigarette burns," Shelly said. "I don't understand any of these injuries. What should I write on my report?"

"I got knocked down during a basketball game."

"And the fellow who knocked you down was smoking and accidently stuck the cigarette into your chest ... two times?"

"Just write that I fell down during a basketball game."

"Are you sure?"

"Yes." Ira pulled his shirt on and buttoned it.

Shelly went to her desk and opened a folder. She began writing. Jamal Pritchett knocked on the door and walked into the room. He stared at the bandage above Ira's eye.

"Will he be all right?"

"Sure," Shelly said, closing the folder. "Are you his friend?"

"Yes."

"He needs someone to take care of him." Shelly walked to the table. "And you, Mr. Ira Hayes, stop smoking in bed or whatever it is you're doing. Now get out of here."

"Thanks," Ira said. He and Jamal left the infirmary. The sun was bright. Taking a deep breath, Ira paused on the steps. Jamal hovered next to him.

"Luther and Max knocked you around yesterday morning. Then someone beat you up last night. Who was it?"

Ira didn't answer. There was shouting from the basketball court. He looked at the mass of bodies under the rim, shoving and pushing each other.

"I'm okay."

"I'm sorry I wasn't around."

"You shouldn't get involved, Jamal."

"I'm already involved, Ira. That's the way it is in North Philly." Jamal smiled. "The Thunder and the Penguin. We'll get through this together."

The engine grinding, smoke shooting from the exhaust, Pastor Andrew Brooks drove the Holy Waters Church van through the gate and stopped in front of the Green Hollow administration building. Pastor Brooks got out and met Dan Boonie on the steps. Dan limped slightly. They went into the building, and a secretary ushered them into the director's office, where they sat at a large oak desk. There was a shiny picture of Ronald Reagan on the wall. In the picture next to it, attired in a gray suit, white shirt, and red tie, relaxed and smiling, Pennsylvania Governor Dick Thornburgh stared across the room.

The door opened. Stan Williams walked in and politely shook hands with Boonie and Pastor Brooks. Sitting down, he pulled some papers from a folder and leaned back in his chair.

"I understand, Pastor Brooks, you have offered to hold a service for our inmates. Well, not really inmates ... troubled teenagers."

"Yes, for the last six years, we've had services at Holy Waters Church."

"How many attended last year?"

"Ten," Pastor Brooks answered. Director Williams scanned the paper.

"I read here that six of the ten boys have been released and are back working in their home communities."

"Yes," Pastor Brooks said. "The church has a positive influence on their lives."

"Of course, it does," the director said. He studied the paper. "I read here that you want to hold a service this Sunday. It's Friday now. Why so little notice?"

"Thanksgiving's coming soon, sir. We want to have the camp service before we get too busy."

"I see," the director said. "I'll run this by Luther Cicconi, but I don't see any problems with the request. What time is the Sunday service?"

"Our van will pick up the boys at seven thirty a.m. The service is at eight o'clock. We'll be back at the camp by ten o'clock."

"Guards have always taken part in the service?"

"Yes."

"I assume you'll attend the service, Dan."

"Yes, but not on official duty. I pass the collection basket every Sunday."

"It's good to see you're involved with church activities." Director Williams looked at Andrew. "Pastor Brooks, I appreciate your interest in our troubled teenagers."

"Thanks," Pastor Brooks said. He and Dan got up, shook hands with the director, and left the office. Reaching the van, Dan looked down the road and saw the two figures standing in front of the infirmary.

"Pastor Brooks, there's Ira now. He was just treated in the infirmary."

"He looks beat up. What happened?"

"I don't know who hit him. But you can bet Luther and Max were behind it. They'll be after him until he tells them where Lisa is."

"Does Ira know she's at my church?"

"He was really worried. I told him Lisa was safe."

"Then he does know." Pastor Brooks frowned. "Will Ira say anything about us?"

"He's been burned and beaten. He'll never say anything. Luther and Max really enjoy hurting him. Is it always that way, Pastor Brooks?"

"What way?"

"That a person has to be hurt, even killed, so someone else can be happy?"

"No, Dan, it doesn't have to be that way. I realize it's happening here, but we'll put a stop to it." Pastor Brooks spoke with conviction. "Come this Sunday, Ira will be a free man."

"Great," Dan said.

Chapter Fourteen

Twin River
Friday Afternoon

Pennsylvania State Police Sergeant Delaware Smith sat at the desk in the principal's office. Gene was next to him, and Arthur Port, a worried expression on his face, sat in his cushioned chair. Sergeant Smith, the only Negro officer in the Huntingdon barracks, was six feet four inches tall, had a thick neck, and weighed two hundred and forty pounds. The sergeant wore dark sunglasses with metal frames.

"How did this happen?" Mr. Port asked. "Heather's missing. I thought you caught the kidnappers."

"No, we didn't catch anyone. We released four girls. We locked up two cabins and confiscated all kinds of sophisticated video equipment. But we never found out who was responsible. One source told us that the gang leader was Nathaniel, the owner of a State College car dealership. Well, we checked all the car dealerships in State College and the surrounding counties. We didn't find any trace of Nathaniel."

A siren sounded from the road, and the sheriff's car turned into the school. Lights rotating, flashing red-and-white beams against the side of the building, the car stopped at the front entrance. Students jumped up from their desks and stared out the windows. Pulling up his gun belt, Sheriff

Parks stepped out of the car. He pushed through the front door and went directly to the principal's office.

"Sheriff Parks," Mr. Port said. "I'm glad you could make it. We were just discussing—"

"There's no time for discussion," the sheriff interrupted. "What we need now is action. The students at Twin River are being abducted. And I intend to stop it."

"You have a plan?" Sergeant Smith asked.

"Of course I do," Parks said. "The mistake we made last time was to post someone on school grounds. But the threat of kidnapping wasn't at the school. The girls are being taken off school property. So, first, I intend to shadow the busses when they start their route in the morning and when they leave off the kids in the afternoon."

"How many deputies do you have?" the principal asked.

"One," Parks said. "Deputy Wright."

"How will you and your one deputy shadow eight busses?" Principal Port asked. He stared at the sheriff, who was momentarily silent.

"I'll get volunteers."

"Will they be armed?"

"Yes. How else can they apprehend the kidnappers?"

"Sheriff." Sergeant Smith got to his feet. "Will you check their backgrounds, train them in police procedures, and test their accuracy with a handgun?"

"I see what you're getting at. We won't take just anyone off the street. We'll select qualified hunters and marksmen—"

"Excuse me," Sergeant Smith interrupted. "I have to make some phone calls. I'll let you and the principal go over plans." Sergeant Smith looked at Principal Port. "But be sure to clear everything with my office."

"Of course," the principal said. Sheriff Parks opened his mouth to comment, but he remained silent. Sergeant Smith left the office. Gene followed him to the hall.

"Gene," he said when they reached the door, "that man's dangerous."

"I found that out years ago," Gene said. "Any news from the Wainwrights'?"

"We were at their house last night and most of today. All they know is that Heather never got back from chorus practice." Sergeant Smith took off his sunglasses and wiped them with a tissue. "Gene, I need your help on this."

"How can I help?"

"You had this contact inside that video porn gang. He gave you good information. We were able to free the girls, but the gang is still loose. I think they got Heather. We have to find her before they start up their video production again. What can you tell me?"

"Not much," Gene said. "My contact was from State College. We met and became friends quite by accident. He quit the video business and left town."

"Gene, we have to stop this gang. Heather's parents are scared to death. Her mother's in shock. Carol couldn't get out of bed today." Sergeant Delaware finished cleaning his glasses and put them on. Gene looked up and saw his reflection.

"I know Heather. She's friends with Conner and Cindy. I often see her in the hall. She always smiles." Gene paused. He stared at the dark outline of his face in the tinted glass. "I was in the auditorium last night when the chorus was on stage. Heather was practicing a solo. I stopped in my tracks. Heather has a lovely, haunting voice. She sang beautifully about *heading for Pennsylvania and some homemade pumpkin pie* … There wasn't another sound in the auditorium."

"Thanksgiving's in a couple of weeks, Gene. Heather won't make it home … unless you help." The tinted glasses remained motionless. Gene lowered his gaze.

"My contact gave me a number in case there was an emergency. I'll call him today. If he remembers anything about the kidnappers, I'll get back to you."

"Thanks, Gene." Sergeant Delaware Smith straightened his glasses and walked to his cruiser.

Sitting comfortably on a stool at the Screwballs Sports Bar & Grill in King of Prussia, Jeffery Turner watched the large TV. Jeffery was twenty-one years old. He was six feet tall and had a trim physique. He wore a blue-and-white Penn State sweatshirt and a faded pair of jeans. The bartender brought him a Philly steak and Coors draft. While watching the noon news, Jeffery finished the steak and was drinking his second Coors when Angel Rogers walked through the door.

A sophomore at Villanova, a varsity member of the swim team, Angel was five nine, had light brown hair, and had a sleek swimmer's body. She wore a white blouse and tight blue slacks. Angel moved quietly behind Jeffery and kissed him on the neck. Turning, his blue eyes brightening, he kissed her on the lips. She laughed and sat down.

"You shouldn't be drinking beer," she said.

"Why?"

"We're going to the pool. You promised to pace me on my backstroke."

"Let's go to my apartment. I'll pace you on your backstroke in bed."

"No, thanks," Angel said. "Let's get your bag and do the pacing in water."

"The mattress would be softer and more comfortable."

"Yes, I know that, trainer Jeffery. But I need to practice."

"With that dedication, you're going to have the best backstroke in Villanova."

Jeffery paid the bartender, and he and Angel walked to the door. Located next to the Screwballs Sports Bar, his apartment was on the second floor directly above the Flowers and Antique Charms shop. Jeffery grabbed a red rose off the display table and unlocked the door. As he climbed the steps, he slid the rose through the open bosom of Angel's blouse.

"I'll swim for that later."

"I swear, Jeffery. You only have one thing on your mind."

"You're studying psychology. Is there a technical word for my condition?"

"Two words," Angel said. "Very horny!"

Jeffery laughed. He unlocked the door, and they went inside. The apartment had one large window that faced the parking lot. The living room was sparsely furnished. There was a sofa, a desk with a computer and telephone, and a twenty-one-inch TV on a stand with wheels. A wooden counter separated the living room from the kitchen. There was a bathroom and a small bedroom in the back.

Barking noise sounded from the bedroom. A golden retriever with soft white fur and long flopping ears dashed across the floor. Jeffery picked up the puppy.

"Skippy, I'm busy now. I'll take you out later." Jeffery lowered the puppy into a brown box that had a towel, a yellow ball, and a rubber biscuit inside. He patted Skippy on the head, walked to Angel, and buried his face in her bosom. When he straightened, he had the rose between his teeth.

"Let's try something different." Jeffery lifted the front of her blouse, placed his hand on her stomach, and slid the stem across the tight, incredibly soft skin. Thin pink lines formed. Then disappeared. Jeffery pressed the red petals lightly against her belly button.

"It tickles." Angel laughed. She stared into Jeffery's face. "I love your eyes. They're an ocean of blue. It's the only color I see when I swim."

"Angel, forget about swimming," Jeffery advised. He was lowering his hand to the button on her slacks when the phone rang. He stood there, letting it ring.

"It could be important," Angel said. "It could be a job interview." She walked to the desk and picked up the phone. Her eyes on Jeffery, she said, "Yes, he's here." Shaking his head, dropping the rose on the counter, Jeffery walked over and put the phone to his ear.

"Gene," he said. "I didn't expect to hear from you again."

As Jeffery listened, his lips closed tightly; his face turned pale. He took a deep breath and sat on the edge of the sofa. After a minute, Angel joined him. When Jeffery spoke, there was a nervous tension in his voice.

"Yes," he said in a whisper. "Nathaniel introduced me to two men who worked for him. Yes … I remember them. When I was slow getting started on the video, they punched me around pretty good. I can help you find them." Jeffery talked for a few minutes. Then he put the phone down; there were beads of perspiration on his forehead.

"What is it, Jeffery?"

"I have to go back to Twin River. I have to go now."

"Why?" she asked. "What happened?"

"I made a bad mistake. I thought I had fixed it, but I was wrong. I have to go back and fix it for good." Jeffery went to the bedroom, then to the bathroom, and returned with his gym bag. Angel stood in the middle of the room; the puppy growled from the box.

"Can you take care of Skippy?"

"Of course. Please wait a few days. We can spend the weekend together."

"I can't wait," Jeffery said. "A girl's life is in danger. Don't worry. I have a good friend there. He helped me before. He'll help me now."

"How long will you be gone?"

"I don't know."

"If you're not back in a few days, I'm driving up to get you."

"You don't have—"

"Give me a telephone number and an address," Angel said quickly. She reached into her bag and pulled out a small notebook. Jeffery wrote down the information and returned the notebook. Then he kissed her for a long time. She held him close.

"Jeffery, please don't go."

"I have to." Jeffery grabbed his jacket and left the apartment. When he reached the display table at the flower shop, he grabbed a bouquet of roses and rushed back upstairs. Angel was standing at the door. He gave her the bouquet and kissed her again. She pressed her body tightly against his.

"Please stay," she whispered, kissing his ear.

"But …" Jeffery began. His heart was beating faster. A sudden warmth flushed his face. The heat, the throbbing electric sensation, flowed through his body. It settled in his groin. The hardness was immediate, stretching the soft fabric of his jeans. She slid her hand down, gently massaging with her fingers, and he moaned.

"Just stay tonight and Saturday," Angel said. Keeping hand pressure on his jeans, she led Jeffery to the bedroom. Skippy growled from the box when the door closed.

Chapter Fifteen

Philadelphia
Friday Afternoon

Wesley Palladin sat in his office on the third floor of the Yummy Noodle House. The office had a desk, three wall cabinets crammed with books, a gray sofa minus a front leg, and a row of wooden chairs. The desk was cluttered with folders and loose papers. There were two video monitors and a telephone on the desk. One of the monitors had a clear view of the street; the other had a shadowy view of the staircase.

There were two other rooms in Palladin's office. The side room was small and narrow. It had a sink, a wall cabinet with a mirror, a shower, and a toilet. The back room had three metal cabinets, a cot, and folding chairs. His buff-and-blue uniform soiled and bloody, his mouth taped shut, Cody Romano sat on the cot with his hands taped behind his back. Caesar Romano was bound tightly to a folding chair. His eyes were closed; his head rested on his chest. There was a deep gash above his right eye. The lines of blood under the eye were dry and crusted. His pants had dark stains.

Palladin watched the door swing open on the monitor. Two boys stepped inside. They walked under the harsh glare of an uncovered light bulb and disappeared.

His hand resting on the golden grip of his Colt .45, Palladin listened to the light knocking sound. He got up, walked across the room, and opened the door. Shoulders together, the boys stood there. The shorter, thin boy dropped his mouth open, staring at the Colt. The tall athletic boy, eyes narrow and straight, studied Palladin's face.

"Who the hell are you?" Palladin asked. The thin boy stepped forward.

"I'm Matt Henry. And this is my friend, Conner Brooks. I read your notice, "Have Weapons Will Travel," in *The Philadelphia Inquirer*. I've traveled a long way to meet you, Mr. Palladin."

"It's pronounced *Pall*-adin, kiddo. Try to remember that. You can come in." Palladin walked to his desk and sat down. "Bring those chairs over here. Tell me what you want and make it snappy. I'm leaving soon."

The boys each carried a chair to the front of the desk and sat down. There was a groaning noise from the side room. Conner turned and looked at the closed door. Matt stared at Palladin, who hit the desk with his hand.

"Well, what are you waiting for? Why are you here in my office?"

"Mr. Henry, he's the owner of the bank, wants to hire you. He would provide free housing in his guesthouse in Barree."

"What the hell is a *berry*?"

"It's *Barr*-ee," Matt said. "It's where I live. There's fifty acres, a mansion, a large guesthouse, and a barn. The guesthouse is furnished. There's a golf course behind it. That is if you like to play. Either way, you would be very comfortable. You can bring anyone, your wife and family."

"I don't have a wife, kiddo." Palladin looked at Matt. "I'm interested in what you say. Tell me about this job."

"That's why I came to Philadelphia," Matt said, sliding his chair closer to the desk.

Matt began in an excited voice. He explained that the bank in Alexandria was planning to hire a security officer. He explained that the man-in-charge and owner, Mr. Henry, went on an extended vacation. The assistant, Mr. Abrams, and the two tellers knew nothing about bank security. So Mr. Palladin would be in complete charge. Palladin would also set up a security system for the estate. Matt continued speaking without a pause.

"Plus, you would be paid extra to teach personal security."

"Teach who personal security?"

"Teach me," Matt answered. "I want to know everything about weapons—how to use them, how to protect myself."

"Why do you feel the need for protection? Are there killers in Berry?"

"*Barr*-ee," Matt said. "Yes, we have our share of killers." Palladin leaned over the desk, studied Matt's face—the bland composure, the large eyes that were now dark. Then Palladin looked at Conner.

"What about you? Got your tongue tied in a knot? What do you have to say?"

"I don't like being here," Conner answered. "I hate this place."

"You can't hate Philadelphia. This is the city of brothers and love."

"Philadelphia isn't a city. It's more like an ocean."

"A what?"

"An ocean. An ocean of crazy people swinging their hands and kicking their feet. You could get knocked off the sidewalk and drown here. No one would pay attention. No one would care if you drowned."

"No one's drowning here," Palladin said. "But that's good. That's a clear answer. My daddy always said if you got something bothering you, get right to the point. Anything else on your mind?"

"Who do you have in the back room?"

"Alert and to the point." Palladin smiled, fingering the end of his mustache. "If I take this employment, you're going to be easy to work with. But Matt here … I'm not so sure about him."

"Why?" Matt asked. "Why say that?"

"Something's bothering you, kiddo. You work hard at keeping your face blank and expressionless. You're hiding something. And there's a shadow over those innocent rabbit eyes. There's mountains of unrest behind that shadow. You say you want to learn how to defend yourself, maybe even to kill someone. But thinking about killing and doing it are two different things."

"I already know about killing," Matt said. "I caught a snapping turtle with my bare hands. I killed a fish with razor-sharp choppers. I know stuff about killing."

"I'm sure you do. But knowing how to kill isn't always a strength. It can be a weakness, also. You need moral direction to control the urge to kill."

"Is that what you have, Mr. *Pall*-adin, moral direction?" Conner asked; Palladin smiled.

"No, moral direction is something I'm paid not to have." Palladin sat back in the chair. There was a groaning sound from the side room. Palladin stood quickly.

"Shut the hell up in there!" he shouted. Matt jumped in his chair. A horn sounded in the street; a car door slammed. Palladin rushed to the window and saw the man hold out his hands. Stopping the traffic, he ran across the street.

"Hell!" he growled, turning to Matt and Conner. "Pick up your chairs. You're going to have to stay out of sight for a while." He walked across the room and opened the door. Palladin pushed the boys inside and forcibly sat them down.

"It smells like shit in here," Matt complained, covering his nose.

"Shut up! And don't move!" he warned them. "That means you too!" he yelled at the bound figures. Then he walked across the room, slammed the door, and sat at his desk, his eyes on the monitor.

Palladin watched the man jump the steps. Within seconds, there was a quick knock, and the office door banged open. JJ Jackson stomped across the floor and put both hands on the front of the desk.

JJ Jackson was a trim thirty-three-year-old Negro. He had a serious, hard face. JJ wore a black suit, black tie with the words *Dinky Dow* written vertically down the front, gray shirt, and a pair of black Converse sneakers. He had a Colt M1911 on his belt.

"Where the hell's Caesar Romano?" JJ asked. He hit his fist on the desk, rattling the TV monitors. "You burned his estate to the ground! The firemen found three bodies! None of them a woman's! None of them Caesar Romano's!"

"There's been a change in plans, JJ."

"Say what! I didn't authorize no change! Romano should be dead now. And you should be in solid with Scavone and his family."

"It ain't going to happen that way! I'm finished with Scavone."

"What ..."

Listening to the shouting, his eyes riveted on the two bloodied bodies, Conner glanced at Matt and got to his feet.

Waving his hands and mouthing, *No, No,* Matt motioned Conner back to the chair. Conner sat down. The racket in the office intensified.

"Protective custody … witness protection! What the hell are you talking about, Palladin?"

"I'm talking about the Romano family. They're in danger!"

"Forget danger! They're already dead! As we speak, Scavone's goons are looking for Romano, the wife, and the kid."

Shaking his head, Conner got up and walked to the cot. He ripped the tape from the boy's mouth and started to free his hands. Matt rushed over.

"What are you doing?" he whispered. The boy looked up. His lips were cracked and bleeding. The shouting in the office became high-pitched.

"Romano's where?" the man bellowed. "In this office!"

Shoes pounded across the floor; the door banged open. Staring in disbelief, JJ Jackson stopped abruptly. Palladin rushed past him and grabbed the boys by the arms.

"I told you not to move." Palladin pushed them back to their chairs. Entering the room very slowly, JJ stared at Conner.

"I never forget a face. I know you, kid. You're Gene Brooks's son." He turned and looked at Palladin. "What the hell's going on?"

JJ didn't wait for an answer. He rushed to the window and signaled with his hand. Within seconds, two broad-shouldered men in dark suits ran through the office, grabbed Romano and the boy, and dragged them to the staircase.

The door opened. Street noise echoed up the staircase. Then the door closed. In the sudden silence, Palladin stared at JJ.

"You got Romano and his son. Now what?"

"We'll pressure Romano to talk. He could put Scavone away for a long time. My advice for you is to close shop and get out of town." JJ moved quickly and grabbed Conner by the arm. "You, kid, you're dead if you stay here. You're coming with me." Conner twisted free of his grasp.

"I'm staying." Conner pointed a shaky finger at Matt. "I'm with him."

"It's okay," Palladin said. "I'll take care of them. We're leaving Philly together."

"You fine with that?" he asked Conner.

"I'm fine," Conner said. Palladin pulled JJ to the side.

"Where's Jane Romano?"

"We picked her up at the estate. She's in good hands … for now. She kept screaming about Cody. I thought it strange she wasn't showing much interest about her husband."

"I'm worried about her. Can I see her?"

"Hell, no!" JJ answered sharply. Palladin spoke in a serious voice.

"I'm *really* worried about her!"

"You can't see her. There's no time. You have to get out of Philly. Call me when you find a safe house." JJ stared at Palladin. "Conner's like family. Nothing better happen to that boy." Straightening his *Dinky Dow* tie, JJ stomped to the staircase.

"What a fiasco," Palladin said. He looked at the boys, pointed at the thinner one. "What did you say your name was?"

"Matt."

"After what you've seen here, kiddo, do you still want me to work for you?"

"Yes, of course."

"Then let's get the hell out of Philly." Palladin went to a wall cabinet, pulled out two bottles, and gave them to Conner. "Here, you carry these. And be careful. They're Bollinger Grande Annee."

"What?"

"Champagne," Palladin said. "I haven't eaten anything today. I'm starved. How long a ride to your place, Matt?"

"It's over two hundred miles. Mostly turnpike."

"That's three hours. We have to eat first."

"I'm starved too," Matt said. "Can we stop at McDonald's?"

"No."

"Maybe Burger—"

"We don't eat fast food here, kiddo. I'll order some take-out from Yummy downstairs." Palladin, followed by the boys, walked into the office and picked up the phone on the desk. "Hey Boy," he said, shouting a series of numbers. "Yes, delivery." Palladin replaced the phone and motioned to Conner.

"How do you know Mr. JJ Jackson?"

"He was in Vietnam with my dad."

"Who's your dad?"

"Gene Brooks."

"Never heard of him."

"Mr. Palladin," Matt said. He had a concerned look on his face. "What's *Dinky Dow* mean?"

"Blood and bodies all over the room, kiddo, and you inquire about some stupid Vietnamese slang on a person's tie!"

"I thought it might be important."

"Of course, it's important. It describes you to a *T*, kiddo. In Vietnamese, *Dinky Dow* means you're crazy. Is that how you see yourself?"

Matt didn't answer. The door opened, and a thin Oriental man with a pointed beard, wearing a long white apron spattered with grease, walked into the office and put three bags on the desk. Steam rose from the openings in the bags.

"Thank you, Hey Boy," Palladin said. He gave the man some twenties. Then he counted out five one-hundred-dollar bills. "I'll be gone for a long time. Can you take care of the office?"

Hey Boy nodded, took the money, and walking backward, scrutinizing and counting the bills carefully, he left the room. Matt made a face.

"My nose burns," he complained. "The bag smells funny."

"It doesn't smell funny, kiddo. The bag smells Yummy. Hot spices are good for the digestion." Palladin pointed to the refrigerator. "You'd better get some bottles of water."

While Matt walked to the refrigerator, Palladin went to the window and stared at the traffic below. The sidewalk was crowded with pedestrians. Some people started crossing Tenth Street. Palladin noticed a man wearing a fur-collar trench coat. The man pushed people out of the way and walked toward Yummy's Restaurant.

"Victor," Palladin muttered. He grabbed a leather carryall from under the desk and shouted at Conner and Matt. "We got to go now. Grab the bags and the water, and don't drop the bottles of champagne."

Palladin led Matt and Conner to the stairs, unlocked the door, and went down the back steps to the garage. The massive hood of the Cadillac Eldorado was inches from the wall. Palladin got in the passenger door, tossed the carryall in the back, and slid across the seat. Matt stared at the car.

"This can't be your Cadillac!"

"You bet it is. I see you're impressed. Everyone's impressed with it."

"I'm not impressed," Matt said. "I hate it."

"Mr. Henry owned a Cadillac," Conner explained. "Matt has issues with that car."

"What issues?"

"Sometimes I got sick. Once I got so sick I threw up over his windshield. That's when he hit me."

"I'll clock you hard if you throw up in here," Palladin said. "Conner, you're in the back. Be careful with those bags of food and the champagne. Matt, you're in the front. I need you close by. I need to talk to you about my employment."

Matt sat down cautiously and placed the water bottles on the floor. His chest scraping against the door, Conner squeezed into the backseat. Palladin started the engine, clicked the remote on the garage door, and backed out quickly. He was pulling away when he looked in the rearview mirror and saw Victor crossing into the alley. Victor opened his trench coat and pulled out a Beretta. He began screwing on a suppressor; Palladin floored the Cadillac. Victor aimed and fired as Palladin turned the corner. A bullet hit the rear fender; Conner turned at the thump sound.

"What was that? Something hit right behind my seat."

"That was a bullet. You didn't hear much noise because the bastard used a silencer."

Palladin pulled onto Cherry Street and made a quick left onto Ninth Street. Within minutes, he was through the traffic and on the Vine Street Expressway. The lane approaching the Schuylkill Expressway was bumper-to-bumper. Palladin turned on the radio; a deep, melodic voice announced:

"You give us twenty-two minutes. We'll give you the world."

"What's this?" Conner asked.

"KYW 24 Hour News. Be quiet and listen."

> *Traffic not moving on the Betsy Ross Bridge ... Two lanes on the Walt Whitman Bridge closed due to construction ... Plan to arrive late if you're going west on the Schuylkill Expressway ... Be prepared to change lanes because of pothole maintenance.*

"It looks like we're not going anywhere," Palladin said, turning off the radio. "Let's eat. Pass a container and the utensils up here." Inching forward in the traffic, Palladin took the pint-size container and chopsticks from Conner and flipped the top open. With the traffic in both lanes stopped, Palladin lifted the container and began shoving meat and gravy into his mouth. Matt eyed him curiously.

"You don't chew your food?"

"Don't have time." Palladin stuck the chopsticks in the container and lifted out a dripping piece of meat. "Here, you have to try this."

"No, thanks. It's burning my nose."

"Quit being such a wimp." Palladin stuck the chopsticks between Matt's lips and shoved the piece of meat inside.

"Ahhhh!" Matt began screaming. Tears formed in his eyes. "Dinky Dow!" he shouted at Palladin. Matt reached for a bottle, screwed off the cap, and began gulping water. A horn blew behind them, and Palladin drove forward.

"What's the matter, kiddo?"

"I can't eat that stuff. What the hell is it?"

"Yummy's specialty dish … spicy pig ears."

"Dinky Dow," Matt said again. He finished the bottle of water. In the backseat, Conner ripped off the flaps. He held the container to his mouth and was using the chopsticks to push noodles and meat inside.

"Not bad," he commented. "What's this I'm eating?"

"You've got Yummy's noodles and beef tripe."

"What's tripe?"

"The first stomach of an ox."

"How many stomachs are in an ox?"

"Just two," Palladin said. "The first stomach and the second stomach. There's some disagreement, but I always thought first stomach tasted better."

"Oh," Conner said.

Palladin finished eating and gave the empty container to Conner. The traffic picked up to forty miles an hour at the Route 1 exit. Reaching the Valley Forge Toll Plaza, Palladin took the ticket from the meter, rounded the wide curve, and sped onto Interstate 76. He moved to the passing lane and accelerated to ninety miles an hour.

"Let's get down to business, kiddo," Palladin said. "You're talking about bank security, right? That's a big job nowadays. Say I agree to work for you. What's my recompense going to be?"

"I haven't thought about it too much. How about a thousand dollars a month?"

"You're talking chicken feed now, kiddo. Is your bank run out of a barn?"

"No." Matt shook his head. "How about a thousand dollars a week?"

"Still not enough. I should get a look at this bank. Then we can discuss salary."

"Sure," Matt said. "Once we agree on an amount, I'll clear it with Mr. Henry. He manages the bank."

"Why don't I just talk with the boss?"

"Mr. Henry went on vacation," Conner answered, leaning his chin over the front seat. "Matt's in charge of the bank until Mr. Henry comes back."

"Isn't Matt kind of young to be running a bank?"

"No," Conner and Matt answered simultaneously.

Palladin was approaching two trucks. The trailing truck put on a blinking red turn signal and started to move into the passing lane. Palladin floored the Eldorado. The boys were knocked back in their seats; the Eldorado zoomed past both trucks. Palladin got the cassette out of the door pocket and slid it into the player. Soon the voice of Paul McCartney and the lyrics of *Live and Let Die* filled the interior of the Eldorado.

Chapter Sixteen

Barree
Friday Afternoon

Gene Brooks was on the porch when the phone rang. He rushed into the kitchen and picked it up a second before Lucy reached the table. Recognizing JJ Jackson's voice, Gene pulled out the chair and sat at the table. Lucy sat opposite him. Jackson talked loudly in quick bursts. Shaking his head, Gene listened intently.

"Are you sure about that, JJ?" he asked. JJ answered in a loud voice.

"No, I'm not sure! I said the man was extremely competent. That's all! Conner and Matt should be safe, but there's no guarantee with Palladin." JJ Jackson hung up. Gene replaced the receiver. Lucy stared at him.

"Where's Conner?"

"He went with Matt to Philadelphia."

"That's impossible. Conner's never been out of Barree. How could he get to Philadelphia?"

"By train," Gene said. "JJ found Matt and Conner with someone called Palladin. JJ says Palladin's a contract killer for the mob."

"A killer?" Lucy gasped, raising her hands to her mouth.

"That's what he said. JJ's not sure, but he thinks the boys will be safe. They left Philadelphia. They're on their way home."

"We'd better go to Matt's house."

"We don't know how long—"

"We can wait there," Lucy stated. She and Gene went outside and got in the jeep. It was a short drive through Barree and up the hill to the mansion. Gene stopped at the locked gate, went to the security panel, and punched in some numbers. The doors swung open. Gene got back in the jeep and drove inside. Lucy looked at Gene.

"How do you know the code?"

"I just do," Gene said. SenSay came barking and running down the lane. Gene slowed and opened the door, and the collie jumped in his lap. With SenSay licking his chin, Gene drove under the portico and parked. Then he and Lucy got out and sat on the porch steps. Tail slapping the wood, SenSay slid between them.

"This is on you, kiddo," Palladin said, stopping the Cadillac at the Harrisburg West Toll Booth window.

"Why me?"

"Because the boss absorbs all travel expenses," Palladin explained.

Shrugging his shoulders, Matt searched his pockets for the exact fare. The trucker behind the Cadillac blasted his horn, and Matt jumped, dropping change on the floor. Matt counted the remaining coins and gave a handful of bills and coins to Palladin, who paid the attendant. Then Palladin drove around Harrisburg, crossed Clark's Ferry Bridge, and headed west on Route 322.

Racing past a FedEx truck on a straight stretch of road outside Watts, Palladin looked at the river, which glistened blue in the afternoon sun. He nudged Matt in the shoulder.

"What do you know about this river?"

"It's the Juniata River," Matt said. "It flows right by Barree."

"That's where you live, right?"

"Yes. Conner lives there too."

"Then we'll have to get to Barree real quick and do some fishing."

"I don't like to fish."

"I wasn't asking a question, kiddo. I was stating a fact. You see, I excel at fishing. And right now, I'm on vacation."

"You're not on any vacation, Mr. Palladin. You said I was the boss. I'll be paying you to work at the bank."

"You call $60,000 a year payment for the quality of work I do?"

"It's not $60,000," Matt said. "Fifty-two weeks. I figure it's more like $52,000."

"Is that what you figure, kiddo? While you're at it, figure this too. $52,000 is about half of what I make in Philadelphia. Who's getting a bargain here? If you expect me to work that cheap, then fishing will be part of my job."

It was late afternoon when Palladin drove up the hill to the Henry estate. The front gate was open. Palladin stopped the Eldorado.

"Is this always open?"

"No," Matt said.

"Then you have visitors," Palladin said.

"I have an idea who they might be," Conner whispered from the backseat.

Palladin went through the gate and entered a dark grove of pine trees. Driving slowly, he saw the massive outline of the mansion. An orange jeep was parked under the portico. The wheels of the Cadillac making a light crushing sound, Palladin stopped behind the jeep and shut off the motor. There was loud barking, and a dog raced toward the Eldorado. Two people—a man and a woman—rushed down the steps. Conner and Matt opened their doors and got out.

His door cracked open, Palladin sat behind the wheel. He watched the lady grab and hug Conner. He saw the dog jumping around Matt. The man walked slowly, studying the Eldorado, scrutinizing Palladin through the windshield. The man brushed his hand through Conner's hair and pointed to the back fender.

"What's that?" he asked.

"A bullet hole," Palladin said, getting out of the car.

"Yeah, Dad, we got shot at."

"You what?!" Lucy exclaimed.

"It was nothing, Mrs. Brooks," Matt said. "It was cool. The *bastard* used a silencer." Matt had a smile on his face; Lucy pulled Conner closer. Conner broke his hand free and pointed at the tall, mustached stranger.

"Mom and Dad, this is Mr. Palladin. His motto is 'Have Weapons Will Travel.'" Conner watched his dad and Palladin. Both stood straight and relaxed; neither one lifted his hand.

"What are you doing here?" Gene asked.

"He's here to work for the bank," Matt answered. "He's planning to live in the guesthouse until Mr. Henry comes back from vacation."

"Whose idea was this?"

"Mr. Henry's." Matt spoke in an emphatic tone; Gene had an incredulous expression on his face. He started to say something, paused, and turned to Palladin.

"Who shot at you?"

"A man in a trench coat," Matt answered again. Gene looked at both of them.

"Is Mr. Palladin permitted to talk?"

"Sure, he can speak. I was just trying to be helpful."

"It's been a long day," Lucy Brooks said. "And it's late. Do your talking tomorrow. We're going home now." She held Conner's hand and led him to the jeep. Gene followed. SenSay started barking.

"Keep that mutt quiet!" Palladin ordered.

"It seems your Have Weapons Will Travel guy doesn't like dogs."

"Palladin doesn't like people either," Conner stated. Gene got in the jeep and started the motor. As he pulled away, he saw Matt struggling to hold SenSay. Talking in a loud voice, Palladin pointed a finger at them.

"I don't trust that man," Gene said, staring at Conner in the rearview mirror.

"Don't look at me," Conner said. "He's Matt's friend. Not mine."

"Leave the boy alone," Lucy said. Then she added in a strident voice, "Let's get home so I can inform Conner why he's grounded for a month!"

Taking the carryall from the back seat of the Cadillac, Palladin entered the mansion and glanced at the massive chandelier glittering silver and light in the middle of the room. There was an elaborate entertainment center along the wall, a plush sofa, and two reclining lounge chairs. Copies of the *Wall Street Journal* and *Financial Times* were on the table next to the sofa. A large painting of a boy with large eyes and a somber countenance hung on the wall.

"Gainsborough's Blue Boy," Palladin commented. "He looks like you." Matt didn't say anything. Palladin looked past him to an ornate gun cabinet in the corner of the room. He went over and flicked on the switch. Light flooded over six scoped rifles. A gold NRA plaque was in the upper corner. *Live Free or Die* was engraved in the center. Palladin pulled on the knob, and the door opened.

"Why's the cabinet unlocked?"

"Mr. Henry wanted it that way. Sometimes SenSay would bark. Mr. Henry would race for his gun."

"Was he a good shot?"

"Mr. Henry was a son of a bitch," Matt said matter-of-factly. "He waited for the deer or turkey to come real close to the house."

"But opening the door, running to the porch, it would spook any animal."

"Mr. Henry shot from the open widow," Matt explained. Light from the cabinet gleamed off his face; his large brown eyes glistened. Closing the door to the cabinet, Palladin shook his head.

"Do you know how to use a rifle?"

"Yes," Matt said. "Mr. Brooks taught me how to shoot. Soon I'll be as good a marksmen as Conner. And he's the best." Matt spoke in a confident tone. Palladin looked at the set of golf clubs leaning against the side of the cabinet.

"Do you golf too?"

"I'm a good driver but terrible putter," Matt said. "Mr. Henry build the clubhouse and golf course for his wealthy friends. He didn't like it too much when I invited my friends to use it. Once Conner and I were racing the golf carts and mine smashed into the fence. That's when Mr. Henry put stronger locks on the front gate." Matt walked to the spiral staircase. "My room's upstairs. You have the whole guesthouse. Mr. Henry furnished it with everything you could think of. He wanted his banker friends to be comfortable."

"I need to make a phone call."

"You have your own line in the guesthouse."

"Good," Palladin said, stopping at the staircase. He noticed the belt looped over the fleur-de-lis at the end of the railing. There were dark stains on the leather.

"How long has the belt been here?"

"Not long," Matt answered, picking up the belt. "Do you want me to show you the guesthouse?"

"I think I can find it." Palladin walked through the house, checked out the kitchen, and went out the back door. The guesthouse was a modern, one-story, log-framed building with a wide porch. Tail wagging, the collie followed Palladin across the yard. Palladin went inside, turned on the lights, dropped the carryall on the table, and walked immediately to the phone on the counter. He dialed, waited, and relaxed when a familiar voice answered.

"Amos," he said.

"Palladin, I've been calling your office all day."

"I left Philadelphia in a hurry. Everything's gone to hell."

"I figured that. Do you need me up there?"

"No, not yet. I'm keeping a low profile. Stay out of Philadelphia for a while. Enjoy your vacation."

"I will," Amos said. "My cousins are here. We're going to Disney tomorrow." There was a pause. "Palladin, you know how kids are. They don't easily forget their pets. Jenny, she's the youngest, asked me about the puppies. About Purgatory."

"I'll visit Purgatory this weekend," Palladin said.

"Thanks. I'll tell her to stop worrying so much. Call me if you need anything."

"I will," Palladin said. Hanging up the phone, he heard a scratching noise and saw SenSay's nose in the screen door.

JJ Jackson sat at the Anastasi Raw Bar located in the center of the Italian Market. He slurped in the last Blue Point Oyster and dropped the shell in the dish. The bartender appeared with his second Blood & Sand, orange peel draped over the chilled cocktail glass.

"How's the drink, Mr. Jackson?" he asked.

"Joe, I can honestly tell you. It's not bloody. It's not sandy. It has a perfect smooth, smoky, and sweet texture."

"I'm glad you like it. You know Rudolph Valentino made this drink famous. You planning to get romantic tonight?"

"I wish," JJ smiled, taking the glass. He looked at the months-old newspaper on the counter. The 1980 World Series Championship team picture and the jocular faces of Steve Carlton, Tug McGraw, and Mike Schmidt were on the front page. Joe removed the dish of oyster shells and pointed at the paper.

"Wednesday, October 22, that was a great day for the city. Governor Thornburgh issued a proclamation declaring it *Philadelphia Phillies Day*. We had thousands of people here all night."

"I know," JJ said. "I was here with my son. The next day he was excited to play in the city championship. He had two homeruns. When he came up again, I saw the coach nod to the pitcher. The kid threw pretty hard. He hit my son with a fast ball."

"You're talking about game four when Dickie Knowles aimed a fast ball at George Brett's chin. Knocked him right on his ass. That pitch got everyone's attention."

"It sure did. Dickie said he was *trying to take his head off.*"

"The brush back must have worked. The Phillies won the World Series."

"But at what cost? A pitcher does that on the street, if he purposely aims and seriously injures a motionless person, he'd be arrested. But ignorant amateur coaches don't understand this. It's *win* at any cost. Devin, he's my son, has a shattered elbow. He'll never play baseball again."

"I'm sorry to hear that," Joe said. He left with the dish, the oyster shells rattling back and forth. JJ drank the Blood & Sand. His phone buzzed. He checked the ID and answered it.

"What is it, Jake?"

"The kid's hungry I showed him the refrigerator. He said he didn't want anything frozen. We drove by Pat's on the way here. He wants a cheesesteak."

"Does he always get what he wants?"

"He's Main Line," Jake said. "I think he gets everything and then some."

"I'm on 9th Street now. I'll pick up a cheese steak."

"Cody wants two."

"Wit' or wit'-out?"

"Wit' and wit' a lot of Whiz too."

"Cody's a real headache," JJ said.

"He sure is," Jake agreed. There was a pause. "Can you get me a few of them steaks too?"

"Damn it, Jake. You filled the freezer with your favorite foods."

"I know that, JJ. But there ain't nothing like those cheese steaks. And maybe you should get two for Buzz. He's set up at the back entrance."

"What about Mrs. Romano. Isn't she hungry?"

"She didn't say anything. She's been very quiet ever since we came in with the boy and the husband. She did ask about Mr. Palladin. Of course, I didn't tell her anything. But the kid got real angry. He said he hates Mr. Palladin."

"Cody has reason to hate him. How's Mr. Romano?"

"He's still in the shower. He was smelling pretty bad."

"I don't trust him," JJ said. "Stay alert. I'll be there in thirty minutes. I'll use the back entrance."

JJ ended the conversation, drained the Blood & Sand, placed two twenty-dollar bills on the counter, and left the restaurant. He walked down 9th Street to Geno's. The tables were filled, and there was a long line on the sidewalk. Shaking his head, he noticed the line of patrons moving quickly at Pat's King of Steaks. JJ checked the traffic and hurried across the intersection.

Chapter Seventeen

Polecat Hollow/Redemption Mountain
Friday Evening

Listening to the clamor of construction noise, Mr. Wilson finished the barn work and walked up the road. Stopping at the top of the hill, he saw the parked trucks and crowd of contractors. Workers were attaching chain-link fencing to the line of cement poles that now circled the Calvin property. A group of men loitered around the front arch. They raised a thick, finely crafted oak sign, "Happy Hollow Hunt Club," into place.

A 1979 gray BMW E23 came from the Calvin house and stopped at the gate, and a heavyset man in a dark suit got out. He started talking to two men wearing Green Hollow Correctional Camp uniforms. They began arguing. Shrugging his shoulders, Mr. Wilson went back to the house, walked upstairs, grabbed the scuffed Hush Puppy off the floor, and took the Smith & Wesson from the bed stand.

"What the hell's going on here?" Nathaniel asked. Nathaniel's fleshy cheeks swung spasmodically when he was irritated. He had large ears, a bulbous nose, and thin red lips. He was tall, corpulent, and wore size thirteen leather loafers. Nathaniel had two gold rings on his right hand and a Piaget Polo watch on his wrist. Shoving his hand in

Luther's face, he shouted through the flashing display of gold.

"There are two trophy hogs in the yard! And they're dead! I planned to use them hogs in a Happy Hollow hunting commercial! Who killed them?"

"I don't know," Luther said. "It happened last night. Max and I were in the Winnebago snatching Heather like you ordered." Luther shuffled his feet in the dirt. "The carcasses are stinking up the place. Shouldn't we bury them?"

"No, hell no," Nathaniel said. "Get one of the tree cutters. Take him and his chainsaw to the barn. Tell him to cut the heads off and spray clear varnish over them." Nathaniel pointed to the gate. "See those two pillars in front of the entrance? Stuff a head on each one. Wire them tight. We don't want any poachers sneaking into the hunt club and stealing our trophies."

"But they're still gonna stink," Max said. Nathaniel glared at him.

"Our guests are not going to smell them. They'll be relaxing in an air-conditioned Winnebago. Now get going."

Max and Luther walked to the group of workers at the front gate. After a brief conversation, one of the men dropped a chainsaw in the truck and raced toward the barn. Nathaniel got in the BMW and drove down the road. As he approached the Wilson house, he saw Mr. Wilson standing next to his black truck. When Nathaniel looked closer, he could clearly see the gun in the man's hand. He noticed a shoe in the other hand.

Mr. Wilson looked at the shiny BMW. When it was out of sight, he stuffed the Hush Puppy in his jacket and got in the truck. The sun dropped lower behind the distant hills. Headlights on, construction vehicles raced past the house.

Mr. Wilson slid the Smith & Wesson under his belt and zipped his jacket. He waited while a white Henry Moore Construction van went by; then he started the engine and turned onto the road.

The horizon was dark. Then the lights flickered, and the cross at the summit of Redemption Mountain burst upward and outward in an ascending line of brilliance. Mr. Wilson looked at the expanding halo through the windshield.

Cain Towers, Wilson thought to himself, staring at the bright beacon of light.

The Reverend Jeremiah Towers walked down the path to the Flaming Cross. When the electricity turned on and the cross ignited with incandescent splendor, the reverend was temporally blinded. His legs wobbly, he sat on the bench. A silver crutch was propped against the bench. It glimmered in the light.

Cain and Abel, the reverend whispered and sang silently. *Waiting for the harvest*. The reverend paused. The incessant blaze from the cross brought moisture to his eyes. The reverend rubbed his face and continued singing the hymn in a fierce voice. *Waiting for the harvest. And the time of reaping … time of reaping*, he repeated solemnly.

Shielding his eyes, staring into the center of the cross, the Reverend Towers glimpsed his wife. Irene smiled to him approvingly. A dense fog descended, diffusing the brightness. Irene's smile dissipated; the face disappeared. The air was still and heavy with moisture. Getting up from the bench, the reverend walked to his car.

The majestic stone tablets along the road protruded through the fog. Driving down the mountain, the reverend caught glimpses of the Commandments. As he raced by the Sixth Commandment, "Thou shalt not kill," he accelerated, the tires sliding off the road, spraying dirt and gravel in the air.

The Flaming Cross glowed in the night sky. Cain Towers parked the poppy-pink Ranchero in the drive and walked with a slight limp across the yard. When he stopped at the edge of the pond, koi began splashing at the surface. Cain struck the glass Chiclet bowl with his fist; nothing happened. He gave the bowl a solid kick with his good leg, and rabbit pellets poured from the opening. Laughing with pleasure, scraping up a handful of pellets, Cain went to the large eastern hemlock and pulled a sharpened stick out of the branches. Bodies alert and crouched low to the ground, the two sleek black cats waited in the shadows of the mountain laurel trees.

"Time for fun and games," Cain said as he limped back to the edge of the pond. Poised there, stick raised at a perfect angle, Cain tossed the pellets skillfully, strategically. They hit the water in an ominous line that began at Noah's Ark and ended at his feet. The frenzied feeding activity immediately commenced at the ark. Then, slurping pellets ravenously, the koi swam closer to the bank. One plump, graceful golden body, silky fins fanning the water, swam toward the last floating pellets. As the koi's mouth sucked at the surface, Cain thrust down with his spear. The sharpened point splashed through the water and pierced deep into the golden stomach.

"It's dinner time!" Cain broadcast loudly. He lifted the stick, lofted the koi high in the air, and turning quickly, he flung it over his shoulder. The cats raced across the grass and were on the golden body when it hit the ground. Clapping his hands, Cain limped to the house, opened the front door, and turned on the lights.

"Abel!" he called. When there was no answer, he called again. "Abel, it's time for rehab! You chickenshit! Get your ass down here!"

The house remained quiet. Cain went to the spacious living room and opened the cabinet in the corner. Bottles of wine were stacked neatly on the shelves. He grabbed a bottle of Finger Lakes Zinfandel, uncorked it, and hastily gulped the wine. The warmth spreading through his body, Cain flexed his knee.

"Feels good," he said. Cain heard a clonking sound on the porch and went to the window. Through the mist settling over the light posts, he saw a black truck racing down the lane. Cain took another drink of Zinfandel.

"Abel!" he shouted. "I'm not waiting forever!" Walking to the hallway, Cain noticed the crack in the door. When he pushed it open, he saw the shoe on the floor.

"My Hush Puppy," Cain whispered. A folded paper was next to the shoe. Cain picked it up and read, "I'll be at Blood Mountain. I want to do the rehab there."

"Fuck you, Abel," Cain said angrily. He went down the steps and across the yard to the garage. Going inside, he saw both Honda three-wheelers along the wall.

"What'd you do, Abel?" Cain muttered. "Did you hobble to Blood Mountain?"

Stuffing the bottle of Zinfandel inside his jacket, Cain got on one of the ATVs. Racing on back roads, he soon reached the river. Cain slowed, saw the trail that led up the side of Blood Mountain, and stopped. Taking a long drink of Zinfandel, he threw the empty bottle against the rocks and began the arduous climb.

The path had sharp turns and steep inclines. Cain drove recklessly, the vehicle sliding precariously on the loose gravel. There were beads of perspiration on his face when he reached the summit. The replacement knee was a burning, heavy weight. Cain attempted to straighten his leg, but the rock-hard muscles were locked.

"Fuck this," he said, scowling. Cain maneuvered the ATV around huge boulders and thick brush. He stopped when he saw a fire next to a towering pine tree and a massive ant hill. Beyond the fire, in the shadows, a hooded figure stood in a field of chest-high Indiangrass. Head lowered, the figure moved out of the shadows and sat at the fire, his back to Cain.

"Abel," Cain shouted. He drove to the fire and was sliding off the ATV when the hooded figure stood and turned. Swinging a branch with tremendous force, the figure hit Cain and knocked him off the ATV. His head cracked against the trunk of the tree; his foot smashed into the ant hill. Clicking mandibles, emitting a trail of scent pheromones, ants streamed out of the hill and crawled over his body.

Black clouds covered the moon. In the darkness, Mr. Palladin and Matt walked along the stretch of rapids at the base of Blood Mountain. Palladin carried a flashlight and a fishing rod. Wearing fluorescent orange sneakers, Matt carried a large Ziploc plastic bag filled with groundhog stomach and intestines. Once they were past the roaring rapids, the sounds of croaking frogs and cricket chatter echoed up and down the bank.

"Why are we doing this?" Matt asked in an angry voice.

"On the ride up from Philly, I told you I wanted to go fishing. My daddy always said don't put off for tomorrow what you can do today."

"It's not today anymore. It's night. And it's cold."

"It's not cold. It feels great. We don't get this quality of air in Chinatown."

Palladin flashed the light on a walled spring, waves of clear water gushing over the side. The water formed a stream that flowed the length of a sandy peninsula jutting into the river. Palladin walked to the end of the peninsula and sat on a log. There was a cool breeze. The clouds moved past Blood Mountain; the current glittered in the moonlight.

"Right here," he said. "There's a deep hole where the stream meets the river. That's where we'll catch our channel cat."

"Why do we need groundhog guts? The animal lay in the field for days. Even SenSay wouldn't go near it."

"Catfish are scavengers. They prefer rotting food. Here, hold the flashlight so I can see what I'm doing."

Matt grabbed the light. Palladin took a small tackle box from his pocket and removed an 8/0 hook with two-foot leader. He tied the leader to a swivel below a six-ounce slip sinker. Taking the Ziploc bag from Matt, Palladin pulled out intestines and stomach. When he skewered everything on the hook, blood and a thick liquid dripped on the sand. Matt made a face.

"That's too big," he said. "Ain't nothing in the Juniata River going to eat a whole groundhog stomach."

"Remember this, kiddo." Palladin leaned the fishing rod on the log and stood. The bloated intestine swung back and forth. Matt grimaced and looked away.

"What should I remember?"

"Big bait for big fish." Palladin threw the remains of the groundhog in the current. "That's called chumming. It'll bring the catfish right to those toes in your orange sneakers. Now shut off the flashlight."

"Why?"

"If you want light, do your fishing during the day. At night, live with the darkness like the fish you're trying to catch."

"I don't like this," Matt said, switching off the light.

"Are you afraid of the dark?"

"Maybe a little. I've never been night fishing before."

"Just relax." Palladin washed his hands in the stream. His eyes adjusting to the darkness, Matt stared at the dark shadows rising up the lofty cliffs of Blood Mountain. Then suddenly a dim light flashed at the summit.

"Mr. Palladin," Matt said. He stood straight, his eyes focused upriver at the distant rapids and mountain. Orange sneakers sinking in the sand, he walked to the end of the peninsula.

"Mr. Palladin, can you see it?"

"See what?"

"There's someone on Blood Mountain." Matt pointed to a flicker of light at the summit. It grew bright, then dim, then bright again.

"You live here, kiddo. Who goes to Blood Mountain in the middle of the night?"

"No one," Matt said. "Bad things happen up there. Did you bring your gun?"

Palladin didn't answer. He picked up the fishing rod. After casting the groundhog intestine and stomach into the river, he held the reel out to Matt.

"I need to show you something before we start. This knob in the front of the reel controls the drag."

"What's drag?" Matt asked.

"How the line goes off the reel, either very smooth or tight." Palladin turned the knob counterclockwise and pulled on the line. Nothing happened. "See how the line stays tight?" Palladin turned the knob clockwise and pulled on the line again. The line clicked out smoothly. "See how it works? When you have a big fish on, you keep the drag loose and let the fish run and tire itself out. Do you understand that?"

"Yes. That's easy."

"Then listen carefully. In that deep hole out there, little fish will swim around nibbling on your groundhog. They will send out vibrations and attract a bigger fish … a monster fish. This monster will scatter the little fish and inhale the groundhog."

"The entire groundhog?"

"Yes, Matt. Big fish are just like people. To stay big, they are greedy and take everything for themselves. So your big fish will suck in the entire groundhog. Then it will swim away. As it swims, it'll naturally chew and swallow. The hook will go deep in its stomach. The fish will not know it is hooked because the line is going smoothly through the slip sinker. But you will hear the clicking sound, and you will know."

"How long before all this happens?"

"I have no idea when a fish will eat your groundhog," Palladin said. He leaned the fishing rod on the log.

"I'm freezing," Matt complained.

"Here." Palladin removed a flask from his pocket and handed it to Matt. "Take a little sip." Matt raised the flask to his mouth and swallowed a mouthful. It scorched his tongue and burned the lining of his throat. Matt sat down on the log.

"Wow! What was that?"

"Ole Smokey. How was it?"

"I don't feel cold anymore. I feel warm all over." Matt took another drink. "Wow," he said again. Hand jittery, he returned the flask to Palladin. "Maybe night fishing will be fun. Mr. Henry never took me anywhere. This is like a whole new experience." Matt leaned clumsily; the log wobbled under him.

Palladin sat down, steadying the log. Frogs chirped from the darkness. Stars reflected sparkling dots of light on the river. The Big Dipper was suspended deep in the current. Palladin took a drink of moonshine. Smacking his lips, he looked at Matt.

"Matt, what happened to Mr. Henry?"

"Why do you ask that?"

"I was curious."

"Mr. Henry's on vacation."

"A manager doesn't leave his bank unattended. What happened between you and your dad that he had to leave?"

"I never talk about Mr. Henry." Matt reached for the flask and drank again. He returned the flask and sat quietly. When he spoke again, his voice was barely audible. "Can I ask you a favor, Mr. Palladin?"

"What kind of favor?"

"There are three bedrooms in the house."

"I know. I went through the house. I saw Mr. Henry's master bedroom. I saw a smaller bedroom with a Peter Pan mural on the wall."

"That was my room."

"I noticed Captain Hook had his eye scratched out."

"I did that."

"I figured you did," Palladin said. "Now what's the favor?"

"Can you stay in the main house?"

"Why?"

"Sometimes I have nightmares."

"What kind of nightmares?"

"I don't know," Matt spoke warily. A cloud slowly drifted across the moon. Matt looked at the moon's reflected glow in the river, the cloud dimming then cloaking the bright orb. "It's always late … and dark like now. It's quiet too. The door opens. I can hear it creaking. I see someone standing in the shadows. He's huge. He fills the doorway." Matt's body was tense. He sat stiff and motionless.

"Does he hurt you?" Palladin asked. Matt was quiet. He raised his head slowly and stared at Palladin. His eyes were glassy in the starlight. His lips began to move.

Just then there was a click; Matt jumped to his feet. There was another click, followed by another one. The rod tip bent slightly. Palladin smiled.

"Pick up the rod, kiddo, and walk to the point."

Matt moved quickly. He grabbed hold of the fishing rod, cupped the reel in his hand, and began walking. The clicking noise became steady. Matt reached the water's edge. The current splashed dark waves at his feet. Eyes bulging open, muttering incomprehensibly, he turned to Palladin.

"Tighten the drag," Palladin instructed calmly. "Then pull back with all your strength."

"Okay," Matt said.

The rod was heavy in his hands; the clicking became a shrieking crescendo, silencing the frogs, shattering the darkness. Matt took a deep breath and turned the knob. The clicking noise stopped abruptly. From the murky depths of the river, a heavy weight pulled at the line. Matt reared back, setting the hook; the rod bent sharply.

"Money!" Palladin exclaimed. The sudden surge and power of the fish jerked Matt off the bank into ankle-deep water. Matt crunched his feet deep in the mud. He tightened his grip on the rod and shouted in an alarmed but excited voice.

"Son of a bitch!"

Just them, as the fish raced upriver, Matt saw a fiery light at the summit of Blood Mountain. The light flashed and grew brighter. Hands swinging wildly, feet kicking through black space, a burning figure fell from the cliffs and dropped into the rapids.

Screaming loudly, Matt lost his grip on the rod. It splashed vertically in the water. Matt reached down, but the rod jumped in the air. He stared hopelessly as the rod and reel zipped across the water's surface before sinking in the river. Matt straightened slowly. He looked at Blood Mountain, now in total darkness. Then he looked at Palladin.

"Was that a body?" Matt asked.

"Yes," Palladin said. He led Matt back to the log and sat him down. "You dropped my fishing rod in the river."

"I'm sorry," Matt said. "I was scared."

"Sorry don't help none." Palladin picked up the flashlight and shined it on Matt's face. "I should clock you on the side of the head. That's what my daddy would do."

"I said I was sorry."

The cloud drifted away. Shoulders slumped, orange sneakers soaked and covered with mud, Matt stared at the river. There was a bright glare of moonlight on the water. Looking past the glare, Matt saw a wisp of smoke curling above a dark lump floating on the surface. A hand rose out of the slow-moving current, waved at him, and disappeared. Matt jumped to his feet and ran through the sand.

"What?" Palladin asked.

"I saw the body," Matt said, searching the current. The hand surfaced again. Matt jumped excitedly and pointed. "There!" he shouted.

"I see it." Palladin removed his shoes, placed his jacket on the log, emptied his pockets, and dropped his wallet and keys on top of the jacket. Last, he slid a derringer from under his belt and gave it to Matt.

"Don't drop this in the river!"

Moving quickly, Palladin splashed to the deep water and started swimming. In front of him, two hands spread over the surface of the water; a dark body popped up between them. Palladin grabbed the closest hand. A layer of skin slid off, wrapping itself loosely around his fingers. Palladin squeezed the skin into a ball and tossed it. The head floated up, exposing jaw bone and a row of perfect white teeth. Patches of scorched hair and blackened skin covered the skull.

"Damn," Palladin said. He grabbed the elbow and swam slowly. At the bank, Matt splashed out and helped him carry the body to the sand. It lay there glistening in the moonlight. Most of the body was black. Strands of T-shirt and blue jean had fused into the skin. Both eye sockets were empty. Palladin noticed the ripped knee.

"Look here, Matt." Palladin pulled away a piece of flesh and pointed to the round metal socket and tube. "This guy had a knee replacement."

"Both Cain and Abel Towers had knee replacements."

"Then it's either Cain or Abel."

"I hope it's Cain."

"You don't mean that, Matt. No one should die like this."

"I do too mean it. Cain was the worst bully. I hated him."

Shaking his head, Palladin went to the log. He put his wallet and keys in his pocket, slid on his jacket, and laced up his shoes. Frogs began croaking again. A fish jumped near the bank. Palladin broke off a low-hanging branch and began scraping away the footprints in the sand. Matt watched him.

"What are you doing?"

"In the business, we call it mopping up. I don't want to leave any traces."

"But everyone will know we found the body."

"How would they know that?"

"Because we're calling the police and reporting it."

"We're not reporting anything, kiddo. We're going straight home."

"But why—"

"I can't attract any police or newspaper attention, that's why. Let some fisherman find the body tomorrow. He can get his picture on the front page." Palladin flashed the light on the trail, and they started walking.

"Mr. Palladin, how big do you think the fish was?"

"To pull you into the river so easily, I would say it was about your size."

"Wow," Matt said. "I'm sorry he got away."

"I'm sorry he took my fishing rod." Palladin turned and faced Matt. "Do you have my derringer?"

"Yes. I'm still scared. Can I keep it for a while?"

"No." Palladin stopped and held out his hand. Matt placed the derringer in the palm. They started walking again.

"The gun's so small. Did you ever have to use it?"

"I use it quite often," Palladin said. "The last time was the day before you met me at Yummy's. I really surprised this man. He pulled out his Beretta—that's a bigger gun—and was aiming it at me."

"What happened?"

"I shot him. Since I use a small gun, the hole in his forehead was very small."

"Oh," Matt said. They continued their walk in silence. The path followed the river; the current made a gentle, rippling noise bubbling over the rocks. Redemption Mountain came into view. The Flaming Cross was brilliant in the night sky. Palladin slowed his pace.

"Matt, I've been with you all day. I haven't seen you smile or laugh once."

"So?" Matt said. "What's there to laugh at? Tonight wasn't funny. It was scary. Philadelphia wasn't funny." He walked silently for a moment. "Mr. Palladin, you shouldn't criticize me. You're no different."

"What do you mean?"

"With your sense of humor, you should manage a funeral home. You never smile either."

"I have reasons for that. I'm older and work in a life-and-death business. But you, you're young. You should take the time to laugh, to enjoy what you're doing." As they approached the rapids, Palladin stopped and faced Matt. "Do you know Bob Hope?"

"Who's he?"

"A famous man, a comedian. He's on a lot of evening TV shows."

"I don't know Hope. I don't watch much TV." There was a low humming noise. Matt looked past Palladin at the cascading rapids in the distance. Clouds of mist rose off the water, sending gray fingers upward along the stone cliffs of Blood Mountain. "Mr. Palladin, you're always so tough. I don't see this Hope guy or anyone making you laugh."

"Oh, he made me laugh," Palladin said. "It was during the war. Every Christmas holiday Bob Hope would entertain the soldiers in Vietnam. He brought singers, professional athletes, and he also brought Miss. America. I saw him at Long Bien. Thousands of us sat on a hillside at the edge of the jungle. The wounded soldiers had benches in front of this make-shift, bamboo stage. Ten minutes before the show began, the monsoon rains hit the base. There was no place to go for cover. We were drenched."

"That doesn't sound funny."

"It wasn't funny," Palladin agreed. "I was just a teenager. I knew back home so many people were against the war. It was hard to take. Bob Hope joked about the mess we were in. He thanked us for being there. He made us feel good. In his own unique way, he gave us *hope*." Palladin had a smile on his face. Matt watched him closely.

"Being in a war, sitting in the mud and rain, none of what you say is funny."

"You weren't there, Matt. You don't know anything about it or Hope. He had a great show. He brought the Ding-a-Lings with him."

"What's a Ding-a-Ling?"

"The Ding-a-Lings were four gorgeous girls from the Dean Martin Show. They climbed onto General Westmorland's jeep. They danced around and sang *Proud Mary*. With the rain pouring down, it was better than any wet T-shirt contest. The Viet Cong in the jungle probably heard the loud cheering and clapping."

"I would like to see the Ding-a-Lings," Matt said. "I would whistle and cheer, but I wouldn't laugh too much."

"Just pay attention. Bob Hope always carried a golf club. He swung it in the air when the Ding-a-Lings sang *Proud Mary*. The Ding-a-Lings were good. They changed the lyrics to fit the situation. Stroking the end of his moustache, Palladin mumbled the words:

> *Left a good job in the city*
> *Killin' for the man every night and day*

"Not funny."

"I'm not done. Listen to this. And don't you dare forget it. The day before Bob Hope arrived, the Viet Cong bombed the hell out of our base. Hope got on the stage and right away joked, 'I love the airport you have here. Great golfing country ... even the runway has 18 holes.'" Matt had a frown on his face. Palladin laughed.

"You don't think that was funny?"

"A little," Matt answered. "Conner wants Alice and me to go to Huntingdon and watch *Caddyshack* with him. I might see something to laugh at in the movie."

"*Caddyshack* is hilarious. If you don't laugh at Chevy Chase, Bill Murray, and Rodney Dangerfield, you're a lost cause."

"Maybe that's it," Matt said. "Maybe I am a lost cause. Other than Alice, and, of course, SenSay, and sometimes golfing, I don't enjoy many things."

"Not even fishing?"

Matt shook his head. Palladin paused for a moment. Then he turned and started up the trail. As they approached the base of Blood Mountain, the rapids filled the night air with a roaring noise.

The moon and stars reflected a bright glow on the Juniata River. Lumbering down the trail, mouths spewing foam, the dogs headed for the spring. The lead dog, a one-hundred pound Rottweiler, raised its head, sniffed, and raced across the peninsula. When it came to the body, the Rottweiler bit deeply into the shoulder. Snarling, baring teeth, the other dogs surrounded the carcass. They ripped off burned flesh and chunks of muscle. A black husky, its fur covered with briars, chewed off an arm and ran into the woods. A German shepherd chased after it, snapping viciously at the trailing fingers. The dogs feasted until the sun rose over the mountain. Then they wandered off slowly, stopping at the spring, lapping at the water.

The morning sun rose with streaming brilliance over Twin River. On the summit of Blood Mountain, the vultures flew from the branches of the ancient pine tree. They glided swiftly downriver, circled the peninsula, and descended on the blood-smeared bones, skin, and ripped tendon. Extending necks and yellow beaks, the vultures squawked and bunched together, forming a dark feathered blanket over the skeleton. In minutes, the bones were picked clean. Fighting furiously, two large vultures dragged the rib cage into the river. When the last vulture flapped its wings and flew off, a solitary light shone from the edge of the peninsula. Protruding from the sand, the round metal socket gleamed silver in the sun's rays

Chapter Eighteen

Barree
Saturday Morning

A thin fog settled over the banker's four-story mansion. The air was chilly; frost covered the lawn. Glistening when the sun rose, the wet blades of grass drooped low to the ground. The curtain on Matt's second-floor bedroom window was open. Rays of sunlight streamed into the room. The crystal coating of frost on the glass turned to moisture. A warmth filled the room, settling over Matt sleeping soundly on the bed.

The Colt .45 tight on his belt, Wesley Palladin was in the kitchen of the guesthouse. Pouring freshly brewed coffee into a cup, he listened to birds chirping and the distant crow of a rooster. He shook his head and smiled. The aroma of coffee filling his nostrils, he lifted the steaming cup.

"Country living is great," Palladin whispered into the cup.

Sipping the coffee, Palladin looked up when he heard barking from the yard. He hesitated a moment; the barking stopped. Palladin drank the coffee, the dark liquid warming his mouth, and he smiled again. Suddenly, shrill yelping blasted the serenity of the morning.

"Damn it," Palladin muttered. Placing the cup on the table, he rushed to the door, pushed it open, and stepped onto the porch. In a glance, he saw SenSay. Drawing in a swift, smooth motion, Palladin aimed the Colt .45 and shot the collie. Seconds passed. His hand shaking, Palladin holstered the Colt and returned to the kitchen. Taking a steak knife from the drawer, testing its sharpness, he stomped down the steps to the yard.

"SenSay," Matt whispered. He opened his eyes when he heard the barking. The yelping noise followed. Matt got slowly to his feet. The sudden crack of the gun knocked him back a step. His mind racing, Matt stood motionless for long seconds. Then wiping the perspiration from his forehead, he walked to the window. Looking through the opaque drops of moisture that dotted the pane of glass, Matt saw SenSay on the ground. Blood covered the fur on his chest and neck. A knife in his hand, Palladin stood motionless over the dog.

"No!" Matt screamed. He gasped for air; his legs weakened. Falling forward, Matt grabbed the curtain, ripping it off the rod. Palladin looked up, and their eyes locked.

A cool wind blew from the Juniata River; white-crested waves rolled along the bank. Staring at the tree that leaned over the water, Gene Brooks wore a blue-checkered, long-sleeved shirt, jeans, and old army boots. He pulled the Arkansas toothpick from the holster strapped to his back. Aiming at the chipped section of trunk, he effortlessly threw the knife. It sailed in a straight line and sliced through the wood. Splinters flew in the air. The tree made a cracking noise, swayed downward, and fell into the river. It held steady in the current for a moment and then drifted into the existing jumble of fallen trees. Water splashed in the air; branches thrashed in the current. Gene walked to the stump and removed the Arkansas toothpick. He turned when he heard shouting from the house.

"Dad!" Conner was running across the yard. He stopped in the middle of the road. "Dad, Matt just called. He was crying. He said Palladin shot SenSay!"

"That bastard!" Gene slid the Arkansas toothpick into the holster, and he and Conner ran to the jeep.

Matt was standing on the porch when Gene parked at the mansion. His face was drained of color; his eyes were moist. He spoke in a weak, tired voice.

"Palladin killed SenSay. He went to the barn."

"You two stay here," Gene said. Adjusting the harness, he walked around the side of the mansion. The boys ran through the door to the kitchen. Reaching the window at the same time, they bumped heads in front of the glass pane. Holding a crude wooden cross in one hand and a shovel in the other, Palladin walked casually from the barn. The shovel dragged along the ground. Gene came into view.

"There's Dad," Conner said.

Moving slowly, Gene approached the dark lump in the grass. The collie lay motionless, his brown fur matted purple in the bright sunlight.

"Mr. Palladin," he said in a strident tone.

"Mr. Brooks," Palladin said. Studying the harness and knife on Gene's back, he paused and leaned casually on the shovel. Then Palladin lowered his hand, tightening the leather holster on his belt. The Colt .45 reflected a golden glow in the morning light.

"What brings you out here?"

Gene didn't answer. He heard the buzzing noise and stopped. A scattering of flies circled around the collie and the pool of blood. Larger black-and-green horse flies swarmed from the barn and alighted on the soft fur.

"Is this your doing?" Gene asked, pointing toward the collie.

"Yes, it is."

"You shouldn't have shot the dog," Gene said. The buzzing noise grew louder; Gene breathed the stale, dead air. He slowly moved his right hand forward, palm open, fingers stretched and lithe.

At the house, Conner watched the hand movement closely. He rubbed away a smear from the window and nudged Matt in the shoulder.

"I've seen Dad do that when he's practicing," Conner said quietly. "He's getting ready to throw the knife. Don't blink, Matt."

"Why?"

"You won't see the toothpick until it hits Mr. Palladin in the heart."

"But Palladin has that gun!"

"It don't matter what he has," Conner said. "It don't matter at all."

Palladin removed his hand from the shovel. It dropped to the ground with a dull thud. He tossed the wooden cross next to it. Palladin's face was expressionless.

"Matt says you're fast with those knives," he said in a calm voice.

"Fast enough," Gene said.

"There's a better way to do this. Are you good with your fists?"

"Good enough," Gene said.

"I'm pretty good myself." Palladin unbuckled his gun belt and dropped it to the ground. Gene slid off the harness, glanced down, and began to wrap it around the Arkansas toothpick. He heard a shuffling noise in the grass, and when he looked up, he saw Palladin in front of him.

Gene swayed to the side, but Palladin's fist moved lightning-fast and made solid contact above Gene's ear. Gene fell hard on his back. The Arkansas toothpick and harness landed in the grass. Palladin looked down at Gene.

"You shouldn't drop your guard."

"I expected a fair fight."

"Your mistake, country boy. You wouldn't last long in North Philly."

Palladin kicked his boot into Gene's stomach. When he kicked out again, Gene slid out of the way and caught the boot in his hand. Jumping to his feet, he twisted the boot and threw Palladin on the ground. A frown on his face, Palladin stood. In a low crouch, fists clenched, he began circling Gene. Then in a burst of energy, he aimed a solid right at Gene's mouth. Gene blocked it and powered a right hook into Palladin's stomach. Air escaping from his mouth, Palladin was knocked back a step. Gene moved in and swung another solid right. Palladin's recovery was fast. He ducked under the fist and punched Gene in the ribs.

His lungs collapsing, Gene gasped for air. Palladin cocked his fist and leveled a straight jab at Gene's face. Gene was quick to deflect it, but hard knuckles glanced off his forehead. Stretched forward and off balance, Palladin left a small opening, and Gene smashed his fist into Palladin's nose. Blood spurted, spraying over Gene's shirt.

"You fucker," Palladin said. He straightened and wiped his nose with his fist, covering the knuckles with a red sheen.

Gene glared at the smashed nose and the blood streaming over Palladin's mustache and lips.

"You done yet?"

"Hell no, I ain't done!"

Grunting and spitting blood, Palladin feigned with his right hand and grabbed Gene by the shirt with his left. Crunching his neck and shoulder muscles into tight bands, he jerked Gene closer and head-butted him. There was a resounding crack as their skulls met. At the moment of impact, Palladin had the higher angle; Gene dropped heavily to the ground.

"This can't be happening," Conner whispered. His breath steaming the glass pane, Conner stared bleakly at the figure on the ground. Turning away from the window, he ran across the floor and opened the door. Matt rushed over and slammed the door shut.

"You can't go out there."

"I have to help Dad."

"Stay here," Matt said. "It's not over yet."

Matt took Conner by the arm and led him back to the window. Swiping his hand across the glass, smearing the moisture, Conner had a distorted view of the two figures in the yard. Palladin stood broad-shouldered and tall. Gene was on the ground. Conner watched his dad slouch to the side and slide his hand toward the Arkansas toothpick. The grass barely moved when Gene picked up the knife.

Palladin wiped the blood from his nose. He saw Gene sit up; he saw the flash of silver in the grass. When Gene staggered to his feet, he had the Arkansas toothpick firmly in his grip. The blade reflected the morning light. Palladin dropped his hand to his holster and stepped back.

"Are you planning to use that?"

"I damn near fell on it," Gene said. "I got my hands full with you. I don't need a blade stuck up my ass." Gene tossed the Arizona toothpick; it landed in high grass. A black, droning swarm of flies rose in the air. Touching the knot on his head, Gene winced.

"You can stop now, you know," Palladin said.

"No, I don't know," Gene said. "Let's get this over with."

When Gene made a hard fist, minute but bright explosions began exploding in his head. Gene smiled and crouched cunningly in a boxer's stance. His vision suddenly blurred, and he hesitated. The swarm of flies buzzed around him and moved away. Rotating his head slowly, Gene followed the sound. The swarm settled on the ground, settled on a long, copper-colored shape. Gene saw the shape was broken, not entirely connected. Blinking, focusing hard, Gene looked closer.

"I'll be damned," he muttered, identifying the rattles on the dismembered tail. The six-foot snake was laid out in sections. The copper-and-black banded skin was partially flayed. The triangular-shaped head was smashed. Two ivory fangs protruded from a cleared space on the ground.

"I'll be damned," Gene said again. "Why didn't you say something?" Unclenching his fist, the sparks in his head diminishing in brightness, he stared at Palladin. "Why didn't you say SenSay was bitten by a rattler?"

"My daddy always taught me that when you do the right thing, you don't have to explain yourself to no one."

"Your daddy was a smart man," Gene said. The buzzing sound became monotonous. His vision clearing, Gene looked at the thickening cloud of flies. Edges of the swarm kept breaking away and darting from one bloody area to another. Pieces of skin curled in the sun. The elongated liver was stretched in a straight line. The sac that had encased the heart was cut in half. Lifting his head in a careful manner, Gene stared quizzically at Palladin.

"What?" Palladin asked.

"You could have killed the snake with one shot! Instead, you butchered it?"

"Yes, I took my time. I felt the need to prolong it."

"I'll be damned," Gene said for the last time. Reaching for the holster and Arkansas toothpick, he shook his head and walked back to the house. Conner and Matt met him on the porch.

"What happened, Dad?"

"Nothing. It's over. We're both going home."

"I saw Mr. Palladin talking to you." Conner hesitated, his eyes searching his dad's face. "Then you stopped fighting. What did he say?"

"Palladin didn't have to say anything. He was in the right." Gene pushed Conner by the shoulder. "Get in the jeep." His eyes downcast, Conner glanced at Matt.

"I'm real sorry about SenSay," he said. Matt stood there, his lips trembling.

"But you can't leave like this, Mr. Brooks. You—"

"It's not what you think," Gene interrupted. He put his hands on Matt's shoulders and stared in his face. "You need to go out there and find out for yourself what happened. Then you need to apologize to Mr. Palladin." Gene released Matt and left the house.

Matt walked slowly down the porch steps into bright sunshine. Blinking rapidly, he saw the swarm of flies; he saw SenSay in the high grass. Then, holding his hand over his forehead, squinting against the bright glow of light, he saw the mangled, bloody pieces of rattlesnake.

Matt took a deep breath. Tears filling his eyes, he picked up the shovel and began digging in the earth. When he finished, he lowered SenSay into the hole, replaced the dirt, and slammed the ground flat with the shovel. His face dripping water, Mr. Palladin came from the barn. He picked up the makeshift cross, two branches nailed together, and stuck it into the grave.

"You should rest a moment," Mr. Palladin said. Matt made an attempt to straighten the cross, but it tilted at an angle. Sitting next to the grave, he pulled his knees to his chest. Mr. Palladin sat opposite him.

"I heard SenSay yelp," Matt said in a whisper. "Did he suffer?"

"No, not for a moment."

"I'm sorry for what I thought about you. I didn't know you were doing a good thing." Matt wiped at his eyes and peered over his knees at Mr. Palladin. "It hurt so much when I saw SenSay. I was afraid." Wiping his eyes again, Matt pulled his knees tighter to his chest. "Did you happen to bring that flask with you?"

"Ole Smokey?"

"Yeah," Matt said. "I need something. I'm all beat-up inside."

"Just a sip." Palladin reached inside his shirt, removed the silver flask, and handed it to Matt.

"You always carry this with you?" Matt asked, taking the flask.

"Always."

"I hope you like it here in *Berry*." Matt attempted to smile. "I hope you work for the bank a long time." Matt drank from the flask. His face flushed; he coughed and gave the flask back. "Thanks, Mr. Palladin."

"You're welcome." Palladin took a drink and held the flask toward the boy. "Matt, I'll let you finish this Ole Smokey if you explain something to me."

"Sure," Matt said. Taking the flask, he drained the smooth liquid in one gulp. When Matt lowered the flask, his nose turning a bright red, he had a dull expression on his face. "What can I explain to you? Please don't make it difficult."

"I think it'll be real difficult," Palladin said. "Just do your best. Last night you didn't care when this Cain fellow was burned to death. Yet now you're very upset about SenSay, a dog. Why is that, Matt?"

"That's easy enough to explain, Mr. Palladin. Dogs, you treat them right, they're the best friends you'll ever have. People, you treat them right, they turn around and bite you. They bite you real bad."

A cloud crossed over the sun, throwing a dark shadow over the grave. Matt sat perfectly still, his eyes staring at the cross that slanted out of the dirt. Palladin waited a moment before he spoke.

"I know you've been through a lot, Matt. But I've got something to do this evening. It's important. I could sure use your help."

"What is it?"

"It's a three-hour drive to a place called Purgatory in Lancaster County."

"You really think I could help?"

"Yeah, I'm a hundred percent sure you could help."

"Then I'll go," Matt said. He got to his feet. "Mr. Palladin, is your nose okay?"

"It's fine. It's been broken many times."

"Mr. Palladin?"

"What is it, Matt?"

"Thanks for making the cross for SenSay. And thanks for the Ole Smokey."

Gene stopped the jeep in front of Holy Waters Church, and he and Conner walked inside. Joyce saw the bruises on Gene's face and rushed to the medicine cabinet.

"Sit down," she said. "What happened this time?"

"Dad and Mr. Palladin beat the shit out of each other," Conner answered. "I've never seen anyone get head-butted like that before. It was great, better than *Magnum, P.I.*"

"Forget *Magnum, P.I.* Who's this Mr. Palladin?" Joyce asked. She poured hydrogen peroxide on a gauze pad and smeared it over the gash on Gene's forehead. Conner stepped closer and watched.

"Palladin's from Yummy's in downtown Philadelphia. He's a pretty scary guy. Matt's employing him to work at the bank. He's going to live in Matt's guesthouse."

"I don't understand half of what you're saying." Joyce put the cap back on the peroxide bottle. She looked closely into Gene's eyes. "Do you feel dizzy or nauseous?"

"No"

"Is your vision blurred?"

"He drove in and out of the gutter twice on the way here," Conner said.

"No," Gene answered irritably. "My vision is not blurred!"

"You have a concussion," Joyce said. "I'd take it easy for a few days."

There were footsteps on the stairs, and Andrew walked into the room.

"What happened to you, Gene?"

"He got—" Conner began.

"Nothing happened," Gene interrupted.

"I'm glad you're here. I was about to drive over to your place. I just came back from Green Hollow. Eight kids have already signed up for the church service. Ira Hayes is one of them. We're breaking him out of prison this Sunday, Gene."

"If all goes well."

"It has to go well," Andrew said. "I know what we're planning to do here at Holy Waters Church, Gene. But I don't know anything about Philadelphia."

"I called JJ. I'll get Ira and Lisa on the train, and JJ will pick them up at Amtrak's Thirtieth Street Station."

"I've been there," Conner interjected. "And I know JJ." Seeing the look on his dad's face, he stepped back.

"What's going to happen when Ira and Lisa meet JJ?" Andrew asked.

"I'm not sure. We'll figure something out."

"Dad," Conner asked. "What's going on?"

"Nothing you need to know about," Gene said. "Let's go home. You're still grounded." He turned to Andrew. "You know exactly what you have to do?"

"Yes," Andrew said. "I know the whole plan. I just don't know what I'll do if there are any surprises."

"Oh, I can tell you what will happen if there are surprises." Pushing Conner toward the staircase, Gene stared at Andrew. "You'll be arrested and put in the Huntingdon County Jail." Gene thanked Joyce and left Holy Waters Church.

It was late afternoon. His gun belt on his waist, Palladin was standing at the garage when he saw Matt walk from the house. He pushed the garage door up and called.

"Matt, can you come here a minute?" Matt walked over and followed Palladin into the garage. Palladin pointed at the white Cadillac convertible.

"Matt, I saw this Cadillac in the garage. The windshield's smashed. The headlights are knocked out. The hood's dented. What happened?"

"Oh, I did that. I *dispatched* Mr. Henry's Cadillac with my Roman death hammer." Matt opened his jacket and pulled the hammer from under his belt. The handle was short and solid; the head was polished steel. One side of the head was flat and smooth. The other side had a sharp tapered point. Matt lifted the hammer proudly.

"I call it Dis Pater."

"The Roman god of death," Mr. Palladin said.

"Then you know about him."

"Yes, I've read about the Greeks and Romans. What are you doing with Dis Pater?"

"He's my main weapon. Dis Pater *dispatched* mortally wounded gladiators who fought bravely in the Colosseum. He killed them painlessly and with mercy."

"Let me see Dis Pater." Palladin took the hammer and swung the pointed side into a wooden post. Splinters flew through the air. "It doesn't look painless to me."

"Maybe the victim feels some pain. But it's over fast."

"Your logic has me confused." Palladin gave the hammer back to Matt, who slid it under his belt. "Why smash the Cadillac?"

"Mr. Henry loved the Cadillac. He hurt me in it. I hated it. I hated him."

"You're too damn impulsive, Matt. You don't give any thought to what you do. The Cadillac was nothing but a substitute for Mr. Henry. You wanted to hurt him. He wasn't available, so you trashed his car."

"Maybe that's right. But it's not like you said. I gave it a lot of thought. Every night I thought about it. After thinking about it so hard, I didn't want to hurt Mr. Henry anymore. I wanted to kill him." Matt spoke in a casual voice; Palladin stared at the boy.

"When you thought I had shot SenSay, you were angry. You hated me. If you still had the derringer, would you have used it?"

"I imagine so," Matt said without hesitating. "I remembered right away how good the derringer felt in my hand." Grumbling to himself, Palladin walked to the Cadillac and opened the door.

"Get in," he said.

"I hate that car."

"I said get in!"

"Where we going?"

"For a short ride."

Dragging his feet, Matt got in the front seat. Palladin turned the key. The engine started smoothly. Pieces of cracked glass and a hubcap broke loose and fell onto the cement floor. Palladin backed the Cadillac out of the garage. He drove across an open field and stopped at a line of trees. He and Matt got out and walked thirty-five yards.

"This is far enough," Palladin said. He turned, removed the Colt .45 from his holster, and gave it to Matt. "You still hate the Cadillac, don't you?"

"Yes."

"The Cadillac brought us up the hill. It's still alive, Matt. Dispatch it for real this time." Palladin stepped back. Matt made a face; the gun wobbled in his grip.

"It's heavy."

"The heavier the gun, the less the kick," Palladin said. "Steady your wrist with your off hand. Lift the Colt to chin level. Lock your elbow. Hold your arm straighter. Aim at the center of the Cadillac. Now, do your thing. *Dispatch* that damn convertible!"

"But—" Matt's eyes were open wide. He stared at Palladin, who shouted.

"It's what you want. Do it!"

"I … I …" Matt moved his lips. Palladin began shouting.

"Don't stutter at me! Don't look at me! Look at your target!"

Matt's shoulders were slumped. He raised the Colt higher. Squinting, he stared at the Cadillac. Then he grimaced and exerted pressure on the trigger. Nothing happened. Matt glanced at Palladin, who had a disgusted expression on his face.

"Pull the hammer back," Palladin instructed. "You know what a hammer is, don't you? It's just like your Dis Pater. You can't just hold it. You have to pull it back before it's any good."

Matt reached up and pressed the hammer down. It clicked into position. Gritting his teeth together, Matt clutched the golden Colt with both hands. A look of cold determination on his face, he squeezed the trigger.

There was a loud explosion. The Colt jerked in the air. Fierce vibrations started at Matt's wrist, tore through the length of his arm, and ripped into his shoulder. Matt fell backward into Palladin.

"Wow," he said. A ringing sound echoed in his ears. He shouted above the noise, "Did I hit it?"

"No, not even close. And stop yelling at me. Do you want to try again?"

Matt straightened. He hesitated for a moment. Then shaking his head, he handed the Colt .45 to Palladin. Palladin holstered the Colt, and they walked back to the Cadillac. Before getting inside, Matt looked closely at the side and the fenders.

"I said you didn't hit it," Palladin said. They got inside the convertible. Palladin drove down the hill to the garage and parked the Cadillac. Matt looked at him.

"Mr. Palladin, when you took me up the hill, you had something on your mind. What was it?"

"What I had on my mind wasn't important. It's what's on *your* mind, Matt. Trashing Mr. Henry's Cadillac won't solve anything. You have to face your problems, or they'll get worse. Why don't you have a long talk with Mr. Henry when he gets back?"

"I can't do that," Matt said. He opened the door and stepped out. "What time are we going to Purgatory?"

"Around seven o'clock."

"Can I ask Alice to go with us? She's my girlfriend. She lives here in Barree too."

"I guess," Palladin said. "We'll be back late. Make sure she tells her parents that."

"I will," Matt said. He turned and walked out of the garage.

Chapter Nineteen

Purgatory
Lancaster County
Saturday Evening

It was ten o'clock when Palladin exited the Pennsylvania Turnpike at the Denver Interchange. Wearing loose-fitting sweatshirts, Matt and Alice Byrd were snuggled together in the backseat. They stopped whispering when Palladin paid the toll.

"Are we there?" Matt asked.

"No."

"Where did you say we were going?" Alice asked.

"A place called Purgatory," Matt answered. "Mr. Palladin asked me to go. Then I asked you."

"I'm glad you did. This car is luxurious." She smiled; Matt put his arm around her and kissed her lightly on the cheek.

"Matt, we have important work to do." Palladin turned onto Route 222 South. "Will you please control yourself for another thirty minutes?"

"Okay," Matt said. He moved slightly away from Alice. Palladin glanced at the hammer protruding from under the sweatshirt.

"Why did you bring Dis Pater with you?"

"I always carry a weapon. Don't you?"

"No," Palladin said. "I always carry two weapons."

Traffic was light on the four-lane highway. Palladin drove at a high rate of speed for twenty miles and then turned east on Route 30. The truck traffic became heavier. He slowed down. It was ten thirty when he turned onto Skunk Road.

The narrow road meandered past houses, large barns, and long sections of white wooden fencing. Lantern bouncing in the darkness, a horse-and-buggy trotted in the opposite direction. Then there was no traffic for the next two miles. When Palladin noticed the dimly lit sign "E & V Kennels" clamped to an open gate, he backed the Eldorado onto a dirt road.

"Wake up back there."

"We're awake," Matt said, sitting straight, looking through the front window.

The road beyond the gate circled a pond and ended in front of two massive barns. A yellow security light was mounted on the corner of each barn. Headlights flicked on, and a truck came down the road. The driver went through the gate and stopped. He got out and secured the two gate sections with a chain and padlock before driving off. Opening the front compartment, Palladin pulled out gloves and ski masks with slits cut in the front. He gave them to Matt and Alice.

"They have video cameras at the barns. So we'll wear these in case they're turned on. And wear the gloves at all times." Alice had a confused look on her face; Matt slid the ski mask over his head.

"Cool," he said.

Palladin took a bolt cutter from the floor, opened the door, and walked across Skunk Road. After cutting the chain and opening the gates, he returned to the Eldorado.

When Palladin drove through the gate, Matt jumped out quickly, closed the gate, and ran back to the Cadillac.

"I didn't give you any orders to close the gate," Palladin said. "You're pretty quick. Have you ever broken into a house or barn before?"

"No," Matt said. "This is a first. I'm not sure what we're doing here, but I like it so far." Matt sat in a ready position and straightened his ski mask. Headlights off, Palladin drove up the road, stopping in the shadows of the first barn. He opened the door, and a burst of putrid air swirled inside the car. Alice covered her nose.

"Something's rotting or dead," she said. "What's that smell, Mr. Palladin?"

"You'll see in a minute," he said. "Wait here."

Palladin walked the length of the barn to the security room and pushed the door open. Without making any sound, he stepped inside. Back at the Eldorado, Alice watched him disappear and nudged Matt in the shoulder.

"What's he doing now?" Alice asked.

"Palladin's a security expert," Matt answered. "He's checking to make sure we're safe to …" Matt hesitated.

"Safe to do what?" Alice asked.

"I don't know." Matt looked at the row of screened cages along the side of the barn. "It probably has something to do with what's inside those cages."

"When he got out of the car, I saw one of his weapons."

"It's a Colt .45. He's teaching me how to shoot it. In my first lesson I almost hit the bull's-eye. Mr. Palladin said I would be an expert in no time."

Palladin moved quietly across the floor. A board squeaked under his feet, and lowering his hand to the Colt, he paused. Leaning forward, his back to Palladin, a whiskered man, wearing black trousers, wide black suspenders, and a black hat, sat at a table that held four TV monitors. An open *Penthouse* magazine was on the table.

Sliding behind him, Palladin cuffed the man in the back of the neck. The man's head fell over the steamy body of the blonde centerfold and was still. After stuffing a rag in the man's mouth, Palladin taped his body to the chair. The man groaned; his eyes opened, and he stared at Palladin.

"You'll be fine," Palladin said. After smashing the TV monitors with his Colt, Palladin returned to the Cadillac. Matt watched him closely

"What's the plan?" he asked.

"It's simple," Palladin said. "This is a puppy mill. The owner raises purebred dogs in the most deplorable conditions and sells them for considerable profit. So we're going to open all the cages and release the dogs. Also, Matt, since you lost SenSay this morning, you can pick out any puppy. We'll take it back to Barree with us."

"My own puppy!" Matt exclaimed. "That's fantastic! Where do we start?"

"The wire cages are latched to the sides of the barn. There may be five or six puppies in a cage. Be careful when you put them on the ground. Their paws will be raw from standing on wire all day. The breeding dogs are inside. I'll release them."

"Any puppy I want?" asked Matt.

"Yes," Palladin said. "Let's get started. Put on your gloves."

Palladin walked to the row of screened wooden cages along the side of the barn. Glassy eyes stared through the wire; a few of the puppies began to whimper. Palladin swung open the screened door at the top of the cage, and reaching inside, he lifted a puppy that had black fur and white paws.

"This is a miniature schnauzer," Palladin said. He put the schnauzer on the grass. The puppy stood perfectly still.

"It's adorable," Alice said. "It's just adorable. But why doesn't it run around?"

"They never exercise the dogs. And they don't bother to feed them much because of the cost. It will take a while before the dogs adjust to all this freedom. Let them alone. Let them do what they want." Palladin reached into the cage, brought out two more puppies, and placed them next to the first one. One licked at the other's neck. Palladin turned.

"You can get started," he said. "We don't have much time."

Matt and Alice hurried to the next cages and swung open the doors, the edges banging against the side of the barn. Soon there were puppy bodies all over the grass. A white furry American Eskimo with black eyes and black nose yelped and chased a brown, floppy-eared beagle in a circle. Enthusiastic and smiling, Matt handled the puppies with extreme delicacy. Alice caressed many of the puppies before she put them on the ground.

Palladin went to the barn and pushed the door open. Coughing at the burst of tepid air, he saw the two rows of wire cages. Excrement lay in dark piles under the cages. Varying in color from yellow to dark crimson, urine dripped from the wire. Palladin walked to the bags of food piled along the wall and ripped them open, spilling small biscuits and pellets over the floor. Then he opened the cages and carefully lifted the heavy breeders to the floor. Some followed him around; others went to the ripped bags of food.

Toward the middle of the row of cages, Alice read the tag on a screened door: "Great Pyrenees." She swung the door open, reached inside, and lifted out a puppy with small dark eyes and fluffy white fur. Alice noticed the fingers on her glove were smeared with blood. Checking the puppy, seeing the gashes on its paws, she turned to Matt.

"Many of the puppies have cuts," Alice said sadly.

"I've seen injuries too."

"It's horrible," Alice said. "The owner is a criminal, the worst kind of criminal. What should we do?"

"Release them like Mr. Palladin said."

"Can't we do more?" Alice pleaded, her eyes tearing up.

"Yes, we can do more." Matt felt the burning sensation against his skin. Sliding his hand under his sweatshirt, he gripped the arrowhead. He watched Alice lower the puppy to the ground; the puppy yelped and collapsed on its side. The green stone burning his palm, Matt removed his hand and walked past her.

"Where are you going?"

"I'll be right back."

Matt walked to the barn, opened the door to the security room, and stepped inside. Taped to the chair, the man with the black hat and long whiskers made groaning noises and breathed heavily through his nose. His chest expanded, stretching the black suspenders. As Matt approached, he heard a light scratching sound from a large, double-wide garbage container in the corner. He walked to the container, slid off the lid, and saw the crushed piles of small bodies. Two glassy eyes stared at him and then flicked shut. His body tensing, Matt pulled Dis Pater from under his belt and hastened toward the security guard, only slowing when he heard her voice.

"Matt," Alice called from the cages. "Matt, I found the cutest collie. He looks just like SenSay!"

Gripping Dis Pater tightly, Matt saw movement at the door. There was a Dalmatian staring at him. One side of the puppy's head was perfectly white. The other side was black. Tiny dark spots dotted its fur. The Dalmatian yelped, and using its front paws, it dragged its body into the room. The puppy's right hind leg was twisted and trailed behind. Matt glared at the bound security guard.

"You rotten son of a bitch!" he spat out. Matt swung Dis Pater savagely into the side of the man's head. The black hat popped in the air. The tape ripped from the chair, and the man fell heavily to the floor. Sliding Dis Pater under his belt, Matt left the room and joined Alice, who was holding the cutest collie he had ever seen.

It took Palladin twenty minutes to empty all the cages. When he left the second barn, he saw puppies wandering over the yard. Some were in groups; some were solitary; some were at the pond. Many just lay on the grass. Palladin went back inside the barn and lifted two large bags on his shoulder. Returning to the yard, he spilled heaping mounds of colored biscuits on the ground. The puppies yelped and chased each other to the food.

Walking to the Eldorado, Palladin saw Matt and Alice in the backseat. He got in the Cadillac, drove down the road, and bumped through the gate. As soon as Palladin braked, Matt jumped out again, closed the gate, and rushed back to the Eldorado. Palladin turned onto the main road and accelerated. Looking in the rearview mirror, he glanced at the couple in the backseat.

"Did you get your puppy?" he asked.

"Yes," Matt answered.

"What kind did you pick?" There was a whimpering sound from the right side. Alice spoke in a soft voice.

"Cute," she said. "Matt picked a cute one."

"I mean the breed. Did you get a collie like SenSay?"

"Yes," Matt said. There was another whimper from the left side. Then a yelp sounded from the floor.

"What's going on with all that noise?"

"I'm sorry," Alice said. "It's my fault. Matt took his collie back to the car. Then I saw this golden retriever. It had big eyes and cuddled in my hands and wouldn't move. I made Matt take him back to the car too."

"I hear more than two dogs."

"You hear right," Matt said. "But it was an accident. When I released the dogs from the last cage, two of them followed me back to the Eldorado. I opened the door, and they jumped inside before I could do anything."

"You have four puppies back there?"

"Yes."

"We already named them," Alice said excitedly. "The collie is SenSay."

"The golden retriever is Fluffy."

"And the other two, we named Hombre and Dolly. Hombre looks tough. He's a German shepherd. Dolly is ..."

"A Dalmatian," Palladin finished.

"You're right," Alice said. She picked up Hombre and Dolly and petted them. "Are you angry, Mr. Palladin?"

"No," Palladin said. "I'm not angry." He turned onto Route 30. "Matt, you'll have to buy tons of food tomorrow. You'll have to buy dog houses and build a pen."

"I don't think I'll need a dog house or a pen. I plan to keep SenSay and Dolly inside."

"What about Fluffy and Hombre?"

"Alice is keeping Fluffy and Hombre can stay in the guesthouse with you." Matt and Alice both laughed. Palladin accelerated. When he reached Route 222, he stopped at a

Sunoco Station and went to the phone booth. Palladin made three quick calls and returned to the Eldorado. As he drove away, Matt leaned over the seat.

"Who did you call, Mr. Palladin?"

"First, I called 911 and reported to the Purgatory police that there had been vandalism at the E & V Kennels. Then I called *The Lancaster News* and *The Philadelphia Inquirer* and reported that disgruntled customers had freed the dogs at the kennel. They were protesting the poor treatment and abuse. It should draw attention to the problem. Maybe something will be done about it."

"Something has already been done," Matt commented. He leaned back in the seat. SenSay crawled softly up his chest and licked his face.

It was two in the morning when Palladin dropped Alice off in Barree. The porch light was on. Alice held Fluffy in her hands. Matt walked her to the steps and pulled her close, kissing her on the lips. Fluffy made a whining noise.

"Can you leave your bedroom window open?"

"But it's so late."

"I need your company," Matt said. "I'm too excited to be alone."

"Maybe it would be good if you stayed here tonight. I've been worried ever since Heather was kidnapped."

"Then I'll be right back. I'll bring Dis Pater. I won't let anything happen to you." Matt kissed Alice and stood there waiting, watching as she entered the house and closed the door. Then he rushed to the car. The puppies made yelping noises and jumped on him when he got in the backseat. He began brushing their fur, hugging them to his chest, and laughing when they licked his hand and face. Palladin drove off, glancing in the rearview mirror. Matt's face was flushed; his eyes wide and bright.

"It's after two in the morning, Matt. Why aren't you sleepy?"

"I don't know. Maybe it's all the excitement."

"Did you get into my Ole Smokey? You got a buzz?"

"No, it's more than a buzz. Much more." Matt reached down and lifted SenSay and Dolly to his lap. Dolly moved energetically even though its hind leg was slightly twisted. The two puppies rolled around making whimpering noises as Matt petted them and tickled their fur. Hombre stayed on the floor and made a growling noise.

"Mr. Palladin, thanks for taking me to Purgatory. I love these puppies."

Palladin drove up the hill to the fence, opened the security gate, and entered the property. Moonlight filtered through the pine trees and cast shadows over the lane. The headlights flashed on a herd of grazing deer, their bodies stiff and alert, their eyes frozen in place. The Eldorado cruised silently past them. It was two thirty when Palladin reached the portico and shut off the motor.

The main road in Barree was dark, deserted, and quiet. A Minnie Winnie was parked in the shadows along the river. Slumped in the front seat, Max Wright opened his eyes when the headlights stopped in front of the house. Sitting straight, he watched Alice, who was holding some kind of dog, and the boy step out of the Cadillac. He watched the couple caress and kiss on the porch.

You two are so sweet, Max thought. *That's the kind of action we're looking for.* He felt the tingling sensation in his groin. Max groaned, lowered his hand, and began massaging his fingers into his pants.

"Our clients will be doin' just what I'm doin' and lovin' it just as much," Max announced to the windshield. He took a deep breath and laughed. Humming quietly, slobbering bubbles on his lips, he sang his all-time favorite song. *I guess we're all gonna be what we're gonna be. Yeah, what do you do with ol' horny bastards like me?* His face flushed, his hand moving feverously, Max sat in the dark for a long time.

Chapter Twenty

Green Hollow Correctional Camp/Barree
Sunday Morning

The morning air was cold and dry when the Holy Waters Church van bounced over the security bump, passed through the gate, and stopped in front of the dormitory. Pastor Andrew Brooks got out of the driver's seat and opened the door. Nine Green Hollow juvenile inmates stood at the steps in an uneven line of shapes and sizes.

Wearing a white shirt and tie, black slacks, and blue-and-gold Twin River varsity jacket, Dan Bonnie stood off to the side. The fabric over his left leg was ripped from the knee to the shoe, exposing the cast. In front of the line, Earl Jones held a clipboard with a computer printout on it. The printout had the names of the prisoners and two columns. The first column had a square for the check-out time, and the second column had a square for the check-in time.

Earl Jones was forty-nine years old. He was unshaven and gaunt, wore a heavy jacket with deep pockets, and had a black wool pullover on his head. Maneuvering chew in his mouth, Earl wrote down seven thirty in the squares as the inmates boarded the van.

All the inmates wore identical gray hooded sweatshirts. Dark, shadowy eyes stared out from under the hoodies. A wide, clean bandage above his eye, Ira Hayes had a Pittsburgh Penguins cap under his hoodie. The hulking figure of Jamal Pritchett was in front of Ira. Chocolate Thunder was sketched with artistic flair on his sweatshirt.

The boys quietly filled the front and middle rows of seats inside the van. A skinny, frail boy, Hector Jimenez, the only inmate wearing a red sweatshirt, a wooden cross wrapped in a circle of thorns stenciled on the shoulder, was the last inmate to board the van. Hector wandered down the aisle and slumped down on the rear cushioned bench. When Dan Boonie approached the door, Earl hit him in the chest with the clipboard.

"Why ain't you in uniform?"

"I'm off duty. I'm helping Pastor Brooks with the church service. After that, I'm going straight home. Do you think you can handle this Barree trip all by yourself, Earl?"

"Just stay out of my way, or I just might bring you back with the inmates."

Dan boarded the van, dragged his cast and leg down the aisle, and sat next to Hector Jimenez. Behind the wheel, Pastor Brooks checked the rearview mirror. He glanced nervously at the rows of inmates. His eyes locked onto Ira's Penguins cap. Spitting a lump of chew on the step, Earl Jones got on the van and scrutinized the hooded figures.

"Okay," he grumbled. "You all remember where you're at today. You're in the house of God. The law-abidin' residents of Barree will be watchin' you. So no shittin' around. No cussin'. And no puttin' your dirty paws on the pretty girls."

Walking down the aisle, counting in a raspy voice, Earl rapped each boy on the head with the clipboard. Reaching seven in the count, he stopped in front of Jamal, who glared at him. Jamal's countenance was a dark shadow of menace. Earl skipped over him and cracked Hector on the head.

"*Nine!*" he shouted, sitting next to Boonie. "Let's go to Holy Waters and do some serious prayin' in order to save your rotten, miserable souls!"

Wincing, Pastor Brooks started the engine and drove the van around the athletic field. At the administration building, Max Wright ran down the steps waving his hands. Pastor Brooks stopped the van, and Max stomped inside. Scrutinizing the rows of inmates, Max walked to the rear and sat next to Earl Jones.

"What are you doing here?" Earl asked. "I can handle this job."

"Luther didn't want anything to go wrong. He said I had to keep my eyes on Ira."

"I ain't blind. I can do that myself."

"Sure you can." Max tapped his fingers off Earl's coat pocket, pinging a hard object. "I see you're carrying that flask as usual."

Church bells rang through the empty streets of Barree. Sitting at the piano, a petite elderly lady in a plain white dress, Mrs. Eleanor Stevens began playing softly. Some of the keys on the piano had smooth grooves; some had thin cracks the length of the ivory. The eight-o'clock service at Holy Waters Church was crowded. Mostly elderly men and women, the parishioners sat in small groups. The women wore heavy coats, some with flowers in the lapels. The men wore black suits and ties. There were a few families; women held small children in their laps. A baby started to cry and was hushed into silence. Conner and Cindy were in a middle pew. Matt and Alice arrived late and sat next to them. They pushed together and began whispering.

Heads lowered, eyes dark under the hoodies, the inmates sat in the front pew. A space heater made a humming noise and fanned warm air in their faces. Waiting until everyone was seated, Max Wright and Earl Jones took their positions in the empty last pew. Earl coughed, removed his wool pullover cap, and slid it into his pocket. When he retrieved the pullover, it was wrapped around the flask. Looking over the heads of the parishioners, Earl took a long drink, burped, and gave the flask to Max, who smiled and took a drink.

The pulpit in front of the prisoners was on a platform. A wooden cross hung above the pulpit. Narrow tables on either side of the pulpit held burning candles. There was a large stained-glass window behind the cross. Rays of sunlight streaming through the panes showed Jesus with arms outstretched to a group of children. The inscription underneath the window read,

> Suffer the little children to come unto me.
> For such is the kingdom of heaven.
> —Mark 10:14

Bells sounded, and Pastor Brooks walked to the pulpit. Standing, holding ancient hymn books, the parishioners sang *Majesty*. The inmates shuffled to their feet. Glancing back at the rows of people, Ira saw Earl and Max sitting in the last pew. Earl had his black cap over his nose and lips. Max happened to look up. His eyes narrowing, he met Ira's gaze for a moment. Then he reached for Earl's pullover and lifted it toward his mouth. The space heater blazed red. Ira turned to the pulpit; waves of heat rolled across his face.

After the hymn, the parishioners sat, replaced the tattered books in the wooden slots, and turned their eyes to the pulpit. Pastor Brooks spoke in a clear voice. He welcomed the special guests from Green Hollow. While he introduced them, complimenting them for their attendance, Dan Boonie limped down the aisle with a long-handled collection basket. Coins and crumpled bills were dropped in the basket. When Dan reached the last pew, he shoved the basket toward Max and Earl. Eyes bloodshot, Earl stared at Dan.

"Piss off," he said.

What an asshole, Dan thought. He retrieved the basket and limped down the aisle to the staircase. When he entered the basement, Dan gave the collection basket to Joyce Brooks. Removing his jacket, Dan pulled nervously at the knot on his tie.

"Let me do that," Joyce said. Placing the basket on the table, she reached over, deftly loosened the knot, and lifted the tie over his head. Dan unbuttoned his shirt.

"Are you ready?" she asked.

"Not yet," Dan answered. He limped forward a few steps, the left leg stiff and unyielding. "It won't work with this cast on." Dan slid off his slacks and stood there in his boxer shorts. The cast was thick and white the length of his leg. "Can you remove it?"

"Sure," Joyce said. "But it's going to be sore." She took a pair of scissors from the wall cabinet, cut the cast down the middle, and pried it off. Dan's leg was swollen, the skin pale and wrinkled. A dark scar cut across the knee.

In the church, the parishioners sang *The Old Rugged Cross*. The words drifted down the staircase: "*I will cling to the old rugged cross and exchange it someday for a crown.*" There were heavy footsteps on the stairs, and Jamal appeared.

"Are you ready?" he asked, looking at the swollen leg.

"Good-to-go," Dan said. Jamal walked to the bathroom. When Jamal exited, the sound of rushing water lingering, he walked up the stairs.

After a short time, Ira came to the basement. He hurriedly took off his hoodie and jeans and gave them to Dan. In exchange, Dan gave him his white shirt, ripped slacks, and Twin River varsity jacket. He brushed his hand over the TR.

"I worked hard for this," Dan said. "Take good care of it."

"I will," Ira said, putting on the jacket. "What sport?"

"Sports," Dan said, dressing quickly. "Football, basketball, and track." Dan straightened and pulled at the folds of the gray hoodie. Ira's jeans pressed tight against the swollen leg. Ira took off his cap and placed it solidly on Dan's head.

"You're a Pittsburgh Penguin now," Ira said. "No one's tougher than a Penguin." He grabbed Dan's hand and shook it vigorously. "Thanks."

"Don't thank me yet," Dan said. Grimacing, putting full pressure on the left leg, he started toward the staircase.

"Wait!" Joyce rushed to the wall cabinet, returned with a double-wide bandage, and stuck it above Dan's left eye. "Now you can go."

Dan pulled the hoodie over his forehead and climbed the staircase. On each step, he gritted his teeth and bent the knee lower. Dan's forehead glistened with perspiration when he reached the front pew. Jamal looked up and patted his hand on the bench. Glancing quickly at Pastor Brooks and then at Earl and the slumping Max in the back pew, Dan sat in Ira's vacated seat.

Gene Brooks stopped the jeep in the alley behind Holy Waters Church. In the basement, Joyce led Ira across the room, opened the door, and pointed to the jeep. Ira caught a glimpse of the girl in the backseat and took off running.

"Lisa," he said, crossing the yard. The jeep door swung open, and Ira jumped into Lisa's arms. They hugged and kissed; tears flowed down Lisa's face. Gene got out and closed the door. Glancing at the church, he waved at Joyce, got back in the jeep, and drove quietly down the deserted alley.

Pastor Brooks tapped the microphone. Sliding closer to Alice, Matt Henry glanced back at the last pew. Earl had the wool pullover pressed against his mouth again. Breathing heavily, Max lay sideways on the pew, dribble on his lower lip, his face flat against the wood. Except for the humming sound from the heater, the church was quiet. Pastor Brooks began the sermon in a strained but hopeful voice.

> Rejoice in the hope of the glory of God. And not only that, but we also glory in tribulations, knowing that tribulation produces perseverance; and perseverance character; and character hope. *Now hope does not disappoint.*

Pastor Brooks expostulated for long minutes about *hope* and *tribulation*. Sitting straight, his leg throbbing, Dan Boonie listened to every word. Matt stopped whispering to Alice and was attentive to the sermon.

When the pastor finished, Mrs. Stevens began playing the piano. The parishioners stood and sang *Amazing Grace* in loud, resonating harmony. Jumping to attention, Earl shoved the pullover into his pocket and nudged Max in the shoulder. Eyes blinking open, Max stood awkwardly. The singing finished, the piano notes resonating in the church, the parishioners moved toward the aisle. Nodding to some,

Pastor Brooks watched their progress for a few moments. Then rushing through the back exit, he jumped in the van, sat at the wheel, and lowered his head.

Remember the prisoners as if chained with them, Pastor Brooks reflected. He drove around the corner and parked the van in front of the church. Earl and Max stood at the door while the inmates boarded. Earl checked off the names with precision. Disguised in the hoodie, Dan Bonnie walked stiffly but solidly down the aisle, sat on the brown cushion, and was crushed into the window seat by Jamal's body. Earl and Max stumbled by and sat on the rear bench.

Pastor Brooks drove with haste to the Green Hollow Correctional Camp. At the checkpoint station, the guard stood, looked through the window, and waved the van on. Driving slowly, Pastor Brooks saw Luther Cicconi hurry down the steps of the administration building. The pastor braked; Luther stepped forward and opened the door.

"How was the service, Pastor Brooks?"

"Great," he answered enthusiastically. "Just great!"

Luther stared at the pastor for a moment and boarded the van. Walking down the aisle, scrutinizing the inmates, he stopped in front of Jamal. Luther leaned forward and snarled at the Penguins cap.

"I hope you prayed real hard, Ira, because this was your last taste of freedom. Come Monday morning you're in isolation until you tell us where to find Lisa."

"Leave him alone," Jamal muttered in a low voice.

Luther straightened. He stood there for a moment. Then he left the van. Max got up and followed him to the administration building. Pastor Brooks drove to the dormitory. Earl stepped off the van first and wrote the time on the printout as the inmates walked past. His red sweatshirt bright in the sunlight, Hector was the last inmate on the list. Swinging the clipboard, Earl waved at the van.

Closing the door, Pastor Brooks held his breath. As he drove through the camp, his chest began to hurt. Seconds after he bounced the van over the speed bump at the exit, Pastor Brooks exhaled a great quantity of air and pounded his fist off the dash.

"Yes!" he shouted thankfully. *"Hope! Hope! Blessed hope!"* The pastor accelerated, spinning tires, kicking up dust on both sides of the road.

"All clear," Jamal said. Looking through the screened window, Jamal scanned the porch, the athletic field, the road to the administration building. A smile on his face, he turned toward Dan. "No guards in sight." Jamal glanced at Dan and the Penguins cap tilted sideways on his head. "Officer Boonie, do you think Ira will be okay?"

"Everything's worked great so far," Dan said. "The guard won't check the beds until lights-out tonight. Ira will be long gone by then. I appreciate all your help, Jamal."

"Just tell Ira hello from the Thunder. You planning to leave through the locked gate in the back fence?"

"Yes, I have the key."

"Wouldn't it be better if there was a hole in the fence that maybe the prisoner could escape through? Then Luther and Max wouldn't think he had inside help."

"Yes, it would be better," Dan said. "But the bolt cutters are locked—"

"I grabbed a pair after yesterday's work detail." Jamal took the long-handled bolt cutter from under his bed and walked to the door. As Dan turned to follow him, he noticed Ira's brown Pittsburgh Penguins work shirt hanging from a hook on the wall. Pulling it off the hook, frowning at the two charred holes, he went out the back exit. There was loud barking from the pit-bull pen.

"You work fast," Dan said, looking at the cut links. Jamal pushed against the fence, creating a wide gap. Dan slid through and straightened painfully on the other side. The barking from the pit bulls became louder. Staring at Dan, Jamal grinned and tapped his finger on his forehead.

"I forgot all about it," Dan said. He ripped off the bandage and put it in his pocket. Jamal shoved the bolt cutter through the gap in the fence.

"Better take this and toss it somewhere."

"You think of everything," Dan said, grabbing the handle. "You're smarter than all the guards, Jamal. You could break out of Green Hollow anytime. Why haven't you?"

"There's nothing but miles of woods and packs of wild dogs on the other side of this fence. I hear them at night. I'm in no hurry. I'll leave when it's my time to leave."

"We couldn't have done this without your help. Tomorrow when I come to work, I'm bringing you a steak, the biggest one I can buy."

Jamal laughed. Dan waved and limped forward a few steps. After a short distance, exerting great effort, he began walking naturally. The narrow path twisted through dense woods. Mosquitoes buzzed around his face; a heavy, gray squirrel jumped across the path. Stopping, Dan dropped Ira's brown shirt and Penguins cap in the middle of the path; he heaved the bolt cutters into the brush. Emitting shrill whistling cries, freezing Dan in his tracks, two bobwhite quail frantically flew in the air. Dan laughed and stared at the path. Then reaching down, he picked up the Penguins cap and put it proudly on his head.

No one's tougher than a Penguin, Dan thought. Mosquitoes buzzing around his head, he walked down the path. After ten minutes, Dan saw the Kawasaki leaning against a pine tree. He wiped the needles off the seat, kicked the starter, and drove away. When he cleared the forest, Dan accelerated, and wind blowing though the hoodie, he roared the Kawasaki down Mountain Road.

Luther Cicconi waved at the guard at the gate and raced the car over the speed bump. Sitting in the passenger seat, Max was knocked against the dash.

"What the hell, Luther?"

"Don't *what the hell* me, Max! Cousin Earl said you slept through the entire church service. You were supposed to keep your eyes on the inmates, especially on Ira."

"Nothing happened at church. Nor on the bus. You saw Ira yourself."

"That don't change the fact that you were sleeping. And Cousin Earl said you drank all his whiskey."

"Fuck Cousin Earl! He's a lyin' weasel." Max sat quietly for a moment. "Hell, why wouldn't I be tired? I was up all night in the Winnebago spyin' on the girl."

"You were supposed to grab Alice, not spy on her."

"How was I to do that? There was this boy and this big guy in a Cadillac. They took her right to her doorstep. And that same boy came back later on his bicycle and climbed through the window into her room. I was gonna sneak over and watch them getting' it on, but I decided not to."

"Good thing you made that decision," Luther said. "That's all we need is for you to get arrested as a peeping tom."

"My brother Oliver would never arrest me for a little bit of peepin'. He does it all the time himself."

"There'll be no more fooling around, Max. Nathaniel wants you to deliver Alice to the Happy Hollow Hunt Club tonight. She's always riding her bike on that hill to the banker's mansion. You can grab her there ... if you stay awake!"

"I'll be awake for her. She's a cute little bitch." Max squirmed in his seat. "Pull over. I got to take a piss."

Shrugging his shoulders, Luther turned the car into the trees, and Max jumped out. Moaning while he unzipped his pants, Max walked to a large bush. A thick swarm of mosquitoes found him. He began pissing and swinging his hand at the strident buzzing sound over his head, urine spraying the bush and spattering off his shoes.

"Shit!" he said, rushing back to the car. Luther watched the clumsy motion.

"Damn fool," Luther muttered. There was a roar of noise on the road; a motorcycle zipped by. Through the cloud of dust, Luther saw the hoodie flare open; he caught a glimpse of the Penguins cap and the profile of the driver's face. Max sat down and slammed the door.

"Who the hell was that? He was wearing a Green Hollow hoodie."

"You ain't going to believe this, Max."

"What?"

"It was our friend, Officer Dan Boonie."

Gene Brooks stood outside the Amtrak station in Lewistown. A tall, Amish boy tended two horses and buggies parked along the sidewalk. Amish loitered in groups on the platform, the women wearing bonnets and blue dresses, the men in black jackets, black hats, and black suspenders. Off to the side, Ira and Lisa were whispering and holding onto each. Gene motioned to them. They broke free and approached him.

"The train will be here soon," Gene said.

"Why did you drive so far?" Lisa asked. "We went by the train station in Huntingdon."

"Someone may have noticed my jeep," Gene explained. "They may also have noticed two suspicious teenage passengers boarding the train."

"You're right," Ira said. "It was very dangerous. You could have been arrested."

"My brother, Pastor Brooks, guaranteed me that you were both worth the effort. He's usually right about people. Now, you'll need new identities. You'll need to leave the state. You can never come back here."

"We have no reason to return," Lisa said. "You never told us where we're going."

"I meant to," Gene said. "I meant to tell you right away. But you were so busy in the backseat I had to slant my rearview mirror."

"I'm sorry," Ira said, eyes downcast. "It was my fault. I haven't seen Lisa since they separated us in Pittsburgh."

"The important thing is that you're together now. The train will take you to Philadelphia. A friend of mine, JJ Jackson, will meet you in the station. He's a very fit middle-aged Negro. He'll be wearing a dark suit and a stupid tie with the words *Dinky Dow* on it. You can't miss him." Gene took a brown envelope from his jacket. "Here are the train tickets. Also, there's a key. Don't lose it."

"A key for what?" Lisa asked.

"I wanted it to be a surprise," Gene said. "But you should know now, so you won't worry too much. It's a key to a beach house in Wildwood. JJ will take you there. You can stay at the house as long as you want."

"Whose house is it?" Lisa asked.

"It's mine. It's comfortable. It's furnished. JJ will stay with you tonight. He'll take you shopping and make sure you have everything you need."

A horn sounded down the tracks; the people on the platform began to move forward. Taking Ira's hand, a worried look on her face, Lisa looked at Gene.

"How will we live in Wildwood?" she asked. "I mean, how will we get a job?"

"I talked with JJ. He'll get you each a work permit, a driver's license, and a Social Security number. He'll get you all the important paper stuff. You'll be starting a new life."

The train screeched to a stop; the doors flew open. Passengers began to disembark. Lisa glanced at the people waiting to board the train. Her face beamed; her body became electric. Ira also relaxed, the glow of excitement showing on his face.

"That sounds great," Ira said. "How can one man do all those things?"

"JJ's with the government, and he's very talented," Gene said. "He can do 'most anything."

"Then he's just like you." Lisa kissed Gene on the cheek; Ira pumped Gene's hand profusely. Then they rushed to board the *Pennsylvanian*.

The groups of Amish began to leave the station. They walked slowly to the horses and buggies. The horn sounded again; the train jerked forward with a loud clanking noise. When Gene searched the windows as the cars went by, he saw a row of strangers with tired faces. Then he saw Ira and Lisa, their smiling faces pressed against the glass, their hands waving back and forth.

Like kids going on a vacation, Gene thought. A smile on his face, he stood on the platform, his hand waving high in the air, until the train left the station. Then, breathing deeply, exhaling a quiet sigh of relief, he walked back to the jeep.

Chapter Twenty-One

Barree
Sunday Afternoon

Gene drove down River Road. Approaching his house, he saw the Cadillac in the drive and Palladin on the riverbank. Palladin was in the process of pulling a big brown trout out of the water. When Gene parked the jeep and crossed the road to the river, he saw four trout flopping in the grass. Palladin tossed the fifth one next to them.

"I got tired of waiting for you," Palladin said. "I saw the fishing rod and all those neat lures in the garage. I thought I might as well experiment a little. This minnow lure of yours works pretty damn good."

"You're breaking the law."

"For using your minnow lure?"

"For keeping five trout," Gene said. "You're over the limit."

"You have limits up here? My daddy always taught me that if you're hungry and eat what you catch, there are no limits."

"Your daddy would have been arrested. What brought you out here, Mr. Palladin?"

"It's mostly about Matt. Do you know him well?"

"As well as anyone. He stayed here for a while."

"Matt said you taught him hunting skills. He asked me to continue the lessons."

"Are you?"

"That's one of the reasons he hired me. But I can't teach Matt anything until I know him better. Matt has serious issues."

"What issues?"

"Something's bothering him. I told him that. I told him that he was restless, dangerous in a way. If he had a weapon, I'm sure he'd be quick to use it. What's bothering Matt that he's so unsettled?"

"Why don't you ask him?"

"I did. At first he was reluctant to say anything. So I gave him some Ole Smokey, and that loosened his tongue."

"You'll try anything to get what you want?"

"It's my job," Palladin said. "After a drink or two, Matt began to explain about having bad nightmares. Then we were interrupted. I think his dad's a big part of Matt's nightmares, and now he's gone missing. What happened to Mr. Henry?"

"I can't say anything behind Matt's back."

"I guess you're right. My daddy always taught me that I should never talk about people's problems without them being present."

"But you're doing it anyway."

"That's because Daddy's not here to clock me a hard one." Palladin walked over and handed Gene the fishing rod. "Thanks for letting me catch trout in your backyard." Palladin pulled a black garbage bag from his pocket and began sliding the trout inside. "I also borrowed one of your bags. All these fish bodies would leave a rank smell in the Eldorado."

"Was there anything else you needed?"

"I got a good look at your Arkansas toothpick on the wall. With that Gillette-sharp blade, it would do a nice job on people, but it was way too much knife for gutting trout. Besides, Matt's got a kitchen full of utensils." Palladin wiped his hands on the grass, walked to the Cadillac, and put the garbage bag in the trunk. Opening the front door, he turned to Gene.

"I meant to ask you. Is there in a store in the area where I can buy *The Philadelphia Inquirer*?"

"Homesick already?"

"No, I love it here in the country."

"There's a bed-and-breakfast resort, Edgewater Acres, on the river. It's not far from here. It's internationally famous. They have newspapers for their guests. When I had coffee there this morning, I glanced at the *Inquirer*. There was a headline about a brutal attack in Amish country. A security guard was beat up pretty bad in a place called Purgatory. Did you hear about it?"

"No," Palladin said, cursing under his breath. "That little son of a bitch." He stood there awkwardly for a moment. Birds sang from the trees; crickets chirped from the grass. Paladin's face turned dark. Getting in the Cadillac, slamming the door, he backed out of the drive. As he pulled away, Gene walked to the porch. Climbing the steps, he saw a cardboard box next to the door. "Hombre" was written on the top flap. Gene opened the flaps and heard a low, growling noise.

On Sunday afternoon, the Green Hollow administration building was empty except for Luther Cicconi and Max Wright. With a large cooler between their chairs, they sat in front of the TV. The Penguins/Bruins game was on the screen. Drinking ice-cold Heineken, they watched Rick Middleton slap the puck past Penguin goaltender Greg

Millen. The Boston Bruin fans went wild. Max finished his Heineken and tossed the empty bottle in the cooler.

"Seven to four—Penguins lose again. They suck!" Max shut off the TV. "I'm goin' home. I need a nap. I might be up all night chasin' after Alice."

"I'll be waiting at the hunt club. Everything's set up in the barn. Nathaniel's put a lot of money into this project. It's looking better than any of those fancy bunny ranches in Nevada. Don't let Alice get away again, Max. I plan to make her comfortable in the Winnebago."

A shrill whistle sounded from the yard. There were footsteps on the porch, and Earl Jones burst into the room. Flakes of chew were stuck to his chin.

"What's going on, Earl?" Luther asked.

"Bad news," he announced, panting loudly. "I took Jasper out to walk my rounds just now. He was barkin' and pullin' me behind the dormitory. That's when I saw the hole in the fence."

"What the hell you talkin' about?" Max exclaimed.

"I'm talkin' about a big-assed problem. Junior's lining up the inmates now. I was plannin' to count heads to see who might be missin'." Earl stomped out of the building. Luther and Max followed him.

The boys ran from different directions and formed rows on the assembly field. Luther and Max walked past them. When they reached the fence behind the dormitory, Max pushed it open, and Luther stepped through. He and Max started down the path. Luther took the pack from his pocket and lit up a Marlboro. Max watched him anxiously.

"Who—"

"Ira Hayes." Luther blew smoke in the air. "Ira broke out." After a few minutes on the path, Luther picked up the brown camp shirt with Pittsburgh Penguins scrawled on the front. Max shook his head.

"That Penguin bastard! I knew somethin' was gonna go wrong. Damn Earl was drinkin' way too much in church and could hardly keep his eyes open."

"Don't worry, Max. We'll have Ira back in no time. He's a city boy. He's a stranger in these parts. No one will help him." Luther started walking at a faster pace. After trudging down the path another six minutes, he stopped and pointed at the tire tracks.

"A bicycle?" Max said.

"A motorcycle," Luther corrected.

"You mean Ira had an accomplice with a motorcycle?"

"Think about it, Max. Try to put two and two together for once in your life. Someone escapes from Green Hollow on a motorcycle, and who did we see riding a motorcycle wearing a Penguins cap?"

"Dan Boonie."

"That's right. Ira made his escape from the church. To cover for him, Boonie changed clothes with him and took his seat on the bus. Boonie cut a hole in the fence, and now Boonie thinks he got away clean. Well, he's in for a surprise."

Luther dropped the Marlboro on the path, crushed it with his shoe, and walked back down the path. Earl was dismissing the lines of inmates when Luther and Max returned. Shaking his head, he approached them.

"Ira Hayes ain't here," he said, a gloomy look on his face. His mouth swelled, and he spit chew on the ground. Luther glared at him.

"Why don't you go search for him at Holy Waters Church?"

"What do you mean by that?"

"I mean you had so much to drink this morning you wouldn't have known if Ira was praying or escaping."

"But—"

"Shut your fuckin' mouth!"

Luther brushed past him. Grinning in Earl's face, Max hurried to catch up. When they reached the administration building, Luther unlocked a wall cabinet and removed a tranquilizer gun and a box of darts. The .50-caliber dart had a hypodermic needle loaded with sodium thiopental. He placed the gun and dart on the table.

"Are we goin' huntin'?" Max asked.

"Yes. Call your brother, Deputy Oliver. Tell him to pick us up. We're going to take a trip to the Brick Yard."

"Okay," Max said. He made the call and returned to the table. Luther had finished loading the gun and was aiming it, checking its balance. Max quickly shuffled behind him. "We're all set with Oliver," Max said. "Who you plannin' to put down?"

"Not who, but what. Boonie exercises that wolfhound on Mountain Road the same time every day. We'll wait for him there. The dart will silence the mutt."

"That dog's huge," Max said. "You'd better use double dosage."

"Why take chances?" Luther said. "I used triple dosage."

The Penguins cap pulled tight on his head, Dan Boonie drove the Kawasaki down the middle of the dirt road. Ruggs loped at his side. When Dan approached a wooden bridge, he saw a black-and-white police cruiser blocking the road. He braked the Kawasaki; Ruggs began barking. Deputy Oliver Wright jumped out of the cruiser and held his palms out.

Dan skidded to a stop; Ruggs kept barking and running forward. Luther stepped out from behind the car and shot the dog. Ruggs yelped and fell to the ground, the feathered dart protruding from his neck. Jumping off the Kawasaki, Dan lunged clumsily in Luther's direction. Max tripped him, and when Dan got to his feet, Luther shot a dart in his thigh. Grabbing his leg, Dan collapsed on the road.

Oliver and Max shoved Dan in the backseat of the police cruiser. Then they dumped Ruggs in the trunk. Luther got in the passenger seat; Deputy Oliver started the engine and drove down the road. Max followed behind on the Kawasaki.

The center of the Brick Yard, four acres of abandoned rock and stone hidden in the immense tracts of Rothrock State Forest, was a pit of placid blue water. Sheer cliffs slid into the pit on three sides. The open edge of the pit was rock, sand, and flat, green lily pads.

The police cruiser was parked next to a two-story wooden platform painted with graffiti. The Kawasaki was on the open edge of the pit, its front wheel buried in three feet of water. Dan's body was crunched low on the Kawasaki, his arms stretched forward, his wrists handcuffed to the handlebars. A wooden raft was ten yards out from the bank. Head flat against the wood, chest heaving, Ruggs lay on his side on the raft.

Max slapped Dan in the face. After the second slap, Dan opened his eyes. Sharp pain crossed his chest. Gasping for air, he began to slide off the seat. Deputy Oliver and Max grabbed him by the shoulders and held him. A jovial expression on his face, Luther stepped closer and shouted in his ear.

"Welcome back, Boonie! There was a question whether you would survive or not. The drug is only for large animals. When it's shot into humans, they hyperventilate and then they die. The antidote is at Green Hollow, but I forgot to bring it."

"What do you want?"

"Ira, and, of course, Lisa."

"Go to hell," Dan muttered.

"There's a sudden drop-off in front of the Kawasaki," Luther said. "There's no bottom to this pit. That's where you're going if you refuse to talk."

"I said go to hell!"

"Don't push your luck, Boonie. You survived the first accident. I'm surprised to see you on a motorcycle so soon. You don't even bother to wear a cast on that broken leg anymore. It must be feeling a whole lot better." Luther reached down and picked up a rusty pipe. Then he stepped next to the Kawasaki. When Max moved out of his way, Luther smiled and began tapping on Dan's kneecap. Dan's body began to tremble. Luther's voice came from a long distance.

"I'm going to ask you one more time. Where's Ira?"

"I don't know," Dan said. The heavy tapping shot fire the length of his leg. He lowered his head, fighting tears.

"Well," Luther said. "You decide."

"I don't care!" Dan shouted. "I'm not saying anything!" Dan closed his eyes, and his muscles tensed.

"I was afraid you would be stubborn," Luther sneered. He lifted the pipe and brought it down savagely on Dan's kneecap.

Dan's scream echoed across the water; his body lifted off the leather seat. The handcuffs cut bloody grooves in his wrist. Deputy Oliver and Max pressed hard on Dan's shoulders, forcing him down. Dan heard barking and stared through teary eyes.

Ruggs stood on wobbly legs and shook himself vigorously. The raft seesawed, sending waves across the surface of the pit. Regaining his strength, the Irish wolfhound stretched to his fullest height. His frame a shimmering, angelic silhouette against the bright blue sky, Ruggs glared at the figures on the bank. Then growling, eyes riveted on Dan, the wolfhound stepped to the edge of the platform.

"Stay, Ruggs," Dan whispered.

"The mutt can't hear you. You'll need to raise your voice." Luther cracked Dan's leg again; Dan cried out. In a flurry of motion, Ruggs leapt off the platform. Paws churning the water, the Irish wolfhound swam toward Dan. Luther laughed.

"Not this time," he mumbled. "No rescue this time." Dropping the lead pipe, Luther picked up the tranquilizer gun.

"Wait!" Dan pleaded. "I'll tell you everything! Please don't hurt Ruggs."

Hearing Dan's voice, Ruggs surged forward. Luther aimed the gun. Dan heard a popping sound, caught his breath, and saw the dart sticking in Ruggs's neck. The dog growled, his eyes closed, and his head dropped in the water.

"You bastards!" Dan shouted. A fierce energy tore through his body. Planting his feet firmly, he ripped up his arms, straightening the chain links of the handcuffs. The front tire lifted out of the water.

"Damn it!" Max growled, tripped backward, and fell in the sand. Stumbling, Deputy Oliver lost his grip on Dan. Luther measured the distance, stepped closer, and swung the gun barrel into Dan's head. Dan collapsed on the seat; the motorcycle slid downward at a sharp angle.

Within moments, Dan's face hit the water. Then the weight of the motorcycle pulled Dan's body under. Water whirled around his face and poured inside his ears, creating a hollow roaring sound. Bright, vertical rays slanted down from the surface. Dan saw Ruggs, the massive body of the wolfhound descending in a halo of light.

Dan lunged and grasped handfuls of hair. Pulling Ruggs to him, he buried his head in the dog's neck. Dan felt the weak heartbeat. Streams of bubbles lifted around them. The Penguins cap slid off Dan's head and drifted away with the bubbles. There was a sudden temperature change. The water turned ice-cold. Ruggs shuddered.

Don't worry, Ruggs. I got you, Dan whispered silently, burying his face deeper in the wet fur. *It's only a game. It'll be over soon.*

Tightening his arms around the Irish wolfhound, Dan felt the slightest movement in the dog's chest; then Ruggs was still. Dan began crying, gulping feverously for air. Tears and water filled his lungs. Buoyed upright by the increasing pressure, the Kawasaki sank into darkness.

Standing on the bank, Luther, Max, and Oliver stood silently. The Penguins cap floated to the surface. The bubbles popped lightly around the cap and then disappeared.

Chapter Twenty-Two

Wildwood, New Jersey
Sunday Evening

A moist salt breeze blew off the ocean. Screeching gulls flew overhead. Except for a few people on bicycles and joggers bundled in sweat suits, the Wildwood boardwalk was empty. Relaxing on their boards, a line of six surfers in wet suits faced the horizon. Whitecaps appeared, and two of the surfers dropped on their stomachs and started to paddle rapidly.

Holding hands, Lisa and Ira walked down the boardwalk. Lisa wore a yellow Wildwood sweatshirt. The front of the shirt had an expanse of sand, a large umbrella, and a folding chair open to the sea. The tranquil scene was highlighted with the caption, LIFE IS BETTER AT THE BEACH. Ira wore the blue-and-gold Twin River varsity jacket.

"You look good in Dan's jacket. I don't remember you getting any varsity letters."

"I would have, but the school didn't think street hockey was a real sport."

"The TR letters are special. Dan earned them. Maybe you should return the jacket."

"I'm never going back to Twin River, but I can get JJ to return it. Or Mr. Brooks could." The setting sun cast a golden glow over the ocean. Shouts and laughter from the surfers carried up the beach.

"Can you teach me how to surf?" Lisa asked.

"Sure can. I'll buy you a board tomorrow. But will you have time? You're a working girl now."

"You're working too. Mr. JJ Jackson introduced us to the owner of the Shamrock, and presto, we both start work on Monday. JJ said he'd bring down our new identity cards next week. Our past will be erased. We'll be starting new lives." Lisa spoke in a soft voice. Ira squeezed her hand tightly.

"I can't figure how everything changed so fast. Just this morning, I was in Green Hollow Camp. I was nothing but a punching bag for Luther and Max. Now I'm on the beach with you." They walked silently for a few minutes. Lisa stopped at the railing and stared at the ocean. Her face glistened with tears.

"I …" she began, seeing the alarm on Ira's face. "I'm happy. I'm just so happy."

Lisa and Ira went down the steps, removed their shoes, and strolled to the edge of the waves that were crashing the length of the beach. Thin-legged sandpipers scattered in front of them

"The air's chilly, but the water's so warm," Lisa commented. She released his hand and raced along the edge of the breaking waves. Ira chased after her. They left a deep line of heel-to-toe prints in the sand. Behind them, a splashing sound, sometimes a low roar, the incoming tide rolled waves over the prints, erasing them as they ran.

Cheering for each other, their bodies low and balanced, two of the surfers jumped up on their boards. The lead surfer lost his balance, and arms swinging wildly, he dove headfirst into the churning water. Lisa and Ira laughed and clapped their hands. At the horizon, the sun set with a dazzling display of color and light that spread across the face of the ocean and splashed luminous silver-tipped waves at their feet.

Chapter Twenty-Three

Barree
Sunday Evening

The two puppies circling, yelping at him, Matt sat in the middle of the backyard. Dolly was dragging behind, attempting to keep up with SenSay. Matt stopped the Dalmatian and studied the hind leg. Palladin came down the steps from the guesthouse and shouted angrily. Both Dolly and SenSay yelped and scampered out of his way.

"Matt, what the hell's wrong with you?" Palladin reached the boy and jerked him off the ground. Holding Matt steady, Palladin raised his fist in the air. "I'm going to *clock* you so hard you'll forget the time of day."

"Go ahead. Hit me. I don't care. You're just like Mr. Henry."

"This has nothing to do with Mr. Henry!" Palladin responded loudly. He stared into the oval rabbit eyes, unblinking and bright in the light.

"Go ahead," Matt said. His chest expanding, Matt lifted his chin and closed his eyes.

"Damn it," Palladin muttered, releasing his grip on the boy's arm. There was a dark hand print bruised into the pale skin. Palladin unclenched his fist. Paws stretched out, heads low to the ground, the puppies sat on the grass. Dolly's hind leg twisted to the side.

"I should have *clocked* you real hard," Palladin said.

"But—"

"I don't want to talk about it. I can't stay in Barree with you acting crazy." Palladin glared at the boy. "You can't club people with that Dis Pater weapon."

"I'm sorry."

"*Sorry* doesn't help. What you did in Purgatory was bad. The man was unarmed and helpless." Palladin stood quietly, opening and closing his fist. Dolly yelped weakly and limped toward Matt. Palladin shook his head. "I admit that some of it was my fault. I recognized that recklessness in you. Yet I took you along."

"I didn't plan it," Matt said. "It just happened." Matt lowered his head and spoke softly. "For the good that I will to do, I do not. But the evil I will not to do, I do." Matt reached down and scooped up the puppy. Palladin studied the boy closely.

"What's that you said?"

"St. Paul in Romans." His eyes clear and gleaming, Matt petted the Dalmatian. "Mr. Henry made me read the Bible to him every night. I memorized some of the scripture. I think I am impulsive like you said. My *will* is weak."

"You're transparent in many ways, Matt. You're sincere. You're honest to a fault. You do what you say you're going to do. There's nothing phony about you. Then you change. I see something I don't understand. I don't know who you are."

"During the bad times I don't know either. When I swung Dis Pater, I wasn't me anymore. I was someone else."

"Can you explain that?"

"Yes," Matt said. "It started when Mr. Henry came to me. I pretended I was someone else. I pretended I was somewhere far away. Only Captain Hook knew. He watched me."

"So it was the banker Mr. Henry who caused those nightmares. It sounds to me like you were afraid. You should never be afraid, Matt. You were running away when you needed to stand up and be strong."

"I was just a boy," Matt said, anger rising in his voice. "And I wasn't running. I was trying to hide." Lowering his head, Matt spoke in a contrite voice. "Please don't leave, Mr. Palladin. I have the letter from Mr. Henry. You can take it to the bank and start your job. In the letter Mr. Henry explains everything to Abrams."

"Sure I can stay if that's what you want. But let me explain something to you, Matt. You have to change the way you handle problems or it won't work. When I look at you, when I look deep in those eyes, I don't like what I see."

"What's so bad? What do you see?"

"The same thing I see in the people I kill. Nothing but gloom and fear. You're dead inside. There's no sign of hope."

"What's hope to me?"

"Don't ask me. That's for you to learn on your own." Palladin studied the boy and the crippled Dalmatian in his hands. "You might be able to do it. *Where there's life, there's hope.* Cicero said that. He was a Roman. The Romans honored Dis Pater. Cicero knew the god of death just as you do. When the time comes, you'll have to decide."

"Decide what?"

"Between Dis Pater or hope."

"I always carry Dis Pater," Matt said reflectively. "But I'll try to be better. I'll try really hard to make the right decision *when the time comes.*" Matt carefully maneuvered Dolly in his hand and showed Palladin the Dalmatian's twisted leg. "I'm going to take her to the vet tomorrow morning."

"No, you're not," Palladin said. "Tomorrow's Monday. You're going to school. Then you can take Dolly to the vet. Do you understand?"

"Yes, Mr. Palladin." Matt petted the Dalmatian. SenSay wandered over and chewed on Palladin's pants leg. Matt looked up. "I'm sorry for what I did in Purgatory, Mr. Palladin. Please don't hate me."

"I don't hate you. I can't judge what you did." Dropping to his knee, Palladin petted the collie. "How old are you, Matt?"

"Fourteen."

"In a way, you and I are alike. I was fourteen when I started hurting people. Well, I actually killed a person when I was fourteen. I clubbed him in the head pretty hard."

"That's what I did. I wanted to kill this man. I was careless. He was lucky."

"It wasn't luck, Matt. Someone was looking out for him. And for *you*." Palladin straightened and walked to the guesthouse. Stopping at the steps, he turned and stared at Matt. "Do you remember how you felt last night?"

"Sure. I'll always remember … I felt good, full of energy. I mean, really alive."

"Then we have that in common. I've never understood it. I've never felt comfortable with it, but that's how I felt too."

"Dinky Dow," Matt said in a low voice.

"Are you calling me *crazy*?"

"Yes."

"Why?"

"Because you felt good after doing a bad thing."

"Yes, I felt good. And I've felt good about all the bodies since then. Maybe we're both a little crazy." Palladin was quiet for a moment. The puppies scampered around, growling, crashing soft, furry bodies into each other. "But all my contracts were rotten criminals. They deserved to die."

"What about your first one?"

"I guess he deserved it. Dad called him a *scumbag*. His name was Henry. I'll never forget that name. Sometimes I have nightmares like you do. Nightmares about Henry. In the worst ones, I hear his wife's voice. She's calling Henry from that damn dock. Actually, it's more of a shriek than a call. I can't shut her up."

"I hear voices all the time. They only stop when I wake up screaming. I hate nightmares. Sometimes I feel I'd rather be dead."

"No one would rather be dead, Matt. That's the easy way out. You're young. You're strong. And you're no phony. You'll get over those nightmares. If you need help, I'll be here. Your girlfriend Alice ... she definitely can help. She was great at Purgatory."

"Yes. she was great at Purgatory," Matt said. "She's great everywhere. I'd be lost without Alice."

Crickets chirped back and forth across the yard. Matt clapped his hands; SenSay growled and ran to him. The Dalmatian moved playfully in front of the collie and was knocked down. Rolling over in the grass, Dolly made a whining noise and struggled to stand on the crippled leg. Matt reached down and gently picked up the Dalmatian. Palladin climbed the steps and walked into the guesthouse.

When Mr. Wilson pulled into the lane, he saw Wayne shooting baskets at the barn. He parked the truck and stood there watching ball after ball drop through the rusty rim. Wayne saw him and walked over.

"Dad, can I have six dollars to buy a net? The old one was all ripped up."

"I'll buy you one when we come back." Mr. Wilson saw the expression on Wayne's face. "We're going to stay with my brother for a couple of months."

"What about school?"

"I explained everything to Mr. Port. He said it was all right. Go pack some stuff."

"What about basketball?"

"It can wait. Now do as you're told."

Head lowered, Wayne walked into the house and returned with his gym bag bulging at the sides. Mr. Wilson turned on the porch light and locked the door. When he got in the truck and started the engine, Wayne noticed the hard features on his face.

"Is this about our trouble with Cain and Abel, Dad?"

Mr. Wilson didn't answer. He accelerated down Polecat Hollow Road and turned onto Route 22. He drove through Huntingdon, through Mapleton, but slowed when he approached the Narrows along the Juniata River. Cars were pulling into the parking area next to the Thousand Steps Trail. Wayne saw people carrying gallon jugs from the spring at the base of the trail. Two hikers walked to the steep trail that zigzagged more than a mile up the side of Jacks Mountain.

"The Thousand Steps are crowded today, Dad."

"The quarries on that mountain are what brought your Wilson kin to this area," Mr. Wilson said, taking a quick glance at his son. "At that time, the railroad, glass, and iron industries needed our silica bricks. You wouldn't know anything about that because you weren't born yet. Cousin Jeb, who was fifteen and nothing but skin and bones, fell off those steps with a sack of sandstone strapped to his back. The mountain cut his face so bad his own ma couldn't recognize him. The Thousand Steps are cursed with the blood of the workers."

Mr. Wilson drove through Mount Union in silence. It took him twenty minutes to reach Burnt Cabins. A gravel road led to a two-story wooden house. There was a large garden in front of the house. The wire fence that enclosed the garden was rusty and leaned close to the ground. As Mr. Wilson parked the truck, the front door opened, and Becky stepped onto the porch. She wore the same pink dress with the large red roses. Holding the railing, walking carefully, she descended the steps and hugged her dad.

"Where's the family?" Mr. Wilson asked.

"Out shopping," Becky answered. She rushed over to Wayne and hugged him, brushing her hand across the cut on his chin. "What happened?"

"It's nothing."

"Walk with me," Becky said, taking his hand. They went around the garden and down a path into the woods. Dry leaves cracked under their feet. A crow cawed from high in the trees.

"I miss you," Wayne said "What do you do down here?"

"Nothing," Becky said. "Just waiting for the baby." She managed to smile. "Uncle Hector don't talk to me at all. He's a severe Christian. He doesn't like my condition, but he puts up with me because of Dad. His wife Louise talks to me some, but she never smiles." Becky squeezed Wayne's hand. "I don't like it here. It's scary. The Rubeck farm where Bicycle Pete was killed is on the other side of the ridge."

"That happened ten, fifteen years ago, Becky. The man was deranged. He kidnapped that schoolgirl. He killed that FBI man. But they chased him down. They say that Larry Rubeck—he was just a kid no older than me—shot Bicycle Pete."

"Uncle Hector was one of the chasers."

"Does he brag about it?"

"Sometimes he does. Uncle Hector claimed he ran out of bullets he was shooting so fast and furious. He keeps his rifle loaded and right above the door. He said it's wild and dangerous in these mountains. He said *bad things were comin' to Burnt Cabins!* He was looking at me ... looking at my stomach when he said it."

"He's crazy."

"He's watching for signs. Yesterday near the garden a possum bared its teeth and came after him. He shot it but wouldn't bury it. I told him the possum had rabies and all the critters eating it would get rabies. He still wouldn't go near it. Last night I took the shovel, dug a hole in the woods, and buried it."

"You shouldn't have gone near it."

"No one else would," Becky said.

They walked to a circular pond in the middle of a clearing. The water reflected blue sky; lily pads grew thick along the edges. Frogs croaked and sprang in unison the length of the bank, splashing through the leafy pads. Becky and Matt sat on a wooden bench. Her face was blushed, bright in the light."

"I have a beautiful sister," Wayne said. Becky laughed and placed Wayne's palm on her stomach.

"Can you feel anything?"

"Yes," Wayne said, spreading his fingers open. "Your stomach is, I think, getting rounder and rounder."

"It's getting bigger. Too big. I think there's more than one baby."

"Twins!" Wayne said loudly, an astonished expression on his face.

"At night, I feel them struggling. It's like they're fighting each other. Then there's nothing for days. It's hard for me to understand. I know part of them, the Wilson part, will be normal and strong. But I'm not sure about the other part." Becky was silent. A breeze blew; orange-and-yellow leaves fell from the trees, glided downward, and landed lightly on the water. Wayne removed his hand.

"Cain was asking about you."

"I don't want to talk about Cain. I'm scared of him. I'm scared of the Reverend Towers and the whole family."

"There's nothing to be scared of," Wayne said. "Dad and I will help you through this." A car horn sounded from the house. They sat there quietly. When the horn sounded again, they got up and walked toward the path in the woods.

Alice Byrd drove under the portico and left her bicycle next to the Eldorado. She knocked on the door, and when no one answered, Alice went inside.

"Matt," she called as she walked from room to room. She heard music and opened the kitchen door. *Live and Let Die* drifted across the yard from the guesthouse. "Matt," she called again. Wearing a white apron, Mr. Palladin appeared on the steps.

"Matt's not here. I think he went to Conner's. Do you want to wait for him? I'm cooking trout. There's plenty. You can eat some."

"No, thanks," Alice said. "I don't understand him sometimes. I thought we were going to the movies with Conner and Alice. We all wanted to see *Caddyshack*. But it's too late now. When Matt shows up, tell him I went home."

Alice waved, walked around the house to the portico, and got on her bicycle. She pedaled down the lane and through the gate. Approaching the steep incline that dropped into Barree, she saw the outline of a vehicle backed into the trees. Alice braked, pedaled forward slowly, and stared curiously at the Minnie Winnie.

"I got you this time!" Max shouted. Panting heavily, he charged out of the brush and stuffed a rag soaked with chloroform in her face. She fell into his arms. After dropping her body in the Minnie Winnie, Max carted the bicycle deep into the woods. Returning to the Minnie Winnie, he started the engine and coasted down the hill. The sky was gray when he drove past the two massive hog heads in front of the Happy Hollow Hunt Club.

Max blew the horn at the barn, and Luther came to the door. They carried Alice to a yellow Winnebago Chieftain and took her to the bedroom. The room was lavishly furnished. Luther placed Alice on a king-sized bed under an ornate canopy. Gold-framed mirrors slanted down from the corners. Eyes shifting from mirror to mirror, Max watched as Luther undressed Alice. Tossing the clothes in a basket, Luther pulled a silk sheet over Alice. He gave the basket to Max.

"Burn these with the trash."

"She's real pretty, isn't she?" Max asked. They walked outside.

"She sure is. You did good tonight, Max. Nathaniel will be pleased."

"I'm plum tired out with all these jobs. I've been thinkin' about vacation."

"I already told Nathaniel that we'd be gone for a few weeks."

"We vacationin' in Wildwood like we always do?"

"You bet," Luther said. "My cousin Albert has those spare rooms available for us. Wildwood Beach during the day and Atlantic City during the night. That's the plan."

"I can hardly wait," Max said. "You can't find nothin' like Wildwood in these mountains. There's always fun and new surprises. Life is way better at the beach." They walked outside, and Luther locked the door. Max grabbed Luther by the arm.

"Can I see her? Can I see Heather?"

Shaking his head, Luther walked to the neighboring Winnebago, put the key in the lock, and pushed the door open. Max rushed past him and clicked on the lights. Heather was in the bed, her body covered by a silk sheet. Startled, she opened her eyes, saw Max, and began crying. Luther clicked off the lights and pushed Max outside.

"That's enough," he said.

"But the fun was just startin'," Max complained. "I like it when they cry."

"I know you do," Luther said. "I told Nathaniel that Heather has a good voice. He plans to have her do some singing on the video. It adds a different twist to the product."

"It sure does," Max said, fingering the clothes in the basket. "Nathaniel's pretty smart that way. Maybe I can teach Heather to do some singin' for me."

Max laughed and walked outside to the trash barrel. Taking the clothes out of the basket one piece at a time, he dropped them in the barrel. When he came to the pink panties, Max held them to his nose and breathed deeply. Then he shoved them in his back pocket. Lighting a match, he tossed it in the barrel. Max backed away as flames boiled over the side, sending sparks in the night air.

Chapter Twenty-Four

Huntingdon/Barree
Sunday Evening

After buying four tickets at the Huntingdon Theatre, Gene handed one to his wife, one to Conner, and one to Cindy. They entered the theatre together.

"We're sitting here in the last row where we can watch both of you," Lucy said.

"Oh, Mom, we're not going to do anything."

"Just make sure you don't." She dropped into the seat. Gene sat next to her.

"I'd better enjoy this movie," he said. "If I don't, you're in a lot of trouble."

"Oh, you'll enjoy it, Dad. *Caddyshack* is hilarious. You and Mom will be laughing all the way home."

Conner led Cindy to the side aisle and looked back at his mom, who was watching them. Conner waved, and he and Cindy shuffled to the last seats against the wall. Holding hands, they sat down. Cindy had a smile on her face.

"I saw Hombre at the house. How did that happen?"

"I don't know, but Mom likes the dog. And Dad does too. He said he had a pet German shepherd when he was in Vietnam. He named that one Hondo."

"He did seem happy. How did you get out of being grounded?"

"It was Dad," Conner explained. "He told Mom that he ordered me to stay with Matt, that I was obligated to go to Philadelphia and watch out for him. Dad said that's what friends do. Mom agreed with him right away. She said she was sick from worrying, but she was happy that everything worked out. When I saw that relieved look on her face, I knew I had to try. I asked her if she would take us to see *Caddyshack*. When she said yes, I was surprised. Dad was surprised too. So here we are."

"What about when the guy shouts out, 'We're all going to get laid'?"

"Oh," Conner said. "That's not until the end. We'll have gotten our money's worth by then." The lights dimmed; some people clapped. Conner leaned back and put his arm around Cindy.

Palladin finished eating the trout, dropped the dish and fork in the sink, and walked to the portico. He had begun wiping off the Eldorado when he heard squealing tires. The blue Pontiac Sunbird raced down the lane and screeched to a stop. The passenger door flew open. Wearing jeans and his blue Valley Forge Academy shirt, Cody Romano jumped out. Clenching his fists, Cody ran at Palladin.

"You bastard!" he shouted.

Palladin didn't move; he squinted slightly as the fist angled toward his face. The punch landed solidly and knocked him down. He looked up at Cody.

"I guess I deserved that," Palladin said. Cody was red-faced and fuming. Jane got out of the Sunbird, walked over to Palladin, and reached out her hand.

"I don't know whether to kick you or kiss you," she said. Palladin took her hand and got to his feet. Feeling his swollen jaw, he spoke with some discomfort.

"Let's try the kiss first." Palladin pulled Jane to him. Her body was soft and warm, and hinted of fresh lilac. Meeting no resistance, Palladin kissed her. Cody attempted to squeeze between them.

"Move back, Mom. I want to smash him again."

"You only get one of those," Palladin warned.

"But, sir, you punched me three or four times! Our house burned down! Then you kidnapped me! And ..." Cody hesitated.

"And what?"

"Sir, my Corvette burned in the fire!" Cody blurted.

"You still only get one punch." Palladin turned to Jane. "Where's your husband?"

"He's with Scavone. Two men broke into the safe house. They killed the guard. Caesar left with them."

"How did you get away?"

"Mr. Jackson, you called him JJ, took us out the back exit. He was worried. He said he didn't know how long he could protect us. He sent us here."

"I'm glad he did. There's plenty of room." Palladin looked at the teenager ... the glaring eyes, the angry face. "Cody, you have to relax. Sure, I knocked you around a bit. But I had to make it look real. It was for your own good."

"Sure it was."

"I'll tell you what, Cody. It's not the same as your Corvette, but you can drive the Eldorado whenever you need to get out."

"I can?"

"Yes," Palladin said. "Now come inside. I'll show you your rooms. And if you're hungry or thirsty, there's plenty of food and soda in the kitchen." Palladin opened the door for them. "Not you, Cody, but, Jane, if you need something with a little more kick, I have stronger drinks in the guesthouse."

"I need that kick right now," she said, a smile on her face. "Do you think we'll be safe here?"

"We're a long way from Philly, but no, we won't be safe here."

"How long before Scavone finds us?"

"That depends on what your husband tells him."

"Dad will tell him anything he wants to know," Cody said. Palladin and Jane both looked at the boy.

"What makes you say that?" Palladin asked.

"I was in the kitchen. I heard Dad talking to Mr. Scavone on the phone just before the men broke into the house. Dad said he was going to return all the money. Then he said he would wrap up his beautiful wife in yellow ribbons and hand her over as a gift." Cody lowered his eyes. "I'm sorry, Mom, but that's what he said."

"What did he say about you?"

"He told Scavone that he would train me. I could work for the mob."

"Then you got off easy," Palladin said.

"I would never let them hurt Mom. I grabbed a chair. I was about to smash it over his head when the men came. They were quick. They had the key to the door and killed Mr. Jake. I don't know his last name. We were lucky Mr. Jackson was there."

"Or I would be wrapped in yellow ribbons," Jane said. She hugged her son. They went into the house. SenSay and Dolly came yelping across the floor.

"I hope you like puppies," Palladin said.

The sky was darkening; the sun was low on the horizon. Wearing jeans and a blue V-neck sweater, Abel walked down the gravel path to the Flaming Cross. His green eyes were bright, his face tan, chiseled smooth. Abel slowed when he saw the Reverend Jeremiah Towers sitting on the bench.

The gaunt figure was dressed in his pitch-black suit, black shirt, and black bow tie. Holding the crutch in his hand, digging the pointed end into the dirt, the reverend stared across the river at the grand Twin River vista of pastures, hills, and forests. Abel approached slowly and positioned himself in front of the bench; the reverend looked up.

"I found your crutch."

"I don't need it anymore."

"You did an excellent job with the music this morning."

"That's the first time I did it alone. I was surprised. Where's Cain? Why wasn't he at church?"

"Cain's on a trip," the Reverend Towers said softly.

"When's Cain coming back?"

The reverend didn't respond. He dug the crutch into the ground; a coned circle appeared at his feet. Lifting the crutch with both hands, the Reverend Towers brought it down hard in the middle of the cone.

"Abel, how did you like the sermon this morning?"

"It was powerful. The people were like … spellbound." Cain looked at the crutch. "But I thought you spent a lot of time talking about the Catacombs."

"Was my talk long?" the reverend asked. "I didn't notice."

"You invited the parishioners to take a tour, to walk through the Catacombs of Rapture. You invited them to see the blessed dead."

"Yes, I did that."

"You asked them to visit Irene's memorial. You asked them to listen to her hymn, to talk with her, to join her in prayer for all sinners."

"Yes, I did that too."

"Then I played *Amazing Grace*. The church was dead-quiet."

"Abel, I believe that was the only time during the service that I was disappointed with you."

"Why? What was wrong?"

"I expected you to play *Bringing in the Sheaves*."

"I'm sorry. I hit the wrong button."

"I know. I listened to *Amazing Grace*. It made me feel uncomfortable."

"Why, it's a beautiful hymn."

"It is," the reverend agreed. "Very beautiful. But it's wrong to play it now."

"I don't understand. How can it be wrong?"

"It's wrong because grace is dead in Twin River. *Grace* died when Irene died. It died when you stood here and watched your brother push her off the cliff into the darkness."

"Dad—"

"Please don't call me that."

"Reverend Towers, it didn't happen that way. Irene tripped and fell."

"Is that how she died?" the reverend asked. He took a cassette player from his pocket. "I had a recorder placed at her memorial. It was reassuring to listen to the people's voices, so sincere in their praise, so blessed in their prayers. It brought tears, proud tears, to my eyes."

"I didn't know."

"Of course you didn't know. Neither you nor Cain knew. The other night while I was listening, I heard familiar voices." Standing, the reverend hit the button; the tape began to play. The last notes of *Bringing in the Sheaves* sounded. Then the voices began:

"Damn it, Abel. Why did you put in that damn sensor?"

"The reverend likes to listen to Mom's gospel music … That day on the mountain, Cain, why'd you do it? Why'd you push Mom?"

"The opportunity presented itself."

"But why? She was loving it here."

"She was always ordering me to do things. When she squeaked, 'In one ear and out the other' for the hundredth time, I nudged her just a little."

The echo of Cain's laughter lingering on the mountainside, the cassette player clicked off. The sun dropped behind the distant hills; Twin River was in darkness. Suddenly, there was a blinding glow. The Flaming Cross ignited in brilliance. The Reverend Jeremiah Towers lifted the crutch and stuck the pointed tip into Abel's chest.

"Please," Abel whispered.

"We are cursed," the reverend muttered. "And the Lord said to him, 'Therefore whoever kills Cain, vengeance shall be taken on him sevenfold.'" The reverend stepped forward; the point of the crutch tore the fabric of the sweater and pierced the skin. Abel tripped backward.

"Please stop." Abel's voice was a whimper. The Reverend Jeremiah Towers turned toward the Flaming Cross. The incandescence scorching his eyes, he shouted to the light.

"For these are the days of vengeance!"

"It was Cain," Abel pleaded, his shoes scraping against the loose stone at the edge of the cliff. Dark patches of blood smeared through the blue fabric of his sweater. "You heard it on the tape. Cain pushed her. Cain killed her."

"You were his twin. You and Cain were one in thought and spirit." The crutch trembled in the reverend's hands, the tip cutting deeper into Cain's skin. "Irene was precious to me. To God. For what I am about to do, I accept His vengeance *sevenfold*."

"You can't harm me. I'm your son!"

"Isn't that interesting?" the Reverend Towers sneered. "Cain said the exact same thing before he died." Moving closer, the reverend delivered a powerful thrust.

"You killed Cain!" Abel exclaimed, planting his feet firmly on the stone. The point of the crutch dug into his skin. "You killed my brother!" His lips twisted grotesquely with the words; a fierce loathing disfigured his face. Grabbing the crutch, he ripped the metal point away, tearing the sweater, leaving a deep gash.

"You shouldn't have killed my brother," Abel muttered. He wrenched the crutch from the reverend's hands, stuck the rubber support under the bony armpit, and hurled the fragile body over the cliff.

Nothing but a scarecrow, he thought. His arms swinging through the air, the Reverend Towers fell with a whimper of an echo. His body cracked into the rocks and slid into a deep crevice, a bloody sock and the heel of his shoe protruding from the crack.

Abel stood in the radiance of the Flaming Cross. Bats flew in and out of the light. A wolf howled from the abyss. Abel's chest burned. Tears began forming in his eyes; he blinked them away. Abel brushed his hand across his torn sweater and raised bloody fingers to the cross.

"I never cry," he whispered. Tears streaming down his face, Abel stood transfixed. The quiet at the summit of Redemption Mountain was stifling. Breathing heavily, his vision blurred, Abel heard the slightest hint of laughter. The laughter, more of a cackle, was replaced by a clear, sonorous voice. Abel recognized the voice immediately. Turning from the light of the cross, staring into the looming silhouette of Blood Mountain across the river, Abel marveled at the sound that had guided him all his life. The voice was clear and strong; Abel listened to the directives.

Yes, he mumbled. *Yes, I'll find Becky.* The rapids echoed a low moaning noise; clouds of mist billowed up the side of Blood Mountain. *Yes, I'll bring her and the child to the Catacombs of Rapture.* The Shadows of Death increased in size and cast a dark shroud over the summit. *Yes, I will see your son born, and I will call him Cain.*

Abel wiped the moisture from his face and took deep breaths. Turning, humming softly, *When our weeping's over, He will bid us welcome; we shall come rejoicing, bringing in the sheaves*, Abel walked down the path to the Catacombs of Rapture. His thoughts were on the small chapel in the back corner of the catacombs. Bereaved relatives would kneel with the Reverend Towers and pray devoutly. It was a holy room.

And now a prison, Abel thought. *I'll need to start right away. The room must be ready for Becky and the child.* Abel smiled as he approached the entrance to the catacombs.

The Huntingdon Theatre was packed. The sky on the screen was blue and clear. Dressed in khaki pants, long sleeved red-and-black striped golf shirt, teenage caddie Michael O'Keefe stood with Chevy Chase in the middle of the tree-lined fairway. His brown, wavy hair curling low over his forehead, Michael looked with concern at Chevy, who was nervously brandishing a golf club.

"See your future," Chevy pleaded. "Be your future." Gesticulating with the driver, Chevy pressed the iron shaft into Michael's body. "Make your future." Chevy spoke in bursts, his hands moving erratically.

"Take it easy," Michael said. He took the driver from Chevy and walked to the ball on the fairway. Michael positioned his feet in a wide, comfortable stance. A rolling hill, two sand traps, and the flag were in the distance. Michael swung the driver with power and grace. The ball sailed over the sand traps and landed on the green.

In the glare of bright sunlight, club members and caddies surrounded the last hole. Judge Smails pulled a putter from the bag, shook his head, and replaced it. The judge looked at his caddie.

"This calls for the old Billy Baroo." The judge waited. When the caddie handed him the putter, Smails removed the royal purple custom-woven wool cover and pressed the putter to his lips. "Billy, Billy," he repeated several times in a prayer-like voice. "This is a *bigee*! Don't let me down, Billy."

His mouth still mumbling in prayer, the judge positioned himself, swung the club smoothly, and sent the ball in a fast, straight line to the bottom of the hole, putting his team ahead by one shot, dooming the young caddie's existence. The finely-attired club members were ecstatic.

The packed crowd in the Huntingdon Theatre fell into a hushed silence. Conner sat on the edge of his seat. Cindy gripped Conner's hand tightly. On the screen, Michael surveyed the green, surveyed the line of the long putt. He stepped back.

"$80,000 on this one putt," Cindy whispered. "It's for college. It's for his future!"

"He sinks it," Conner said. "Or the poor kid works in a lumberyard for the rest of his life."

"I can't look," Cindy said, placing her hand over her eyes. Fingers split open, Cindy squinted at the screen. "Please, God," she prayed.

Chevy Chase casually walked up to Michael and handed him the putter. "Don't worry about this one," he said, nudging the caddie on the shoulder. "You miss it. We lose." Chevy didn't smile.

Low, white clouds now covered the sky. Out of sight, crouching on a nearby green, wearing a wrinkled camouflage hat, groundskeeper and gopher exterminator, Bill Murray, leaned over an old splintered blasting box. He had a frown on his face when he carefully tightened the rusted wing nuts. Studying the wires that led to his unique concoction of plastic explosives buried in the gopher holes, the groundskeeper twisted his lips in anguish, and with a hint of sorrow, he mumbled the stirring notes: *Silver wings upon their chest. These are men, America's best.*

Michael waited alone on the green. The caddies encouraged their fellow low-waged employee with nodding heads and whispered words of support. "You can do it," one said, pointing at Michael. Smiling with exuberance, Rodney Dangerfield waved his hand in approval. His face wet with perspiration, Michael walked up to the ball and settled himself comfortably into position. Focusing with steely determination, he swung the putter, tapping the ball forward. The ball rolled smoothly across the perfectly-trimmed green, slowed to a crawl, stopped, and tottered at the edge of the hole. Michael O'Keefe lowered his head. At the Huntingdon Theatre, Cindy gasped; Conner collapsed in the seat. A suffocating pall hung over the packed rows of stunned viewers.

His head turning suspiciously to the right and to the left, the groundskeeper appeared on the screen again. Bill Murray mumbled *four* in a respectful tone, vigorously pushed down on the plunger, and detonated the plastic explosives. Flames and smoke erupted over the Bushwood Country Club. Trees swayed; the earth shook. Making squeaking noises, a furry gopher scampered down the burrow, a wall of flames behind it. Above, alarmed at the fire clouds and billowing smoke, the crowd of spectators panicked. Then everyone quieted and focused on the ball in the middle of the green. A series of vibrations moved across the grass. Tilting precariously, the ball dropped into the hole.

Cheering and yelling erupted in the theatre. Hands swinging wildly, people jumped high in the air. Cindy pulled Conner off the seat and hugged him. Animated on the screen, leading a raucous crowd, Rodney Dangerfield broadcast loudly.

"We're all going to get laid!"

"Yes!" Conner shouted as the theatre thundered with laughter and jubilation. In the last row, Lucy Brooks was clapping her hands. Gene leaned close and whispered.

"Let's get the hell home and follow Rodney's advice."

"You wish," Lucy said. "I never laughed so much. I just wonder where Matt and Alice are. Conner said he called them."

"They're probably out having a good time. Matt's a good golfer. I bet they'll both want to see *Caddyshack* after talking to Conner and Cindy. We'll all come back and watch it again."

There was a lull in the noise for a moment. Making squeaking noises, a gopher emerged from the hole in the center of the green and danced around. As fire and smoke lifted in the air around the trashed golf course, loud whistles and cheering echoed off the theatre walls. The credits began scrolling to the lyrics of Kenny Loggins, *I'm Alright!*

> *I'm alright*
> *Nobody worry 'bout me*
> *You got to gimme a fight*
> *Why don't you just let me be*

Music from the surround-sound speakers bombarded the theatre. Conner and Cindy pushed their way into the jammed aisle. When they reached the last row, Gene and Lucy were laughing. Conner shouted, "Did you like the movie?" The noise was too loud; his parents continued talking and laughing. Reaching the lobby in the crush of people, Conner held onto Cindy's waist. The boisterous music and lyrics followed them into the street.

> *Do what you like*
> *Doing it nat'rally*
>
> *It's your life*
> *And isn't it a mystery*

Chapter Twenty-Five

Blood Mountain
Sunday Evening

Dressed in a loose-fitting Twin River sweatshirt and old jeans, Matt Henry stood on the porch of Conner's house. He hugged and petted Hombre, and then put the puppy inside the screen door. A green Dodge Colt came down the road and pulled into the drive. The door opened, and a tall man wearing a Penn State sweatshirt stepped out. Matt walked down the steps and called out in a surprised voice.

"Jeffery," he said. Reaching the car, he shook hands. "I thought you had left for good. Mr. Brooks said you were never coming back to Twin River."

"I have to see him. Is he here?" Jeffery's gaze swept past the empty garage. He looked at the house. "Is he here?" Jeffery asked again.

"No," Matt answered. "No one's here but me." He stood there awkwardly silent, his mind racing, the palm of his hand resting nervously on Dis Pater. "But I know where Mr. Brooks is."

"Where?"

"Blood Mountain," Matt said. "I can take you to him."

"I don't like Blood Mountain," Jeffery said. "In fact, I hate Blood Mountain. I was nearly killed there. I still have a scar. I'll wait for Mr. Brooks right here." He started toward the house; Matt stepped in front of him.

"Mr. Brooks said he had something important to do. He won't come back until late tonight. Maybe tomorrow morning. We can go to Blood Mountain together. Nothing will happen. I'm sure Mr. Brooks will be glad to see you." A frown on his face, Jeffery hesitated a moment.

"Okay," Jeffery said. He and Matt got in the car. When they reached the base of the mountain, Matt jumped out and rushed down the overgrown path to the utility shed. Taking the key from under the rock, he unlocked the door and pulled out the red four-wheeler. Matt quickly returned to the car. He motioned to Jeffery.

"I can drive," he said.

"Isn't this Mr. Brooks's ATV?"

"Yes."

"Why didn't he take it up the mountain?"

"I don't know," Matt said. "You can ask him when you see him."

Shrugging, Jeffery slid onto the seat. Matt gunned the motor down the straight section of trail, slowing slightly when he started the ascent. Jeffery held on to Matt's shoulders on the sharp bends. Matt drove at a fast speed. The sun dropped lower on the horizon. Dark shadows formed along the trail. When Matt reached the summit, he stopped a short distance from the towering pine tree.

"I don't see anyone," Jeffery commented, getting off the four-wheeler. The bed of pine needles snapped under his shoes. Emitting a dull glow, the sun set; the sky turned black. Then on Redemption Mountain, the ascendant light flared, one bulb flashing after another, forming the brilliant Flaming Cross. His face smooth and bright, Jeffery stood transfixed in the warming, incandescent glow. He raised his hand and pointed.

"Look," he said. Jeffery turned slowly. Matt lifted Dis Pater. When he brought it down, the silver hammer radiated an ominous, portentous beauty.

I am the grim reaper, Matt thought with complete satisfaction. *Doing what Mr. Brooks did before he changed. Doing what Mr. Palladin does now. Slaying those who have sinned.* The death hammer struck Jeffery in the head. His eyes closed, and Jeffery fell heavily to the pine needles.

In the evening darkness, a heavy mist lifted over the Juniata River. It cloaked the Flaming Cross and rose in thick layers around Blood Mountain. Standing on the edge of the cliff, Matt faced the Shadows of Death. The wind stirred; the shadows swirled around him. He saw the man again; Mr. Henry had not aged. His face was sickly pale and wrinkled with dark lines. A sudden stench of tepid air struck Matt. The shadows rose from the abyss.

> *The shirtless, flabby figure of Mr. Henry materialized. Mr. Henry pinned the boy to the bed and tore away his pajamas. When Mr. Henry crushed him with his weight, Matt smelled the stench of whiskey and sweat. Eyes disfigured, Captain Hook stood motionless behind Mr. Henry. The shadows darkened, and the grinning god of death, Dis Pater, stepped forward.*

Finding it difficult to breathe, Matt slid his hand along the rawhide cord and clutched the green arrowhead. The sharp point cut into his palm. He saw a thin line of blood flow between his fingers. Releasing the arrowhead, Matt turned and walked with heavy, scraping steps. The narrow path wound through a field of chest-high Indiangrass, shrubs, and large boulders. A fire flickered in the darkness. Flames rose in the air, casting light on the massive pine tree and the shirtless body of Jeffery Turner lashed to it.

Avoiding two large ant mounds, Matt stopped at the tree. Jeffery's wrists were bound behind the tree; his shoulder muscles were taut and bulging. A thin scar cut across his ribbed abdominal muscles.

"I was here when Mr. Brooks gave you that scar," Matt said. Jeffery lifted his head painfully and stared at the boy.

"Why are you doing this?" he asked.

"Mr. Brooks was supposed to *dispatch* you for what you did to the girls. Instead, he was weak. He let you go. But I'm not like that. I'm not weak." Matt slowly, resolutely slid out the death hammer.

"Don't."

"But I have to." Matt glared at Jeffery. "Another girl has gone missing."

"Mr. Brooks told me about the kidnapping," Jeffery pleaded. "That's why I returned. I want to help."

"You can't help," Matt blurted. Dis Pater was heavy in his hand. The fire cracked; a cinder rose in the air and landed next to the tree. An owl hooted high in the branches.

Then there was a thunder of noise, and the Shadows of Death spilled over the summit. Matt watched the ballooning clouds creep across the open ground, darkening the field of grass and large boulders. A roaring noise filled Matt's ears. He felt extreme pressure in his nose. A blood vessel broke. The crimson liquid flowed over his lips into his mouth. He gagged and coughed uncontrollably, spitting blood over Jeffery.

"Don't," Jeffery murmured again, blinking against the spray.

Whirling closer, morphing incandescent at the fire, the shadows enveloped Matt and Jeffery. The roaring noise grew louder. Matt shook his head. Dis Pater tingled with electricity. His entire arm trembling, Matt spoke through the dull crescendo of sound echoing through his head.

"Someone must protect the girls. Or it will go on … and on . . ." Matt's voice trailed off to a whisper. His countenance turned vicious.

"But I know their names!" Jeffery shouted, purple veins bulging on his neck. "I can stop the kidnappers!"

"What?" Matt asked. Jeffery's words were mute, unrecognizable in the roar.

The fire flared; the flames threw a flickering glow across Jeffery's face. His eyes were glassy, the irises a perfect shade of blue. Beads of moisture streaming down his face, Jeffery breathed deeply; his lips quivered.

"What?" Matt asked again. A bewildered expression clouded his face. Lifting the death hammer, he stepped closer.

"Please …" Jeffery said weakly.

Screaming out, Matt swung Dis Pater with a savage quickness. Blood spattered across Matt's face, dripped onto his sweatshirt. Crimson droplets formed irregular patterns on the ground. Matt shuddered, shaking his head. He heard a popping sound. The roaring noise in his ears stopped suddenly.

In the eerie silence that followed, there was the lightest of clicking sounds. A streaming line of ants emptied from the coned mound of dirt and pine needles. The lead ants crawled over Jeffery's shoes and onto the exposed skin. The fire blazed and cracked bright cinders in the air. The Shadows of Death dissipated. The North Star and the Big Dipper glittered brightly in the night sky.

Dis Pater, a cumbersome weight in his grip, Matt backed away from the tree, turned, and walked around the boulders and shrubs and into the field of Indiangrass. The grass was blue-green and supported large golden seed heads. The death hammer made a sinister hissing sound going through the blades of grass. Stomping forward, Matt found himself at the edge of the cliff. The river below shimmered brightly; the faint, flashing lights of a train glowed over the vaulted arches of the darkened bridge.

Feet unsteady on the moist, grainy stone, Matt hesitated. He was confused, dizzy at the ominous vacuity in front of him. There was a sudden weakness in his legs. A beckoning murmur echoed from the distant rapids. Matt leaned awkwardly on the slippery precipice.

So easy to fall, Matt thought. A heavy wind blew over Blood Mountain. Behind him, Matt heard a rustling sound; he sensed Mr. Henry crushing through the Indiangrass. Matt shivered uncontrollably as he always did in his nightmares. Closing his eyes, searching for his safe hiding place, he was an easy step away. Dis Pater pulled at him.

Matt felt Mr. Henry nudge his shoulder blade; an abhorrent odor of decay rose around him. Wobbling precariously close to the void, Matt wished himself free … slid his foot forward. Then a fierce, unfathomable force moved through his body. His eyes opening wide in bewilderment, Matt *caught* himself. He slowly, carefully regained his balance and straightened to his fullest height.

The dull lights of the train moved off the bridge. A wolf howled. Matt turned and looked back. Through a distance obscured by the slanting dry stalks of grass, he saw the pine tree and the shadowy body lashed to it. A sliver of stone cracked at his feet and fell into the shadows.

"I'm not afraid anymore!" Matt screamed vehemently. On the summit of Redemption Mountain, the Flaming Cross radiated a brilliant glow.

"And I'm not crazy!" he broadcast loudly to the light. A dead weight, Dis Pater tugged at his shoulder. Matt moved away from the ledge. His mind raced, inexplicably filling his head with images of Palladin, the golf club, and the TV comedian he had never fathomed as a boy. Matt slid his feet into his most comfortable golfing stance. When he lifted Dis Pater over his shoulder, he repeated in a steady voice the words he had heard—*even the runway has eighteen holes.* Visualizing briefly the craters and blasted runway, Matt relaxed. A smile cracked the hard features of his face.

"I didn't forget, Mr. Palladin," Matt whispered, his lips barely moving. "Just like you said, Hope was … is funny. Hope feels good."

Concentrating with steely determination, taking a smooth, flawless swing, Matt flung Dis Pater over the cliff. The death hammer spiraled through the air, disappeared briefly in the lingering Shadows of Death, and splashed into the river. Protruding from the swirling current, its sharpened edge spattered with crimson, Dis Pater cast a black, pulsating shadow over the fast-flowing water.

Standing motionless, Matt stared at Dis Pater for the longest time. Then he heard a sound, a weak moaning sound coming through the field of Indiangrass. Listening intently, Matt turned away from the cliff. The words were obscure at first. Then he heard the name clearly—*Matt. Matt.* Without any hesitation, he began running full stride, his whole body disappearing inside the field of flowing, fragrant grass. Sprinting forward, his hands swishing loosely through the dry, slender blades, Matt ran with purpose and hope toward Jeffery and the tree.

To be continued …

Coming soon: *Twin River III*
A Death at One Thousand Steps